Much Obliged
The Brent Boys
Book 3

D.P. Clarence

Much Obliged

This is a work of fiction. Names, characters, places, and incidents either are the product of the author's imagination or are used fictitiously. Any resemblance to actual persons, living or dead, events, or locales is entirely coincidental.

Copyright © 2026 by D.P. Clarence

All rights reserved. No part of this book may be reproduced or used in any manner without written permission of the copyright owner except for the use of quotations in a book review. For more information, address: dan@dpclarence.com.

First paperback edition March 2026

Book design by Bailey McGinn

ISBN 978-1-7395509-8-1 (paperback)

ISBN 978-1-7395509-9-8 (ebook)

ISBN 978-1-918476-00-2 (Amazon)

www.dpclarence.com

Content Warnings

Please be aware this book contains:

- A few wobbly body parts, lovingly described
- Strong, heavy and endlessly energetic profanity
- Some very off-hand drug references
- Chain smoking
- A little homophobia (only very little)
- The death of family members (off-page)
- Judgy and overbearing parental units
- Mental and physical health themes
- Thoroughly over-the-top references to the occult
- Characters experiencing financial distress
- A sexy English rugby jock who wears very, very little for *most* of the book
- Posh people
- A journalist from *The Bulletin*.

Buckle up, my sweet, because things do get a bit bawdy.

Glossary

Here we are again, my friend. I know the Britishisms sometimes leave you diving for your dictionary, so here's a cheat sheet.

- **AWOL** – Absent without leave
- **BAFTA** – British Academy of Film and Television Arts
- **Barrister** – a specialist courtroom lawyer who represents clients in higher courts
- **Bellend** – an insult, used to mean "idiot"
- **Boxing Day** – the day after Christmas, a national holiday
- **Brummie** – a person from Birmingham, a city in the British Midlands
- **Bruv** – London roadman speak for "brother"
- **Chambers** – a group of barristers who share offices and administrative support (but are not a firm)
- **Coach House** – originally a building for carriages and horses
- **Dower House** – a smaller house on a large estate traditionally used by the widow of the former lord

Glossary

- **Folly** – a decorative building constructed for ornament rather than practical use (often tower-like)
- **Gaff** – house
- **Grand National** – a famous British horserace
- **HMRC or His Majesty's Revenue and Customs** – the UK government department responsible for tax collection
- **Innit** – "Isn't it"
- **Johnnies** – condoms
- **King's Counsel** – a senior barrister recognised for excellence
- **Lolly** – a candy, a sweet
- **M25** – the motorway (highway) that encircles London
- **NHS** – the National Health Service, the UK's free-at-point-of-use healthcare system
- **Old Bailey** – London's Central Criminal Court
- **Pointless** – a TV game show that airs at 5pm
- **Public school** – an elite, private, fee-paying school
- **Quid** – slang for one pound sterling (£)
- **Vauxhall** – both the name of an area in London notorious in the gay community for its permissive nightclubs and venues and the name of a British car manufacturer
- **Village undertaker** – funeral director
- **Wormwood Scrubs** – a prison in London.

For Beejay.
A nerdy gay teenager's knight in shining armour.
And the only person I know to have buried a Bernese mountain dog by hand.

Chapter 1
Petey

If I'd known what Eva Pilotti breaking her leg on a skiing trip would do for my career, I'd have pushed her off the chairlift myself. I'm not as evil as that makes me sound, I promise. I don't know Eva, I've got nothing against her, I hope she made a full recovery. But TV is a dog-eat-dog industry, and if you want to make it, you've got to fight for every opportunity you can get. The fighting isn't always fair. There's certainly no room to be sentimental about someone else's misfortune.

Fighting for an opportunity was precisely how I found myself in a rickety old lift, headed up to the office of Monkey Ginger Productions in a building on London's Golden Square. It was a fresh Wednesday afternoon in spring. My hair was freshly bleached, I was wearing my favourite blue boiler suit and my lucky earrings, and I was clutching a laptop loaded with ideas to pitch to the company's boss, legendary TV producer Indira Murray. The lift rattled to a halt at the fifth floor.

"You're a blethering idiot, Eva," a woman with a strong Glaswegian accent shouted. It was, unmistakably, Indira herself.

"My five-year-old nephew has got more fucking brains than you, and my sister can't stop him eating the chewing gum he finds under the seats on the bus," she continued.

This was not a great sign. I checked the time. Five minutes early. Not really long enough to go back downstairs and come up again in the hope things had calmed down. I tried to extract myself from the lift as quietly as possible but got caught in the old-fashioned grille door, and it slammed shut behind me.

"I have another meeting, I have to go," I heard Indira say.

I stood in the vestibule, staring at the reeded glass door with its gold lettering. My stomach was jittering so much I almost checked to see if I'd left my vibrator in. I took a deep breath and stepped into the reception area. No one sat behind the counter, but Indira's office door was open.

"It goes without saying, you're off the show."

Indira raised an arm and waved me in—beckoning me to sit in the chair opposite her.

"This has sod all to do with morality. We're filming in a five-hundred-year-old manor house. The job means running up and down stairs all day. You're in a moon boot. How are we going to get you up to the top floor? Fire you out of a fucking trebuchet and hope for the best?"

Indira looked directly at me for the first time, mouthing "sorry." I dismissed the need for an apology with a sweep of my hand.

"You need six weeks to recover, minimum, and it's a four-week shoot." Indira pulled a packet of cigarettes out of the drawer, put one in her mouth, and lit it. She shook her head. "Well, you should have thought about that before you did something so incredibly stupid. I'm sorry, my decision is final."

Indira ended the call, took a long drag of her ciggy, craned around to open the window, and blew the smoke out into the cool air. Her eyes flicked back to me, inspecting me, sizing me up. She was every bit as terrifying as her reputation. Before starting her own production company, Indira Murray had done ten years on *Make Me a Pop Star*

—the behemoth of all reality shows—starting as a runner on season one and working her way up to executive producer. You had to be made of pure steel to thrive in an environment so toxic.

"Word of advice. If anyone ever offers you five grand and an all-expenses-paid week at a Swiss ski resort in exchange for filming their risky, frisky al fresco OnlyFans content, please, I beg of you, remember that lube will make a chairlift *really* fucking slippery."

I burst out laughing. Indira sucked on her cigarette.

"Remind me who you are?"

"P... Peter," I spluttered. "Peter Topham. We met at the BAFTA—"

"The kid from *Wake Up Britain*. I remember now."

Kid?

"I'm twenty-seven." I needed her to take me seriously. At least she remembered me. I'd met Indira a few weeks earlier at an after-party for the ritzy industry awards night. Fuelled up on free champagne and egged on by my best mate, Jumaane, I'd plucked up enough courage to introduce myself and ask for a meeting. Fighting for my opportunities, and all that.

"Do you *like* working on breakfast television?"

She sounded like my parents. I had no idea what answer Indira wanted to hear, so I opted for the truth.

"The hours are hell, but it's fun."

She was eyeballing me like she was planning a dissection, so I kept talking, desperate to win her over.

"I've done five years. Started as a runner. Did two years as an assistant producer. Now I'm a field producer. But what I really want to do is produce big reality shows like yours. I heard you might be looking for fresh ideas?"

"Every production company in the country is looking for fresh ideas," she said, blowing a grey stream of smoke through the open window.

"Exactly, and I—"

She cut me off. "Since Channel Three cancelled *Make Me a Pop Star*, it's opened a shit ton of prime time slots in the Christmas run-up. We need to fill them with something suitably addictive or the great British public won't know what to do with themselves on Saturday nights and there's a risk they'll open their phones, disappear down a rabbit hole of ultranationalist conspiracies, and end up voting for total fucking fascists at the next election. And that's not a country I want my nephew growing up in. So, yeah, I'm on the lookout for fresh ideas." She knocked the ash from her cigarette into a mug. "What have you got for me?"

This was it. This was my moment. I opened my laptop and turned it to face her.

"OK, so the first one is called *Inner Circle*."

"Terrible."

"Er—"

She took another drag. "But go on."

"The idea is, couples match with each other on dating profiles, but when they go on their first date, instead of finding the person they matched with, they find the person's parents, best friends, colleagues, and so on. Instead of getting to know the person directly, they get to know them through their fam."

Indira huffed. "You're single, aren't you?"

"Um, yeah. Why?"

"You've never had a girlfriend or boyfriend or theyfriend, have you?"

I swallowed. "How'd you know?"

"No one who'd ever had in-laws would suggest this. What else you got?"

I took a deep breath, pulled myself together, and scrolled through my presentation to the next idea.

"This one's called *Sweet, Sweet Love*. Imagine it's a bit like *Blind Date*, with one person asking questions and three or four anonymous contestants on the other side of a wall answering them to win their heart. Only as well as answering questions, they're making desserts, and the one who made the dessert she or he likes best gets to go on a date with them. So, it's a cooking show and a dating show combined."

Indira shrugged. "Not enough tension. Next?"

I swallowed and flicked through to idea number three.

"*Gays Off Grid* is like a gay *Survivor*. We send a group of hapless gay guys who think they could survive without electricity, running water, and TikTok into a remote forest—"

"If you want to film an orgy, I'll give you Eva's number." Indira blew a lungful of smoke out the window. "Listen. Peter, was it?"

I nodded.

"How good are you at fuckwit wrangling?"

I didn't know what she meant. Indira huffed impatiently.

"Handling big egos. Juggling ridiculous demands. Politely telling self-important twats you're going to rip their heads off and turn their skulls into novelty Skittles decanters if they don't sit the fuck down, but doing it in such a way that they come back years later and ask you to be godfather to their children. That kind of thing."

I nodded like a plastic dog on the dashboard of a Vauxhall Astra. "We've had a lot of big-name celebrities on *Wake Up Britain*'s famous yellow couch over the years." This was true. I'd seen it all. The Silicon Valley CEO who sprinkled ketamine on his doughnuts and went live to air in a K-hole, but nobody noticed because everyone thinks tech bros are weird anyway. The ageing Hollywood legend who dragged me into the make-up room and made me pull all her neck skin back behind her head until she had a visible jawline, then made me duct tape it in place to hold it. Or—and this was peak—the Tory health minister who flopped his cock out in the green room and asked me if, in my professional opinion, I thought he had the clap.

"And did he?"

Apparently, I'd said that aloud. "No idea, but I said yes on principle. Then told the geezer I was taking the whole story to the newspapers unless he doubled the funding for the Gay Men's Sexual Health Clinic."

Indira laughed—actually *laughed*. She sat back in her chair and, from the corner of her mouth, blew a heavy fog of smoke out the window.

"I like you," she said. "You have initiative."

She liked me!

"Listen, I have a show with a two-and-a-half-million budget that starts filming up in Leicestershire on Monday. I'm short an assistant producer. I need someone who can juggle the egos of a dozen online influencers without collecting them all up in a sack and drowning them in the lake. The job is yours, if you want it."

My pulse stuttered. This wasn't what I came here for. My mind was racing, calculating what this opportunity meant and where it could lead.

"What's the show?"

Indira shuffled through a pile of papers, pulling out a booklet in a plastic cover. It landed with a slap on the desk in front of me.

"*The Love Manor*. Shit name, but then it's a shit concept. Can't believe Channel Three went for it, to be honest with you."

The cover showed a group of people in Regency costumes standing in front of a very grand manor house.

"It's basically *Love Island* in fancy dress," Indira said. "*Pride and Prejudice* with promiscuity."

I snorted.

"I've got twenty-four spoilt-brat twenty-somethings signed on to do it. They're all absolutely fucking stunning and Instagram famous. Thick as shit, obviously. They're descending on an old manor house in the middle of buttfuck nowhere on Monday. Twelve lads. Twelve lassies. The lads all think they're Mr Darcy. The lassies all think they're Daddy's fucking princess. What they don't know is we're splitting them into upstairs and downstairs." Indira pointed at the booklet. "You can take that with you, it explains everything. But the gist is, we're putting a heap of horny models into a castle together, making half of them pretend lords and ladies, half of them pretend maids and menservants, providing them with a bucket full of johnnies, and giving them a list of rules about who's allowed to bang who. Then we're going to film them breaking the rules and put it all on the telly."

I flicked through the booklet. This could be either television's lemon of the year or an absolute winner. But it was also a chance to work with Indira Murray—the best in the business. I'd be mad to turn it down.

"I mean, I would *literally* watch this," I said.

Indira smiled. "Do you want the gig?"

It would mean either begging my boss for a month off with zero notice or quitting my job with zero notice. Either way, I would be leaving my team high and dry, and I might have nothing to come back to after filming finished. My heart was thudding so loudly it was rattling the window. I tried to slow down my breathing. This was a major decision.

I put the booklet down. "What about my ideas?"

"Your ideas need work." Indira leant forward and stubbed out her cigarette. "But that's precisely why you're in the right place. You do this job for me, keep working on your ideas, and in a month's time, when filming is over, come back to me with the best idea you've got. We'll see if we can do business."

I was so excited I had to clench every clenchable body part I had. This was an incredible opportunity. This was my dream. My boss at *Wake Up Britain* would have to find someone else. It was the risk employers took when they kept you rolling along on exploitative casual contracts, year after year, rather than providing job security. Flexibility cut both ways, I decided. I really wanted to do this. But I had to play it right. Indira clearly respected ballsy, so I went with ballsy.

"If you accept my idea, I want an original concept credit and I want to be an executive producer on the show. A real one. Not just a name on the screen."

Indira tapped a finger against her cigarette packet, eyes never leaving mine.

"Can you be in Leicester by Sunday night?"

"I can."

Indira stood and extended her hand.

"Then we have a deal, Peter."

Chapter 2
William

I was the wrong way up in the toilet when I smelt smoke.

"Bramley!"

No reply.

"Bramley!"

That's the trouble with having seventy-eight rooms. It can be terribly hard to locate your staff. Harder still when you only have one member of staff. Until my great-grandfather's day, we had a bell system for this kind of thing. But even if it still worked, it would have been useless to me. I was in the lavatory in the old servants' quarters—the end where the bell rings, not the end where the button is pressed to ring the bell. I took my frustration out on the toilet, jabbing the plunger at the ancient porcelain like the blockage was personal and I could beat it into submission. To my surprise, the toilet fought back. As I thrust forward, the rubber slipped, spraying foul, stinking water all over my face and shirt.

"Bastard!"

"You called, my lord?"

I slumped against the wall of the water closet and came to a rest on the filthy tiled floor. Eyes closed against whatever muck I was covered in, I wiped my face on my shirtsleeve.

"Ah, Bramley. Just the man. Can you smell smoke? Tell me, are we finally burning the place down? Only the artwork is no longer insured, so we might want to save the Holbeins. You know, for the nation. Or whatever."

"It's the bonfires, my lord."

Once my face was satisfactorily dry, I looked up at my employee.

"Bramley, why are you wearing a crown of flowers?"

"It's Beltane, my lord."

I sighed.

"Of course." I looked at my watch. I don't know why. It doesn't chime whenever there's a pagan festival. Although it would be handy if it did.

"The dowager baroness said I looked very smart."

For a moment, I considered jamming my head back inside the toilet. This time on a more permanent basis.

"Let me check I've got this right. We've got fifty people arriving over the next few days. Two dozen of them expecting to live within the walls of this crumbling ruin you and I have the misfortune to call home. We have a to-do list as long as the Bayeux Tapestry. And my mother is currently running around a bonfire, in the middle of a stone circle, in the middle of the forest, in the middle of the night, wearing nothing but old muslin curtains?"

"That's about the size of it, my lord."

"Brilliant. Glad we've all got our priorities clear."

Bramley pointed at the lavatory. "Do you want me to call the plumber up from the village, my lord?"

I dropped the plunger to the ground and put my head in my hands. The bill for a call-out to fix faulty Victorian plumbing on this scale, at this time of night, would be eye-watering. The production company's initial instalment cheque for allowing *The Love Manor* to be filmed at Buckford Hall had already been spent on emergency roof repairs. It was the only way we could guarantee our guests and their expensive camera equipment would stay dry. The money had been a godsend. We'd had a tarpaulin on the roof ever since a big storm at Christmastime, when the chandelier in the Long Gallery began doing a splendid impression of the waterfall thingy at Changi Airport. My grandfather, the fifteenth baron, would be horrified we were letting a television programme be filmed in the old ancestral pile. The night I signed the contract, I swear I could hear his screams drifting over the hill from his crypt in the family mausoleum. But needs must, Grandad. And it was hardly the worst place this family had found the money to keep the roof on over the centuries.

"No," I said firmly, sitting upright. "I'm not giving up yet. There's bound to be a YouTube video covering this exact situation."

Four hours later, I slumped into an armchair in the East Drawing Room. I was exhausted and smelly but reasonably confident I had saved the estate a plumber's bill totalling several hundred quid. I knocked the top off a well-earned bottle of beer, put my socked feet up on the coffee table, and stared up at a portrait of the ninth baron. He'd earned a fortune investing in the railways in the Victorian era— enough to think nothing of more than doubling the size of the original Jacobean house. It was his arrogance, his largesse, his bloody ego, that'd had got us into this mess. Maintaining a house of this size had been a millstone around the neck of every baron who'd come after him. I sipped at my beer and flicked on the TV, hoping to watch the rugby on catch-up. As the wheel of death began slowly loading, my eyelids started to feel heavy. I closed them, briefly, while I waited.

* * *

Something wet splashed across my face. I recoiled, wiped my cheek, and blinked into the light streaming in through the drawing room window, bright and yellow. I must have fallen asleep on the sofa. I closed my eyes against the sun, only to become aware of a loud, repetitive thudding across the floorboards.

"Morning, darling!"

I opened one eye enough to see my mother and her best friend—my godmother, Aunty Karma—wafting around the room like geriatric ballerinas, muslin trailing behind them. The smell of smoke had drifted in with them. I clamped my eyes shut before I could be confronted by naked breasts.

"Beltane's blessings upon you," my mother said, her voice now right behind me. She planted a kiss on my forehead. Wetness splashed across my face again.

"Stop it! What is that?" I nearly opened my eyes but thought better of it.

"It's morning dew!"

"Why? Why is it morning dew?"

"It keeps you young and beautiful."

"I'm twenty-five!" I bleated. "Surely a pair of withered old crones could find a more urgent use for your precious morning dew than waking me up with it?"

"But it's Beltane!" Mum said, her voice drifting around the room. Thundering footsteps continued to dance around me, testing the strength of whatever the woodworm had left of the floorboards. At any moment, either of these women might plummet through to the wine cellar. With any luck, both. Mum and Aunty Karma were in their late fifties. They'd been up all night dancing around the stone circle on the top of Buckford Hill. Where the hell did they get their energy?

"The great goddess of the earth is at her fullest," Aunty Karma said, adding her two pennies' worth to the madness. "Her womb is ripe. She awaits the seed of new life."

"How ghastly."

A pair of hands grabbed my knees. "This is a time of abundant fertility. Of sexual energy!"

"Stop, please. This is too much."

The hands released their grip. A smoke-scented breeze hit my face as my mother danced away again.

"This is a time of passion, of *sensuality*," she said.

"Any chance it's also a time of sleep? What time is it, anyway?"

"Time?" Aunty Karma said, her voice drifting past me accompanied by the sound of bare feet padding across the room. "It's a time for passion. For vitality. For love."

"*For love!*" my mother cried.

"Have you two been foraging for mushrooms in the dark again?"

"The great goddess wants you to find a lover, William."

I groaned. "Does she?"

"She does. She *spoke* to me."

"Incredible how you and the great goddess share exactly the same opinion. That's a bit of luck, isn't it?"

For the past two years, my mother had been obsessed with finding me "a lover" (which is, to be clear, the most horrific word a parent can ever use to describe a son's potential partner). She was relentless, insisting "every generation for centuries found a true and enduring love match at Buckford Hall" and it was time I had found mine. I'd considered asking Bramley to pretend we were an item, merely to get her off my back. We'd see if a fifty-year age difference shattered her "love is love" sensibilities.

"The goddess sees a tall, handsome stranger in your future, William," Mother wailed.

My eyes were still clamped shut. "And how does she suppose I'm going to meet this tall, handsome stranger out here in the middle of nowhere? Did she give you any clues? Are they going to wander in off the street and drift up the stairs to find me drowning in debt and stinking of lavatory water, and fall head over heels in love with me?"

"Open your heart," Karma wailed across the room, "to the great passion the goddess is sending you."

"Any chance she could send my breakfast instead?"

I shouted for Bramley.

"Listen, I'm going to open my eyes now, because I need to find my way to the door without stubbing my toe on whatever bits of forest you two geriatric wood nymphs have dragged in along with you, and I'd quite like to start my day without the trauma of seeing whatever's left of your mouldering carcasses. You've had your fun. Go on, shoo."

Mum made a kissing sound, and her hand tapped against my forehead.

"Very well," she sighed. "See you at breakfast, darling."

Two pairs of leaden feet danced their way out the door. I finally opened my eyes.

"You don't even live here!" I shouted after her. "Why am I feeding you?"

Not half an hour later, I was down in the kitchen, knocking the top off my fourth soft-boiled egg. A newly installed camera hung like a bat from the corner of the ceiling, ready to film Buckford Hall's celebrity guests. Yesterday's mail sat unopened in a pile on the table in front of me. A brown envelope marked *His Majesty's Revenue and Customs* lay on top, the words URGENT: DO NOT IGNORE stamped across it in red ink leaching any joy out of an otherwise beautiful morning, feeding off my spirit like a succubus. I wondered whether the chaps with a financial domination kink enjoyed it when the King's tax collector came to drain their bank accounts. As my account was already empty, I supposed I'd never find out.

I was idly weighing how hard fin-dom could possibly be as a career choice when I heard footsteps on the stairs. I quickly flipped the stack of letters over and forced a smile. Mother drifted in, freshly showered, wearing her tatty old Chinese silk dressing gown.

"You literally have your own house, why is your robe here? Wait, which bathroom did you use?"

"You have fabulous bed hair this morning, darling," Mum said, standing behind me to run her hands through it.

"Technically, this is sofa hair."

She kissed me on the forehead. "I love it when the sun catches the red. It reminds me of your father."

Sadness, or guilt, or something like it, stabbed through me, and I craned up to peck her on the cheek.

"Ooh, coffee," Mum said, launching herself towards the pot. She shouted up the hallway for Aunty Karma to come down, then plonked herself in her usual spot, sharing the corner next to me. The lights above our heads flickered. Mum fingered the mail. I picked it up and lobbed the whole stack onto the counter by the butler's sink before she could spot the notice from HMRC. She reached for the coffee pot and poured the steaming black liquid into her cup.

I told her about fixing the toilet as I cut another piece of toast into soldiers.

"Good for you, darling! That's a few pennies saved."

"Pennies?" I was so indignant I put down my knife. "I've saved us hundreds of pounds."

"Congratulations, darling!"

Aunty Karma appeared in the doorway in a white terry towelling dressing gown.

"And whose robe is that?" I asked.

Karma selected the chair opposite Mother. "What are we congratulating?"

"William," Mother said, pouring out the coffee. "He managed the toilet last night, all by himself."

Aunty Karma frowned.

"Six hours it took me," I said, dipping my soldier into my egg. "I didn't think I was ever going to winkle it out."

Aunty Karma grimaced. "Do you think it's your diet?"

Mother laughed. When I explained I'd spent my night coaxing a dead wood pigeon out of a two-hundred-year-old S-bend, Aunty Karma howled, too, which made Mother start up. It was like an incontinence commercial. Then something caught Aunty Karma's eye, and she stopped.

"Is that a camera?" She folded in on herself, shielding her face.

I glanced up at the corner of the ceiling.

"They've set them up all over the house. Don't worry. They're not turned on yet. No one's filming you in your nightie."

"Every camera is filming, if someone wants it to be filming." Karma shuffled around to turn her back to it. "You never know who could be watching."

I sat there in astonishment, toast soldier poised in mid-air.

"Aunty Karma, you don't *have* to tell me, of course. I make no judgement. Who among us hasn't sinned? But... are you on the run?"

Mum rolled her eyes and cut into a grapefruit. Aunty Karma shook her head. To have seen her the previous night, at her paganest witchiest, you would never have guessed my mother's best friend was a weekend warrior of the dark web. To be honest, Mum and I normally took extreme care to avoid any topic that might bring up the subject. Everyone's tedious when they're on their soapbox. Ask me whether Brandon Osmond's *A Kingdom of Vipers and Valour* series is better epic fantasy than D. R. R. Fanshaw's *Knights-Errant* trilogy, and you'll see what I mean.

"If you'd seen the things I've seen online," Aunty Karma said, "you'd be more protective of your privacy. Someone could easily hack into the system. Someone could be watching us right now."

"I wish you'd told me earlier. I'd have done my hair."

"You can laugh, William, but—"

I held up a hand. It was time to change the subject or we'd be here all day. "The correct form of address is 'my lord,' if you please, Aunty Karma."

"You cheeky little upstart, I used to change your nappies! You might be built like a shire pony, William Winters, but you're not too big to put over my knee."

"In front of the cameras? What would that footage be worth on the dark web? If it's enough to rewire the west wing, I'm game."

"William, really!" Mum said, horrified.

"Needs must, Mother."

Aunty Karma shook her head. "I don't know how you can voluntarily live with cameras everywhere like this."

"I'm not. I'm moving up into the folly this afternoon. There are no cameras up there."

"The folly?" Mother said, her eyes glazing. I hadn't had the heart to tell her until now. I knew how she'd be. Avoiding her gaze, I went to dip my soldier but discovered I'd run out of dippy egg.

"Do we have any more soft-boiled eggs?"

"Why the folly, darling?" Mum asked.

I sighed. "They need my bedroom for filming."

The folly was the one cool thing the ninth baron had built. It was an Italianate tower on the eastern side of Buckford Hall, rising two floors above the rest of the house. It had been my father's study. It was, in fact, a bit of a bachelor pad. Over three floors, it had all the essentials—a bed, a library, a kettle, and an oak desk with a genuine secret drawer. The top floor was a belvedere with a spectacular view. "Has anyone seen Bramley?"

The kitchen lights flickered and stuttered again.

"Why don't you move into the Dower House with me? Think of the fun we could have! We could stay up all night playing whist, charades, Scrabble—"

"I think you've answered your own question, Mother dearest."

"*Dungeons and Dragons*, then? We never did finish our last campaign—"

"*Bramley!*"

Mum reached across to muss my hair. "Golly, I must have been such a terrible mother."

I shrugged her off.

"It's vital everything goes smoothly," I said, and caught myself glancing over at the stack of mail, trying not to imagine the vast sums of money the letter said I needed to find and the consequences if I didn't. "We need this show to be a success. If I'm living on-site, I can make sure everything's working exactly as it should. No clogged plumbing, dicky electrics, or falling masonry."

Mum wasn't giving up. "Why not move into the old servants' quarters instead? You'd have a lot more space."

"They need it for filming. The cast who are playing servants will be living in it. *Bramley!*"

I knew why Mum didn't want me moving into the folly. It had been my father's lair, and we'd left it untouched these past three years. For my mother, I think it was a kind of memorial. For me, there simply hadn't been much reason to go in there. It stirred up too many emotions I didn't want to feel. But now, needs must.

"You bellowed, my lord." Bramley stood in the kitchen doorway, covered in cobwebs and dust.

"Good God, man, have you been wrestling the ghosts?"

"I've been in the cellar, my lord. I fear the television equipment might be overloading the circuitry."

As he spoke, the lights flickered off, then on, then off again—which was how they stayed. This was not good news.

"Oh dear," Mum said.

I stood, my breakfast apparently over. "Well, at least you can stop worrying about the cameras, Aunty Karma."

Bramley cleared his throat. "Shall I get the electrician up from the village, my lord?"

"Why are you so *obsessed* with calling the local tradesmen?" I muttered, heading for the cellar and certain electrocution. "Are you on commission or something?"

Chapter 3
Petey

The DJ at Hades, London's iconic gay nightclub, had the bass cranked so high my sphincter was pulsing in time with the subwoofers. The boys and I were up the far end of the ground floor bar—the quietest part of the venue we could find that was wheelchair accessible for Nick. Hades was not my favourite venue. The glasses were plastic, the drinks were mostly ice, and the crowd always looked like they'd somehow given their babysitter the slip. But it was my last Saturday night in London for a month, and the Brent Boys—Jumaane, Dav, Nick, Sunny, Ludo, and Stav—had organised an impromptu leaving party. I looked at my watch. It was gone half one. Jumaane was buying another round of drinks. I thought about everything I had to do later that day and suddenly felt incredibly tired. I was catching the 3:00 p.m. train up to Leicester, but I had Sunday lunch with my family to get through first. Jumaane passed around our drinks, and when we all had something in our hands, he raised his cup of vodka and soda into the air.

"Congratulations to our incredibly talented friend. You are living your dream, and we are all *so* proud of you!"

"Absolutely!" Ludo said, lifting his plastic flute of champagne.

"Chuffed for you, mate," Stav added, raising his red wine.

"Well done, pal," Nick said.

I felt a warm glow and for a moment I thought I might cry, but it would have ruined my tough-as-Mrs-Thatcher-in-a-tank image, so I raised my glass instead.

"Cheers, fam!" I said, and everyone clinked their unclinkable drinking vessels together.

The DJ changed the music to a Cole Kennedy club remix. The shrieks of delight from the hordes of twinks could have shattered glass, if the venue had any. The children streamed past us, beelining for the dance floor like there was a Boxing Day sale at a toy store.

"Tune!" Nick said. "Who wants to dance?" Without waiting for an answer, he downed his drink in one gulp, handed his boyfriend the empty cup, spun his wheelchair around, and disappeared into the sea of twinks.

"Sometimes I forget how incredibly Scottish he is," Dav said, putting both their cups on the bar and following Nick into the crowd. Jumaane and Stav went, too, leaving me with Sunny and Ludo. All the boys and I, with the exception of Ludo, had been at uni together in Leeds. Sunny was a journalist for the BBC's current affairs programme *Compass Point*, but used to write for Britain's trashiest tabloid newspaper, *The Bulletin*. His fiancé, Ludo, was a reporter for a theatre magazine and, I supposed, probably technically the heir to the *Sentinel* media empire. His family were, as Sunny often said, "proper minted." I mean, my family were well off, but Ludo's father had bought a helicopter to cut his commute.

"Any luck finding a gaff for your wedding yet?" I asked.

"Nope," Sunny said, grabbing Ludo's hand and squeezing it. Ludo's grandmother had been unwell, and the boys were trying to bring their plans forward to make sure she could see them get married.

"It's proving jolly difficult," Ludo added. "All the decent venues are booked out three years in advance."

"That's 'decent' according to Ludo's father," Sunny clarified. "We'd be fine with the registry office, but Hugo seems to think this is going to be the society wedding of the year. And he's paying for it, so..."

I shrugged. "Can't you get hitched on a beach or in a park or something?"

"English law," Ludo said, shaking his head. "You can only get married in a registered venue. We can't get a marriage licence until we have a venue. Those take six weeks. And now my idiot brother Jonty has announced he's going travelling and will be uncontactable for at least a month..."

Ludo was starting to spiral. This was one of a thousand reasons I never wanted to get married—the stress weddings cause is even more outrageous than the expense.

Sunny put his free hand on my shoulder. "Did I overhear you telling Stav your new show is being filmed up in my hometown?"

I nodded. "Just outside. In some spooky old gaff near a haunted little village called Newton Bardon."

"Not Buckford Hall?"

"You know it?"

Sunny laughed. "How do you *not* know it?"

"Well, I don't come from Leicester, so I've never had to beg the local lord for potatoes in winter, or whatever you had to do to survive growing up."

"You've never heard of the Bisexual Baron Buckford?" Sunny asked.

I winced. "No? Why would I care who some sticky old duke is shagging?"

"Oh, he's not old," Ludo said. "He's a couple of years younger than us. He was in the same year as Jonty at Petersham. Fabulous rugby player, as I recall. An excellent equestrian too. Thighs so thick I always worried he might accidentally snap the horse."

"You're kidding?"

"No, he's a proper dish," Sunny said.

This I could get on board with. "How do you know he's bisexual?"

"To be fair, I don't," Sunny said. "But it's the nickname *The Bulletin* gave him after he was caught on a park bench in Berkeley Square at four in the morning with his tongue down some lass's throat and his hand down her lad's pants. It was a whole scandal. He'd only inherited the title a few weeks earlier. His old man was barely cold."

"Have I been lied to about the aristocracy?" I said, stifling a yawn. "I don't remember anything like that happening in *Pride and Prejudice*."

"But seriously, the whole thing was a terrible tragedy for the family," Ludo said. "Their plane went down. One of those little fixed-wing jobs. The elder brother died too."

"Jesus," I said. "So, suddenly, he's the duke? And he's bi? And he's fit?"

"Baron," Sunny corrected.

"*That's* the problem you had with what he just said?" Ludo chimed in.

The next month was going to be all long days and hard work, but I certainly wasn't going to complain about a bit of eye candy on set. Stav came bounding back up to us from the dance floor, sweat running down his face. The DJ was now playing Chappell Roan.

"We need to change venues," he said. "It's like a kindergarten out there. I literally found someone's lollipop stuck in my chest hair."

I pulled open Stav's shirt and peered down at his gloriously furry belly.

"What are you doing?" he asked.

"Checking the twink's not still stuck down there, trying to get his lolly back. They can easily fall between the gaps, if you're not careful."

As we laughed, the rest of the gang rejoined us, their faces betraying various levels of exhaustion.

"That's it, I'm done," Jumaane said, puffing. "Let's head to Vauxhall."

Vauxhall was where Jumaane and I belonged. The grittier, grimier clubs under the railway arches south of the River Thames were our spiritual home, our natural hunting ground. We could find our way around the darkroom at Crucifix with the precision of bats. We'd spent many a night trawling it in search of, um, let's call it, er, *love*... I guess?

I checked the time. Two o'clock. I shook my head. "I'm going to bail."

Six pairs of eyes glared at me, like this had literally never happened before.

"Are you OK, pal?" Nick said.

"Did you come off the PrEP or something, babes?" Jumaane asked.

"I'm tired," I said.

Jumaane clicked his fingers in my face. "You're leaving for a month. Who you think you banging while you're out in the sticks, babes?"

"Oi, that's my hometown!" Sunny said.

"Sorry, babes, no offence."

"Are you saving yourself for the bisexual baron?" Ludo asked.

"No!" I said, a little too quickly. "This next month is all about my career. This is my big shot. I don't have time for boys."

"All the more reason for one last hurrah, babes," Jumaane said.

I sighed, deeply. "I also have lunch with Sir Edward and Angelica tomorrow." I used my parents' first names to really drive home the full horror. The boys cringed in unison. "It'll be easier to cope with them if I've had a good night's sleep. I love you, fam. Thanks for tonight. But I'm off home to crash. See you all in a month, yeah?"

"What is even happening?" Jumaane said, as I pecked him on the cheek.

"Your wee pal has finally discovered something more important to him than cock," Nick said, as I went around the group kissing everyone goodbye. "I'm so proud."

Dav smacked his boyfriend on the shoulder with the back of his hand. "Why couldn't you have said 'personal growth' or something, like a normal person?"

Chapter 4
William

I swung by the folly, my heart thumping as I opened the door. Bramley had been in and dusted and vacuumed, stocked the little pantry cupboard with tea and biscuits, and put fresh linen on the bed. My clothes were all neatly hanging in the wardrobe. Suddenly, I was five years old again, running up these stairs in my pyjamas to my father's office to kiss him goodnight. My hand went to the ring on the chain around my neck. His ring. I closed my eyes and breathed him in, sucking the essence of him into my lungs before it disappeared forever—replaced by whatever it is I smell like. I missed him. Terribly. When I wasn't furious with him. My hands started to shake, so I rummaged through the wardrobe, put on my riding gear, and dashed out to the stables.

I'd barely got Achilles saddled up and his girth strap tightened when from behind me, I heard one of those not-so-subtle throat-clearing noises people make to announce their presence.

"Hello, Dub-Dub!"

At the use of my old school nickname, I spun around, quick as lightning, to see my greasy-haired bespectacled horror show of a neighbour, Horatio Blunt, standing in my stables. In all the commotion of the TV crew setting up, I hadn't heard his Range Rover drive up. If I had, he would not have found me.

"What do you want, Horatio?" I grabbed Achilles's reins to lead him out into the yard, impatient to get away.

"Nice, is that how you greet an old friend?"

"Of course not," I said, in all honesty. "It's how I greet real estate agents."

Horatio laughed. "I'm a premium property adviser, actually. But it's an easy mistake to make. I think you'll be interested in what I've got to say."

"You're emigrating?"

"I've got an offer for you. One that could make all your money worries disappear."

A pulse of anger rippled through my body. Of course this arsehole knew I had "money worries." People in high places talk, and Horatio's father was very well connected. He probably knew more about my financial situation than I did. But then, that wouldn't be hard. I shook my head, put my foot in the stirrup, and launched myself up into the saddle.

"If you're going to make another offer to buy the village, the answer is still no. It will always be no."

Horatio and his property developer father had been trying to buy Newton Bardon and the land around it back from the Buckford Estate for years. Ownership of the village had bounced back and forth between our two families for centuries. Most recently, my grandfather had snapped it up for a song in the early 1990s, when the Blunts' original property development empire went bust during the recession. The family had been forced to abandon horrendous plans to build a two-thousand-home housing estate on the village common. They had to liquidate their assets. They lost everything. Horatio's grandfather had gone to prison.

I let Achilles feel the squeeze of my legs, and we walked towards the gate into Home Field.

"I'm not interested in the village," Horatio said. He waved a plastic pocket of documents in the air. "I've got a client who wants to buy Buckford Hall."

I pulled on Achilles's reins and we stopped, dead still. I kept looking straight ahead, feeling my blood slowly begin to boil at the impertinence. I refused to make eye contact with the silly little man.

"It's not for sale," I said, through gritted teeth.

"Are you sure?" Horatio stepped in front of us. "It's a very generous offer."

"The answer is no."

Achilles walked on, forcing Horatio to stand aside.

"Sensible opening negotiating strategy, Dub-Dub. Of all people, I can appreciate that." He was trotting along beside us now. "My client is very serious. They're a cash buyer. A reputable international hotel chain."

The idea turned my stomach.

"Buckford is not for sale. It never will be." It was time to put the boot in. "And if your father thinks sending you to do his dirty work, just because we went to school together, is going to make me sell, then he's an even bigger idiot than you are."

Horatio winced. A point to me.

"Oh, come on, Dub-Dub, everyone knows how hard up you are," he said. "I mean, I saw the TV crews as I was driving in. You must be getting desperate. It can't be long now, surely?"

The words tightened around my chest like a corset. The scoreline was even. It takes a lot to get me angry. I was raised on a diet of yoga and meditation by a pair of carefree well-heeled hippies, after all. But Horatio Blunt knew how to press my buttons. He'd been doing it since school. I was now absolutely raging. I eyeballed him.

"Look, Horatio. We're friends, aren't we?" (This was a lie. We absolutely were not friends.)

"Of course, Dub-Dub! Oldest chums."

Achilles and I negotiated the gate.

"Then as an old chum, I know you won't be offended when I say this, but the only person I want to see coming down my driveway *less* than you is the village undertaker. And next time I see you coming down my driveway—and mark me, this is a promise—the very next person coming down the driveway after you will, in fact, *be* the village undertaker. Do we understand each other?"

I let the gate slam shut.

Horatio blinked. "I can see you need time to think about it. Perfectly understandable. It's a big decision. I'll leave this folder in the tack room for you, shall I?"

I could barely breathe. I leant forward in the saddle, dug my heels in, and clicked my tongue. Achilles took off at a trot.

"All you have to do is sign and all your money worries will be gone," Horatio called after us.

I clicked again and Achilles broke into a canter, then a gallop. I rode him hard, the white stallion's hooves thundering across Home Field and up the winding trails of the ancient oak woods to the top of Buckford Hill. It was only once we reached the stone circle which crowned the estate that I could rip off Horatio's corset. I dismounted, let Achilles's reins fall, and sucked the fresh spring air deep into my lungs. As I stared out over the green expanse of everything my family had achieved in five hundred and forty years, I knew Buckford wasn't mine to sell. It was mine to save. Horatio believed selling up would solve all my problems, but he misunderstood something fundamental—something he, of all people, really should have known. Selling wasn't the easy answer. It was the hardest answer of all.

Chapter 5
Petey

Come Sunday lunchtime, I was sitting around the table in the dining room of my childhood home in Pinner, in posh, suburban North London, sharing an awkward meal with my parents, my brother and sister, their spouses, and my gran. My father was droning on, lecturing the whole table about some boring detail of law. My gran's shoulder pressed into mine, no weight behind her birdlike frame.

"Fetch us the gravy, will you, Petey Boy," she said.

I reached across for the gravy boat. "Do you want me to pour it for you, Gran?"

"Pour it?" she whispered, loud enough for only me to hear. "I'll pay you ten quid to hold me head under in it until the bubbles stop."

I had to smother my laughter with my napkin. Gran winked, eyes full of mischief. Except for Gran and me, everyone around the table was a lawyer. It was the family trade. My father, Sir Edward Topham, was a renowned barrister and King's Counsel, and he'd been an unbearable snob long before he got his beloved knighthood. My mother was a youth court judge who lamented nothing so much as the abolition of hanging. My brother and sister were barristers in the family chambers. Their partners were soulless corporate lawyers. It was like having lunch in the Old Bailey canteen. Sunday roast was practically a staff meeting, and the conversation almost never shifted from legal industry gossip. Which is why I rarely turned up. Well, that and the fact I was usually either too hungover, still too drunk, at a drag brunch with the boys, or still trying to prise myself out of a Vauxhall sling. I was only here now because I was going away and it was my last chance to see my gran for a month. Plus, I had exciting news to share.

"A what, sorry?" my father said.

"A reality TV show," I replied. "I start this afternoon, actually. Totally gassed for it."

"Oh, Peter!" My mother was visibly horrified, as if I'd revealed I'd been slaughtering schoolchildren instead of landing an opportunity that could make my career. "Why must you consistently degrade yourself like this?"

I'd known it was going to be like this, but somehow, I always held out hope my parents might at least be pleased for me, if not impressed.

"It's a real opportunity, innit?" I said, trying to stay upbeat, trying not to sound like I was pleading. "If this goes well, I could get my own show."

"Good God!" my mother cried.

"Will you stop talking like a bloody barrow boy," my father roared. "You had a very expensive education."

My brother nearly choked on his wine. "Your own reality show? What's the concept? Stick a dozen of your bum buddies in a room, turn the lights out, and use contact tracing to work out who had the super gonorrhoea?"

His wife dug him in the ribs and winced apologetically in my direction. I'd long since given up on my brother's appalling homophobia, and misogyny, and insert-outrage-here.

My father shook his head. "You could be a mid-level associate by now. Instead, you're wasting your life on *this*."

Under the table, Gran squeezed my knee. Gran was born in Bethnal Green Tube station during an air raid. She and my late grandad had spent their entire lives grafting on a market stall in London's East End, selling fruit and veg, saving every penny they could to send their two sons to university and give them a better life. Unfortunately, the result was my emotionally stunted father. Fortunately for me, my parents being so busy with their careers when I was a kid meant, after my brother and sister went to boarding school, I spent all my time at Gran's house in Tower Hamlets, where love was never in short supply. Unsurprisingly, I grew up wanting to be more like Gran and Grandad, and less like Sir Edward and Angelica. I belonged in the gritty East End, not in comfortable, suburban, middle-class Pinner. The way I chose to speak was the outward expression of that. It didn't hurt that it drove my parents bananas.

My parents looked furious. Mum was gripping her napkin like she was wringing the blood out of it.

"Have you even thought for a second of the damage you're doing to the family name?"

"Quite!" my father said. "When you begged me to give you permission to read 'media studies' at university—"

My brother scoffed. "I don't think they 'read' at Leeds, Dad. It's not a real university."

I rolled my eyes. This was old ground too.

"—you stood on the carpet in my chambers and you promised me a brilliant career in journalism awaited you," my father continued. "You would be the next Dimbleby, you said. A journalist with the intellectual heft of a Paxman or an Andrew Neil. Instead, you've wasted your life making *breakfast* television—a concept so ghastly I can barely conceive of its existence—and now *this*?"

In my fantasy version of this lunch, my father would have raised his glass to toast my success, my mother would have leapt up and hugged me, and my siblings and their partners would have all begrudgingly nodded and smiled and said they were proud of me, while secretly hating their own life choices and seething with jealousy I was doing something so wildly exciting with mine.

"Millions of people watch reality shows every single week," I said, going on the defensive. "It's an incredible opportunity, innit?"

"Too right," Gran said, throwing up her arthritic hands and pulling my face to hers for a kiss on the cheek. "Well done, Petey Boy. You've made your old gran very proud."

"Proud!" My father almost choked. "Your grandson is wasting his potential. Look at him! He's twenty-seven. He's hungover. He's dressed like he works in a factory. He speaks like a South London gangster. He's a miscreant, leading a totally wanton lifestyle and showing absolutely no signs of settling down. He's throwing his life away making trash entertainment for the kinds of people who eat dinner off a tray on their lap in front of the television. If he doesn't get serious, he's never going to amount to anything."

My throat tightened. This was exactly why I never came to Sunday lunch. I bit my bottom lip to stop it quivering—as I always did—and swallowed my rage. I am the way I am, I thought, because the alternative is to be like you.

"That's a bit rough, Dad," my sister, Kathy, said.

"You all know I'm right," he said, wrapping his sausagey fingers around his glass of Bordeaux. He took a swig to wash down the bile.

Gran was indignant. "I eat my tea off a tray in front of the telly!"

"Do you, Gran?" Kathy said, without looking up from her carrots.

"It's not too late, Peter," my father barked. "You could go back to law school now. I'll pay for it. I'd be willing to let you specialise in media law, if you like. Best of both worlds. What do you say?"

I could feel tears trying to well, but I would have died before I let my family see me buckle. I shook my head. I couldn't speak. No one else said anything either. The table was unbearably quiet.

Finally, my sister cleared her throat. "What's the show about, Pete?"

I explained the Regency dating premise. The whole table fell about laughing—except for my mother, who looked like she'd found a turd in her Riesling. Gran, forever Team Petey Boy, loved the idea.

"It's being filmed at Buckford Hall in Leicestershire," I added, hoping this detail might appeal to my parents' entrenched snobbery. "I'm going to be living in a real-life manor house for the next month, how cool is that?"

My father's eyes boggled. "The family are letting you film this... this... *nonsense*... in their ancestral home?"

I nodded. "Of course."

"This country is going to the dogs," my mother declared.

My father shook his head, poured himself another glass of red, and turned to my brother-in-law. "Did I tell you we're taking the Jag' Club on a drive up to Chatsworth House for the annual Father's Day run next month? Now, *there's* a stately home..."

And just like that, the conversation moved on. After a few minutes, my mother got up and started clearing the table. I sat there in silence, stewing inside, listening to my father witter on about his beloved North London Jaguar Car Club—the only subject on which he was more tedious than the law. My sister, apparently also bored by the subject, turned to Gran.

"How's the new home, Gran? Are you settling in all right?"

"It's marvellous, Kathy," Gran said. "The lads in the kitchen are magicians with a blender. It's so secure too. I ain't seen security like that since I used to visit your Great-Uncle Frank when he was doing seven years in Wormwood Scrubs."

"Well, that's... good," Kathy said, unsure.

The noise of my family babbling away washed over me. The faint clattering and clanking of my mother stacking the dishwasher drifted through from the kitchen. I couldn't wait to get out of there. I stared at the clock on the mantel. Every second was a minute, every minute an hour. I couldn't bear it. Mum hadn't even come in with the coffees when Gran leant over and whispered in my ear.

"You do whatever you have to do to prove 'em wrong, Petey Boy," she said. "You show them."

My jaw tightened. A rod of steel seemed to slide up my spine and click into place. I sat taller. Gran was right. Nothing was going to stop me getting my own reality show and proving my family wrong. *Nothing*. It was my first and last priority. My family might not approve of what I did for a living, but I was going to make bloody sure they had to at least respect me for it.

"And get me out of here, will you, Petey Boy?" Gran said. "Before I lose the sodding will to live."

Gran was right. Even prison was better than this. I had to get to work.

Chapter 6
William

The carriage court hadn't seen this much action since my parents turned Buckford Hall into a base camp for fox hunt saboteurs in the early 2000s. There were lorries and vans everywhere and dozens of people dashing about, lugging everything from lighting rigs to period dresses into the house. In the middle of all this organised chaos stood the four-foot-nothing mini firecracker who'd sold me on the idea of filming a TV show at Buckford in the first place, Indira Murray. She was, in turns, barking orders at her underlings and sucking on a cigarette like she was extracting its soul. Desperate to make sure she felt welcomed, I marched towards her with my hand outstretched and professed how glad I was to see her.

"There's a madwoman by your front gate whacking our vehicles with flaming tree branches as we drive in," Indira said.

"Ah, that'll be Mother."

"Has she escaped from somewhere?"

"The Dower House." I nodded. "I'm not technically allowed to lock her in. Fire regulations, and all that."

"What the fuck is she doing?"

I grimaced. "She'll be burning sage. It's meant to cleanse you of negative energy."

"Well, can you put a fucking stop to it? Because half my team are burnt-out millennials and the other half are permanently freaked-out Gen Z, and we're already filming around forty different fucking mental health diagnoses. One of the sound technicians has brought his emotional support duck with him. Some of these kids have never been outside the M25, so having an actual witch greet them at the front gate is going to cause permanent fucking trauma, and I don't want that on my conscience. More to the point, I don't want it on my insurance."

The sage wasn't working, then.

"I'll have a word."

"Thank you."

Without dropping eye contact, Indira took a deep drag of her cigarette, then blew her smoke out in a long, steady stream.

"How are you feeling about all this?" Her tone had completely changed, as if the tobacco had achieved what the sage could not.

"It's all terribly exciting," I said. I meant it. I wasn't only thinking about the balance of the £250,000 fee and what it would mean for saving the estate. It was genuinely thrilling to have so much activity and energy around the old place. There hadn't been much of that around Buckford lately. Not since the accident and the terrible months that followed.

Indira smiled. "Good. Is the house ready?"

"Absolutely." Instinctively, I turned to stare back at the crumbling family pile, which was looking glorious in the spring sunshine. "We've moved all the important artefacts into storage—anything fragile, irreplaceable, readily nickable, or important to the nation—as requested." I turned back to Indira. "Including Bramley, who I've shipped off to the Dower House for the duration. Mother's terribly pleased."

Indira sucked on her cigarette, her gaze fixed on the house. "I'll drop him five grand if he locks her inside for the duration."

I thought it politic to pretend the woman with the big cheque hadn't suggested imprisoning my mother and pushed on. "Your set dresser fellows have been beavering away like absolute champions these last couple of weeks. Everything looks good to go. If you need me for some reason, at any time, if there's an emergency, I'll be lodging up in the folly." I pointed to the tower. "There's no phone reception anywhere around the house, and the Wi-Fi doesn't reach up there for some reason, but send someone up to knock on the door if you need me."

Indira glowered. "You're staying in the fucking house while we're filming?"

"Well, I, um, er, I *am*, actually. Is that a problem?"

"Can't you go somewhere else?"

"Not really," I said, trying not to sound too tentative. "You've booked up all the accommodation within a ten-mile radius. And if you make me move in with my mother, I'll cancel this deal and give you your deposit back."

It was a bald-faced lie, and on the inside I was flapping my hands and screaming in panic she would call my bluff. Indira threw her cigarette to the ground and stamped it out with the toe of her pink Adidas trainers. My fingers were itching to pick it up, but I resisted that too.

"Fine," she said. "But if you get in my shot, or if there's so much as a stray mouse squeak from your fucking Rapunzel tower—anything that ruins my footage—I'm taking you, your mother, your butler, your dog, and the emotional support duck, and I'm inserting one of you inside the other like a human turducken. Are we clear?"

I was becoming slightly obsessed with this woman. She was so completely terrifying that I didn't dare mention that I didn't have a dog.

"Absolutely," I said. "There are at least a thousand books up there. You won't hear a peep out of me. I'm planning to reread the entire *Knights-Errant* ser—"

"Your butler's trying to get your attention," Indira said, nodding.

"Oh, he's not my butler," I said, turning to look over my shoulder. "We don't use that term, he's actually the estate's chief operating off—"

My eyes landed on Bramley. He was stumbling across the gravel of the carriage court, completely drenched, plunger in hand.

"You've got to be joking."

"I'm afraid not, my lord," he said, pulling up beside me.

"What's happening?" Indira asked, straight-backed and alert.

"Victorian waterworks," I explained. "Bit temperamental."

Indira rolled her eyes. "Get a plumber on it, pronto."

"No need to call a plumber, I can fix it. I've already fixed it once."

Indira's eyebrows shot up. "Lord Buckford, if you've fixed it once and it's still broken, you haven't fixed it. You've unfucked it for five minutes. Now it's fucked again. Need I remind you your contract says all facilities used by cast and crew must be in good working order? The crew is already here. The cast is arriving in the morning. I suggest you get a professional onto it, toot suite, or, believe me, I'll soon wipe that posh pretty-boy smile off that ruddy-cheeked face of yours—because the cost of every delay you cause is coming off your cheque. Are we clear?"

I was a bit taken aback, to be honest. But she'd said all that without taking a breath, and smoke was billowing out of her nostrils like a dragon despite the fact she'd stubbed her cigarette out at least a full minute earlier.

"I'll get right onto it," I said, turning to dash towards the house. Bramley trotted along behind me, plunger aloft.

"Shall I call down to the village for the plumber, my lord?" Bramley asked, as we shuffled through the entrance hall towards the grand staircase.

"Absolutely not!"

It was bad enough I'd had to stump up to pay the electrician.

Chapter 7
Petey

The taxi rumbled down the drive, and Buckford Hall came into view. It was far from the poshest stately home I'd ever seen. Angelica and Edward had dragged us all around every Treasure House in Britain when we were kids, so I knew at a glance this Leicestershire manor was no Blenheim Palace. But Buckford Hall, with its red brick, creamy sandstone, and Dutch gables, was undeniably charming. Like, if you saw it standing alone in the corner of a bar, you'd definitely walk up to it and ask if it wanted a drink, before subtly prodding to see if it was a top. Whereas the architecture of Blenheim Palace leaves you in no doubt. It grabs you by the throat and calls you its little bitch.

The cabby took my case out of the boot, and I said my thanks.

"Sorry about the scorch marks, bruv," I said. "No idea what that madwoman was thinking."

He grunted, got back in the car, and drove off. I was smoothing out the creases in the legs of my favourite boiler suit when Indira Murray came marching across the gravel towards me with a folder in her hand.

"Peter, not before time."

"My call time was five o'clock, wasn't it?" I asked, worried I'd already screwed up somehow.

"The secret to being a successful assistant producer is anticipating the needs of the production. I could have used you by two."

My stomach dropped. "Sorry. I had Sunday lunch with my family and—"

She raised a hand. "Say no more. Last time I had Sunday lunch with my family, I spent my entire afternoon in the emergency department waiting for my nephew to have baked beans scooped out of his ear. You're here now. That's what matters." She passed me the folder. "Here's your production bible. Shooting schedule, photos and bios of the cast—it's all there. Don't lose it, and *don't* let the cast see it."

I flicked through the folder while Indira lit a cigarette. The page fell open to a photo of a face I recognised.

"Oh, hello! That's Jonty Boche."

"You know him?"

I nodded. "His brother, Ludo, is a good mate."

"Is this going to be a problem?"

Only in the sense that he's mad as a march hare, I thought.

"No, ma'am."

"Good." Indira blew out a heavy nicotine fug. "Because he's one of your charges. You're going to be looking after the twelve servants. Six of each. All their pronouns are listed. Everyone's cisgendered, obviously. This is Channel Three, not Channel Four. They're all absolute twats, of course. Sorry, no offence to your twat friend. They're used to living the high life." She pointed at a photo. "That blonde one with the tits hasn't so much as rustled out a sneaky queef in the last two years without Instagramming it. This is going to be murder for the lot of them, but they've all signed up for it. Which reminds me, there's no reception, so we're on walkie-talkies and headsets. Go pick yourself up a set from the production office in the Old Coach House."

"Gotcha."

"There's a map of the house and grounds in the back of your bible," Indira said, anticipating my next question the way only someone who has spent a career as a producer can. "The servants' quarters are highlighted in pink. You've got your own small production office off to the side. I think it used to be a cleaning cupboard or something. That's where you're kipping too. Go familiarise yourself with your patch."

"Roger!" I said, trying to sound both as keen as I felt and as efficient as Indira expected. Then, to my eternal shame, I saluted. She rolled her eyes.

"I'll crack on then, shall I?"

"If you would."

I smiled.

"You've got a lot riding on this," Indira said. "Don't make me regret giving you a shot."

Brutal. I nodded, pretending she hadn't winded me completely. I was going to have to work hard to earn her respect. I turned to walk into the house.

* * *

The bathrooms in the servants' quarters were completely flooded.

"You have got to be kidding!" I had been on the job less than ten minutes, and there was already a disaster.

Rapid-fire cursing echoed out of one of the stalls. I walked along the row until I found a man standing on a toilet seat, arms reaching into a cistern high up on the wall, apparently screwing in some kind of black plastic ball. He was wearing a pair of brown loafers, obscenely tiny shorts, and a tattered old Polo Ralph Lauren rugby shirt. He was drenched.

"You're making a right mess, mate," I said.

"Hang on."

"Have you got any idea what you're doing there?"

"I said hang on."

The plumber finished playing with his little ball and turned to look at me over his shoulder. His face was as wet as the rest of him. Strands of his mid-length auburn hair were stuck to his forehead and cheeks. He was, to be clear, bloody gorgeous.

"Who the hell are you?" he said.

His rudeness jogged me out of my trance. I had a job to do.

"I'm the bloke whose job it is to make sure the toilet's fixed!"

He turned back to what he was doing. "Well, it's fixed. I've just fixed it. Probably."

Water sploshed over the side of the cistern and onto his shirt. It ran in rivers down his legs. His thighs were so meaty they belonged in a butcher's window. Frankly, he did not look like a professional plumber.

"Mate, are you even qualified to fix that?"

"Qualified?" He laughed. "I have a degree in English lit. I'm singularly *unqualified* to fix this. I'm unqualified to do anything remotely useful at all, truth be told. But it's never stopped me fixing the plumbing in this house before."

I was shocked, to be honest. "Breaks down regularly, does it?"

"You'd be surprised."

"I don't think I would." Not if this was the quality of the tradesman sent to fix it.

The plumber sighed, stood upright, and cricked his back. His wet clothes were clinging to him like he'd been vacuum-sealed into them. He turned to look at me, and his face, still ridiculously gorgeous, looked seriously annoyed. His cheeks were as red as apples. He had an extremely wet cloth in his fist, which was dripping water as he jabbed a finger in my direction.

"I told Bramley not to call you," he said. "Sorry, but you've had a wasted trip. I don't need your help. You can leave."

"Pardon?"

"And don't even think about charging a call-out fee, because I'm not paying it. I didn't call you out."

He'd lost me now. "Why would I charge you a call-out fee?"

He sighed. "Look, I don't have time for this. I've fixed it. I don't need any help."

I roared in frustration. "You *do* need help. Blind Freddie can see this job needs an actual qualified plumber."

"I'm not paying you to do a job I can do perfectly well myself."

"Why would you pay *me* to do it?"

"Because I've never heard of a plumber working for free. Unless you're some magical plumbing fairy my mother has accidentally summoned with one of her ridiculous herbal concoctions?"

He was winding me up now. "I'm not the plumber. You're the plumber."

"No, *you're* the plumber."

"I am not!"

"Well, you're dressed like a bloody plumber," he said.

I looked down at my boiler suit. "This is *fashion*. This is my signature look."

The plumber looked exasperated. "This is insane. I'm going insane. If you're not the plumber, then who are you, and why are you up here badgering me about needing a plumber?"

That was it. If my whole future in TV depended on this job going well, I wasn't going to fail in my first ten minutes on set.

"Who am I?" I raged. "I'm the bloke who's going to report you to Trading Standards, bruv."

The plumber frowned. "Now listen here—"

"Yeah, that's got you worried, hasn't it?" I felt myself grow two inches taller. "Got your attention now, haven't I? You've got no business calling yourself a plumber if you're not even qualified."

"I never claimed to be a plumber."

"Look, I'll make you a deal," I said. "If you immediately pack up your things and leave quietly, I won't call the authorities. But if you don't leave, I'll have no choice but to get my boss up here to sort you out—and she's a very angry Scotswoman with the temper of a chain-smoking Chihuahua. Believe me, that's the last thing you want."

The man's face cracked into an enormous, shit-eating grin. Then he roared with laughter. I couldn't believe it.

"You must be one of the crew!" He stepped down from the toilet and extended a hand. "I'm Wi—"

"You're a con artist, mate," I said. "I've got your number."

The plumber was grinning like an idiot. "Actually, I'm Will—"

"You think this is funny? You're putting a two-and-a-half-million-quid production at risk," I growled. I was in full flight now, giving him a real piece of my mind. "That's it. If you don't leave this property immediately, I'm calling the police. You've got no business being here."

"No, you're quite right," he said, leaning against the wall of the toilet stall. "Please, be my guest. Do call the police."

"I will!"

"Oh, good. This should be fun."

I pulled my mobile phone out of my pocket.

"Oh, there's no coverage anywhere in the house," he said, smiling. "You'll have to use the landline. It's in the kitchen. You go out this door, turn right, go down three flights of stairs, turn left, go all the way down the hall, and the kitchen is on your right. The phone is on the wall by the refrigerator. Alternatively, the Wi-Fi code is 'Buckford1485,' with a capital *B*. But at this time on a Sunday, the cops will have to come all the way in from Leicester, so it might be a bit of a wait. We could always go direct to the local magistrate to sort this out instead, I suppose. Although as she's my mother, she might need to recuse herself from passing judgement. Alternatively, how about we, you know, sort this out like gentlemen?"

Oh God. Realisation dawned. Heat flushed my face. The silence between us was so far beyond pregnant it had already been sewn back up and was cracking on with the breastfeeding.

"You're... not a plumber, are you?" I said, swallowing.

"Afraid not." A disarming smile lit his face, and his grey eyes sparkled with mischief. He was staring at me through the silence, smirking. His skin was unbelievably clear and smooth. A vision of ruddy good health. His auburn hair was bouncing into curls as it dried. His lips were plump and pink. He was built like he'd spent his whole life on a rugby field. Which, I now realised, he had.

"You're... going to make me ask, aren't you?" I said.

"Oh, I absolutely am." He threw the wet cloth he'd been holding across the room and into the sink. It landed with a splat.

My courage failed me. I decided to build up to the inevitable humiliation, bit by bit.

"So, do you... *live* here, then?"

"I do!" He folded his arms and leant against the stall wall, a broad smile across his face.

"Is this... *your* gaff?"

He shrugged. "We're only ever custodians of the house for our lifetimes. It's never really *ours*, you know? We keep it in trust, for the next generation... and the nation."

I swallowed so deeply my Adam's apple plunged all the way into the pit of my stomach and had to take the elevator back up.

"Keep going," he said, nodding enthusiastically. His loose curls bobbed around his face. "You're doing so well. You're nearly there."

I took a deep breath to summon my courage and closed my eyes. "Are you... Baron Buckford?" I squinted through one eye.

"Got it in one!" His hand shot out once again. "And you are?"

"Peter Topham," I said, sheepishly. I grabbed his hand. "But you can call me Petey Boy."

Why did I say that? The Bisexual Baron Buckford's eyebrows shot up. The mischievous sparkle was back in his eyes. My hand was still in his.

"I'm William," he said, his gaze holding mine.

I faked a smile. I was dying inside.

"But you can call me 'my lord.'"

Jesus, that was hot.

Chapter 8
William

W hy would anyone voluntarily call themselves Petey Boy? I don't actually make anyone call me "my lord," to be clear. Bramley's the only person who does, and that's mostly a habitual tic. I only said that to Petey Boy to break the tension. I'd intended for him to laugh, but instead he went as red as an English rose and bobbed like he was meeting the Prince of Wales.

"No, please don't do that," I said. "It makes me incredibly uncomfortable."

"I'm sorry, my lord."

"No, don't do that either. It's William."

I smiled to reassure him, and his eyes met mine again. They were the most intense Mediterranean blue, behind long lashes. His short-cropped hair was dyed a white blond. He stood up straight, and for the first time, I clocked he was also unbelievably tall. I'm six foot two, and he had at least four inches on me. He must also have been about half my weight. He was built like an animated hair ribbon. He wore a diamond stud earring in his left ear. It was terribly sexy. There was a rebel edge to Petey Boy I found... intoxicating.

"Listen, William, you won't tell Indira I bawled you out, will you? It was a genuine mistake. Please, I—"

"I won't tell a soul." I drew a cross over my heart with my finger to seal the deal. Petey Boy sighed in obvious relief, and for the first time, a smile cracked his face. It absolutely took my breath away. He was beautiful.

"Oh my God, bruv, thank you," he said, holding his hand to his chest. Why was he speaking like that? It didn't sit right, somehow. "This job's bare important. I can't afford for a single thing to go wrong on my watch."

"We have something in common, then," I said. "Bruv."

I thought it might make him smile, but it didn't even register.

"True?" he said.

"Of course! I—" It was on the tip of my tongue to say how much I desperately needed the cash. I had to stop myself. What was it about this majestic feline stranger that had me nearly spilling all the family secrets? "—I want *The Love Manor* to be a raging success too."

"OK, phew." Petey Boy mimed wiping the sweat off his forehead. "That's, like, a huge relief, innit?"

"I want the show to keep coming back year after year," I said—and the more I spoke, the more Petey Boy smiled, the happier he seemed, the more relaxed he appeared, the more I thought perhaps we were maybe kind of flirting? I leant into it. "I'll do whatever I can to make sure this thing goes off without a hitch."

"That's really reassuring," Petey Boy said, bouncing on his heels. "Like, I can't even tell you."

"We're on the same team here," I said, hitting him between the eyes with what I hoped was my cheekiest smile. "Anything you need, please ask."

"Perfect, thank you. The plumber will do for now. Where did you say the phone was?"

He stood there, eyebrows raised, expectant, like he hadn't

knocked the wind out of me. He hadn't been flirting with me at all. It was merely gratitude I was willing to help.

"We don't need a plumber," I said. "I've got this."

He sploshed the lake of water on the floor with the toe of his boot. "What about this situation makes you think you've got this?"

"I know how to fix a toilet. It's not hard."

That was the precise moment the ball float shot loose from the ballcock, opening the valve and sending litres of water shooting out across the room—again. The water hit the stall wall and showered down on me like a thunderstorm.

"The phone?" Petey Boy said.

"In the kitchen," I said, staring at the floor, letting the water run down my back.

Chapter 9
Petey

Early next morning a fleet of taxis collected the first nine contestants from the world's ugliest Travelodge (quite an achievement) and took them to a marquee on the edge of the Buckford Estate. Here, they would be ushered through a well-ordered production line of costumiers and hair and make-up artists until their transformations into Regency-era maids and menservants were complete. The first to arrive was Liverpudlian fashion TikToker Kiki Galapagos, who couldn't say her own name without covering you in spit. I checked her arrival on my clipboard and asked her to follow me into the marquee.

"Is it you I need to speak to about my lady name?" she asked as we stepped inside the big white tent.

"Sorry?"

"Don't I get to be the duchess of somewhere?"

"You're asking if you get a title?"

This was awkward. Not only did she not get to be the duchess of anywhere, in about three hours' time, she was going to learn she was a servant. Those destined to be lords and ladies weren't arriving until this afternoon. (Indira had decided to hold back six of the twenty-four contestants to sprinkle them in later, to stir things up.)

"Only, I'm a brand ambassador for Amphora, you see, so I wanted to be the Duchess of Amphora." She extended a wrist, jangling with bracelets. "They've got this gorgeous new jewellery range—"

"It ain't possible, babes," I said, shutting her down firmly but politely. Kiki looked hacked off, but I didn't have time to deal with her now—another taxi was already pulling up outside.

"What about the Duchess of Clermont-Ferrand, then?" she asked. "I've been representing their new range of heels for summ—"

"You won't be the duchess of anything," I snapped. She straightened, like she was preparing either to ask to speak to the manager or to punch my teeth down the back of my throat.

"Not until you marry a duke," I said, in a brainwave. "It's a dating show, that's the whole point, innit?"

I ushered her in the direction of the costumier and raced out the door to greet the next taxi. That was close. I needed to be more careful. I'd already made an idiot of myself with the baron, I couldn't afford to mess up with the cast as well.

"Can I at least wear the bangles?" Kiki shouted after me.

The next to arrive was Lola Q, an English Korean YouTuber who did make-up tutorials. She screamed when she saw the three gold-trimmed horse-drawn carriages lined up to take the contestants down the drive to Buckford Hall, then she screamed again when she got into the marquee and saw Kiki. Then Kiki screamed when she saw Lola. Then the two of them screamed together, and I felt a trickle of blood roll from my ear.

The cast started to arrive thick and fast. The first of the lads was Theo, a carpenter from Luton, whose social media content suggested he didn't own a shirt and who took me aside to ask if anyone had bagsied being "the Lord of Carhartt" yet. Next was a travel blogger called Zoë, whose social accounts indicated her wardrobe was entirely bathing suits and things that wrap around bathing suits and who demanded to be Lady Lauren by Ralph Lauren. It was about then I realised I'd crossed an invisible bridge into a bizarre new world. Ellie from Essex, who had her own vegan cooking channel, arrived and asked to be the Comtesse Le Creuset. For a moment, I thought things might be getting back to something like normal when "hot farm boy" Tom, from Somerset, turned up and beelined for the horses like it was 4:00 a.m. and the club was closing and he still had a few chat-up lines ready to go. But then he quietly pulled me aside and suggested he'd like to be "the Earl of G. W. Gimpson and Sons Saddlery and Stock Feeders Taunton" and I realised we'd hit peak batshit. It was a relief when the next taxi door finally opened to reveal Ludo's little brother.

"As I live and breathe!" Jonty Boche said, pulling off his sunglasses. "First the taxi flies past a sign for Buckford Hall, and I think, oh hello, it couldn't possibly be, could it? And sure enough, it turns out we're filming this whole shebang at old Dub-Dub's place. Then whose is the first face I see but none other than that scandalous homosexual Petey Boy *Doesn't* Topham."

"Surprise!" I said, meekly. Jonty threw his arms around me, wrapping me up in a bear hug. Then he stood back, held my elbows firmly, and shook his head in what seemed to be genuine disbelief.

"The last time I saw you, I was falling out of the Ritz at one in the morning, and you were being carried off into Green Park by an off-duty Grenadier Guardsman."

"I remember."

"With your legs wrapped around his face."

"I recall."

"How'd that all end up?"

"With a Distinguished Service Medal for him and a visit to a clinic for me," I said.

"Mixed results, then. Shame. It all looked so promising."

I ushered Jonty into the marquee and gave him the onboarding spiel I'd been giving all the others. Turn your phone off and put it in this paper bag. You'll get it back at the end of the show. There's no contact with the outside world during filming. Did you tell anyone other than your emergency contact where you are? No taking any personal belongings with you onto the set. While on set, please ensure you're wearing your microphone pack at all times, except when bathing. And so on.

"Do you have any questions?" I asked.

"Actually, I do." He was perched against a trestle table with his arms folded. "Do I get a title? Because I'm an ambassador for the Hazel Dormouse Protection Trust…"

Chapter 10
William

The buzz in the carriage court as filming got underway was absolutely electric. It was like those tense few minutes before you run out onto the rugby pitch—anticipation in the air, grunts of encouragement flying around everywhere, adrenaline pumping through your veins, and tears streaming down your face because you were careless about where you put your hands after slapping on the Tiger Balm. Well, maybe not the last bit. It was a bright sunny day, right after luncheon, and I was standing well back, under a tree, where Indira was staring at a bank of monitors. I was under strict instructions to remain totally silent.

"It's costing sixty grand to film this one sequence," Indira explained. "So you're welcome to stand here and watch. But if you fuck this up for me in any way, I'll pluck your family jewels from betwixt your impossibly thicc thighs and I'll crush them with my bare hands until they turn into diamonds. Your future baroness will think you've had a fucking vajazzle. Do I make myself clear?"

"Crystal." I swallowed. "You won't hear a peep. We're on the same team. I'm here to make sure this whole thing goes as smoothly as possible."

Indira did not look convinced.

Members of the crew were zipping around everywhere, all wearing headsets with little microphones. At least five cameras were set up on tripods around the carriage court, the operators standing on boxes, heads bowed downwards, staring intently into their viewfinders. There was a bloke with a big boom microphone who, on closer inspection, I realised was carrying a duck in a baby sling. There was absolutely no sign of Petey Boy, thank God. I wasn't sure I was ready to see him again, knowing he must have thought I was a bumbling incompetent. But in the centre of the carriage court, standing on a small stage covered in red velvet, was someone I was thrilled to see—*The Love Manor* host, and national treasure, Dorinda Carter. Big, Black, and Brummie, she looked like a queen in a massive hooped dress of electric blue silk. She was glittering with diamonds (acquired, I imagined, from Indira's previous victims). A stylist bustled around her, adjusting a tiara sparkling out from an improbably tall afro puff.

"Right, let's go," Indira said into her headset. "Get the drone up."

Someone yelled, "Places, everybody!"

The stylist bolted from the set. Dorinda stood a little taller.

Indira, eyes flicking between the monitors, nodded and pressed the button on her headset. "Action!"

"Wait!" someone shouted from behind us. "I've brought acorns!"

"CUT!"

I turned to see Mum and Bramley running towards us across the lawn from the Dower House, carrying wicker baskets.

"Reset, everybody." I could feel Indira's eyes boring into the back of my head. "Lord Buckford…"

If I didn't turn around, I couldn't meet her gaze and she couldn't turn me to stone.

"I'll handle it."

Mum pulled up in front of us, huffing and puffing.

"Gosh, you don't realise how big that lawn really is until you try running across it," Mum said. "I guess that's why we call it the Great Lawn."

Over her shoulder, I could see Bramley about twenty feet back, bent over, hands on his knees, trying to catch his breath. "If you've killed Bramley—"

"Oi," Indira barked. "I'm trying to make a fucking TV show here. Do you know how much it costs per minute to keep thirty crew standing around doing bugger all?"

"Well, exactly," Mum said. "That's why I've bought acorns for everybody."

"Mum, that's enough," I said through gritted teeth.

"They're a symbol of good luck," she continued. "Only they're not fresh. I collected these last year, obviously, because acorns are out of season right now. But I thought if everyone had an acorn in their pocket, it might—"

"Is she a fucking squirrel?" Indira muttered.

Mum blinked, clearly taken aback. "I'm sensing some negative energy. Perhaps some pranic breathing exercises, as a group, might be in order?"

I turned to face Indira. "Just take them."

"Pardon?"

"It'll be quicker if you take them," I said, sotto voce. "Imagine she's your nephew."

Indira reached out her hand and took the basket. "*Where* are my manners? Very thoughtful. Thanks ever so much, et cetera. I'll distribute them to everyone later. I hope there's enough for Derek's duck. I know he'd hate to miss out. Will you be staying to watch the filming?"

The sarcasm was thick in the air, but Mum completely failed to smell it. She nodded. So did Bramley, who'd caught up and was collapsed on the grass beside his own wicker basket.

"Fine," Indira said. "But if I hear a peep out of either of you, I'm sticking every last one of those acorns up your arse, sideways, until you're shitting expensive cabinetry. Do you hear me?"

A few minutes later, three black landaus, each drawn by a team of four magnificent Cleveland Bay mares, circled into the carriage court. As if out of nowhere, Petey Boy was at the centre of the action. He had a clipboard in one hand, while the other was constantly playing with the button of his headset. He looked so *in control*. Like he was completely in his element. As the cast members sat in the carriages, dressed in their finery, Petey Boy issued instructions about how they should line up in front of Dorinda and what would happen next. He oozed calm authority. A gust of wind picked up, and from the stables, Achilles neighed loudly—as far as the stallion was concerned, a busload of new girlfriends had turned up. About three of the mares whinnied back. My eyes darted to Indira, but she didn't say anything. Then there was a flurry of activity, and Petey Boy dashed over to stand with our little group. I raised my hand to wave hello, but he ignored me completely to stare at the monitors.

Indira called, "Action." Actors dressed as footmen bustled about, helping the contestants down from the landaus. I spotted Jonty Boche, dressed in full coat and breeches, jumping down onto the gravel. Before I could engage my brain, my hand shot up to wave hello to my old school chum. Unfortunately, Jonty did the same.

"If it isn't old Dub-Dub!" he bellowed, marching across the carriage court with his hand extended.

"CUT!"

Indira and Petey Boy both turned and glared at me, heads tilted. I'd seen the velociraptors do that in *Jurassic Park*.

"Petey Boy, go deal with your twat friend."

"I'm on it," he said. Unless I'm terribly mistaken, he scowled at me—actually *scowled* at me—before dashing away to head Jonty off at the pass. It was clear I was no longer considered merely a bumbling incompetent but a serious liability. So much for being on the same team.

"Seeing as we've all stopped," Mum put in, "would anyone like some tea?"

Bramley produced a thermos from his basket and raised it aloft like a trophy.

"NO! We need to crack on." Indira turned to face me. "Lord Buckford, if you, or your people, cause me one more delay, I promise you I will be adding a pair of very small, very inbred, very high-carat diamonds to my jewellery box. Are we clear?"

My head was in my hands. This was not going well. When everyone was back in their positions, Petey Boy dashed back over to our tree by the monitors. I smiled as apologetically as I could manage and received a death stare in reply.

"Action!"

In the carriage court, it was time for Dorinda Carter to deliver the day's coup de grâce. The smiling faces beaming back at her as she welcomed them to *The Love Manor* turned to looks of horror as the first nine contestants learned they would not be lords and ladies after all.

"Upstairs, in the servants' quarters, you'll each find a bedroom with your name on the door," Dorinda said. "Inside, you'll find the uniforms appropriate to your new roles, as maids, housekeepers, cooks, valets, butlers, and footmen."

"You what?" Ellie from Essex spat.

Kiki Galapagos shook her head. "Yous are takin' the piss."

Tom the hot farm boy raised a hand. "Can I be a stable boy?"

Indira's jaw was clenched, her eyes bulging with delight. On the monitor, I could see cameras moving in and out on the contestant's reactions. This was exactly what she wanted.

"So, go upstairs, find your rooms, get changed, and get to work," Dorinda said. "Because…" She paused for dramatic effect. "Tonight, you're hosting a ball for the lords and ladies of the ton. They will be here in four hours' ti—"

A duck quacked, loudly.

I barked a sharp, nervous, involuntary laugh—and slapped my hand to my mouth, horrified. There was a beat of silence. Dorinda and all the contestants fell into giggles. The carefully built on-screen tension had evaporated. Off-screen, the tension was thicker than ever. I looked at Indira, waiting for her to explode. She was silently staring at the monitors. I glanced over at Petey Boy, who was practically white knuckled, waiting for Indira's reaction.

Dorinda didn't miss a beat.

"So you've got a lot of work to do," she said, taking charge of the moment. "Cos I don't reckon that duck's in the oven yet."

Jonty's familiar laugh bellowed across the estate, like a hyena having an asthma attack. The contestants cackled like hens. My eyes flicked to Petey Boy. His gaze met mine for an instant before we turned to face Indira.

We waited.

And waited.

Then she smiled, and her shoulders started to bounce up and down.

"CUT!" she bellowed. She took her headset off, rubbed her eyes with her hands, and *laughed*—a real gut-busting roar of a laugh. It was joyous. Then she turned to Petey and sank a finger into his chest.

"And *that*," she said, "is why we always work with the best. Dorinda Carter. What a fucking pro."

Petey's face transformed, the tension evaporating—replaced by a glorious smile. He really was beautiful.

Chapter 11
Petey

Filming for the Welcome Ball was a triumph—which was a huge relief after the fiasco that bumbling aristocrat caused earlier in the afternoon. The Great Hall looked spectacular, as did the contestants in their empire-line dresses, dapper waistcoats, and smart uniforms. But *The Love Manor* was a dating show, and the Regency conceit only went so far. No one danced a quadrille. What we wanted was gossip and intrigue. So Indira was thrilled when we got footage of the contestants sizing each other up, chatting shit about one another, and deciding who they wanted to shag and in what order.

Two hours later, they were all safely tucked up in their beds—and all I wanted was to have a shower and do the same. I was studying the map to work out where my allocated bathroom was when there was a knock at my door.

"You decent, Petey Boy?" They were the unmistakable tones of Jonty Boche.

I opened the door, annoyed by the interruption. "Yes, I'm decent."

"First time for everything, I suppose."

"Jonty, I'm asleep on my feet. You're not meant to be here. What do you want? And where's your microphone pack? You're supposed to wear it at all times."

"It's old Dub-Dub."

I yawned. "It's what?"

"Dub-Dub," he said, swinging into my room and plonking himself on the bed. "Winters Minor."

"I'm too tired for this shit, Jonty."

"I was hoping to see William."

Dub-Dub? What a ridiculous nickname. But then, he was a ridiculous man. Hot. Stunning, in fact. But ridiculous.

"Is he about? I haven't seen him in an absolute age. He never comes to London anymore. I've been up on secret dormouse-related business, of course, but... feeling a bit guilty about not making more of an effort."

"Jonty, you're not allowed contact with the outside world. It's in your contract. Go back to bed."

"Outside world? Petey, Dub-Dub is Lord Buckford. This is Buckford Hall. Dub-Dub's not the outside world. This is quite literally *his* world. If anything, we're the outsiders. If you think about it. We're inside his world, if you see my meaning? How can he possibly constitute the outside world?"

Exhausted, I held the door open and pointed out into the hall. "Jonty, it's been a really long day."

"Right! Of course!" he said, jumping up. "But... is he here?" His eyebrow cocked, eyes squinted, as he studied my reaction. "Or is he... staying at the Dower House? Or... in town, perhaps?"

"I notice you're not moving to the door."

"Yes, I noticed that too."

"Jonty."

"If he's still on the estate, nod, and I'll promise I'll leave you be."

I gave him nothing. Jonty frowned.

"Is that you *not* nodding, meaning he's not on the estate, or is that you not wanting to answer me because you're a cuck who believes in obeying the kinds of silly rules that keep old chums from catching up?"

I groaned. Indira had been very clear about not letting the cast know the actual lord was living in the house. But Jonty obviously didn't intend to leave until he got the information he wanted, and my body ached for my bed.

"Come on," he said, wiggling his thick black eyebrows. "Be a sport!"

I sensed that he sensed my resolve was waning. But if I was going to risk the wrath of Indira Murray, I was going to get something for my trouble.

"I'll make you a deal."

"Anything. What do you need? Daniel Craig's telephone number? Henry Cavill's discarded underpants?"

"It's William, actually," I said.

"Oh, hello." Jonty's eyes sparkled. "You're such a horndog, Petey Boy. Honestly, you're insatiable."

I sighed. "What's his deal?"

"You mean, is he as bisexual as the papers say? No idea. Never even known him to go on a date, if I'm honest. I thought he was in a committed throuple with his rugby team and his library books. You could've blown me away with a pheasant when I saw the infamous photo in *The Bulletin*."

"No, it's not that."

"Do you need a character reference?"

"Well, yes, actually. He seems really—"

"Hot?"

I shook my head.

"Sweet?"

"Out of his depth."

Jonty cackled like a hen laying a Rubik's Cube, which wasn't an encouraging sign.

"I've got a lot riding on this show going well," I hissed. "I need to know if he's a liability. Because so far, all signs point to yes."

Jonty took a deep breath, his face turning serious: something I don't think I'd ever seen it do before. That wasn't encouraging either.

"Look, he used to be a lot of fun. Dub-Dub never asked for any of this," Jonty said, swirling a finger through the air. "He's doing his best with the cards he's been dealt. But I'll tell you this for free. While I've known plenty of chaps with bigger brains than William, I've never known anyone with a bigger heart. With Dub-Dub, everything comes from a good place. Always."

Jonty's blue eyes were bursting with sincerity. I was still taking in what he'd said when he transformed back into Ludo's obnoxious brother.

"That was some top-shelf wingmanning on my part, I thought," he said. "No round of applause, I notice. Shame. Still, did you get what you need?"

"I asked if he was a liability."

"Oh, total liability. I'd keep a close eye on him. Don't let him out of your sight. Best to stick to him like shit on your shoe."

I rubbed my temples. This was pointless. I wanted my bed.

"So, is he about?" Jonty asked, eyebrows raised in hope. "Deal's a deal, and all that."

I nodded. "He's lodging in the folly. No one is supposed to know. So if you get caught, you're on your own. I am *not* losing my job over this."

"You're a prince!" Jonty grabbed me by both shoulders and planted a kiss on each of my cheeks. "I'll put in a good word for you with His Lordship."

"I don't need your help, thank you very much," I called after him. "And put your microphone pack back on when you're done!"

I cracked the window to let some air into the stuffy little room. As I scooped up my toiletries bag and my towel, I glanced again at the complicated map to check my route to my allocated bathroom. I stepped out into the hall, turned the corner at the end of the corridor, and counted my way along to the third door, grabbing the handle and flinging it wide open, ready to greet whatever Victorian horrors a Buckford Hall bathroom had in store for me this time.

"Oh, hello there."

"Lord Buckford!"

He was side on to me, one foot up on the edge of the bath, towelling himself down. I couldn't breathe. My lungs scrambled for air.

"I mean, my lord. I mean... William. I mean... oh my God. I'm *so* sorry."

I looked away, but he didn't try to move or cover himself. I looked back. The room was full of steam, and his skin was pink from the heat of the water. His body was athletic, thick from years of rugby, but softened, I guessed, after several years away from the pitch. My subconscious immediately imagined exactly how it would feel to have that weight bearing down on me. Stop it, I told myself. No boys. I was here to work. Keep it professional.

"How'd it go out there today, Petey Boy?"

"You're... completely naked." I shielded my crotch with my toiletries bag, as if I wasn't still wearing my boiler suit.

William put his foot on the ground, stood upright, and turned to face me—his soft, plump cock swinging there—like this was the most normal encounter in the world. I tried to focus on his face.

"Well, I'm in my bathroom," he said, rubbing his towel through his hair. "And so are you, as it happens."

I shook my head. "I counted the doors. This is *my* bathroom."

William pointed past me to a door on the other side of the corridor.

"I think you'll find *that's* your bathroom. This one's mine." A cheeky grin lit up his face.

I looked over my shoulder, face burning with shame. Words failed me. I sucked my lips in between my teeth and made a popping sound.

Then made it a few more times, as I slowly stepped backwards across the corridor. I pointed my thumb over my shoulder.

"I guess I'll..."

William held up his hand and wiggled his fingers in a patronising little wave. I turned on my heel and opened the door to my bathroom, spun back around again to say thank you, then turned, disappeared into the correct bathroom, and slammed the door behind me.

"You're welcome!" I heard William call out from across the hall.

I turned to face the bathroom door and let my forehead slump against it with a thud. I stood there like an idiot, knowing I'd made a massive tit of myself in front of the most perfectly formed man I'd never been under. Worse, I was allowing myself to get distracted not only by a boy but by the biggest liability I'd ever met. From the other side of the door came the unmistakable sound of the liability chuckling.

Chapter 12
William

The cuckoo clock cuckooed midnight. I sank back into my father's old armchair, and the dents and tea stains that had outlived him, intending to read for a half an hour before falling asleep. It was strange, being in here without him. I picked up my beaten old copy of *The Page's Quest* and dug my elbows into the threadbare fabric of the armrests, but my mind soon drifted to the television industry's sexiest animated hair ribbon. Petey Boy had seemed so in control at work, but he was at his cutest when he was flustered and wrong-footed. I smiled, happy to have evened our score. The book fell open, and my makeshift bookmark, the unopened letter from His Majesty's Revenue and Customs, slithered out onto my lap. Sensing danger, the dinosaur part of my brain sent a shot of adrenaline through my chest. I closed my eyes—if I didn't see the tax bill, I could ignore the tax bill—took a couple of deep breaths, and tried to calm my body. It's what I used to do before taking a penalty kick. And it might have worked but for the knock from downstairs. I nearly soiled the red satin boxer shorts that served as my jimmy-jams.

"Bramley, is that you?" He was supposed to be lodging at the Dower House with Mum. The knock came again, this time more insistent. I tucked the envelope back into the book and tossed it onto the coffee table. "Are you missing me already? Or are you annoyed because she's beating you at Scrabble?" I donned my robe and padded down the stairs. "She cheats, you know. Keeps extra letters Blu-Tacked under the table."

I flung open the door to be greeted by a face significantly younger than the withered old walnut of my faithful retainer.

"Dub-Dub!"

Jonty's arms flew wide, and I found myself wrapped in them before I knew what was happening.

"Marvellous to see you," he said, grabbing my elbows. "How are you, dear fellow?"

"What a pleasant surprise." And while I meant it, a new sense of dread washed over me. I adopted a conspiratorially hushed tone. "But what are you doing here?"

"Didn't seem right, sleeping under the old Buckford lead without saying a proper hello." He released me and began wafting around the room, inspecting everything from the floorboards to the rafters.

"Golly, I haven't been in here in *years*! Looks the same." He sniffed the air. "Smells the same. Should we open a window?"

Apart from the bathroom being along the hall, the folly functioned as its own apartment. This level, the downstairs room, was on the third floor of the house and served as a small bedroom. There wasn't much there, only an old wire-framed double bed and a gas ring so you could make tea or boil an egg. It felt quite a lot like my old dorm at Petersham—doubly so, now my old school friend was standing in it.

"We'll get in trouble for this," I said, closing the door as gently as possible, as if someone might hear it click and we'd be sent to see the headmaster for a flogging.

"Remember all those nights we used to sneak out of dorms to go to the cinema in Richmond?" Jonty said, making himself comfortable on my bed.

"We only did that once."

"Did we?"

"You abandoned me halfway through to go hang out by the towpath and fondle Laura Pettigrew's tits."

"Ah yes! Good old Heavy Pettigrew." Jonty disappeared into memory. "Collected virginities like Pokémon. Absolutely relentless. Did she track you down in the end?"

I shuddered. "Mercifully not."

"Oh, shame. Who punched your V-card, then? I know her brother was sweet on you."

I winced. I wasn't ashamed of being a virgin, but I wasn't going to admit my status to Jonty or he'd take it up like a charitable cause. I'd end up as part of an Instagram campaign. Fortunately, Jonty was easy to distract.

"Tea?" I pointed to the kettle on the gas ring.

"Splendid suggestion, Dub-Dub! Don't mind if I do. Have you got oat milk? Lactose intolerant these days. If I get so much as a whiff of an unwashed cow creamer, I'm shitting for Britain. Still, keeps you slim." He flopped back onto the bed. "So, Bunny Winters cheats at Scrabble, hey? Escándalo!"

I'd forgotten how completely overwhelming Jonty's presence could be. While the kettle boiled, I listened to him catching up on old times. The entire time I was terrified either Petey Boy or, God forbid, Indira might burst through the door to make an arrest. There were cameras throughout the house. Surely it was only a matter of minutes before someone noticed Jonty Boche was missing and came to collect their errant schoolboy? I didn't fancy opening the door to either of them with Jonty sprawled across my bed, so I suggested we take our tea up to the study. As Jonty padded up the stairs, wittering on about his beloved dormice, I quickly snuck open the door to check the hall for any sign of rampaging producers. The coast was clear, but the little robot camera mounted in the corner of the hall turned its eye towards me, its red LED blinking. I slammed the door shut.

Upstairs, Jonty was flopped in Dad's old armchair like he owned it, my copy of *The Page's Quest* in his lap, the envelope in his hands.

"I think you're meant to open these," he said, waving it about.

I snatched the letter out of his hand and tossed it onto my father's desk, nearly spilling my tea.

"It looks kind of angry. All those red letters."

"It's nothing."

I perched on the edge of the other chair. Fortunately, Jonty had the attention span of a lobotomised squirrel.

"I adored your old man," he said, looking around a room. "A true British eccentric. I remember he used to go up to the roof to do yoga first thing in the morning. Stark bollock naked. Arse up, saluting the sun, dangly old scrotum visible from space. Must have been astronauts chundering their cornflakes up all over the International Space Station."

He tossed my book onto the coffee table and reached for his tea. "You'll never guess who I bumped into earlier."

I shrugged. "Oscar-winning actor Dame Judi Dench?"

He frowned. "No, Petey Boy. The producer. Chum of Ludo's, dresses like a garage mechanic, looks like he was assembled from a flat-pack. And he was asking me questions about *you*." Jonty's eyes sparkled with mischief. "I'm telling you now, Dub-Dub, he's hot for you. Absolutely roasting. Oiled up, generously salted, and slapping his rump with buttered rosemary. You should get in there."

My pulse broke into a light canter. I couldn't stop it. Not wanting to look too keen, I scoffed loudly.

"Don't be ridiculous. If Petey Boy thinks of me at all, he thinks I'm a nuisance."

Now Jonty scoffed. "Noooooo! No, no, no, no, no, noooooo. Perish the thought!" He batted the idea away with his hand. "He's into you all right. Made a point of asking me what your 'deal' was. If that's not a sure sign his old tip's tingling for you, I don't know what is."

I fidgeted on my chair, feeling uncomfortable. "And what did you tell him?"

"I bigged you up, old chap. Pointed out all your finest qualities! Level six human paladin with an oath of devotion. Brain so remarkable it should be studied by science. So impressively hung the lads all call you the National Gallery. That sort of thing."

I laughed. "Well, he's under no illusions there. He burst into my bathroom uninvited about half an hour ago and saw the whole exhibition for free."

Jonty's hand shot up into his loose black curls. "My God, he moves fast! I can't have left him more than a few minutes earlier. Imagine if the British government had that kind of efficiency. We'd still have an empire." Jonty kicked his feet up onto the coffee table. "So, what happened?"

"He was so flustered he couldn't get out of there fast enough."

Jonty frowned. "This is the same Petey Boy we're talking about?"

"Yes."

"Tall bloke? Bleached hair? Built like a biro?"

I nodded.

"And there you were, all chiselled and as naked as Michaelangelo's David, and you say he couldn't get out of there fast enough?"

I shrugged. "Yes. It's hard to believe it could be the same guy who runs around with a clipboard putting the fear of God into people all day."

"We all contain multitudes." Jonty shook his head. "Petey has certainly contained multitudes. Often in the course of a single evening."

I had no idea what Jonty meant and I didn't really care to ask in case I looked stupid. We sat there in silence for a moment.

"So, what's *his* 'deal,' then?" I asked.

Jonty sipped his tea.

"Well, he's the black sheep of a massively overachieving family—the affliction of so many of us—so he's got a huge chip on his shoulder. He's cursed to spend forever trying to prove himself. He trawls all the wrong places looking for love when what he's really looking for is approval. But he has the brains, drive, and energy of a border collie, and he's every bit as smart, loving, and loyal. No idea if he's any good with sheep, mind you."

I don't think I'd taken a breath the whole time Jonty was speaking. "Golly, that's quite the review."

"Plus, he's widely regarded as the best two-door ride Vauxhall has produced in a century."

I spat my tea out across the coffee table.

Jonty's eyebrows waggled in a disconcerting manner. "Shall I tell him you're interested, then?"

"Absolutely not."

"Why not? You are. It's as plain as the tea running down your face."

I wiped my chin with my wrist and shook my head.

"Come on, Dub-Dub, a little summer fling would do you good. Throw your leg over a few times and give the old glutes a workout."

"I don't want a fling, I wan—"

There was an angry thump at the door, and a Scottish voice boomed from beyond it.

"If this meeting of the Incompetent Nepo Baby Society is finished, I'd quite like a fucking word."

Chapter 13
Petey

By day four it was all kicking off at *The Love Manor*. It was a bright sunny morning, and I was standing on the Great Lawn with one of our roving outdoor camera crews watching three of the female contestants rip each other to shreds.

"Why is you disrespecting her, though?" Lady Cristina, a fitness Instagrammer from London, screeched.

Ellie from Essex raised a hand. "No offence, but it's none of your business, babes."

"Don't 'babes' me, *babes*, I saw what I saw. I'm sticking up for what's right."

Indira was back in our production office, in the Old Coach House, watching the footage roll in. She had to be loving every second. This was TV gold. It was also how I could prove her faith in me was warranted.

The Bookstagrammer, Lady Ridhi, was crying—long manicured nails quivering as she wiped her tears. "But why would you even *ask* Armando to go into the hedge maze with you? He's with me."

Ellie rolled her eyes. "Then you ain't got nothing to worry about, have you, babes?"

"The boys are saying you kissed him!" Cristina cried.

Indira's voice crackled in my headset. "What the fuck is he doing? He's ruining *everything*!"

I looked up, chest tightening in panic, and my eyes landed on him. You couldn't miss him. Of course it was *him*. Riding his horse directly through the back of our shot—shirtless, round arse bouncing rhythmically, erotically, up and down in the saddle. Instantly, I understood why the "horsey girls" at school had been so obsessed with their weekend pony clubs.

"Holy shit," Ridhi said, pointing at William, tears suddenly forgotten. "Girls, cop a look at that. It's straight out of a Jilly Cooper."

Ellie and Cristina turned in unison.

"You must be joking me," Ellie said, eyes glazing.

Cristina fanned herself with her hand. "Who the hell is that?"

We all watched, captivated, as William's wide back and firm buttocks bounced out of view behind the stables. Indira screeched something into my ear, shaking me back to life. I banged my hand against my clipboard to get the women's attention.

Ellie turned around, thumb pointing back over her shoulder, eyes hopeful. "Is he for us?"

"No, he's the guy who owns this place." As soon as the words left my mouth, I knew I'd messed up. "He's completely out of bounds!"

"*He's* Lord Buckford?" Cristina's razor-thin eyebrows were waging a losing battle with the Botox in her forehead.

"Come on, let's focus," I said. "We're all here to talk about Lord Armando, remember?"

Ridhi looked at me like I was an idiot. "Who cares about that badmash when there's a real-life lord right there."

"And he looks like that!" Cristina added.

Ellie was shaking her head. "I ain't never been jealous of a horse before. He can bounce up and down like that on me anytime."

My headset crackled, and Indira's voice came through in my ear.

"Reset. Remind Ridhi we've got Armando on camera saying he's falling in love with her. Find a way to quietly slip it to Cristina we got the kiss on film. That should get us back to where we need to be. You're on your own for five while I go ask Baron Fuckwad whether he's been kicked in the head by a horse or if he's really that fucking stupid."

"Let *me* go," I said. It burst out of me so quickly I surprised myself. But not only was this an opportunity to show Indira I could handle any situation the job demanded, it was also a chance to regain some semblance of professionalism with William.

"We'll finish this scene and I'll go have a word with him," I said. "You've got enough on your plate."

* * *

Half an hour later I was marching towards the stables, clipboard in hand, headset hooked into my belt, going over in my head what I was going to say when I found Lord Liability. The crunch of the gravel under my trainers sounded satisfyingly aggressive. The air was thick with the earthy stench of farmyard. A loud neigh echoed out from the stables. Several other horses joined in. Then I thought I heard William's voice. I made a beeline for an open pair of barn-style doors, ready to give him a piece of my mind. I was still a good ten metres from the building when I decided to fire the starting gun on my rage nice and early, so he'd know he was in trouble.

"Lord Buckford," I called out, sounding fierce.

"Lord Buckford again, is it?" he called back, although I still couldn't see him.

Then, suddenly, I *could* see him. William emerged from the darkness, through the barn doors and into the bright midday sun. He strode towards me, still shirtless, wearing only cream jodhpurs, knee-high black riding boots, and a pair of brown leather gardening gloves. Sweat trickled down the side of his face, his neck, and the line of his chest. A gold chain around his neck sparkled in the sun. He was so... *wide*.

"What happened to William?" he said. He had straw in his hair, dirt smeared across his chest.

"Mate, do you have any idea what you've done?" I managed to bark.

He shook his head, grimaced, and wiped his brow with his forearm. How was I meant to work in these conditions? I was here to give this guy a professional ticking off and all I wanted to do was lap at his armpits like a Labrador at its dinner bowl. I had to remember why I was here. Not at the stables, but why I was at Buckford Hall at all.

"I've been staying out of everyone's way, as requested," William said, turning towards a haystack and sliding his gloved hands under the strings of a bale. "I haven't had any contact with anybody since Jonty came to the folly. Whatever's happened now, I'm not to blame."

He lifted the bale of hay, rested it against a powerful thigh, and disappeared back into the stables with it. I had no choice but to follow—if only so I could keep watching the way the cotton of his jodhpurs clung to his arse like it was polishing a pair of bowling balls. I made a mental note to brainstorm reality TV show ideas centred around horses and stables. *The Riding School*? *Celebrity Riding School*, perhaps?

"Watch your step," William said, giving me barely enough time to skip around a massive pile of horse poo.

"You ruined a really important scene."

William put the bale down, pulled out a pocket knife, and cut the strings. The bale burst open.

"How?"

"We were filming on the Great Lawn. You rode through our shot, bruv."

"What? I'm so sorry." He looked genuinely surprised. "Nobody told me you were filming outside. How was I to know?"

It was a good point. I could see in his face that he could see in my face that I recognised it was a good point.

"Look, when I got that bollocking from your boss lady the other night, I agreed I wouldn't get in the way of filming and I wouldn't fraternise with the cast, and she agreed I'd get to keep my balls."

I nodded. Indira told me she'd threatened to shave £10,000 off his cheque.

"The agreed exception to my imprisonment was that this is a working estate, and there's still work that needs to be done."

He looked... fed up. Tired. I remembered what Jonty had said about William being overwhelmed and felt a twinge of guilt for having been so aggressive.

"Achilles needs exercising, every single day," he said, spreading straw around the stall. "It's non-negotiable."

An enormous white horse popped its head over the side of the stall and neighed loudly.

"That's right, boy. I'm talking about you." William reached up and scratched the animal's jaw. My God, it was sexy.

A volley of neighs shot back from somewhere nearby. Achilles snorted, threw his head around, and stamped his feet. I stepped back.

"Is he mad at me or something?"

"No, he's horny." William chuckled. "Three of your Cleveland Bay mares are chasing him. The handsome devil."

The dozen horses that pulled the carriages down the drive on the first day had been hired for the duration of the production. William stood, took his gloves off, and stretched his back and neck, rolling his shoulders. I couldn't take much more of this. In the name of discretion, I held my clipboard in front of the gusset of my boiler suit. I tried to remember the job I'd been sent here to do—and thought I might be able to do it with compassion.

"We wouldn't have to be so strict if you weren't costing us a bomb in reshoots."

"I'm sorry I ruined your shot," William said, eyes twinkling with sincerity. "I didn't mean to. Believe me, I want this TV show to go as well as you do."

"You keep saying that, but the evidence—"

"Listen, we both want the same thing here." The piece of straw finally fell from his hair. It landed on the sweaty round bulk of his pec, right by the signet ring he kept on his gold neck chain. In that moment, I didn't think we wanted the same thing at all, because all I wanted was for William to ride me like we were belting down the home straight in the last hundred yards of the Grand National. Like, professionally.

"How about you let me know when and where you're filming outside," William said. "And I'll avoid taking Achilles out at those times, or at least avoid taking him anywhere we might be seen on camera?"

I nodded. "That works."

"See, that wasn't so hard, was it?" He smiled, grabbing a rake and leaning on it. "And we did it all without any of the threats of violence you folks from London are so keen on."

I held up a hand. "OK, bruv, but if Indira asks you about this, you'll pretend I had you quaking in your boots, right?"

William snorted. "Quaking, bordering on incontinent."

I laughed, William smiled. A crackle of static burst from my headset. I grabbed it from my belt and stuck it to my ear. I was barely able to make out the words "catfight in the Orangery."

"Sounds like you're needed," William said. I nodded, waved a thank you, and turned to bolt out the door.

"Watch out!" he called as I planted my foot straight into the huge pile of horse shit.

Chapter 14
William

That evening, I was propped up on my bed in the folly with a steaming cup of tea and an ill-advisedly tall and teetering pile of ginger nut biscuits on the bedside table. Excommunicated from my house guests, I had no reason to be wearing anything other than my red satin boxer shorts. The letter from HMRC was shoved deep beneath the pillows, and my copy of *The Broken Crown* was open in my lap. It's the first book in the *Knights-Errant* trilogy proper, and I was getting to the good bit, where young Sir Gawain saves Prince Henry from an assassin's arrow and the unspoken sexual tension between them starts to sizzle and smoke like a dragon's set it ablaze.

There was a knock at the door.

"Bramley?"

The knock came again.

"If that's you, Jonty, I'm not risking a turn on Indira Murray's ducking stool to listen to you bleat on about my father's balls again."

"Sorry?" said a soft feminine voice. It definitely wasn't Indira. Perhaps one of Petey's colleagues had come to ask me to relight the hot water system, or fix a loose stair rod or relocate the newts in the downstairs lavatory? I opened the door to find a woman mid-curtsey, her voluminous breasts practically tumbling out of a black silk dressing gown.

"My lord," she said, standing upright, her wide brown eyes—innocent as a newborn doe's—meeting mine.

"Are you lost?" I asked. "Can I help you?"

She shook her head, then looked at me the way a child looks at a doughnut in a bakery window.

"No, thank you. I've found *exactly* what I'm looking for." She brushed her décolletage with her hand. "My name's Ridhi. Aren't you going to invite me in, my lord?"

"I'm not allowed to talk to strangers," I said—suddenly aware this unsolicited intrusion was going to cost me £10,000. I had to get rid of her.

"But the whole idea is for us to get to know each other, my lord."

"Whole idea of what?"

She looked past me to the bed, her eyes lighting up. "Oh, my goodness, you're a reader. What are you reading?" Ridhi's voice had changed completely. She pushed her way into the room and plucked my book off the bed.

"*The Broken Crown?*" She smiled—somewhat patronisingly, I thought—and sat on the edge of my bed. "*Knights-Errant* is such a classic series. Have you tried Brandon Osmond's *A Kingdom of Vipers and Valour*, though? It's so much fresher."

Well, that was it. I had no idea what this woman wanted, but if it was an argument, she was going to get it.

"I prefer fantasy that doesn't read like the author has already sold the TV rights to a streaming service," I said.

"Please don't misunderstand me, my lord. *Knights-Errant* is a foundational text—"

"Without D. R. R. Fanshaw, there *is no* Brandon Osmond."

"I *so* agree." No, she didn't. She was backtracking. I know an Osmond apologist when I hear one.

Silence fell between us. Ridhi worried her lips with her teeth.

"I think we might have got off on the wrong foot, my lord. Can we start again?" She leant back onto the bed and kicked her legs playfully. "I have just had a vision of the most incredible collaboration. My followers will go nuts for a fantasy-reading aristocrat with a chest like that." She patted the bed. "What would you say to you and I... going viral together?"

I reached out a hand. She smiled, batted her eyelashes, and grabbed it.

"Absolutely not," I said, pulling her upright and shuffling her out the door.

"But... my lord! Please! I think there's been a misunderstanding—"

"No misunderstanding," I said, firmly. "You're a member of the cast. I'm not allowed to talk to you. Please, go. And for the love of God, don't tell anyone you've been here!"

Ridhi frowned.

"Nice to meet you," I said, and gently closed the door.

A moment later came a muffled "*Vipers and Valour* has sold more than thirty million copies, you pretentious wanker!" I heard her stamping up the hall like a petulant child. Well, I wasn't letting her have the last word.

"*Knights-Errant* has never been out of print, you philistine," I shouted back, without opening the door.

"I have sixty thousand followers on Bookstagram!" Her voice was faint now, all the way down the corridor. "I know about books!"

I cracked open the door and shouted through the gap. "I did my dissertation on *Knights-Errant*!" I slammed the door. Then opened it again and shouted: "At Loughborough University!"

Well, I doubted Ridhi would be back. But what the hell had she been doing here in the first place? I returned to my book and stack of biscuits, wondering whether she'd cost me ten big ones. Twenty minutes later, there was another knock, and I presumed I was about to find out. Too fed up to care, I opened the door still clad only in my boxers, ginger nut crumbs tumbling out of my belly button. I was greeted by a blonde woman wearing not very much.

"Is you Lord Buckford?"

"Sadly," I sighed.

She curtseyed.

"No, please don't do that. You need to go—"

"You can call me Ellie." She extended her hand, and on instinct I shook it, which she took as permission to slither past me into the room. "I'm a vegan chef. Maybe you seen my YouTube channel, Eat Like an Ellie Plant?"

"I'm afraid I haven't."

Ellie collapsed on my bed.

"We saw you riding your horse earlier. You looked right fit."

"Ah." I was beginning to see what was going on.

"You're ever so good with animals. That's a very sexy quality in a man."

"Er, thank you. I believe Indira's lined up a dozen men with a range of sexy qualities for you ladies to choose from. She's even dressed them all up like Colin Firth. Or Matthew Macfadyen. Whichever you prefer. You should probably be getting back to them, or you'll get stuck with Mr Collins." I held the door open, gesturing the way out with my hand.

She didn't budge. "Why chase them pretend lords when I've got the real deal right here?"

If she fancied long-term financial security, she might not be so keen. I shook my head.

"Well, I'm afraid I'm gay, so you're out of luck."

It was a spur-of-the-moment thing to say. An unexpected trump card.

Ellie smiled and slowly shook her head. "No, you ain't."

"Pardon?"

"We was talking about you, all us girls, and Kiki—she's like a hotline to *The Bulletin*, don't ever tell her nothing, babes, unless you want it in the papers the next day—Kiki said she remembered a headline about the Bisexual Baron Buckford."

I swallowed. "Don't believe everything you read in the papers."

Ellie eyeballed me squarely and shook her head. She didn't believe me. She pulled her dressing gown up, revealing a remarkable amount of thigh.

"Do you ever eat meat, my lord?"

Dear God, I nearly had a heart attack.

"I could never be with a meat eater, you see. It's unjustifiable."

I jumped on the proffered life raft. "Eat animals? I'm afraid I do. Completely ravenous for them. Got a deep freezer downstairs simply bursting with sausages. Saw a chap walking around with a very tasty-looking duck the other day too."

Ellie turned up her nose, like she'd been crop dusted with the gamiest of meat farts. "You're disgusting, mate."

"Afraid so," I said, pointing again to the door, urging her out.

She shook her head. "I've been thinking all afternoon about the incredible collaborations we could do. My audience would go mad for a vegan lord with a chest like that."

"Sorry. Still, better for you to have found out now, before we both got too invested."

"Hundred per cent." Ellie stood, straightened her dressing gown, and stepped towards the door. I stuck my head into the hallway to check the coast was clear, then ushered her out.

"Lovely to have met you. Safe journey home. Please don't tell anyone you've been here."

I shut the door.

"I bet my cooking could change your mind," Ellie said, somewhat belatedly.

"Sorry, can't hear you over all these delicious sausages."

Ten minutes later there was another tap at the folly door. Were all the female cast members really going to give it a go? If they had any idea what being Lady Buckford entailed—the abject poverty, the unsafe wiring, the unending requests to judge things at the village fair—they wouldn't be quite so keen. I ignored the knock. In *The Broken Crown,* Gawain was about to throw himself in front of the arrow headed directly for Prince Henry's heart.

The knock came again.

"Go away!"

"Oh, sorry, mate." It was a man's voice. At least it wasn't Indira. I opened the door, expecting to see one of the producers. A rugged, shirtless, tanned young fellow with a dirty blond buzz cut stood in the hall.

"No, I'm sorry," I said. "I thought you were someone else. It's been like Paddington Station around here tonight. How can I help you?"

The chap smiled, his hazel eyes twinkling with mischief. "I'm Tom." He held out a hand. His grip was firm and rough, his eye contact unwavering. "Is the white stallion in the stables yours?" he asked, in a deep West Country accent.

I nodded. "Is something wrong? Are you the crew horse handler?"

Tom laughed. "Nothing like that. He's fine. I'm part of the show. I'm a contestant."

"I'm sorry, but you have to go."

I tried to close the door, but Tom slipped a foot into the doorway.

"He's a beautiful beast. Gorgeous temperament. A few of those Cleveland Bay mares seem right taken with him." He stepped into the room, his chest almost brushing mine as he squeezed past me. "But who can blame them?" he said, looking me up and down. "I prefer a big white stallion myself, as it happens."

Then he flopped down onto my bed.

Oh. Unbelievable! That wasn't merely horsey small talk. It was Trojan horsey small talk. First the women, now the men too. Was this because I'd told Ellie I was gay? Was I being tested? Were they all in on it? Christ, how long before Indira found out? How long before my cheque was whittled down to nothing?

"Lovely to chat," I said. "I'm sorry you can't stay."

"What?"

I pretended to yawn. "It's getting terribly late."

"Oh." Tom frowned but sprang up from the bed. "Of course." He hadn't expected that. With a face and body like his, I doubted he got turned down very often. Still, first time for everything.

"Yes, too bad," I said.

Tom squeezed past me, his chest hair tickling my nipples, his eyes locked onto mine. "You must come down to Somerset sometime. I've got a Suffolk Punch at home."

"Beautiful workhorses."

"I'd love to take you up the field and show you how deep I can plough. I can go for hours."

"Sounds exhausting." My voice squeaked out of me like a teenage boy.

Tom's eyes flicked down to my neck. His head tilted. He closed his eyes, leant towards my skin, and breathed in deeply. My nervous system was screaming like an air raid siren.

"You smell really good," he said, opening his eyes.

"Thanks. It's... ginger nuts."

Tom frowned. I opened my mouth like I was at the dentist and huffed air onto his face so he could smell it.

"See? Ginger nuts."

Tom blinked, shook his head, turned, and disappeared down the corridor.

Over the next two hours, there were three more knocks at the door. All women. So if Tom was sent to test my claim to homosexuality, I'd failed. I was getting increasingly frustrated. The best passages of my favourite book were being ruined by interruptions. It was nearly eleven when there was another heavy, urgent thump at the door.

"Oh, sod off! Are you trying to bankrupt me?"
"It's me, open up."
"Petey Boy?"
I threw open the door.
"You and I need to talk," he said, marching into the room.
"We absolutely do," I agreed.

Chapter 15
Petey

By midnight, Indira, William, and I were standing in our pyjamas in the production office in the Old Coach House. This was *The Love Manor* base camp, the nerve centre. Long trestle tables had been set up along both walls, with screens showing the feeds coming in directly from all the fixed cameras set up around the house. My night shift colleagues, Haruto and Thandiwe, were sitting at their desks, logging and filing the day's material. Indira sucked on her cigarette.

"Remind me why you're living in that fucking tower?"

William shrugged. "To make sure everything runs as smoothly as possible."

"Right. How do we think that's going?"

"Listen, I know we had a few teething troubles, but—"

I scoffed. "You're a liability, bruv."

"Hey, I kept to my side of the bargain. What happened this evening had nothing to do with me. If you had *any* control over your cast—"

I wasn't having this entitled himbo throw me under the bus. "This only happened because you rode through my shot!"

"How did they even know who I was? I didn't tell them," William said, throwing his hands wide.

Suddenly, I felt incredibly guilty. That was on me. But I couldn't admit it in front of Indira or she'd give me a bollocking—and I had too much on the line.

"And I certainly didn't tell them where I live. Someone told them, because it takes quite a mental leap to put all those things together."

Indira waved her cigarette. "It could have been your furry friend. The one with a laugh like a jackal fucking an electric power socket."

"Jonty?" I said, leaping on the escape route offered. "Could have been, I guess." After all, it must have been him who'd let slip about the folly.

"It doesn't matter now, anyway," Indira said. "All that matters is fixing it."

I had to come up with a solution. Not only because I'd caused this headache and avoided the blame for it, but I was meant to be Indira's fix-it man—and if I ever wanted my own show, I needed to prove my value.

"We need to remove William from the table as an option for the cast," I said. "Could you live somewhere else for the time being?"

"Absolutely not," he said, stamping his foot. "I want this show to be a success, but this is my home and I won't be pushed out of it."

"It's for, like, three more weeks, bruv."

"I'm not merely the lord of the manor, I'm Buckford's custodian, its caretaker for my lifetime. I have a responsibility to look after it."

This privileged idiot had clearly fallen for the same horseshit "family legacy" speech as my brother and sister. Still, he was very sexy when he was passionate. He was very sexy when he wasn't passionate, too, but there was something incredibly hot about him coming over all masterful like that. Apparently, he was even sexy when he wasn't being very helpful.

Indira blew out a stream of smoke. "We could tell them he's gay. Take him off the table that way."

"I already tried that," William said. "They sent Tom up to test out the theory."

"Tom's into guys?" Indira asked.

"Into, verging on assault, I would say," William said. "And it didn't work, because I had three more women visit me after Tom, one of whom spat so badly when she spoke I had to have a shower. The papers call me the bisexual baron, no one is going to believe I'm off limits based on my advertised preferences alone."

Indira sucked on her cigarette. "Unless we take you off the table like *completely* completely."

William looked horrified. "You want to... murder me?"

"No, you fucking dafty." Smoke was leaking from Indira's head like a Victorian chimney. "We tell them you're already in a committed relationship."

"Genius," I said. Possibly laying it on a bit thick.

William looked wary. "With whom?"

Cigarette burning away between her fingers, Indira pointed at me. *Oh God!* William looked aghast.

"Got a better idea?" she asked.

I looked at William, William looked at me, we both seemed to consider it for a second, then we shrugged in unison. I might not have come up with the solution, but surely the next best thing was to be an integral part of it?

"Go pack your things, Petey Boy, you're moving into that fucking Rapunzel tower with Lord Rumpled Sportsman here."

William threw his hand up into his hair. "Hold on, there's only one *tiny* bed."

I was eager to be helpful. "I don't mind if—"

"No, I'm not having that," Indira said. She pointed at William. "You I don't give a fuck about. But Peter I have a duty of care for.

You've got two hundred rooms, you must have a spare couch you can drag up there."

William wavered. "We might have an old trundle bed in the attic? Bramley will know."

"Problem solved." Indira sucked deeply on her cigarette, one eye squinting against the smoke. "Peter, when you do the morning rundown with the cast at breakfast tomorrow, you're going to announce Lord Juicyballs here is your boyfriend."

William and I glanced at each other. He looked petrified.

"Take him with you. Put on a show. Convince them you're so in love you can't keep your hands off each other. You're up his arse like a rat up a drainpipe every chance you get. Fuck it. In fact, tell them you're engaged. Let's really lock this down. You're both very flattered and all that, but Mr Darcy is shagging Mr Wickham."

"Wickham?" It was a bit much. "Can't I be Bingley?"

Indira, emotionless, sucked on her cigarette like it was sustaining her existence.

"Do you think they'll swallow it?" William asked.

He was right. "It is a bit convenient, isn't it? We're filming in his house and I'm his fiancé?"

"Tell them that's how we got permission to film here." Indira blew out her smoke. "You're a smart kid. Use your fucking imagination. We need you to convince the cast you're in love. It can't be fucking hard. Six of them have already told our cameras they're in love, and they only met four days ago."

* * *

The next morning the whole cast—lords, ladies, and servants, all dressed in their Regency gear—gathered in Buckford Hall's dining room for breakfast. It was the daily routine: The show's catering company laid out all the options, buffet-style, and the cast helped themselves. They could sit with and chat to whomever they wanted. Our installed cameras filmed the whole thing, in case something vital to the narrative happened, but it was understood this footage wasn't generally used. At some point, either I or one of the other assistant producers would interrupt to deliver the rundown for the day. I stood in the hallway with William, summoning the courage to make my entrance.

"Take a few deep breaths," William said. I met his grey eyes, and he smiled reassuringly.

"I ain't usually this nervous."

"Well, it's not every day you announce your engagement."

I rolled my eyes.

"Did you deal with Jonty?" William asked.

"First thing this morning. He won't say a word. You remember what to do?"

"Absolutely." William winked. "You look very cute, by the way."

Heat rushed to my face, and I glanced away.

"Thank you, so do you." There weren't many outfits that could upstage the flamingo-pink boiler suit I'd worn for the occasion, but William in his full riding outfit—the boots, the jodhpurs, the polo shirt he must have had to grease himself up to get into—was right up there.

"Breathe," he said.

So I did.

Then I made my entrance.

"Morning, everyone."

There were the usual whoops and cheers—the loudest of all from Jonty. My heart was racing as I ran through a few important bits of housekeeping. "Now, before I move on to the subject of plans for tomorrow night's ball—" Big cheers from the cast, the balls being the highlight of each week. "I think there's something we need to clear up."

"Is it the pox?" Jonty called out. There were a few laughs.

"This is serious. Rules have been broken."

The cheers died down, replaced by the clatter of cutlery being gently placed on crockery and tablecloths. Eighteen pairs of eyes stared at me intently.

"It's come to my attention some of you—an alarming number of you, actually—broke the rules last night and made contact with someone from the outside world."

Faces were being pulled, sideways glances shared.

"Shocking," Jonty said, shaking his head. "Who would do such a thing?"

"It seems some of you heard a rumour, saw an opportunity, and decided to act on it."

"Disgraceful."

"That's enough with the help, thank you, Jonty."

"Right you are."

I straightened up, gripping my clipboard with both hands.

"I wasn't going to reveal this to you all because, well, it's a private matter... and the news hasn't been made public yet, but..."

On cue, William strode into the room and stood beside me. I turned to look at him, trying to appear completely besotted. It wasn't hard when he looked like that. In return, he stared into my eyes like I was the only person in the room, like I was the centre of his world. I'd have gone weak at the knees if it wasn't also how he looked at his horse.

"For those of you who *haven't* met him yet," I announced to the room, "this is William. Buckford Hall is his gaff."

William slipped his hand into mine, our fingers intertwining. "And we're engaged to be married," he said, bringing my hand to his lips and kissing it.

There was a sharp intake of breath around the room. Jonty leapt to his feet, clapping and shouting "Bravo!" and "Three cheers for the new Lady Buckford!"

Slowly, the stunned faces around the room joined in the celebrations. William and I gazed at each other like we were deliriously happy.

As I looked into his sparkling eyes, I got swept up in the part and threw myself around him. He pulled me into a tight hug. He felt so strong, I sank into him.

"Kiss her!" Jonty shouted. I could have killed him. It was *not* in the script. But now a chorus of "Kiss, kiss, kiss!" was filling the room, and I didn't feel like we had any choice.

"Should we?" I whispered into William's ear.

"You're the producer, not me."

I rested my forehead against his. We smiled at each other like a young couple in love. The calls for us to kiss were now deafening. They wanted evidence—and we needed to give it to them. So I planted my lips on William's and slowly, gently, lovingly, but chastely kissed him. His lips were soft and plump, and the light rasp of his stubble sent electricity through my whole body. Then he grabbed my arse, picked me up, and spun me around—to whoops of applause from the cast. He planted me back on the ground.

"Job done, I'd say," I whispered in his ear.

William turned to face the cast and raised his hand to silence the room. "So, while I'm very flattered by the attention—ladies, gentlemen—I'm afraid I'm off the market. But let me tell you all something. Members of my family have been finding true love in this house, finding deep and abiding connections that last a lifetime, for more than five centuries. If you can find love anywhere, I promise you can find it here, at *The Love Manor*. And I wish that for every single one of you."

I was blown away. His little speech wasn't part of the plan either. The cast cheered. Ridhi, Cristina, and Lola Q looked on the verge of tears. William waved at them, pecked me on the lips one more time, and slapped my arse. Then he marched out of the dining room and presumably carried on to the stables to take his actual one true love, Achilles, out for a ride. I stared at him as he disappeared up the hall, completely in awe. For a moment, I almost forgot I wasn't actually in love with him. I shook it off. I was *not* going to get distracted by a boy.

"Right, settle down, everybody," I said, putting as much authority into my voice as possible. "Are we all excited for tomorrow night's ball?"

More whoops and cheers. The cast was in a great mood. They might have dipped out on marrying a real member of the aristocracy, but they were having fun this morning. It always made for great footage through the day.

"The costume department has been busy, and your outfits for tomorrow are ready to go. You're all going to look spectacular."

"All of us?" Kiki Galapagos sneered. "Or just the toffs?"

"Everyone! Because the theme for tomorrow night is a hunt ball, and servants were traditionally involved in various roles."

There were a few cheers. But not as many as I hoped.

"Which means tomorrow we're out on the horses!" I added. That got a roar from farm boy Tom and Lord Armando, and a few enthusiastic whoops from several others.

Ellie, the vegan chef, raised her hand. "Um, are you making us go fox-hunting?"

"Well, no. For one thing, fox-hunting is illegal. I promise you, no foxes are going to die tomorrow."

"So, how is it a fox hunt?" Tom asked.

"It's quite good fun, actually," I said. "We've hired the actor Samuel Fox to stand out in the woods somewhere, and you have to locate him. We've got a shirt with his scent on it for the dogs to follow. It's worth ten thousand pounds to the prize kitty if you find him."

Ellie looked horrified. "Won't he get ripped apart by the beagles?"

"They're not hunting beagles, Ellie. They're trained actors, we've hired them especially."

She looked confused. "And they're wearing beagle costumes?"

"Who?"

"The actors."

"No, they're *real* dogs. The dogs are trained actors. Come on, Ellie. Keep up."

She shook her head furiously. "You say no one's going to die, but my career's going to die if I go along with a fox hunt. Can you imagine what it would do to my brand? The sponsors? The fans? I ain't doing it, mate."

"It's only pretend. It's not a real hunt."

Kiki stood up. "Yeah, but it's still promoting fox-hunting, isn't it?"

"She's right," Zoë the travel blogger said. "I'm not doing it. It's not only off brand for me, it's wrong. I'm not getting cancelled for doing something I don't agree with in the first place."

"Well, I'm in," Tom said.

Within seconds the cast were bickering about the moralities of filming a pretend fox hunt. I shouted across the room, trying to regain order, but no one was listening. They were all screaming at each other. Indira would be watching this all on the monitor back at the Old Coach House. There was no pretending everything was under control. There were eighteen of them. This rebellion was too much for one person to handle—especially considering that morally, I agreed with the rebels. Admitting failure, I slunk back into the hall, found my headset, and put it on. My finger was shaking as I pressed the button to speak to Indira.

Chapter 16
William

I endured an evening meal at the Dower House with Mum and watched the England v France match on her couch with Bramley, then he and I dragged the only surplus mattress not riddled with carpet beetles up to the belvedere at the top of the folly. He fussed about for a while—making beds, muttering about biscuit crumbs and falling standards.

"Bramley, I hope you realise you've ruined my carefully curated Wallowing Bachelor Aesthetic," I scolded him on his way out the door.

Freshly showered and finally alone, I found myself pacing anxiously about the folly, waiting for Petey Boy's arrival. It was gone 10:00 p.m., and I was the kind of nervous where if I went for a poop, it'd tumble out in cubes.

"Read," I said to myself, and plucked my well-thumbed copy of *The Broken Crown* off the coffee table. My buttocks had barely grazed the fabric of Dad's old armchair when I heard the click of the door downstairs.

"Petey Boy?" I called down casually, as if I hadn't been on tenterhooks for an hour.

"Is it all right?" His voice sounded unsure.

I stood at the top of the stairs. "Of course, come on in! This is your home now. Welcome to the pyjama party!"

My fake fiancé pulled the door closed and kicked off his shoes. He looked tired but as beautiful as ever.

"Cup of tea?" I offered.

Petey turned to look up at me, his eyes suddenly on stalks. "Uhhh, you should probably…" He waggled his finger at me, and I realised he could see straight up my boxer shorts.

"Oh! Right. Sorry." I bounced down the stairs. Petey didn't take his eyes off me the whole way down. "Left my dressing gown upstairs in the belvedere, I'm afraid. I'll try to remember for next time. Was that a yes to tea? Have you eaten? I could boil you an egg."

"I ate at the catering truck."

As I bent over the gas ring, Petey started unbuttoning his pink boiler suit. He had a white vest on underneath, and I kept sneaking glances as his fingers worked lower and lower. When he got to his waist, he tied his sleeves together in front of his groin. Then he flopped onto the bed.

"You look exhausted," I said.

"Tough day. Armando's affair with Ellie came out. He's a lord and she's a servant, so according to the rules, she had to be dismissed."

"Sounds a bit brutal. What does that mean, in practice?" I reached for a couple of mugs from the kitchenette.

"She's currently in the Travelodge with the aftercare team, and she'll be on a train back to Essex in the morning. The cast is a mess about it. It's our first dismissal."

"Golly, I didn't realise that was a thing. What happens to Armando?"

"Nothing. He's a lord."

A laugh barked out of me, my mind flickering to the envelope upstairs.

"Oh, for a world where a title meant no consequences."

Petey Boy was leaning back on the bed—the slender length of him, the porcelain skin, the pink of his nipples showing through his vest. He was breathtakingly handsome. I pointed at the kettle.

"This thing takes ages. Why don't you have a shower to wash away the day, and I'll take these up to the study?"

Petey Boy shook his head. "I think I'll hit the hay. I'm sapped."

"Oh," I said, failing to hide my disappointment. "I was hoping we could, you know, get to know each other." And I winked, for good measure. I don't know why. The mood came over me. Seemed the friendly thing to do.

Petey Boy blinked, his eyebrows bouncing. Then his eyes sparkled through the tiredness, a glorious grin widening across his face.

"OK, sure, why not. We're engaged, aren't we?"

A warm tingle flushed through my body.

Twenty minutes later, he was sitting in the chair opposite me in my father's study, hair damp, wearing a fluffy white robe. I was in one exactly like it, but with tea stains down the front.

"Were you actually christened Petey Boy?" I asked.

He smiled. "It's Peter, obviously. But my gran calls me Petey Boy, so it's what I like to be called. You can just call me Petey, if you like."

"Are you close with your gran?"

"Spent every afternoon after school with her, either at her place in Tower Hamlets or at their market stall in Petticoat Lane."

"Oh, so your grandparents are proper East Enders, then?"

Petey Boy's whole face lit up. "Gran's brothers used to knock around with the Krays. You don't get more East End than that!"

He seemed inordinately proud of this link to London's most notorious gangsters. In the fifties and sixties, the Krays were responsible for armed robberies, money laundering, arson, violent assaults, and even murder. Still, Buckford Hall's Long Gallery was lined with portraits of men whose crime sheets wouldn't have looked so very different. I remembered Jonty saying Petey Boy's family were hugely successful, and suddenly I wondered in what field.

"If you're planning to nick the silver, you should know none of it is real," I said. "The real stuff is in storage. Indira insisted. Come to think of it, you might be the reason why."

Petey laughed, and I enjoyed knowing it was because of something I'd said. It was a shot of endorphins, and I wanted more of it. His eyes locked onto mine, and he kicked out his foot across the coffee table to playfully nudge my knee.

"Why does Jonty call you Dub-Dub? That's what I want to know."

I sighed. "Oh, it's a stupid nickname. From school. I hate it. It's because of the two *W*s in my name."

"In William Buckford? I thought you went to one of the best schools in the country. Didn't they teach you how to count?"

I laughed. "Buckford is only the title. The *W* is for Winters."

"So, you're William Winters?" Petey Boy sipped at his tea.

"Actually, I'm William Stanley Leaf Richard George Winters-de Valois-Winters. If we're getting technical about it."

Petey Boy frowned. "Leaf?"

"It's my godfather's name."

"And *two* Winters?"

"Across five hundred years, you pick up a lot of valuable surnames. You don't simply let the good ones go. Generations of scheming mamas worked so terribly hard to acquire them."

"Should we be worried you seem to have picked up the same one twice?"

"I'll have you know the Winterses are where we get our prominent chins. We have to circle one back into the gene pool every two hundred years or so to top up the old jawline."

Petey Boy laughed, and it was beautiful. He wriggled in his armchair, and the movement loosened his robe a little, letting me glimpse the milky skin of his chest. It took me a moment to remember where I was.

"So, have you always been a reality TV show producer?"

Petey shook his head. "First gig."

I listened while he told me about his years working on *Wake Up Britain*, fascinated by a world about which I knew nothing.

"Five years was enough," he said. "I was sick of the segue sandwich. It was a joy to hand in my notice."

"Is the catering no good at Channel Three?"

"No, I mean writing the presenters' links. Give me any two subjects, totally unrelated—make them as stupid as you like—and I'll write the segue for you."

"Oh, this is fun." I sat upright and loosened my robe to get the blood flowing and the old noodle noodling. "Got it. I bet you can't link former Welsh rugby full back Leigh Halfpenny and Britain's most endangered mammal, the hazel dormouse."

Petey Boy seemed to roll the idea around in his head for barely a second.

"And if the sight of gorgeous golden-haired Leigh Halfpenny wasn't enough to get your ovaries quivering over your cornflakes this morning, it's time to meet another adorable golden furball you wouldn't mind taking up residence in your basement, the hazel dormouse." He clapped his hands and flopped back into the chair. "Too easy."

I bellowed with laughter. "You can't say that on TV!"

"No, but it was worth it to make you laugh." Petey Boy winked and flopped a leg onto the coffee table, his foot mere inches from my bare knee. Extraordinary manners, really. My stomach burst with nervous energy, and my leg started to bounce up and down involuntarily. I wanted to ask him more, but he beat me to the next question.

"You know the hazel dormouse is Jonty's pet project?"

"Where do you think I plucked the idea from? Buckford is where Jonty learned about the hazel dormouse in the first place." I pointed towards the porthole window and Buckford Hill beyond. "The wood is absolutely teeming with the little blighters."

"You're kidding."

"My parents were committed naturalists. And naturists, as it happens. I can never remember which one is which. But during his nineteen years as baron, my father rewilded a third of the estate, created two new forests, and restored the ancient oak woodland. All bare-arsed, of course. Murder in the bramble season, but you get used to it. We were a very naked household. Upon reflection, that's probably why the staff all left."

Petey snorted a laugh. Emboldened by the sight of him enjoying himself, I kept riffing on the theme.

"Long and the short of it, Buckford is practically a nature reserve. A few years ago—before my father and my brother, David, died—Jonty was staying for the weekend when the Hazel Dormouse Protection Trust released twenty dormice into our oak woodland. Now you can't move up there for the furry little bastards. They're taking over. I went for a ride the other day, I kid you not, half a dozen of them—pistols in their paws, bandanas covering their darling little faces—blocked the path and shouted, 'Stand and deliver!'"

Petey Boy was in fits, and my heart was absolutely bursting out of my chest.

His foot brushed my knee, jolting me out of my momentary reverie. Our eyes met. Then, before I realised he'd even moved, Petey Boy was straddling me in my armchair, his soft lips pressing passionately into mine. He smelt like tea and toothpaste and geranium body wash. There he was, this beautiful lithe man, wrapped in a bathrobe, his body hot with expectation, and there was me, underneath him, frozen in horror—my body an explosion of pins and needles.

He pulled away. "What's the matter?"

"Nothing."

He scrambled off me, tightening his robe around his waist. "Did you not... oh my God. I'm *so* sorry."

I jumped up because sitting down suddenly seemed incredibly awkward. "No, I'm sorry, I wasn't expecting—"

"I thought you said you wanted to get to know each other?"

"I do. We were. I mean, I thought we were. The conversation was going well, wasn't it?"

Petey Boy shook his head, his eyes wide in disbelief or panic or something like it. "When you said you wanted to get to know each other, I thought you meant... you know... you wanted to get to *know* each other."

How had we got here? Why was I so bad at reading signals—at *giving* signals?

"I think there's been a misunderstanding—"

"No kidding." Petey Boy's hand was in his short-cropped hair. "I thought you'd been giving me green lights all the way."

"To be fair, I did make you tea."

"I'm, like, *really* good at consent."

"We've hardly met," I said.

Petey Boy was pacing now. "You answered the door with your cock out."

"It was the angle. I'm sorry. I didn't think. I told you, we're a really naked household."

"You told me to go for a shower."

"You seemed like you needed one."

Petey Boy stopped still, staring at me incredulously. "I douched!"

As sentences that can silence a room go, it had to be one of the shortest in the English language. I stood there, staring at Petey Boy, unsure if he was angry or embarrassed or both, and completely unsure how I was meant to respond. Apparently, the squirrel part of my brain, the part that gets distracted easily, thought this was a good time to take over.

"Did... the plumbing hold up OK? There's a plunger in th—"

"I should go to bed," Petey Boy said. His face was unreadable. He spun around and started down the stairs. "I'm sorry. I didn't... I thought... I'm sorry."

"Goodnight!" I called after him. I stood there, staring at the top of the stairs for a minute, as if he might reappear, until the light from downstairs was doused and I heard Petey Boy climbing into my creaky old bed. Disappointed, confused, I grabbed my copy of *The Broken Crown* off the coffee table, turned the light out, and schlepped my way up to my new bedroom in the belvedere, wondering where it all went so wrong.

Chapter 17
Petey

The blast of a fox horn pierced the cool morning air in Buckford Hall's carriage court. Our run of good luck with the weather had ended. The day was grey and threatening to rain. To my left, Armando—dressed in a bright red hunting jacket—put his foot in a stirrup and expertly launched himself into the saddle. To my right, a pack of ten beagles was being loved to death by a dozen members of the cast—including Lola Q, who was following the dogs around with an itchy Instagram finger, and Jonty, who I noticed was following Lola Q like a puppy. The horn blasted again, and I nearly jumped out of my skin. Tom, the hot farm boy, was getting trumpet lessons from the show's historical consultant—learning the different calls traditionally made during a hunt. My headset squawked.

"Dorinda's almost ready. Five minutes."

I checked my watch. Ten thirty a.m.

Despite Ellie's rebellion, we'd managed to get five of the cast to agree to the mock hunt. Tom was so enthusiastic there was a chance he might actually kill a fox if the opportunity arose. Tom was... troublingly intense. Armando was on the Italian national polo team and would have agreed to anything to be on horseback, and I was reasonably certain how good he looked on horseback was exactly why Indira had us here. Fitness influencer Cristina, Theo the carpenter from Luton, and Ridhi the Bookstagrammer had also been willing to take part.

Tom blew on the trumpet again, and a moment later, I heard shouting across the carriage court.

"No! No! NO! Ab-so-lutely not!" It was William's voice. But I couldn't see him. I'd snuck out quietly that morning, desperate not to wake him, unable to face him after the night before. His voice came again. "Stop this at once! Are you mad?" My ears found the direction of his voice, and I looked up to see him shirtless and hanging out a window at the top of his tower.

"Pardon?" I called up, heart in my throat.

A well-muscled arm thrust from the window, pointed finger jabbing in my direction.

"Stay. Right. There," William yelled. Then he disappeared inside the tower, pulling the window closed behind him. Then opening it again. Then closing it. Then opening and closing it several times in quick succession. I think he was struggling with it. He opened it wide again and hung out of it a ridiculously long way. "Don't you dare move, Peter Topham." He slid back inside, slamming the window shut, but it seemed to bounce open again. He continued opening and closing it for a moment before it swung wide open and, given he didn't reappear, I assumed he'd abandoned it. Forty seconds later, he was striding across the carriage court in bare feet, wearing nothing but his tiny red satin boxer shorts and the gold chain bouncing around his neck. His face was as full of thunder as the skies overhead. Every pair of eyes in the carriage court was fixed on him. Even the duck stopped to watch.

"What didn't you understand about what I said last night?" he demanded.

My breath caught in my throat. He had to be kidding. He wanted to do this here? Now? In front of the entire cast and crew?

"Uh-oh, trouble in paradise!" That was Jonty, obviously. Although I wanted to throttle him, it did remind me William and I were meant to be madly in love.

I grabbed the ridiculous aristocrat by his bicep, ignoring the sexy way it tensed under my touch, and turned him back towards the house.

"Not in front of the children, darling," I said, letting my nails sink in as I dragged him away. "Shall we talk about this inside?"

In fact, a few moments later we'd marched all the way through the house to the lake on the other side. William's face looked like it had been boiled in a bag. I was fuming.

"Never *ever* show me up in front of my cast and crew like that again," I barked.

"I can't believe you," William said. He was pacing around on the gravel, shaking his head. "That's what you're worried about?"

"My job requires me to maintain a level of respect and authority," I said.

"So does mine!" I could literally see the veins on either side of his neck pulsing. "And I clearly have neither your respect nor any authority, because if I did, I wouldn't have been woken up by a hunting horn."

"Wait, is that what this is about? We woke you up? Do you still keep Regency hours? Were you up gaming all night at your club?" I couldn't believe my ears. "William, I thought this was about last night."

"This *is* about last night. I could not have made myself clearer last night."

I wasn't having it. "Oh, mate, you absolutely could have made yourself clearer last night. In fact, I really wish you had. Because I made an idiot of myself. I *hate* that I now have to live in a freaking tower with you, that I have to pretend that I'm in love with you, that I'm going to marry you, when in fact all I want to do is never see your stupid, perfect, posh-twat face ever again."

William stopped pacing and spun around to face me, his eyes wide. "You think this is about the kiss?"

"What else could it be about?" I'd barely thought about anything other than my appallingly misjudged workplace assault since it happened. I'd barely slept all night, worrying what to do about it. My only reprieve had been my alarm going off and throwing myself into my work.

"This is about the fact there's a bloody fox hunt meeting in my carriage court. Are you insane?"

I hadn't seen that coming.

"I blathered on for ages last night about my father's legacy, how Buckford is a wildlife sanctuary, how it's my parents' life's work. And this morning I find you organising a fox hunt."

He crossed his eyes, stabbed a finger into his head, and stuck his tongue into his bottom lip so it protruded grotesquely. It was the unmistakable gesture used by children everywhere to tell other children they're too thick to function. Message received. Honestly, this pretend fox hunt had already been far more trouble than the footage was worth. If Indira hadn't spent so much money on the costumes, I'd go back there and talk her out of it—but I knew she wouldn't change her mind.

"It's not real," I said.

"It looks real."

"Fox-hunting is illegal. It's obviously not real."

"Doesn't matter. You're romanticising a brutal blood sport. There are freaks out there who will watch this on TV and think, Oh what a shame, one of the old traditions of the English countryside that's disappeared, let's bring it back."

I hated that I agreed with him because I was still incredibly angry with him. When I say I was angry, I mean I'd been embarrassed and anger was how I was processing it. My headset crackled, and I lifted it to my ear.

"Where the hell are you?" Indira barked. "Dorinda's ready."

Thunder rumbled through the sky. I looked at William.

"There's nothing I can do about it," I said. "Some of the cast raised concerns, too, but they've fallen on deaf ears."

William shook his head. "You know my parents organised the anti-fox-hunting rallies across the East and West Midlands? For years. Buckford Hall was base camp."

"I'm sorry, William. It's not my decision. You can take it up with Indira, but you won't get anywhere." I put my headset on and turned to walk back through the house to the carriage court. "Coming, Indira," I said.

As I trotted up the stairs, I turned back to look at William. He was shaking his head.

"You're going to awaken forces you don't even understand," he shouted after me. It sounded like the ravings of a madman.

* * *

By the time Dorinda had filmed her parts and the hunt got underway, it had started to rain heavily. I joined Indira in the production office in the Old Coach House, listening to the storm thrum against the slate roof tiles. It smelt like petrichor and diesel fumes and Indira's cigarettes, which added an extra frisson of danger to the events about to take place.

"What did Lord Bucknaked want?" Indira asked.

I shrugged. "Nothing I couldn't fix."

We had five crews on electric quad bikes set up on a predetermined course around the Buckford Estate, ready to film our pretend hunt. Except for one fixed camera trained on the actor Samuel Fox, which was livestreaming directly back to the Old Coach House, we had no way to beam the footage back to us live, so we couldn't see what was happening. We had to rely on reports coming in from our crews in the field on the walkie-talkies. Ours crackled into life.

"Base, this is Unit One."

"Go ahead, Hassan."

"Base, uh, we've got company."

Indira squinted, and I wondered if this was how she powered up the lasers in her eyes.

"Define 'company' for me, Hassan."

"We have at least two dozen anti-fox-hunting protesters on set."

"Where the fuck did they come from?" Indira's eyes narrowed further, and I got a sinking feeling her eye lasers would be pointed at me any second. "Can we film around them?"

The walkie-talkie crackled.

"Negative. They're spread out all across Home Field. They have placards, and they're shouting anti-fox-hunting slogans. Even if we can keep them out of the shot, the audio will be unusable."

Indira switched the channel on the walkie-talkie and barked an order at the head of security to send every single person they had to Home Field to deal with our unexpected guests, then switched back to the regular frequency.

"Hassan, push onto Hill Gate. Unit Two, are you there?"

The walkie-talkie crackled, and Su-wei confirmed she was waiting with her crew at Hill Gate.

"Any sign of anyone in the woods?"

"All clear, Base."

"OK, get ready for handover. Once we get the cast through the gate, we should be good to go."

Indira's hand dived into her cigarette packet. She produced a dart and lit it with such fluidity it resembled tai chi. She sucked in the tobacco and held it in her lungs until I thought she might actually have died, then blew it out in a heavy stream that fogged the air around us.

"Any idea how they knew about this?"

My heart was in my throat. "No idea."

The laser eyes were on me. I froze, in case her vision relied on movement.

"What *exactly* was it Lord Fuckstud wanted earlier?"

I shook my head. "Nothing."

Indira wasn't buying it. The lasers were heating up.

"Nothing I couldn't handle."

"And what, specifically, did you handle?"

I tried to swallow, but my mouth was suddenly too dry, so I let my sandpapery tongue rasp down my throat to my stomach and then crawl its way back up again.

"He... had some concerns."

"About anything in particular?"

"I couldn't say..."

Indira sucked on her cigarette, eyes never leaving me. "Was it about fox-hunting, by any chance?"

The jig was up. "He *might* have mentioned that the whole estate is a wildlife sanctuary and very specifically that his parents led the anti-fox-hunting rallies before the ban."

"Shit."

"For the whole Midlands."

"Shit."

Indira blew the smoke out the side of her mouth and closed her eyes, holding them shut. "How much time have they had to prepare?"

I checked my watch. It was midday. "Ninety minutes? He only found out about it when he heard the hunting horn go."

Indira opened her eyes and nodded, slowly. "OK, how much damage could they possibly organise in ninety minutes, right?"

The walkie-talkie crackled. "Base, this is Unit Two."

"Go ahead, Su-wei."

"Base, we've lost the dogs."

Indira and I stared at each other.

"What do you mean you've lost the dogs?"

"Base, the old butler dude turned up with, like, I swear, maybe two hundred cooked sausages. He threw them to the dogs, and, well, have you ever met a beagle? They've scoffed the lot, and they're all passed out across the bridle trail, we can't even get around them on the bike."

Indira shook her head. "Are the dogs OK, Unit Two?"

"Base, I'd say the dogs have never been happier. But they won't be bounding up this hill any time soon."

Indira turned to me. "How do you find and cook two hundred sausages in ninety minutes?" She squinted. "Are you sure you didn't let anything slip last night while you were shucked up in your love turret?"

"I promise. This isn't my fault." Somehow it felt like my fault, but I literally could not be blamed for this.

Indira inhaled on her cigarette like an asthmatic on a Ventolin puffer.

"Unit Two, can you get around the dogs?"

The walkie-talkie popped and squeaked. "That's a negative for the bike. The horses can pick a route through the trees."

"OK, Unit Two, you stay with the dogs. Send the cast up to Unit Three. Unit Three, are you reading?"

"I gotchyu, Base."

"Jameelah, is there any sign of any trouble up there?"

"We ain't seen nothin' yet."

It was a tense ten minutes while our "hunt" rode up Buckford Hill in the pouring rain to the stone circle, where Indira had planned for a stunning drone shot that would show the cast on horseback, in their hunting clobber, looking out over the estate—Buckford Hall glittering in the sunshine. Except we'd lucked a storm instead.

"Base, we got a problem, innit."

"What is it, Jameelah?"

"We got two old women—come out of nowhere—running around the stone circle with their tits out."

Indira's head landed with a thud on the desk. "The mad fucking mother."

The walkie-talkie crackled again.

"Base, Derek's trying to catch one of them." Crackle. "Oop, nearly." Crackle. "Oh shit—"

Indira sat up and grabbed the walkie-talkie, holding it between us.

"Come in, Unit Three. Are you OK?"

Ten, fifteen, maybe twenty seconds passed before the walkie-talkie fizzed back into life.

"Base, we got a situation, innit?"

We could hear screaming in the background. For the first time, I saw genuine worry on Indira's face. "Go ahead, Unit Three."

"Derek slipped and went arse up. I think he's broken his arm."

Indira turned and shouted "Medic!" The sound of it echoed down the Old Coach House. My pulse was racing, but Jameelah wasn't finished.

"That ain't even it, though," her voice came again. "Only when he fell his duck slipped out of its baby sling."

Indira's head was in her hands. "Is the duck OK, Unit Three?" she asked wearily.

The walkie-talkie crackled.

"Scarpered, mate. Flapped his wings, took off, did one lap overhead, and disappeared. To be fair, I think that's why Derek's screaming."

The head medic appeared in the doorway, and Indira barked instructions at him. It was then my eyes caught the monitor showing the live feed from the camera we had trained on our "fox." My heart sank. I pointed to the monitor.

"What now?" Indira barked.

"I *think* someone has kidnapped the actor Samuel Fox," I said.

Chapter 18
William

The footage of the "fox hunt" was completely unusable. We'd cost the production tens of thousands of pounds, which Indira intended to deduct from Buckford's estate hire fee. No matter what demands the cursed letter from HMRC contained, the loss of cash would hurt. But principles are principles, right? Indira said the best sound guy she'd ever worked with had been injured (we had apologised profusely) and was now on leave—although whether he was on leave because he'd broken his arm, his emotional support duck had done a runner, or his first aid had been administered by a pair of bare-breasted, rain-soaked hedge witches was still unclear. What was clear was that the kidnapping charges would not stick. The police found Samuel Fox in the village pub, getting merrily drunk with Uncle Leaf, standing on the bar reciting T. S. Eliot's "The Love Song of J. Alfred Prufrock" to rapturous applause from the locals. So far, so good. But Petey Boy hadn't spoken to me for over a week. The atmosphere when he arrived at the folly each evening was frosty at best. This space had enough difficult memories without this unpleasantness. It was absolutely killing me. I'd wanted to be chums. I'd wanted to get to know him.

I was sitting in Dad's armchair in the study, reading *The Knight's Vow*, the second *Knights-Errant* novel, the brown HMRC envelope shoved down the side of the cushion so I didn't have to look at it. Young Prince Henry was now young King Henry, and the teenage lust between him and Sir Gawain had mellowed and matured into something deeper—a kinship all around them envied.

The door downstairs clicked open.

"Petey Boy?"

I moved to the top of the staircase. Petey Boy looked up at me, his eyebrows flicking an acknowledgement, then he moved out of sight.

"How was your day?"

Still no answer, so I bounced down the stairs. Petey Boy stared, his face clearly unimpressed.

"Do you have anything else you can wear? Anything at all?" he said. Yep, definitely unimpressed. He looked tired too.

"These are my jimmy-jams."

Petey Boy rolled his eyes. "You've been wearing the same pair of red boxers this whole time. It's gross."

"Bramley washes them every other day," I protested. "In Fairy Non-Bio. I assume because I have enough Fairy Bio as it is."

He didn't laugh.

"They barely cover you. It's obscene."

I leant my bum against the kitchenette and folded my arms. "I'm getting the sense you're mad at me about something."

Petey Boy's eyes flared. "You're joking, mate. You know exactly why I'm pissed at you. It's quite the list. For starters, you made me look like an idiot in front of the whole cast and crew."

"In the carriage court, you mean?"

"You know that's what I mean."

I supposed it was why my boxers had set him off tonight; they reminded him of the other day.

"Yes, I'm sorry. I'd meant to pull on some trousers before I went down, but the blasted window—"

"You undermined me. In front of everyone." Petey started unbuttoning his boiler suit, revealing his white vest.

"I'm sorry," I said. "I was angry. I could have handled it better."

"Derek had to be taken to hospital. They've upped his anxiety meds. You know he's off the show?"

"Yes, I'm very sorry about that too," I said. "If there's anything I can do—"

"You sabotaged an entire day's filming." Petey tied the sleeves of his boiler suit around his waist, yanking them tight. I got the sense he wished he was tightening them around my neck.

"To be fair, that wasn't me. I was in here almost the entire day. Reading. Except for when I went to the pub to watch the rugby with Bramley and Uncle Leaf. And Samuel Fox, actually. Did you meet him? He's great. He's thinking about renting a cottage in the village."

Suddenly, Petey Boy roared in unmistakable frustration.

"Shut up! Just bloody well shut up, will you?"

That took me aback.

Petey Boy flopped onto the bed, his head in his hands. Then his shoulders bounced, and I realised he was crying.

"Hey, hey, hey, hey, hey," I said, which I believe comes straight out of all the psychology textbooks. I moved towards him, arms outstretched, instinctively, to hug him. Then I second-guessed myself and pulled away. Then he sobbed and I stepped forward again, but he held up a hand to stop me.

"I haven't cried since I was fourteen," he said, face buried behind his other hand.

"Then you should probably let it out," I said. "That sounds super unhealthy."

Petey Boy slowly shook his head, refusing to look at me. After a few moments, he picked up the end of a sleeve and wiped his face. There were dark rings under his bloodshot eyes, and snot was glistening at his nostrils like a couple of silvery snails who were thinking about popping out for some lunch. His eyes finally met mine.

"If you ever tell anyone you saw that, I will hunt down everything you care about and personally see to it that it is destroyed beyond recognition."

"You'll have to hurry. I've got quite the head start on you," I muttered.

"Huh?" He frowned.

"Nothing. Your emotional vulnerability is safe with me."

He scowled and got to his feet. "I'm going for a shower."

He slunk out of the room. As the door closed behind him, I exhaled a long blast of breath. Unsure what else to do, I checked the water level in the kettle and lit the gas ring. By the time Petey Boy came back from his shower, there were two steaming mugs on the coffee table in the study.

"Up here," I called down when I heard the door click.

"I'm going to bed," he mumbled.

"Come have your tea. It's Scottish. It'll help you sleep."

I heard a few steps, and Petey Boy's head popped up in the stairwell. "I've heard of Irish coffee but not Scottish tea."

"It's my invention," I said, taking a sip from my mug, then raising it to say cheers. Petey Boy continued up the stairs, his slender body hidden behind the white robe. He was always so completely covered, and I wasn't sure why. He sat down in the armchair opposite me and picked up his tea.

"What's that taste?" he asked, nose crinkling. "Is it brandy?" He sipped.

"Valium."

He nearly choked on it.

"Are you for real?"

"No, you goose, it's a shot of Scotch whisky. But it will absolutely help you sleep, and you'll have very sweet dreams. Probably about sexy kilted ginger Scotsmen. The kind who're so hung their foreskins drag along in the heather behind them."

This time Petey Boy did laugh. Oh, I had missed his smile. Then his face turned serious again, and I realised it must be time to pay the piper.

"When we first met," he said, "you told me we were on the same team."

"We are."

"So why does it feel like I'm constantly fighting against you?"

"I promise you, we want the same thing."

"It doesn't feel like it to me. It doesn't feel like it to Indira either. She's on the warpath, mate, and she's got you in her sights."

I gulped down my tea. "And what does that look like when it's at home?"

"Put it this way, if there's going to be a second season of *The Love Manor*, it won't be filmed at Buckford Hall. I can tell you that for free."

This was very bad news indeed. I was kind of relying on the show coming back year after year to keep the estate afloat—and to deal with whatever it was the King's tax collector wanted. My fear at losing a significant amount of future income must have been obvious on my face, because Petey Boy's eyebrows went up.

"Yeah," he said, "it turns out I'm not the only one who unleashed forces I didn't understand."

Well, he had me there. My father always used to say *Don't quote me to me*, and now I understood why. It had seemed funnier when I'd said it.

"How do I fix it?"

Petey Boy leant forward in his chair, cupping his tea on his knees.

"You can start by keeping your word about being a help, not a hindrance, bruv."

He was right. My eyes flicked down to my copy of *The Knight's Vow*, Sir Gawain's oath to protect Henry unto the death flashing through my mind. To be honest, if you'd asked me, I'd have said keeping my word was a defining feature of my personality—right up there with being bookish, horsey, and deathly allergic to trousers. Petey Boy seemed to sense his words had wounded.

"You promised to do everything you could to make this show a success," Petey Boy continued. "So far, you ain't lived up to that promise, mate. It's me who cops it in the neck every time you fail to step up."

My leg started to bounce involuntarily, the way it did when I felt uncomfortable or stressed. I chewed at my thumbnail, looked aimlessly around the room as if my father's dusty books might provide the answer. I needed Petey Boy to know I really would do whatever it took to make *The Love Manor* a success—and to keep future seasons filming at Buckford. My eyes settled on *The Knight's Vow* again.

"That's it!" I said, jumping up.

Petey Boy looked startled. "What's what?"

I put my tea down. "Stand up," I told him, grabbing his hand.

"William, I'm tired, what is this?"

I got down on bended knee, still holding Petey Boy's hand in mine.

"Oh, no, no, no," he said. "No, I don't think that's the answer."

I bowed my head and said the words Sir Gawain had said to his beloved King Henry. More or less.

"I, William Stanley Leaf Richard George Winters-de Valois-Winters, swear that henceforward I will be a faithful man to my lord, Peter..." I looked up. He was smiling. "What's your middle name?"

"Boy." He giggled.

"Fair enough." I bowed my head solemnly once more. "Will be a faithful man to my lord, Peter 'Petey Boy' Topham, and do become your liege man of life and limb in your crusade to make *The Love Manor* a success. I will bear unto you a BAFTA-worthy television programme, to live and to die, against all manner of folk. I will not reveal your counsel to any man, nor any angry chain-smoking Scotswoman, and I will serve you faithfully with worldly honour, until your show is safely 'in the can.' So help me God."

I put my hands together in the prayer position and presented them to Petey Boy, my head still bowed.

"Put your hands around mine," I said.

"This is batshit crazy, bruv."

"Come on, do it. Or I can't be held to my words."

He put his hands around mine.

"Now kiss me on the forehead."

"Are you serious?"

"Do you want my help or not?"

Petey Boy chortled. I looked up at him, and he finally bent down. He closed his eyes, and his gentle lips met my brow. He smelt of Buckford's familiar rose-and-geranium soap. My breath caught. He lingered, perhaps a moment longer than he should have. My pulse raced. Then, suddenly, he was upright again, and my face was almost in his crotch. I stood up, my eyes meeting his.

"Well, that was very dramatic," he said. "Thank you for the tea. If you don't mind, I'm off to bed. I'm so far beyond tired, I've just hallucinated that you swore an oath of fealty to me."

"I did," I said, with a sincerity I hoped he saw.

"I know you did. As odd as it was, I appreciate it. Really. I've been so stressed, it helps to know I won't be fighting all the way anymore." He turned and took the first couple of steps down to his bedroom. "Oh, by the way. It's my day off tomorrow. I'm planning to sleep in for as long as possible. I appreciate this is your home, but do you think...?"

"You won't hear a peep out of me, I promise."

"Thanks."

As he started back down the stairs, an idea came to me. This was exactly the opportunity I'd been waiting for.

"Hey, when you get up, do you want to, maybe, hang out?"

"Huh?" Petey Boy's head reappeared above the level of the floor.

"I thought I could show you around the estate. We could take the horses out? Go down into the village, perhaps?"

Petey Boy was frowning.

"You want to hang out with me?"

"Well, it's not obligatory. But I am your liege man, after all. I thought you might need to get away from the house for a while. It's what I do when it all feels like too much. This house is enormous, but it's also very small. Getting away from it is good for perspective. Clears the mind."

Petey Boy chewed his lip, considering. Then a hint of a smile, and a nod.

"I'd like that."

My heart took off at a gallop, my whole body tingling.

"Great," I said, trying to sound casual. "You sleep as long as you need. When you're ready, I'll get you out of here and show you my world."

Chapter 19
Petey

I didn't dream of ginger Scotsmen. I dreamt of William. Wild, vivid dreams. His red boxer shorts transformed into a tiny red satin kilt that didn't cover him completely, and he breathlessly whispered oaths of devotion into my ears. When I woke at midday, flagpole rigid, drowning in sweat, William was—thank God—nowhere to be found. There was a note on the kitchenette: *Meet me at the stables whenever you're ready. No hurry. Wear these. WW.*

I picked up the garment underneath the note. "Yoga pants?"

I stood under the shower for what seemed like an age, still hard as an iron girder. It had been three weeks since I'd had sex—my longest drought since first year uni. I was missing London. I was missing the clubs of Vauxhall. But I was here to work, not get distracted by hot aristocrats, so I couldn't go riding in this state. Certainly not in yoga pants. I closed my eyes, and William was there. Behind me, inside me, here in the shower. He might have rejected me in real life, but here in my imagination the sexiest, most confusing man I had ever met was all mine. When it finally erupted, my load shot a tile right off the wall.

* * *

William was standing in the stable yard between two already saddled horses, dressed in his riding gear. He looked like a horsey Tom of Finland. Seeing him, I suddenly felt quite nervous. Why did he want to spend the day with me at all? It wasn't like he was interested in me. William bobbed his head.

"Good morning, my liege. My word, don't you look splendid."

I spun around, letting him appreciate the full ensemble.

"I hope you don't mind, I stole one of your tops." I'd found a light blue linen shirt in William's closet and tied the shirt fronts together into a knot—showing off all the goods, front and back, in the yoga pants.

William's face went as red as a postman's sack.

"Not at all. You look... *splendid*," he said, again. Was he permanently awkward? Was that the problem? Because honestly, he wasn't giving me disinterested vibes.

I said good morning to Achilles, and then William introduced me to a dappled grey pony called Pat.

"You named your horses Achilles and Patroclus? I knew you were a book nerd, but this is too cute for words."

William laughed. "Actually, this is Patrick Swayze. Mum named him. Mostly so she could tell her friends she spent all morning riding Patrick Swayze. It's a joke that works well for women of a certain age." William tapped Achilles's saddlebag. "I hope you're hungry, Bramley's packed one hell of a picnic."

After a quick lesson, we rode across Home Field, side by side—me wriggling in the saddle, trying to get comfortable, trying not to look like a massive tit.

"This was the site of the Battle of Buckford Field in 1485," William said, starting his tour. I tried to look impressed. "When I was a kid, you could still find arrowheads. It's all been gone over by metal detectorists now. Haven't found one in years."

William rode ahead to open Hill Gate, and I watched as his

magnificent arse bounced up and down, rising in and out of the saddle. It was going to be a long day.

In the oak woods, the temperature dropped ten degrees. The ancient trees had huge gnarled trunks and fat sprawling branches hung with moss. The air was busy with the sound of bird call. We picked through the uneven ground and overgrown trees for a while until William said it was time to dismount. He grabbed the saddlebag, took my hand—sending my heart into fits—and told me to close my eyes.

"Are you crazy? I'll break an ankle."

"Good point," he said, and crouched down. "Hop on."

"What?"

"I'll give you a lift. Close your eyes. I want this to be a surprise."

I mean, come on, how romantic was this? And this was the man who wouldn't even kiss me? How was I supposed to interpret these signals?

I put my legs either side of William's back and leant down into him.

"Put your arms around my neck."

"This is ridiculous," I said, but I was loving every second of it.

"Tighter. Now squeeze your legs around me."

I sank into William's back. The warmth of his body radiated into mine, like he was charging my battery. Then I felt his weight shift, and he stood like it was no effort at all. He handed me the saddlebag.

"Close your eyes. Hold on tight."

I didn't need telling twice.

William marched through the forest like a machine. I felt like Katharine Hepburn being carried across the river by Humphrey Bogart in *The African Queen*. I could feel every muscle in William's chest, his back, his arms, his shoulders, flexing beneath me. Our bodies were pressed together, the heat quickly turning the clothes between us damp with sweat. I held my face close to William's neck and breathed in the heady mix of shampoo and horse and leather. If I hadn't knocked one out in the shower that morning, I'd have destroyed a perfectly good pair of yoga pants and, quite possibly, have blown William's back out. A waft of an unfamiliar perfume found my nostrils, and a few moments later, William stopped.

"OK, open your eyes."

I blinked, readjusting to the light.

"Oh my God. It's... beautiful."

The entire forest floor was a sea of purple.

"They're English bluebells," William said. "They flower late here. Something to do with the hills. A microclimate or frost pocket or something. My father could have told you. Mind where you step."

I unwrapped my legs and slid to the ground. "I wish I had my phone. Why didn't you say? I could have brought a camera."

William shook his head. "This place should feed your soul, not your Instagram account."

"Does Indira know about this?"

"That's the whole point. This might be the latest-flowering bluebell wood in the entire Midlands. That's what makes it special. But it's also a secret. That's what makes it magical."

I wanted to bawl him out for holding back on something that would look so great on screen, but it was hard to argue with him when he was showing me something so sacred to him.

William laid a blanket down on a large mossy rock overlooking the mauve carpet of flowers, and we ate lunch. Bramley had packed enough sandwiches, apples, hard-boiled eggs, biscuits, and tea for six people. Which was just as well because, as it turned out, William ate enough for five.

"Posh Spice and a red telephone box," William said, passing me a sandwich.

I stared at it, confused. "No offence to Bramley, but I'd prefer egg and cress."

William laughed. "Write me a link."

I loved that William had remembered. I took a bite of what turned out to be cheese and tomato.

"Got it." I cleared my throat. "Posh Spice there, looking fabulous as always. How does she do it? Now, if I'd been married to a man as hot as David Beckham since the nineties, I'd certainly have a clapped-out red box. And mine wouldn't be the only one. A new report has revealed the parlous state of London's iconic red telephone boxes. William Winters filed this report."

William rolled back on the rug, clapping, trying not to choke on his sandwich.

"That is an incredible talent. They should give you your own show."

My tummy fluttered, a tingling pulse of heat radiating up through my body.

"That's the plan," I said.

"Really?" William looked genuinely excited for me, so I explained my deal with Indira.

"All I have to do now is come up with my big idea. One good enough to impress the toughest woman in television."

"What's your best idea so far?"

"*Himbos on Horseback*."

William raised an eyebrow. "It could do with some workshopping. How long do you have to come up with an actual workable, non-offensive, Indira Murray–shattering original idea for this show?"

I sucked air in through my teeth. "Two weeks."

"Two weeks?"

"I have to present it once filming completes."

"Well," William said, slapping his hands on his thighs. "We've got some work to do."

"We?"

"I'm your liege man. I swore an oath. We're in this together."

William's eyes were absolutely sincere, and something inside me crumbled. I'd called him a himbo to his face. Yet he was showing the kind of unconditional belief in my dreams I normally only got from my gran and from the Brent Boys. Who was this incredible, ridiculous, rugby-playing, fantasy-reading, honour-obsessed man who apparently didn't want me for my body but seemed to want to be around me for... well... me?

"So, tell me," William said, a while later. "Do you think there will be a second season of *The Love Manor*?" He was clumsily picking the shell off an egg.

"Wondering if you pledged fealty to me for no good reason, are you?" I nudged him playfully with my shoulder. "It's too late now, you've said the words."

He smiled, but the smile didn't seem to reach his eyes.

"I wondered, in your professional opinion. You're halfway through filming. Is it any good?"

I tried to weigh up what he really wanted to know.

"If you're worried *The Love Manor* is going to trash Buckford Hall's reputation, the time to think about that was before you signed on the dotted line."

"But if there was a second season, would Indira really film it somewhere else?"

I waved a hand. "That's what she's saying. But if we do our jobs well and don't stoke any more revolutions, uprisings, or a peasant's revolt, I'm sure she'd prefer to come back here."

William flicked some eggshell from his finger onto the dirt and held the naked egg up to his face, inspecting it. "If it did come back, would, you know, the same crew return?"

"Worried Derek might seek revenge for his broken arm?" I nudged him again, and the great bulk of William's body swayed away from me, then towards me, then settled back in place.

"Would *you* come back?" He turned to face me, his eyes burning with sincerity. My heart stopped. This was the question he wanted an answer to.

"Would you want me to come back?"

A short huff of air accompanied William's smirk.

"Of course."

He jostled his shoulder into mine, sending me swaying in the other direction. I nudged back into him on the recoil and let my shoulder rest against his. He didn't pull away, so I stayed there, the heat of his thick bicep burning into my arm. Our eyes were locked together. The sea of bluebells, the hum of the bumblebees, the cool soft light of the ancient forest—the producer in me was screaming *This is the perfect place for the most magical first kiss ever*. But the boy inside me was too scared to go for it, in case William pulled away. So I didn't. However, in that moment, I realised if coming back in a year's time was what it would take to earn William's kiss, then I would be back. It was one more excellent reason to make sure *The Love Manor* was a success.

"Then yes, of course I'd come back."

William grinned like an idiot. "Good." Then he popped the entire boiled egg in his mouth. "Thaa maygths me tho hhhhappy."

Chapter 20
William

T he village pub, the Hooray Henry, was standing room only for the big England v Scotland match, but I'd managed to nab a table with a first-rate view of the big screen. I sat on my own, watching the pre-game with three pints of real Leicestershire ale in front of me, looking both like Nobby No-Mates and a certified alcoholic. Petey Boy was outside, making the most of the phone reception to call his gran. The other beer was for Bramley, who had never heard of the term *third wheel*, and had also never taken less than forty minutes to pee. When the pub door opened and Petey's face appeared, I threw my hand in the air, perhaps a little too eagerly, to get his attention over the hubbub. He was walking gingerly, like he still had a horse under him.

"That's why I gave you the yoga pants," I said as he slid in beside me. "Wear anything with an inner seam and you'll be red raw."

I pushed his beer towards him. He winced. "Last time I found myself walking like this, I was staggering back to my hotel from the Folsom Street Fair."

"Is that like a village fair? You know the Newton Bardon fair is coming up soon?"

Petey Boy stared at me. I couldn't read the expression.

"How's your gran?"

"Fuming. She reckons one of the other inmates swapped their dentures while she was asleep, because her teeth don't fit right anymore and someone called Doris now has an eerily familiar smile."

"Did you say inmates?"

"She's in a home. She's not a fan. Still, it ain't all bad news. Chatsworth House cancelled a visit from my father's car club, and he's furious. So that's delicious."

This took me aback.

"I had the impression your father was probably serving twenty-five years to life for the Hatton Garden robbery."

"Sir Edward Topham, KC?"

"A King's Counsel?" I was rapidly reassessing everything I thought I knew about Petey Boy. "So, he's not even a barrow boy, then, let alone a notorious East End gangster?"

"Afraid not."

I let this information settle for a moment. Pennies were starting to drop. All this "bruv" talk didn't sit right because, well, it wasn't really who Petey Boy was. But why the facade?

"Do I get the impression you don't get on with your old man?"

"My parents... disapprove."

"Of?"

Petey Boy waved a hand up and down the length of himself. "All of it."

The family's black sheep, Jonty had said.

I took a cautious stab. "Rebelling against your class?"

Petey Boy pursed his lips. "That's part of it."

"Being gay?"

"To be fair, no, not that. But they have a very set idea of how I should live my life. I never wanted the life they offered, and they've never really forgiven me for it. But then, I've never forgiven my father for defending a lot of the #MeToo accused, so I guess disappointment is my family's love language."

"I'm sorry," I said. My father had been chaotic and irresponsible and frustrating, but I knew he'd have supported me, no matter what I chose to do with my life. Of course, if he'd been less chaotic and more responsible, I might still be doing what I chose to do with my life, rather than what he was supposed to be doing with his.

"Dub-Dub!" Horatio Blunt's voice boomed across the pub, and I flinched. I sensed him moving towards me like an oil slick. Petey Boy's hand went to my knee under the table.

"Are you OK?"

I spoke quickly, through gritted teeth. "It's someone I'd rather not —" A hand landed on my shoulder. "Horatio!" I turned to face him.

"Lovely to see you, Dub-Dub. I was hoping I'd bump into you."

"Were you?" Of course he was. Not only had I threatened him with the undertaker if he turned up at home again, but the TV company had security on the gates, and they weren't letting anyone through—especially twats—so stalking me in the village was his best hope of getting to me.

"I thought you might come in for the big game. Mind if I join you?"

"Actually, we're waiting for—"

But he had already slithered into Bramley's seat.

"I won't take up much of your time."

I mouthed an apology to Petey Boy. He squeezed my knee. Horatio extended a greasy hand towards him.

"Horatio Blunt. Old school chum of William's."

"Peter Topham," Petey Boy said, shaking the offered mitt.

"I say, no relation to the KC, are you?" Horatio looked him up and down, taking in the hair, the ear stud, the boiler suit, and answered his own question. "No, I suppose not. Still, thoroughly sound chap. Helped my poor father out of a spot of bother a few years ago. What's gotten into all these secretaries, hey?"

It was my turn to squeeze Petey Boy's knee under the table. His hand held mine. It was deeply comforting.

"My clients have upped their offer," Horatio murmured into my ear. He slipped a piece of paper onto the table.

"My answer is the same."

"Come on, Dub-Dub. Take a look."

"I don't need to look at it."

Petey Boy leant into my ear. "Are you OK? Do you want me to get him chucked out?"

I was grateful but said I could handle it.

"Fair enough, Dub-Dub," Horatio said. "If you need a little longer to come round, that's absolutely fine." He leant in closer, the heat of his breath on my ear. "It won't be long now. In my experience, once someone sells their family's dignity, it's not long before they're willing to sell their family's heritage too. You've got my number. Call me any time, old chum."

Outrage boiled up inside me. "Who the bloody hell do you think you are?"

Horatio frowned, pretending to be innocent. "I'm not the bad guy, Dub-Dub. I'm the man who holds in his hands the obvious answer to all your problems. I'm here to help."

Petey Boy's hand pressed into my shoulder, and I realised I'd been rising out of my chair, my fists clenched. I'm not a violent person. I've never thumped anyone in my life. But Horatio Blunt could well have been the first.

"Time to piss off, mate," Petey Boy said, standing up—all six and a half feet of him unfolding to tower over my old school bully—and looking ready to start a pub brawl.

Horatio laughed like this was the most ridiculous thing he'd ever seen. "And who the bloody hell are you? His nanny?"

"How dare you, sir!" Bramley's voice boomed through the pub. I hadn't seen him look so incensed since that time I suggested we save on polish by only doing the silverware once a month. "I'll have you know, you're addressing His Lordship's fiancé!"

"No, Bramley, that's only for—" But my protest arrived too late.

"Fiancé?" Horatio repeated, his voice thundering across the whole pub. "Dub-Dub, you dark horse! Congratulations!" He stuck his hand in mine and shook it, then pulled me towards him, slapping my back. "Everybody, His Lordship is engaged to be married!"

A roar of applause went up around the pub. Horatio shouted the entire bar a round of drinks. By the time the congratulations had died down, the match was starting and Horatio had slunk off. At half-time, I stood on a chair and bought everyone another drink on the condition they swore to keep the news about my "engagement" under their hats.

"The last thing we want is for this to make the papers," I said. "We all remember what it was like last time our village was crawling with reporters."

"Gutter scum!" Birdie Craddoch cried out.

"What's the world coming to when you can't even finger a girl in the street without some arsehole taking a photograph?" Noah, the village electrician, added.

"Shame!" someone boomed.

"We saw them off for you, though, William," Gurpreet, the local chemist, said.

Which was all jolly encouraging, but it didn't alter the fact that the lie Petey Boy and I were engaged was never meant to go beyond the walls of Buckford Hall. Now it had escaped, and I feared it might be difficult to contain. I was relying on my community's love and respect for my family to keep it quiet. Because if it hit the papers, we wouldn't be left alone—and I wanted very much for us to be left alone. Almost as much as I was starting to want to add *us* to my list of pronouns. I sat down. Petey Boy leant into my ear.

"Why didn't you just tell them the truth?"

"We couldn't risk the cast finding out."

Petey Boy looked at me like I was an idiot. "The cast that is locked away at Buckford Hall and has no contact with the outside world? Who these villagers are therefore never going to meet?"

"Ah." He had me there. "Yes. That cast."

No wonder he thought I was a himbo.

* * *

Back at the folly, I made my way upstairs with a couple of nightcaps to find Petey Boy sitting at my father's desk, his fingers tracing the ornate carvings. The moon was shining in through the porthole window behind him, giving his white-blond hair an ethereal glow that reminded me of Prince Henry in the *Knights-Errant* trilogy. I presented him with the tumbler, and he took it.

"What is it?"

"Sloe gin. It's about the only thing this estate still produces. Sorry, there's no ice."

We cheersed and he sipped at it, his eyebrows leaping off his head.

"This is *really* good."

I parked my arse against the edge of the desk, pretending to look out the window at the moon but mostly enjoying the closeness of Petey Boy's body.

"Was it a good day off, then?"

He smiled. "The best."

I clinked my glass against his. "I'm glad. I'm sorry we couldn't fit in the otters."

He spluttered into his drink. "I missed out on otters?"

"Didn't I mention?" I knew I hadn't. "Well, it was otters or the rugby, so I made an executive decision."

"I feel like if I'd been consulted, our day would have ended very differently."

As it turned out, that would have been for the best.

"They're very young. Their mother is still teaching them how to swim. There's plenty of time."

Petey Boy looked like he was having a stroke. "*Baby otters*? You withheld *baby* otters? Fuck. I know people who would shiv you for less."

I laughed. "You'll have to hang around a bit longer, then." And with every fibre of my body, I wanted him to. "When's your next day off?"

"In eight days. At which time I demand otters."

"It's a date." I rocked my shoulder gently into his, hoping to placate him.

Petey Boy pretended to be properly sulking, tracing his fingers over the carved woodwork of the desk, right by my thigh. His hand brushed my leg. I rocked into him again.

"This desk is really cool," he said.

A wave of sadness crashed through my body as a thousand memories of my father flashed in my head. I knocked back my gin. It sucked the air out of my lungs and gave cover to the tears in my eyes.

"You want to know what's *really* cool?" I turned, put my glass down, and crouched low. "Come stand behind me. Watch this." I gently pushed the small drawer inwards while my other hand fished around under the desktop. Then I gave the drawer a sharp shove, and a hidden panel thrust out from the desk where Petey Boy had been sitting. He shrieked with delight.

"A secret drawer! That's the coolest thing ever." There was a look of genuine childlike delight on his face. Sadly, there wasn't any treasure rattling around. A deck of cards. A dead spider. I wished there'd been something more interesting so Petey Boy could really understand the magic of it.

"When I was a kid, my father and I used to use it to send secret messages to each other. Stupid things, really. I'd pop in a drawing of a horse or something. You know, kid stuff. He'd leave me sweets or five pounds or, when I was much older, maybe a spliff or a mushroom."

Petey Boy shook his head. "You have *got* to be kidding me."

I laughed, wiping away a silly tear with my forearm. "My parents aren't—*weren't*—like normal parents." I felt the familiar weight in my chest I always felt talking about my father and tried to swallow it down. "I don't think I've opened the drawer since he died. Sometimes there'd be letters from him telling me how proud he was or how much he loved me. I've kept them all somewhere."

Petey Boy's face twitched, and too late, I remembered his terrible relationship with his parents.

"Let me show you how the mechanism works," I said, hoping to distract him—and me too.

I pushed the secret drawer back in until it clicked. Then I grabbed Petey Boy's hand and fed it under the table, feeling for the button, enjoying the feel of his fingertips weaving through mine. When I found it, I slid his hand onto it. His eyes met mine, and electricity sparked through my chest. I shifted in behind him, grabbing his other hand and placing it on the drawer knob.

"Like this," I said. "Now press here." My head rested against his, and Petey Boy leant into it. "Then *shove*." The drawer popped open, and we both looked in total surprise as a joint rolled slowly through the dust towards us.

Petey Boy stared at the spliff, then up at me. "I think your old man wants us to have a smoke." He picked up the joint. "How long has it been since, um...?"

"Three years." I shook my head. "There's no way that's any good."

"Still, your old man sounds like the kind of guy who'd want us to give it the old college try, right?"

Chapter 21
Petey

We went upstairs to William's bedroom in the belvedere so we could open some windows. The belvedere was a bit like a summer house but stuck on top of the tower. It had glass on all sides, giving us an incredible view across the lake, the fields, and the hilltops of the Buckford Estate. William's temporary bed was a mattress on top of some sort of wooden platform. The place was like a fairy-tale castle. We sat opposite each other, cross-legged on the bed—William in his boxers, me in my robe—coughing our lungs up.

"This is rough," I said, passing the joint back to William.

"Gordon Ramsay could attack my lungs with a cheese grater and it would feel smoother than this," he said.

I was getting a very light buzz, but nothing worth losing the lining of my throat over.

William took another small hit and fell about spluttering.

"Now I remember why I haven't done this in years."

He passed it across and leant back on his elbows on the bed, getting some air into his lungs. The shadows of the leaded lighting in the windows cast diamonds over his smooth skin, the curves of his arms and pecs, and the small hump of his softening belly. The sight was doing more to get me high than the dope. I wanted to get the conversation around to Horatio Blunt. I wanted to know who he was and what he wanted—because William had been furious to see him turn up at the pub, and his face had been practically purple by the time their conversation was over. I felt weirdly protective of this beefy horse-riding himbo, and I needed to know what could upset him like that. But William's eyes were still watery—and I knew it wasn't from the gin or the ancient spliff.

"What was he like, your old man?" I asked, giving the geriatric doobie another go.

William sighed and stared out the window while I hacked up the smoke.

"Dad was a hippie. Decades too late to be a real hippie, obviously. He was rebelling, I suppose. Like we all do."

He looked straight at me then. I looked away. I didn't want to talk about Sir Edward and Angelica now. I couldn't help but notice William hadn't actually described what the old baron had been like as a father.

"How do you rebel against a father who leaves pot for you in his desk drawer?"

William laughed. "You become a fantasy-reading, *Dungeons and Dragons*–playing rugby jock."

"How did that go down?" I offered him the joint, but he shook his head.

"He didn't care in the least, as long as I was happy."

My heart wrung itself out in my chest, the way it always did when someone talked about having loving, supportive parents.

"You're lucky, bruv. What was it like growing up here?"

"As childhoods go, it could have been a lot worse. My parents indulged our imagination. They encouraged us to get outside and play. We had four thousand acres and no discipline. I remember, one time, David and I had a fight over—I don't remember—something stupid. I felt slighted and I declared, rather pompously, as I was all of seven, 'I demand satisfaction.' Goodness only knows what I'd been reading at the time. Well, Dad thought that was hilarious. So, our parents acted as seconds while my brother and I fought a duel, over there on the Great Lawn, with pea-shooters made from hollowed-out biros. David and I fired spitballs at each other for five minutes, until I finally managed to hit him square between the eyes with a really gloopy one, and honour was satisfied."

I laughed. "For real?"

"That was parenting the way my folks did it."

"Sounds magical."

"It was. I thought so, anyway. Until I discovered he was as lax with everything else as he was with discipline."

William was opening up. He was quietly crying. Neither of us mentioned it.

"Do you mind if I ask what happened to them?"

"You don't know?"

I said I didn't, and William shrugged. "It's all a matter of public record. It was a light plane crash. David was an amateur pilot. He'd taken Dad up for a joy flight. He liked to do that sometimes. They had engine trouble, David tried to land it in a field, came down too steeply, and instead of skating along the grass, slammed into the ground. They died instantly."

"I'm so sorry." I couldn't think what else to say. William reached for the joint and I handed it to him, grateful to have something to do. "That must have been a really hard time."

"I was on a rugby trip down in London when it happened. There was a train strike, the roads were jammed. I couldn't get home. I was stranded, heartbroken, and alone. I cried myself to sleep in a cheap hotel in Saint Pancras that night. When I finally did get home and someone called me 'my lord' for the first time, I found I was actually rather angry. I still am, sometimes. At Dad. At David. At life. But it is what it is. And here we are."

William sucked the smoke into his lungs, then covered his mouth as he spluttered and coughed. I passed him my drink. "Are you OK?"

"I'm fine. Perhaps it's not a great idea to smoke a joint that's older than your trauma?" He coughed again. "Anyway, we rallied. My godparents—you remember Leaf and Karma?"

"The fox hunt saboteurs?"

"They came down and stayed for a few weeks, to look after Mum. My sister and her husband came up from London with the kids. We had a lot to sort out. Including what it meant for my sister's boy, Callum, who was now the heir. We sat around and drank a lot and talked a lot and had a tonne of meetings with accountants and lawyers and slowly came to the terrible realisation we were all quite fucked."

"Fucked how?"

William shook his head. "Never mind."

He took another hit on the joint, passed it to me, and got up and opened another window. He stood there, letting the cool night air drift over his skin, his body bathed in moonlight. He was beautiful. My stomach fluttered with nerves, and I took a hit to calm them. It was time to shoot my shot.

"The man at the pub today?"

William turned to look at me, resting his buttocks against the windowsill.

"What did he want?"

"He wants me to sell the estate. He's found buyers. Belarusian oligarchs. They're cashed up, and they're determined. They want to turn it into a hotel."

"You're kidding. You're not going to sell it, are you?"

William smiled, a big cheesy grin. He laughed, wiping the tears from his cheeks with the palm of his hand.

"I don't want to. But Horatio's right, it would solve a lot of problems."

At the thought of it, William's face seemed to change. He looked *tired*. Suddenly, I could see the weight he'd been carrying around.

"Your money trouble. Is it... bad?"

William looked up at the ceiling and closed his eyes. The great bulk of his chest grew as he slowly filled with air, then gently deflated again as he slowly released it. When his eyes opened, the moonlight glinted in his tears. He walked across the room, smoothly sweeping the joint out of my hand and sticking it in his mouth on the way. He reached for his book and plucked out a brown envelope. He passed it to me and sat back against the windowsill, sucking back on the last of the joint.

"Open it," he said, coughing. "Do you want any more of this?"

I shook my head. "Not without anaesthetic." He dropped the roach into his glass.

I turned the envelope over in my hands. It was from His Majesty's Revenue and Customs, the words *URGENT: DO NOT IGNORE* written across it in red ink. I'd never seen one like that before. I was horrified.

"You're meant to open these."

William waved a hand. "You open it."

I stared at him, unsure if he was serious.

"Please."

I slid my finger into the corner of the envelope and extracted the letter. It started out boring enough. Then my eyes landed on the number.

"Holy shit, William, you owe HMRC four point three million pounds."

He sighed, his shoulders slumping.

"Did you know about this?"

He shook his head. "I knew we owed a lot. I had no idea it was so much."

I kept reading the letter. "William, you've only got like five months to pay this. The deadline is Halloween."

"That's fittingly ghoulish," he said, forcing a laugh. "Perhaps this year I should dress up as a taxidermied version of myself? Being as I'm so completely stuffed."

I couldn't imagine having that kind of debt. How was William functioning? This letter was dated weeks ago. Why hadn't he dealt with this? He was going to lose everything.

"Do you have the money?"

"Nowhere near it."

"What are you doing about it?"

"Well, I thought *The Love Manor* cheque would help—"

"William, that's not even going to scratch the sides. What else are you doing?"

He looked stricken and lifted his shoulders. "It all helps, right?"

"How did this happen? I thought these sorts of places were always in a trust?"

"It is. But every ten years you have to pay tax on it. My father didn't leave enough. He might have had a plan to pay it, but if he did, he didn't tell me. He might have told David, but..."

The tears were silently streaming down his face, along his neck and over his chest.

"William, I'm so sorry."

He turned and rested his hands on the windowsill, looking out across the estate.

"It costs one point two million pounds a year to keep the lights on and everything ticking over," he said. "Thank God for the rents. I've been doing my best these past three years, but I wasn't raised to do this. I was the spare. I wasted my education playing rugby and reading fantasy novels. David would have known what to do."

I thought of our picnic in the bluebell woods, of all the stories William had told me today, of the obvious pride he took in his family's centuries of achievement at Buckford. This place was so a part of William, I couldn't imagine him selling it. Yet the stress it was causing him was clear.

"What happens if you sell?" I asked, tucking my legs up under my chin.

"After I've paid all the debts, I'd probably walk away with about forty million pounds."

I choked like my throat had rediscovered its gag reflex. *Jesus!* William waited for me to recover.

"I'd have to look after Mum and my sister and her family out of that, obviously." He turned around to face me again, resting his arse against the windowsill. "I know, it's very hard to feel sorry for me, isn't it? It's not exactly Sophie's Choice."

"It's a lot of money."

"I'd be failing my family."

This was something I knew a bit about.

"It's not failing your family to choose a good life for yourself. It's failing yourself to choose the expectations of others over your own happiness."

"You don't understand. I have an obligation to my family, to this place."

I felt my hackles rise but chose compassion. "You don't. You can choose a different life for yourself."

William slapped a hand to his face and wiped at his eyes. I wanted to comfort him but worried a hug might be unwelcome.

"You think I should sell," he said. It was a statement, not a question.

"No," I said, quickly. "I'm saying you need to choose what's right for you. When I finally told my parents I wasn't going to Oxford to study law, that was me choosing my own happiness. It was the hardest thing I ever did. Harder than coming out. But it was the best thing I ever did. I'm not telling you what your decision should be. I'm telling you to choose whatever is going to make *you* happy—and sod whatever anyone else thinks."

William's leg was bouncing up and down. I sensed I'd pushed him too far. We were high. He'd opened up, I'd got behind the himbo facade, seen into his soul. I feared he might push me away now, when what I really wanted was for him to pull me closer.

"You think less of me, I'm sure," he said when he finally spoke. "Now you know I'm not some rich aristocrat but a himbo who's drowning in debt."

"Don't be silly. Of course not."

"If I choose family expectations and debt, though—if that's what happiness means to me—would you think less of me?"

Walking away from £40 million and choosing debt and family expectation? *The Love Manor* had filled this house with two dozen people willing to do anything for cash, and here was William willing to walk away from unfathomable wealth out of, what, a sense of duty?

"Not at all." How could you think less of anyone for that?

"I thought you'd run a mile," he said, looking at me earnestly. "Any sane person would run a mile."

I was high enough that it took a moment to realise what he'd said. William's choice of words only made sense if he was interested in me after all. Had he been holding back because he thought I wouldn't be interested in him when I discovered all was not rosy at Buckford Hall? He might not have known how much trouble he was in, but he knew he was in trouble.

"I'm still here," I said.

William's eyebrows drew together. "Why?"

"No liege man left behind."

He smiled. He lay down on the bed, on his side—his red satin boxer shorts cupping him in all the right places—and held out an arm towards me. His eyes met mine. He patted the duvet cover beside him.

"Come here."

My heart raced at the invitation, adrenaline rippling out from my chest. I wasn't meant to be getting distracted by boys. I was here to work. But I found myself crawling across the bed towards him, my arms and legs wobbling like a newborn deer's. I laid my head down on the pillow, my eyes meeting William's. Was he going to kiss me?

"Turn around," he said, winking.

Christ, he wanted to get right down to business?

"Listen, I haven't—"

"Please, Petey," he said, softly. The way he shortened my name felt intimate. His hand rested on my hip and gently turned me over. The heat of his body, the strength of his touch—I was powerless to resist. I tucked myself up against him, my back against his stomach. Only my robe separated us. I became aware of our breathing, the gentle rise and fall. His thumb traced up and down my chest. Again, I realised how slow I'd been to understand. William hadn't wanted to shag me, he wanted to hold me—and his embrace felt more real than any I'd had from any of the hundreds of men who had gone before him.

"Thank you," he said.

"For what?"

"For not running."

"Why would I run?"

"I can think of four point three million reasons, at least."

The cuckoo clock downstairs cuckooed for ten o'clock. I needed to sleep.

"I'm a producer, William," I said. "We don't run from problems. We solve them."

He snuggled closer into me, his legs and feet entwining with mine. His face nuzzled in behind my ear, his hot breath making my cock as rigid as I could ever remember it being—but he never reached for it. I knew he wouldn't, and I was fine with that. This wasn't sex. This was something else. I didn't understand it, I didn't recognise it, but I realised now it was something I had been looking for, for a long, long time.

"Do you want to sleep up here tonight?" he asked.

I nodded, and I felt William's whole body relax into mine. Then, as light as breath itself, William's lips grazed my skin, and he tenderly kissed my neck.

Chapter 22
William

How do you know if you're falling in love, and how do you know if what you're actually doing is going insane? I couldn't concentrate all the following day. I'd managed to leave a message for my accountant, but between my money worries and thinking about Petey, my brain was mush. Petey was working late, but by early evening I was already sitting in my father's armchair, counting the hours for him to come home. I drummed my fingers against the unopened copy of *Oathkeeper*—the final book in the original *Knights-Errant* trilogy—in my lap. Petey Boy was all I could think about. I kept going up to the belvedere to stare out the windows, hoping to catch a glimpse of him. I kept burying my face in the bed sheets, hoping to catch the scent of him. I'd tried to start reading at least a hundred times, but my thoughts drifted—to the way his body fit so perfectly into mine, to the way his nose crinkled up when he laughed. To the way he didn't even bat an eyelid when he found out what a mess I was in. So *how* did you tell if this was actual, full-blown, shout-it-from-the-belvedere love, or the kind of medically diagnosable, legally inadvisable obsession that gets people put on a register?

The door downstairs burst open.

"Dub-Dub, I'm in love!"

"Jesus, Jonty, could you have knocked? I nearly shat my boxer shorts."

I put my hand to the seat of them to check. I was cautiously sniffing my palm when Jonty came bounding up the stairs, his black curls in a tangle.

"You can't be in here," I bleated.

"You have to meet her, Dub-Dub. She's so beautiful, busloads of supermodels are giving up the catwalk and wolfing down Big Macs to make up for lost time. You should *see* her! Her little ears, Dub-Dub! They're... gah... you've never seen ears like them. They're perfect. It's literally like someone designed those ears specifically for her."

"Jonty, you need to leave." I was thinking of Indira's fines and how much I needed the cash. But I was also thinking of my oath to Petey Boy. Aiding and abetting a lovesick Jonty in going AWOL was not good boy behaviour. I tried to usher him back down the stairs, but he was bouncing around like a toddler on red cordial.

"Her laugh, Dub-Dub! It tumbles out of her like church bells. The sound, I swear, it's... a religious experience. I find myself making goofy little jokes to hear that intoxicating peal. It goes straight to the old beef bayonet, Dub-Dub. In an instant, the plucky little chap's protruding from the gun port, ready to fire hot lead right into her sides."

The cuckoo clock sang for six o'clock. Thank goodness. Cocktail hour. Clearly, I wasn't going to get rid of him, so I poured us a drink while he blathered away about this woman's incredible brain and business acumen. I sat in my father's armchair.

"Jonty, who the devil are you talking about?"

"Isn't it obvious?"

"Well, no. You haven't said her name even once."

"Lola, of course. Who else's ears could I possibly be talking about?"

"Which one is she?"

"The short one. Black hair. Face of a goddess. Extremely popular make-up tutorial channel. You must have watched it. Come on! Father from Seoul. Mother from Cockermouth. Accent direct from Cheltenham Ladies' College. Adorable little ears. You can't miss her."

Jonty is tedious when he's not in love. Jonty believing himself in love could be weaponised by MI6.

"So, what are you doing here, telling me about her, instead of being out there with her?"

"Because we're both servants, and under the rules of the game no one can know about our affair or we'll both be dismissed. I couldn't bear it, Dub-Dub. This forced proximity, it's incredibly special. We can't go home to our day jobs and Tube journeys and squeezing each other in at the weekends."

"Jonty, you don't have a day job."

"You know what I mean, Dub-Dub. She lives in Chelsea. That's a forty-five-minute cab ride, at least. Here, she's in the next room. I can practically hear her sleeping. Do you have any idea how incredible that is?"

Actually, I thought I did. I recognised myself in Jonty's madness. This seemed like the perfect opportunity to ask a few pertinent questions.

"How do you know it's love?"

"Of course it's love, man. She's shut down all my brain function. All I can think about is her. She's commandeered all my senses. I can't smell anything but her perfume, hear anything but her voice, see anything but her face, taste anything but her earwax."

"Probably didn't need quite so much detail," I said. But I understood, because I should have been making some more calls and rustling up a spare £4.3 million but I'd achieved nothing all day because of exactly that.

"Every cell in my body aches for her. She has bewitched me. Do you know what that does to a man?"

If you'd asked me two weeks earlier, I'd have said no. But now, I thought perhaps I did. If that's what love felt like for Jonty, then maybe that meant I was in love too?

*　*　*

Petey was clearly working late, so I had gone to the Dower House for dinner with Mum. Bramley was drizzling custard onto my slice of apple pie so slowly, he must have made it the same consistency as his pee.

"Good God, stop holding back, man. A chap could starve under these conditions."

"It is your third piece, my lord."

"Who died and made you Weight Watchers team leader?"

Mum clattered her espresso cup down into her saucer with finality. "Right, who's for Scrabble?"

I hadn't told her about the £4.3 million. There was no need to worry her. I didn't feel like talking about it, anyway.

"Actually, Mum, I wondered if I could ask you something kind of personal?"

Mother reached out and grabbed my hand. "Anything darling, you know that. Is it piles? Because I have an ointm—"

"Not that kind of personal, Mum." I snatched my hand away, wary of where those fingers had been. "Never that kind of personal."

I shovelled a heaped dessertspoon into my mouth, plucking up courage. Mum sat back in her chair, steepling her hands.

"William, the great goddess has sent you a gift. Exactly as she said she would. What's the matter, darling, don't you know how to unwrap it?"

I spluttered in shock and a piece of apple pie shot across the room, splattering against the window.

"How... how on earth did you—" I coughed and slugged at my water. "I hate it when you do your witchy stuff."

"It doesn't take witchy stuff to see you're completely besotted by that tall streak of bacon in the boiler suit you're pretending to be engaged to. You're almost as bad as Achilles at hiding your attraction."

"Fine, yes. You're right."

Mum's arms flew out wide, and she reached across the table.

"My darling, that's wonderful! How can Mummy help?"

This was mortifying enough as it was. Why did she have to be like this? But I did actually need her help. I asked a starter question for ten points.

"How did you know you were in love with Dad?"

Mum's eyes glazed. She squeezed my hand.

"It was a night like this. Moonlit. I'd come up from university to visit him for the weekend. Your father took me for a walk down by the Long Water. We talked about our hopes and dreams. When we stopped to cross Lady Caroline's Bridge, his hand slid gently onto my cheek. I turned towards him, and his lips found mine. It was a gentle kiss, soft as the flutter of a butterfly's wings. But it caused an earthquake inside me, and thirty-three years later, I'm still riding those vibrations."

Hard to know the appropriate thing to say to that.

"So, my father was basically chaos theory in meat form." I nodded. "Yep, that checks out."

Mum laughed. "No, darling, *love* is chaos theory in meat form."

"So, you think I should kiss him?"

"Yes, William, of course you should kiss him! Go make wild, passionate love to him on every corner of the estate, if it's what your heart tells you is right."

"But what does love *feel* like?" I asked. "Not the sticky bit. I mean the other bit."

Mum smiled. "It feels like a key sliding into a lock. If it fits, you know you belong together. That you wouldn't work without each other."

Bramley reappeared with a damp cloth and a bucket, ready to attack the window.

"Sorry, old chap," I said.

"Think nothing of it, my lord."

Over Bramley's shoulder, I saw a light go on in the distant porthole window of the folly. I stood abruptly, made my apologies, and dashed out of the room.

"That's it, my darling," Mother called after me. "You ride those vibrations."

Running across the Great Lawn, the cool night air prickling against my skin, I couldn't help but notice it was a glorious evening. Almost romantic. Perfect for a walk and a life-altering first kiss on Lady Caroline's Bridge. I burst through the folly door and bolted up the stairs to find Petey sitting at my father's desk, jotting at a notepad.

"You're home early," I said, catching my breath.

Petey could barely contain his laughter as he looked me up and down.

"Where the hell have you come from, dressed like that?"

"Dinner."

His eyes popped. "You went to dinner in your boxer shorts?"

I shrugged. "It was only family."

"I thought the aristocracy dressed for dinner."

"I dress for important things."

"I refuse to believe you don't think dinner is important."

"It's one of the eight most important meals of the day," I confirmed.

"William, do you know your feet are covered in grass clippings?"

"Had to dash across the Great Lawn."

"Why?"

"Because you came home. Early."

Petey smirked. "You rushed home because *I* was at home? Do you still think I'm planning to steal the silver?"

"You're welcome to it, actually. It's incredibly ugly, and it takes a lot of polishing. Listen, it's a glorious night. The moon's out. The air's fresh. The frogs are busy banging each other's brains out, and they're making the most magnificent cacophony. It's like a bloody concert. Shall we go for a walk?"

He shook his head. "I've got work to do. I've got an idea for a show I'm trying to knuckle out."

"That's wonderful! What's the—"

"Then I've got a couple of ideas to help you bring in some cash."

"Help *me* bring in some cash? Petey, that's not really your responsibility—"

"I know. But why don't you put the kettle on, wash your feet, and we can have a chat in a bit?"

This was already going off the rails. But this country didn't become great by chaps giving up at the first hurdle.

"I have a better idea. Why don't we walk and talk? I can help you hash out your show idea."

Petey looked up at me. "Actually, I'd appreciate a sounding board."

"So we're on?"

"Only if you put some clothes on."

Ten minutes later, I'd put on my best chinos, a linen shirt, and some loafers. I'd brushed my teeth and combed my hair. While I did genuinely want to hear Petey's show idea and I was deeply touched he'd been thinking of ways to help me raise funds to save the estate, I was definitely leading him down the path by the Long Water with a singular goal in mind. When we reached the bridge, I was jolly well going to kiss him. With his consent, obviously. I was following my father's lead, not my grandfather's.

"Come on, hit me with it," I said. "Tell your liege man this big idea of yours."

His eyes lit up.

"It's a twist on an idea I pitched to Indira before. A dating show where your friends and family get to choose who you get to date."

"Sounds horrendous. I wouldn't let my mother choose who I dated."

"Exactly. Which is why people will watch it."

"But how do you encourage your victims to take part?"

"Officially? Finding true love."

"And unofficially?"

"A free holiday. If they go on a date and like each other enough, we'll send them to a Greek island for a week together. All of which we film, obviously, to see how they get on." Petey looked at me hopefully. "What do you think?"

I thought I was grateful it was dark out.

"Look, it's no *Himbos on Horseback*—which would obviously rate its socks off—but I think there might be something there." I slipped my hand into Petey's, as smooth as reins sliding through fingers. His hand felt so right in mine. Part one of Operation Snog was underway. I felt brave and bold and it gave me such a hot rush, I thought my aorta might burst right out of my chest and splatter the cow parsley with blood. I looked at Petey, who smiled down at me.

"I'll keep working on it, then," he said.

"How's the other big show going? I had a visit from Jonty today, by the way."

"We know you did. He's been warned. Again."

"You know?" I looked at him. "You don't seem... angry."

"To be honest, we were all quite relieved to be shot of him for an hour. He's been running around with a lit fuse for days now. He's driving us around the bend."

So I wasn't in trouble. That was a relief. I didn't think an angry Petey would be a kissy Petey.

"But it was a big day today. Double eviction."

"Not—"

"No, not Jonty and Lola. Kiki Galapagos and Tom the racist closet case from rural Somerset. But, in welcome news, Ridhi and Armando seem to have turned a corner."

"Bully for them. Three cheers."

As we reached Lady Caroline's Bridge—the covered stone Palladian crossing built by Capability Brown—my heart was thumping so loudly it was causing ripples on the water. Petey sat on the bench looking back along the lake to the house, so I sat down beside him. His fingers were still intertwined in mine. The evening was calm, but the frogs were going absolutely hell for leather. A pair of ducks glided down from the sky and landed on the water in front of us.

"Is that Derek's duck?" Petey said.

"You know, I think it might be. Looks like he found himself a girlfriend."

"Good for him."

We sat there in silence for a minute, me trying to drum up the courage from my loafers, where it was hanging out with my toes.

"All right, your turn," Petey said. "Shall we compare notes? You go first. What ideas did you come up with for saving the estate today?"

"Ideas?"

"Yeeeessssss…"

"For saving the estate?"

"William, did you not come up with any ideas? What did you do all day?"

How could I tell him I stared out the window, hoping to catch a glimpse of him? That I pined for him? Imagined kissing him, spending my life with him?

"Well, I…"

"William, you have a hundred and sixty-five days to save the estate. You need twenty-six thousand pounds every single day or you'll lose everything." Petey stood, his hand leaving mine. He pointed back towards the house. "If I were you, I'd be unable to think about anything else. Have you done *anything* to find that cash today?"

I felt so ashamed, but I couldn't admit I hadn't. I opted for a tiny white lie.

"I thought we could sell the Holbeins. They'll leave sodding great gaps on the wall of the Long Gallery, but that portrait of Queen Elizabeth is the stuff of childhood nightmares. No wonder she died a virgin. I won't miss it. I'm sure we'll be able to fill the spots with something. There's an IKEA up near Nottingham."

Petey's eyes narrowed. "I can't tell if you're joking or not, and to be honest, this ain't the time for jokes. You need to get serious or you're gonna lose everything."

I hated that he was right. But I felt so daunted by the size of the task in front of me. It was crippling.

"I have absolutely no idea where to start."

Petey's eyes softened. He sat back down beside me, weaving his fingers into mine again.

"A kilo of carrots is approximately eight to ten carrots," he said.

"Have you had a seizure?"

"When I was a kid, my gran would sell a kilo of carrots for eighty pence. The profit margin was ten per cent."

"If you're suggesting I sell Achilles's carrots out from underneath him, he'll riot."

"Eight pence profit isn't a lot, but sell enough every day, every week, and at the end of the year you've made about four hundred quid—on carrots alone. Then there's potatoes, beans, tomatoes…"

Petey looked at me earnestly, like he'd made a deeply profound point that would set me on the path to financial freedom.

"You think I should grow carrots?"

Petey's head was in his hands.

"Don't think of it as one lump sum," he said. "Every little bit of cash you can bring in chips away at the total. Every penny you get is a penny you don't have to find. You need to raise cash now, then you need to find long-term diversified revenue streams."

That made sense.

"I do have a couple of ideas for you," Petey continued. "You don't have to agree, but I think you should."

"Spoken like a TV producer."

"You remember I said Chatsworth House cancelled on my father's car club? Well, the club is still looking for somewhere to go. They were going to pay Chatsworth two thousand pounds. That could be two thousand pounds in your pocket."

"It's not a lot of cash, though, is it."

"It's a shitload of carrots, William."

He looked impatient. My panicked brain caught up with his reasoning.

"Would it be OK, though? I mean, you don't like your father."

"Why would I care? I won't be here. It's after the show wraps. I'll be back in London."

My chest tightened, like a fist had gripped my heart. Of course Petey would be back in London by then—and beyond my reach. He didn't live here. He had his own life. But... I didn't want him to leave. Jonty had been right—our time here together was short and precious. I had to do it. I had to kiss him now. He needed to know how I felt about him. I stood, grabbing his hand, ready to pounce.

"Petey, I—"

A loud, insistent chorus of quacks split the night air. I looked around to see Derek's duck shagging his girlfriend. I dropped Petey's hand and let my shoulders fall. This was not going to be the moment I had hoped it would be.

"What were you going to say?" Petey asked when the feathered fornication had finished.

"Nothing. I suppose Bramley could do the tea."

"If you have a different car club come every weekend, that's one hundred and four thousand pounds a year—all money for doing basically sod all."

"And I love earning money for doing sod all," I said, choosing enthusiasm. "Petey, this is genius. Get the telephone book. How many car clubs are there in England?"

"Telephone book? Listen, can we head back? I've got one more idea I want to put to you, and I really need to get back to my pitch."

I felt completely deflated. I'd failed to kiss him. Failed to achieve what my father had achieved with my mother on this very spot.

Which was starting to feel like the story of my life. But I had gained something else: an understanding that this financial mess wasn't going to go away unless I fixed it. Thanks to Petey, I felt for the first time like perhaps I could actually fix it. At least I had to try.

"What's this other idea?" I said as we shuffled down the stone steps to the path that would take us home to the folly.

"How do you feel about weddings?" he said.

Chapter 23
Petey

"Drone up! Get the bloody drone up!" Indira shouted. "They're going to shag in the hedge maze."

We were in the production office in the Old Coach House, watching the footage from the fixed cameras in the house. Ridhi and Armando had been getting closer for days, but Armando had made a special trip to the dining room to raid the punchbowl full of condoms, and he and Ridhi were now hightailing it across the Great Lawn to the yew hedge maze. Indira was bouncing on her feet, pumping her fists.

"Has anyone in the cast clocked it?"

"I don't think so," I said. "Now Tom's gone, Armando's lost his little buddy to confess to."

"Damn. Is there anyone we can tip off? I want that fucking wedding."

Ridhi and Armando were both aristocrats. Under the rules of the game, if they got caught in a compromising position, then Armando could choose either to banish Ridhi from the show or to wed her. Not a real marriage, of course. But a spectacular fake Regency fake wedding, with all the fake trimmings. We were three-quarters of the way through filming. The footage we were capturing now was notionally for episode nine of twelve. We had a ball to film tonight, and two new contestants joining the cast, but it was the perfect spot in the season for a wedding.

"Cristina and Ridhi are too tight, she won't say a word even if she knows," I said. "I miss Ellie and Kiki. They wouldn't have thought twice about sticking their oar in."

Indira lit two cigarettes and sucked on them both. Out of the corner of my eye I saw movement in the yard through the window. William, in his riding gear, headed for the stables. My God, he was fit. But now I was getting to know him, I found myself noticing the depth behind the posh, beefy lughead exterior—his kindness, his passion, his ridiculous but adorable moral code. He caught me staring at him through the window and, from across the yard, waggled a finger at me in the universal gesture for *Come here*. I looked over at Indira, who was shouting orders into a walkie-talkie, and indicated with my thumb I was popping out.

"Are you going to tell me you've come up with fifty-two grand's worth of cash?" I asked, closing the gap between William and me.

"Fifty-two? What happened to twenty-six?"

"You didn't come up with anything yesterday."

"Goodness, all right, Madam Lash. As a matter of fact, I've been on the phone to Wetherby's Auction House all morning. Someone's coming up from London to value the artwork after filming's finished. May as well get rid of all of the spookier portraits. The ones that make the house feel like a creepy museum."

"But how will you fill all those gaping holes?"

(Yes, I know. It flew right over his head. I really missed the Brent Boys at times like this.)

"Mum's got some wonderful Kazimierczuks in the Dower House. Paintings of hedgerows and wildflower meadows and, you know, stuff people actually like to look at. I thought I'd commission the artist to paint a few more Buckford scenes to replace all the creepy bestockinged children by Reynolds. Should raise a couple of million *and* lift the spirits."

That put my story about eight pence on a kilo of carrots into perspective.

"You've been busy," I said. "I'm proud of you."

"Everyone is putting their shoulder to the wheel. Bramley's selling his underwear on the internet."

"Bramley makes underwear?"

"No."

I tried not to process that news. "That reminds me, we need to get you on TikTok."

Achilles neighed.

"All right boy, I'm coming."

I followed William into the stables. He disappeared into the tack room and came out with his saddle.

"How about you, young master Topham, did you have any luck with your phone calls this morning?"

I'd almost forgotten.

"It's a mixed bag. Father said no. I'm sorry." In fact, we'd had a blazing row on the phone. It had taken two coffees to summon the energy to call him, and he could not have been more contemptuous or dismissive. "Said he didn't think the Love Manor was an appropriate venue to host his beloved car club."

"Well, a pox on him!" William flipped the saddle up onto Achilles's back and started fiddling with the leather straps.

"But Sunny and Ludo said yes. They'll come up after filming has finished to have a look at the place. They said it sounds like the ideal venue for their wedding. Sunny's chuffed to bits. He's *very* proud of his Leicestershire heritage."

"Oi, Romeo!" Indira shouted across the yard. "Where the fuck art thou, Romeo?"

"I have to go," I said. "But good work on the art."

William nodded. "Good work on the phone calls."

William's face moved towards mine, and I thought he was going to peck me on the cheek, so I turned—and he kissed me on the ear.

"Petey Boy, we have a fucking wedding to organise!" Indira shouted.

"Coming!"

* * *

That evening, I raced around looking for William. He wasn't in the folly or the stables, so I found myself out of breath and knocking on the Dower House door in desperation. Bramley opened it.

"I'm afraid His Lordship is in the midst of losing a game of Scrabb—"

"Petey?" William appeared behind Bramley—naked, as always, except for his red satin boxer shorts. "What's up?"

"We need your help," I puffed.

"Anything at all." He ushered me past Bramley and into the vestibule, his arm looping around my shoulder. "You look like you've had a fright. Is everything OK?"

"I've been running. I think working with Indira has killed my lung capacity."

Bunny's voice echoed through from another room. "Who is it, darling? Is it my future son-in-law?"

"Oh God," William said. "Look, I apologise in advance—"

"William, this is urgent," I pleaded. "I don't have ti—"

Bunny Winters appeared in the doorway in a diaphanous blue dress, gently greying hair piled up on top of her head. There were now rather a lot of us in a vestibule no larger than a lift.

"Do you know, William, I don't think your lover and I have been formally introduced."

Lover?

Bunny looked at me, and at her son—her face quizzical. William looked at me, and at his mother. I stood there, looking at them both.

Bramley was pretending to polish the doorframe. I didn't have time for this.

I extended a hand. "Lady Buckford, it is a pleasure to meet you. Sorry I can't stay to chat. I have an emergency, and I need William's help—"

She batted that away with her hand. "William tells me he tried to take you up the Long Water last night."

"Mum!"

"I'm sorry?" I looked at my watch. Indira was going to kill me.

"It's my fault," Bunny went on. "I'd been filling his head with stories about what a wonderful lover his father had been—"

"You had not!" William protested.

"William was hoping to recreate a little of our magic and kiss you, but he chickened out—" She turned to William. "Didn't you, darling?"

William was as white as a ghost. I wasn't far off it myself.

"Be patient with him, Peter." Bunny's hand found my chin, her arctic-blue eyes staring directly into mine. "William was a late developer, and he's always swerved life's more powerful emotions. But he's also an incurable romantic at heart. He'll get there in the end."

And with that, she drifted away, leaving me totally speechless.

"I am *so* sorry," William said.

Bramley was still polishing the same bit of doorframe with his cloth. My walkie-talkie squeaked into life, screaming at me in Scottish.

"Forget it. I need your help," I said, springing back into action. "Ridhi and Armando have been lost in the hedge maze for the last six hours."

"That's awful," William said.

"Depends how you look at it. Assuming Armando isn't a total dog, we're having a wedding tomorrow. Indira's delighted. But we need you to find them and get them out. Plus five other members of the cast. Plus six of the crew. In fact, everyone who tried to rescue them is still in the maze. We're meant to be filming a ball in an hour, and there's practically no one left."

Bunny's voice echoed through from the other room. "It's your turn, William. I've just played *JAZZIEST* on two triple word scores for four hundred and thirty-seven points."

William's face set with the grit and determination of a storybook hero. He bowed slightly, as if accepting his mission.

"I shall not fail you, my liege," he said—and I tried not to roll my eyes. Then he slipped his feet into some flip-flops, grabbed a flashlight off a hook by the door, and slid his hand into mine.

"I thought there was only one *Z* in a Scrabble set?" I said as we dashed out into the night.

"There is," William said. "But Mum doesn't really do rules. Not unless they suit her."

We were making a beeline across the Great Lawn for the hedge maze. The grass was damp and slippery and glistening in the moonlight.

"Wait, don't you need a map or something?" I asked.

"A map? I've been trimming those hedges since I was fifteen. I could find my way around them with my eyelids stapled shut."

"That's... vivid."

It took William less than ten minutes to extract all the cast and crew from the maze. The medics were on standby, giving everyone water and checking for cuts, bruises, insect bites, and stray badgers masquerading as fashionable haircuts.

"Is that everything you need?" William asked.

I said it was and thanked him.

"No problem. I'll see you back at the folly." He kissed me on the cheek. "Best keep up the pretence we're in love," he whispered. He winked, and I felt my knees go. Then I watched his magnificent arse disappear into the darkness—like two watermelons wrapped in red satin, bouncing off into the distance on the back of a well-sprung wagon.

My headset crackled in my ear.

"Find out if they fucking kissed," Indira barked. I waved at the crew, pointing them towards the gaggle of relieved cast members. Then I whispered an instruction into Jonty's ear. He repeated his lines like a lamb.

"Come on then, give us the gossip. How was the old tonsil tête-à-tête? I bet he gets the tongue right in there, hey Ridhi? He looks the sort to go ferreting after your lunch."

Ridhi looked straight down the barrel of the camera. "Can we get an interpreter over here, please?"

Cristina rolled her eyes. "Did you snog, babes?"

Armando raised a palm, gesturing widely. "A gentleman never—"

"Snog?" Ridhi wasn't having it. She was straight-backed, palms in the air. "My father's going to watch this. We're not married. Of course I didn't bloody kiss him."

"It doesn't really matter, does it?" Zoë the travel blogger said.

Ridhi and Armando turned to look at her, each with their eyebrows furrowed.

"You spent six hours alone in the hedge maze."

Jonty cleared his throat. "She's right, I'm afraid. Whether Armando slipped you a tongue, a trouser flute, or a few lines of Tennyson, it hardly matters. The fact is, you've been most dreadfully compromised. You've got no choice. You've got to marry him."

Indira's voice in my headphones shouted, "Fuck yes!" At least, I think it was in my headphones. It might have drifted over on the wind from the Old Coach House.

Chapter 24
William

I put a calendar up on the wall in my father's study and crossed off the date. I'd numbered every day until Halloween. In the morning, I'd have a hundred and sixty-three days to save the estate. I picked up my copy of *Oathkeeper* and slid it onto the shelf between *The Knight's Vow* and *To Betray a King*, the first book in Fanshaw's second *Knights-Errant* trilogy. My hand hovered over it, finger poised to tip the spine towards me. Adventure awaited inside. Petey's words echoed through my mind.

"No," I said to myself, to the room, the ghost of my father. "It'll be waiting for you in a hundred and sixty-three days—and not a minute sooner."

Then the lights flickered off.

It was gone midnight when I heard Petey arrive home at the folly. I was sat up in bed in the belvedere, surrounded by candles, my notes for saving the estate strewn all around me. I'd been unable to go to sleep until I'd seen him—needing to explain away my mother's incredibly unhelpful contributions to my love life. I was stacking up my papers when Petey's head popped up in the stairwell.

"Why are you sitting up here only lit by candles?" he said. Even through the soft glow, I could see he looked shattered.

"Atmospherics?" I tapped the wooden structure underneath my bed. "I think the hot tub blew a fuse. I couldn't be bothered walking two miles to the cellar to fix it."

"You have a hot tub up here? You've been holding out on me."

Petey stumbled up the last few stairs and sat on the edge of my bed. His boiler suit was tied around his waist, his vest rumpled, the pale white skin of his arms glowing gold in the candlelight. My breath caught. He was spectacularly beautiful—like a bleached-blond angel.

"How'd it go?" I asked.

"Armando announced their engagement at the ball. Everyone's drunk. Indira put the wedding off till Friday so they can sleep off today's excitement—and so the crew can get some rest."

I smiled. "Good TV, though, I bet?"

"*Great* TV."

He yawned. I presented Petey with a fist to bump, and he duly bumped it. I held my arms out, gesturing for Petey to come to me.

"You do not want to hug me," he said. "I am *ripe*."

"The three best smells in the world are, in no particular order, a stable, a dirty kit bag after a long bus ride home from an away game, and—I'm willing to bet you any money—your armpits right now."

"You're a stink pig?" Petey's eyebrows bounced. "Yeah, actually, that checks out."

I had no idea what he meant. All I cared about was the fact Petey was smiling and crawling up the bed towards me on his knees. He lay down beside me, sinking into my body. He smelt of sweat and pine needles and second-hand cigarette smoke. I twisted around him and buried my face in the milky white flesh of his pit. In a loud, exaggerated manner, I breathed it in.

"Well?" he said.

"Perfection."

"Liar. I should go for a shower." He sat up to go, but I pulled him back by his arm.

"Don't," I said. I needed to explain. I couldn't chicken out on something two nights in a row. That wasn't the way the British won two world wars. "About my mother—"

"It's OK." He moved to sit, facing me, on the edge of the bed—one leg folded in front of him, the other dangling off the side.

"It's not," I said.

"No, it really is. It helped, actually."

"My mother has never helped any situation. Ever. Literally famous for it."

"I didn't understand before," Petey said, his eyes sincere. "But I've been thinking about it, and... I think I get it now."

My heart started to race. Got what? What did he think he understood? I sat upright, crossing my legs. I rested my hand on Petey's ankle. He put his hands on my knee.

"So we're clear: Yes, William, I like you. I think you're gorgeous and hilarious and fascinating, and I really, *really* want you to kiss me. But I want you to know... there's no hurry. I've realised, since getting to know you, that you're worth waiting for. We'll move at your pace. There's no pressure."

My breath quickened. Petey's eyes were looking directly into my soul. I'd never felt so *seen* by anyone before. I knew, in that moment, it had to be now. I reached up and felt the exquisite soft skin of his cheek with my hand, traced the line of his jaw with my fingertips.

"I..."

"It's OK."

"I..."

I closed my eyes and leant towards him, waiting for my lips to connect with his. Instead, I felt Petey's hand slide into mine and turn it. His hot breath and tender kiss grazing the palm of my hand. I opened my eyes.

"What is it?" I said softly. "What's wrong?"

"Nothing at all." He smiled. "But... I have an idea. Do you trust me?"

I wove my fingers into his, unable to keep the grin off my face. "Of course."

Petey kissed the back of my hand and let it go. He stood and turned away from me, plucking off his vest—the smooth alabaster skin of his back glowing in the candlelight. Slowly, he undid the knot of the sleeves of his boiler suit and let it gently slide to the floor, revealing tight cotton boxer briefs in a vivid royal blue. The way they cupped the rounds of his pert little buttocks could have steered ships onto rocks. I was gone. Completely gone.

"What are you doing?" I said, starting to shiver.

"Blow the candles out."

"Petey, I..."

He turned to face me. His body was beautiful. Like a Pre-Raphaelite Narcissus.

"It's OK. Nothing is going to happen that you don't want to happen. Just... blow the candles out so we don't burn everyone to death in their beds, because that would be a massive downer and I would like to avoid it, if at all possible."

I did as instructed. Petey grabbed my hand in the dark and led me down the stairs.

"Where are we going?"

He didn't answer, so I followed him in silence out the folly door, along the corridors and out of the house, down to the path by the Long Water.

"Is there any reason we're in our jimmy-jams?" I said finally.

"William, I've almost never seen you in anything else. I'm following your lead. 'When in Rome,' you know?"

It was a beautiful, clear night—a blanket of stars twinkling in the sky overhead. The frogs had finished their chorus, and the evening was quiet. The air was cool against my skin, but my hand was sweating where it held on to Petey's—where our bodies connected. I was still so high on adrenaline, I giggled as we picked our way barefoot along the path beside the lake.

"This feels so naughty," I said.

Petey squeezed my hand. "Naughty would be pushing you in," he said, with a cheeky grin.

I laughed. "I'd like to see you try."

"Is that a dare?"

"Go on, try." I let go of Petey's hand, folded my arms, and sank my weight into the ground. "Give it a shot."

He chuckled. "I would never."

"Oh, you absolutely wou—"

His palms slammed into my chest, but I didn't move.

"You're going to have to try harder than that," I said.

He tried again, pushing my shoulder this time, and I pretended to wave like a scarecrow in the breeze. "Put your back into it."

Petey's eyes narrowed. He walked behind me, his leg slipping between mine, his arm wrapping around my neck like he planned to trip me up karate-style. There was a lot of grunting and swearing, but I wasn't going anywhere. Then Petey's foot slipped on the gravel, and he was swinging from me like a rope.

"Steady there, Tarzan," I said, sweeping him up in one arm and depositing him back on two feet. "How about we stop before you hurt yourself?" I didn't really want him to stop. I was enjoying the closeness, the feel of his bare skin against mine.

We ambled slowly along the path until we reached Lady Caroline's Bridge.

"After you," I said, letting Petey take the steps ahead of me. The stone was cold under my feet. The air smelt of earth and water, mown grass and cow parsley. The view back to Buckford Hall was breathtaking—the house reflected perfectly in the still water. Then Petey stopped. He stood right in front of me, facing me, his hand reaching out. I couldn't see, hear, or feel anything but him. He was leaning against the pillar of the bridge. My eyes locked into his. But before I could move towards him, his face broke into a mischievous smile—and his foot splashed down into the lake, kicking water up and all over me.

"You didn't."

"I did."

And he did it again. So I wrapped my arms around his shoulders and locked my wrists together. He giggled nervously and tried to wiggle free—but I held him tighter. My plan was to get him away from the water, to sit him down where we'd sat the previous night. But as I shifted my weight to budge him, his leg swept my own out from under me, and before I knew it, I was falling. Petey was falling with me. My body tensed in shock from the cold and the wet and the surprise. My mouth filled with lake water.

"Oh, holy shit, it's freezing!" Petey said as he broke the surface, gasping for air.

"Are you OK?" I asked, flicking my hair back out of my face and treading water.

"I'm fine. You?"

"It's deeper than I remember here. And *really* cold."

"I won," he said with a cheeky grin. He had duckweed in his hair. I laughed, unable to control it—my body looking for every opportunity to convulse, to generate some heat. I moved towards him, intending to pluck the stray greenery, but my inner child took over and instead I put my hands together to make a big paddle and sliced them down into the water, almost drowning Petey with the splash.

"You bastard!"

He splashed me back. So I splashed him back. So he splashed me back, and I was laughing so hard I almost choked on the water. I kicked my legs out and swam maybe twenty, thirty metres out into the middle of the lake—to a spot where I knew I could touch the bottom. I turned to watch as Petey bobbed slowly towards me in a gentle breaststroke, his head never going below the surface.

"Truce?" he said when he finally reached me. He held out a pinkie.

I linked my finger into his. "Truce." I pulled him towards me, and Petey's legs wound their way around my hips, his arms wrapping around my shoulders. He was weightless in the water. My hands held his waist. He was so slender, he seemed almost fragile to me. How was I allowed to hold this gentle, breakable, perfect, precious object? It was cold, and he shivered. I pulled him closer to me, so our bodies could warm the still water between us. Petey squeezed his legs tighter around my hips. His breath was short and sharp, and it felt hot against my face. My heart was thumping in my chest. Every cell in my body was telling me this was it. *This* was the moment. Very slowly, ever so slightly, Petey nodded—urging me on. I leant into him and he leant into me, his eyes flicking down to my lips for a second before he closed them. I didn't close mine until my lips had locked with his.

Chapter 25
Petey

Before that night, I had known lust. I had known sex. I had known the throwaway junk food diet of cheap gratification that was endless hook-ups and meetups and nights under the Vauxhall railway arches. A world where I was comfortable and in control. Where the sex was on tap and incredible and nobody got emotionally involved. I thought I knew everything attraction entailed—a headless torso on an app, a lustful glance on a dance floor, a naked body in a darkroom. But I had no idea. No one had made me ache for them like William had. And all he'd done was kiss me.

We walked back along the path beside the Long Water. The gravel was digging into the soles of my feet. William suggested I walk on the lawn, but the grass was cold and slimy.

"Hop on," he said, and he gave me a piggyback all the way to the house. I expected him to put me down in the doorway, but he didn't. He carried me up three flights of stairs and along the corridor and deposited me on the tiles in my bathroom.

"That's an incredible service, my lord—does everyone get this kind of treatment?"

"I believe we did something similar for Charles the First.

Churchill, probably. Mostly to stop him circling back via the cellar after dinner en route to his bedroom." William leant against the door frame, not taking his eyes off me. "But, no, only really special people get to ride the old Buckford chariot."

Knowing his family's comfort around nudity, I took a punt and let my wet briefs slide to the floor. There was very little William hadn't already seen, or been able to make out, in any case. William looked me up and down like I was a precious exhibit in a glass cabinet. I'd never felt so exposed—or so exhilarated. No one had ever looked at me the way he looked at me. It wasn't lust, which I'd experienced plenty of times before, but wonder. His chest heaved as he breathed. Then he looked over my shoulder and into the mirror.

"You have duckweed on your back."

"Oh." I turned around and watched in the reflection as William stepped towards me and removed it as gently as if he were unlacing a gown. He held it up to show me, then dropped it into the wastebasket. His eyes never left mine. His hands held my hips and he pulled himself towards me, nestling against my buttocks and back. Softly, he kissed my neck.

"Is this... OK?"

"Yes." I felt his wet hair against my neck and leant into it. "It's always OK, William. You don't need to ask."

"You do me an honour," he whispered, like a hero from one of his books—a character from a different time, with a different moral code. From anyone else, it would have sounded ridiculous. A teenager's idea of chivalry. But I knew William meant it. He felt honoured to be allowed to touch me, like it was something he had earned, a gift I had given him. I suppose it felt like that to me, too—because I'd never been touched like this before. A new heat boiled up inside me, molten and intense, like lava.

"Let's get you warm," William said, kissing my shoulder and releasing me.

He let his boxer shorts slide to the floor, turned on the shower taps, and gestured for me to join him under the thundering water. I ached to feel him inside me, to feel as close to William physically as I felt emotionally. But he did not give that to me. He took the bar of rose-and-geranium soap and, as the steam billowed around us, explored my body with what I can only describe as reverence. I had never felt so adored, so desired, in all my life. It felt powerful—and I never wanted it to end.

* * *

Late the next morning, I walked into the production office to a knowing smile from Indira. Indira smiling made me feel extremely uncomfortable.

"I keep meaning to ask how things are going with Lord Cockchug up in that love turret of yours?"

I shrugged, playing it so cool I could have sunk the *Titanic*. "Fine. Why?"

"Anything I should know about?"

"I don't think so." I slid into a chair in front of one of the computers.

Indira turned her screen to face me and hit the space bar on her keyboard. Footage of a basically naked me riding through the house on a basically naked William played out on the monitor. I felt my heart stop. I had been so caught up in the moment, I hadn't given the cameras a second thought.

"Are you sure about that?" she said.

It took me too long to reply. "Of course. We're totally committed to the whole fake-fiancé act."

"Ah, so you were doing this for the good of the production."

I embraced this life raft enthusiastically. "You know me. Anything for the show."

"Petey Boy, I'm not a fucking idiot. He's not a member of the cast or crew. You're not breaking any rules. This isn't an HR issue. I simply want to know if you're banging him."

"Uh..." I wasn't sure how to answer. "Why?"

"Because the team has been running a book, and I've got twenty quid on at five to one to say you are. The odds have now significantly shortened."

Jonty burst into the room—face wild, shirt buttons in all the wrong holes.

"You have to help me, this is an emergency."

I jumped up. "What is it, do you need a medic?"

"A lobotomist, perhaps?" Indira added.

Jonty was flailing. "It can't wait a minute longer. I have to marry her right now or I'm literally going to die."

I sighed. "Jonty, this area is crew only. You know the rules—"

"Sod the bloody rules, Peter, this is an emergency. Zoë is onto us. If you don't let me marry Lola now, she's going to squeal like a stuck pig, and Lola and I will be dismissed. I will not risk being sent home for want of a fictional piece of paper. What Lola and I have is *real*, and it's too precious to end like this. It's unfair. It's unconstitutional. I beg you, remove this sword of Damocles hanging over our heads. Marry us. Today. Please. Before my loins set fire to something."

Indira was playing it cool, but I could see she was screaming internally. *Two* weddings? It was everything she could have hoped for. Under the rules of the show, before two servants could marry, they had to stand before Queen Dorinda to make their case. If she believed their connection was genuine and gave her blessing, the couple could be fake married in the fake Regency style befitting their fake status. If she didn't believe them, they would be sent home. Of course, Dorinda believed whatever Indira told her to believe.

Indira's face was hard, expressionless, and turning a very unhealthy shade of burgundy. It had been turning that colour a lot lately.

"Dorinda's already on standby for Armando and Ridhi," I said, ever the loyal wingman. "Unit Three comes on at two o'clock. Technically we could film it this afternoon."

"Oh, fuck yes. Let's gazump the other two." Indira pumped her fist. "Genius. Ridhi will lose her shit. Let's do it."

Jonty jumped up and down, shouting his thank yous and praising Indira for her common sense. He threw his arms around me, cheering like he'd won the National Lottery. Indira grabbed her walkie-talkie and screeched for the costume department, then fished around in her cigarette packet and, yet again, lit two at once.

* * *

Jonty and Lola Q were fake married by three o'clock that afternoon in a simple but enthusiastic ceremony in the Buckford chapel, then bounced around each other like coked-up bunny rabbits for the rest of the day. Ridhi and Armando were fake married twenty-four hours later. What the latter couple lacked in genuine enthusiasm, the production team made up for in sheer bloody spectacle. It made recent royal weddings look like quickie jobs thrown together from the Argos catalogue. For me, the next few days passed like a dream. I'd work all day, then each evening William and I would sit around in the folly, notepads on our knees, coming up with ideas for shows and ways to make money for the estate.

"Your mum," I said on the third night. William looked up from his notes, bathed in golden light from the reading lamp. "What are her friends like?"

"Every bit as unhinged as you'd imagine. Why?"

"I was thinking about a *Real Housewives*–type concept, but with real lords and ladies all going for each other's throats. Like, *Dynasty* but if Joan Collins was a duchess."

William stared at me blankly. "Who's Joan Collins?"

I had to steady myself in case I fell out of my armchair.

"I can see that was the wrong answer. Shall we pretend I didn't say that?"

I shook my head. "I'm wondering if there's like... a gay school we can enrol you in."

William bucked his shoulders. "In any case, we don't really mix with that kind of society. I think you'd struggle to find anyone who moves in those circles who'd want to, shall we say, let the sunshine in."

Damn. He was right. My own family wouldn't agree to it either. I had five days until filming wrapped up, and Indira would be expecting to hear my big pitch.

"By the way, I looked into environmental and heritage grants today," William said. "I reckon there's a few hundred thousand we could apply for."

"You can't use grant money to pay the tax man."

"No, but if the grants can pay for work we were doing anyway, that frees up capital to send to His Majesty."

William was starting to think like a grifting businessman, and I felt genuinely proud of him.

"Oh, and I've got a woman coming up from the village tomorrow morning to talk about starting a riding school here."

"William, that's wonderful."

The next day was my day off. William got me out of bed early, and we rode out across the estate to see the otter cubs playing in the River Buck. It had been worth the wait to finally see them. The mummy otter appeared incredibly proud—and no surprise. If I could create something so unbearably cute, I'd be pumping out two or three a year myself. William and I spent the day hanging out in the folly, then went into the village pub in the evening to watch the Ireland v England rugby match. As William drove us back to Buckford, he reached across and rested his enormous hand on my leg. My heart almost burst through the windscreen, and my cock was instantly at full mast. I looked over at him, and his eyes met mine briefly.

"I hope you've had a good day," he said, "experiencing all the delights of the estate and village life."

"I did." I let my hand rest on his.

"It gets under your skin, this place," he said. "My father used to say Buckford magnetises the blood, so you constantly feel the pull of the place, wherever you are in the world."

I squeezed his hand, unsure where this was going. "That's very sweet."

"The longer people stay, they more they yearn for the place and ache to return."

"Well, I can understand that," I said.

"You can?" William looked across at me again, eyes bright.

"Of course. I feel the same about London."

William's eyes returned to the road. An oncoming car momentarily lit the cabin of the Range Rover, then it plunged back into darkness.

"I miss it," I said, "being so far away from it. My gran, my mates." I laughed, remembering our big nights out at Miss Timmy's in Soho—Old Compton Street's most popular gender-nonconforming restaurant and cabaret venue. "Have you ever been to a drag show?"

William shook his head. "I've been to a few rugby club revues where the lads dress up."

"Not the same. When you come down to London, we'll get a jump start on your gay education, and you can come to Miss Timmy's and see Sandy Crotch in action."

William stiffened. His hand, which had been tenderly holding my leg, set like stone, resting there like dead weight. I moved my hand from his, and he placed his back on the steering wheel. The atmosphere in the car had suddenly become weird and tense.

"What's the matter?"

"I don't go to London."

"But you've been there before—"

"Anymore." He tapped the steering wheel, keeping his eyes forward.

"Never?" Jonty had said he hadn't visited, but I didn't realise it was policy. William shook his head. "Are you saying when I go back to London, you won't come to visit me?" I couldn't believe my ears. "Like, ever?"

"It's not about you. I just can't go back there, all right?"

This was ridiculous.

"Is this because of the rugby trip? The one when your dad died?"

"Leave it, all right?" He banged the steering wheel with his hand. Then seemed to check himself, balling his hand, then unclenching and tapping it against the wheel more gently. "Sorry. Would you mind if we dropped it for now?"

The headlights of an oncoming lorry lit up the inside of the car, catching the water in William's eyes.

"Of course," I said, remembering Bunny's words about William avoiding life's stronger emotions. I was beginning to realise how massively avoidant he was in general. As we drove along in silence, a very different thought took hold. What kind of future could we possibly build together after the cameras stopped rolling? Was this thing between us over before it even got started?

Chapter 26
William

As the folly was Wi-Fi-free, the Dower House had become the unofficial headquarters of Save Buckford Enterprises Limited. This morning, though, rather than beavering away at Mum's laptop, I was lying on her couch with my head in her lap while she ran her fingers through my hair.

"Stop mourning him before he's even left," she said—a sobering choice of words from a widow, but I couldn't get out of my funk.

"In three days, he's going back to his life in London."

"Exactly! You have three whole days. Live in the moment you're in, William. It's the only thing that's real."

"How can I live in the moment when I know how dreadful the moment is going to be in three days' time?"

Obviously, I had known Petey wouldn't stay on at Buckford after *The Love Manor* finished filming. Unlike me, he had a life outside the estate. But I'd thought maybe he'd want to stick around. Hearing him talk about how much he missed his life in London, I realised he would only be back if the show came back. It was a punch to the gut.

Mum rubbed my forehead with her thumb. "Stop frowning or you'll have a face like a scrotum by the time you're fifty." I batted her hand away. "You know, you could always invite him to stay on for a bit..."

I shook my head. "He's desperate to get back to London."

"I lived in London when I was courting your father, and guess what? We had thirty blissfully happy years together. All spent right here at Buckford. If you don't count your father's year in the ashram—but we're all entitled to a little midlife crisis."

My hand reached for my father's signet ring, hanging from the chain around my neck. Some days I missed him so much it ached in my bones. God only knew how Mother must have felt, losing him and her eldest son on the same day. My chest tightened. "But you stayed."

"I did, my dear sweet boy. Do you know why Mummy stayed? Because Daddy pulled on his big boy pants one day and asked Mummy if she wanted to stay."

"I feel like you're mocking me."

"A bit."

I sat up. "I'm revoking your hair-stroking privileges."

Mum clasped her hands together. "Well, to be honest, it's a relief. You've had one of your testicles hanging out of your boxer shorts for the last fifteen minutes."

"Oh God, Mum. You could have said."

"I couldn't find an appropriate pause in the conversation. You were being so vulnerable with me. I think you're past the age now where a mother can flick it back in."

"You think?"

"I figured Bramley would come along, eventually, and dust it. I thought you'd deal with it then." The laptop pinged with an email notification. The new version of me, Chief Executive Officer William, kicked into gear. I popped my bollock away and slid into the chair at the dining room table.

"Holy shit."

"What is it, darling?"

"It's an email from Petey's father."

"I didn't know you'd met the family."

"I haven't." I read the email aloud:

"*The North London Jaguar Car Club would be delighted to accept your kind invitation to visit Buckford Hall on the twenty-first of June, proximo, for our annual Father's Day Run. We anticipate up to forty cars making the journey and approximately eighty head. Please send payment details to my assistant, here copied. Much obliged, your servant, et cetera.*"

"Guests! How lovely. When did you invite them, darling?"

"I didn't. Petey did. Edward said no."

"Well, he's changed his mind! Isn't that marvellous?" Mum said. "And it's on the summer solstice. We should invite them to come up early so they can join the celebrations."

"Yes, Petey's parents sound like exactly the kind of people who'd gladly step in to perform the human sacrifices."

Mum rolled her eyes. "You know what this is, though, don't you, darling? It's exactly the excuse Petey needs to come back and visit—and in a few short weeks. The great goddess has provided, exactly as I knew she would."

I wasn't so sure. Given Petey's relationship with his family, this might give him more reason to stay away. Besides, a few weeks? I couldn't be apart from him for three whole weeks. A fellow can't go cold turkey: The shock could be fatal.

* * *

That night, when the folly door downstairs announced Petey's arrival, I jumped to my feet.

"I have news," I said as he stomped his way up the stairs to the study.

"So do I." He slapped a copy of *The Bulletin*—the UK's trashiest tabloid newspaper—down on the coffee table. I turned my nose up at it like it was a turd in a teapot. Petey flicked the pages open to a photo of the two of us—walking arm in arm towards the village pub, laughing at something or other, a joyous expression across both our faces. Adrenaline flooded my body. The headline read: "BISEXUAL BARON TO WED TRASH TV TWINK." My hands shook. It had happened again. I took several long, slow, deep breaths, trying not to freak out. It was actually a lovely photograph of us. The first ever photograph of us. But it wasn't ours—it was public property. Cheap entertainment.

"Twink?" I asked, trying to appear outwardly calm.

"Scrub round that bit," Petey said. "When the tabloids start appropriating terminology from gay culture with any accuracy, it's a sign of the apocalypse."

But the apocalypse was already here. I sat down on the edge of my father's chair and picked up the paper, my breath shortening.

"How'd they get this?"

It was all there, the facts and the fiction—*The Love Manor*, Petey taking up residence in the folly, "inseparable for weeks," "very much in love," "secret engagement."

"Horatio Blunt?" Petey asked.

I shook my head. "Horatio might be an unrepentant cockweasel, but he's smart enough to be strategic. This doesn't get him any closer to his goal."

"Then someone from the village?"

"They wouldn't. Besides, they've known for, what, a week or so. It doesn't take that long to call a newspaper."

"Maybe it took the paper that long to get a picture?"

I turned the page over to see if there was any more. There wasn't. I went to flick it back.

"Wait!" Petey said, pinning the page open. There was an article about summer fashion trends featuring a photo of a woman in a yellow dress. I vaguely recognised her face.

"I know how they got the story," Petey said.

I looked at him blankly.

"That's Kiki Galapagos, one of our banished contestants."

Something vaguely flashed into mind—another contestant calling Kiki a hotline to the press. Why had it never occurred to me that inviting all these attention-hungry people into my house would lead to more attention on me? It was the last thing I wanted.

"I'll ask Indira to get the lawyers onto it," Petey was saying, "but I don't know if she's in breach of contract."

The mention of lawyers added a lead weight to my already heavy stomach.

"Petey, I have to tell you, I got an email from your father today."

"I know." He sighed—and I felt relieved he knew about it already. "He called me when I was in the village. In fact, if he hadn't called to congratulate me on my engagement—which he did not bat an eyelid about, by the way—I wouldn't have seen the article."

"He congratulated you?"

"For getting engaged to you. Yes." Petey threw his arms wide. "I know. In twenty-seven years, I've never once won my father's approval for anything I've done. Today, he finally uttered the words 'Well done, son'—and it was for something I *haven't* done at all. Press the buzzer for the irony klaxon, please. Petey Boy has hit an all-time low."

He was dismissing it, but I could see it hurt.

"Petey, I'm so sorry." I stood and wrapped my arms around him.

"Don't be. It's not your fault. My parents are their own kinds of cockweasels."

He pulled away from the hug sooner than I would have liked. My chest hollowed.

"So, now the whole country thinks we're engaged," I said, eyeballing the newspaper like my stare alone could reduce it to ashes. "I'm sure we can explain it to your folks easily enough."

"Yes, I look forward to seeing their faces slide back into permanent disappointment. This can be yet another way I've failed them, depriving them of an aristocratic son-in-law."

I sighed in sympathy. "I'm going to have to explain it to the whole village too. Preferably this side of the village fair, or that'll be unbearable."

"So, is he coming here with his bloody car club?"

"I haven't replied yet," I said. "I wanted to ask you what I should do."

Petey shrugged. "A bag of carrots is a bag of carrots."

"You don't mind."

"Why would I? I won't be here."

Chapter 27
Petey

William looked broken, like the newspaper article was more than he could take.

"Any chance your father's popped another spliff in that drawer," I asked, half hoping to lighten the mood a little, half hoping a spliff might actually be on offer.

"Given there was only one in the drawer and we already smoked it, that's one of those questions with no good answer," he said. "A no means disappointment, but a yes means we'll never truly be able to sleep comfortably in here ever again."

William moved to the makeshift drinks cabinet on the bookshelf and poured us each a sloe gin—no ice, no mixer.

"This'll help," he said, and knocked his back so fast it couldn't have touched his tongue. I took a sip of mine, winced, then did the same. It burnt all the way down, but as the warmth radiated out from my belly, I felt some of the tension leave muscles I didn't know I'd been clenching.

"I need to get my laptop," I said, heading for the stairs.

I still hadn't worked up a presentation for Indira with my best idea for a TV show. I really needed to be working on it.

"Petey, this is going to follow us around," William said, staring out the porthole window. "The last time I was in the papers—"

William paused. I couldn't tell if he was deciding whether to tell me something, or whether he was swallowing his emotions.

I sat down in the armchair, facing him.

"I was down in London for the reading of my father's will," he said slowly. "I was a wreck. My father and brother had been killed three weeks earlier—I'd been in London then, too, as you know. The place is cursed for me. Every time I go there, something dreadful happens."

Was that what his hatred of London was all about? A tragic coincidence? A silly superstition? I couldn't wrap my head around it. A photo like that wouldn't have kept me up at night. It would have horrified my parents, but that was all the more reason to revel in the notoriety. William and I lived in completely different worlds.

"The accident had been all over the papers. A baron and his heir dying in a plane crash. I get that it's news. But I wasn't thinking about that. I was so deep in grief. I'd just inherited all this and been told my father's affairs were an absolute mess and there was *no* money. I'd had to give up my rugby career to move home and deal with it all. My mother was inconsolable."

His hand started to shake, and he put his glass down on the coffee table, slumping into his armchair.

"Some friends, Jonty among them, took me to Annabel's and got me drunk. I was in a devil-may-care mood. It was probably the cocaine. Possibly too many hours on the trot in Jonty's company. So when this couple approached me, bought me a few drinks, and asked me home, I thought, sod it. Why not? Isn't this what normal people do? I can be normal. This is what young men are supposed to do when they're in London, right? My parents were always saying to live in the moment. So we left the club. Got as far as a park bench in Berkeley Square. You know the rest."

He kicked the newspaper off the coffee table and onto the floor.

"I'm sorry that happened," I said. I could tell he had been suffering, that this moment had haunted him all this time.

"Listen," William said, leaning forward and grabbing my hands in his. His eyes were bright with enthusiasm. "Why don't you stay?"

"What?" Had I blacked out for a second?

"I'm telling you, London's going to be a nightmare. You don't want to go back down there, what with the press chasing us. Why don't you stay here at Buckford after filming finishes? After all, Sunny and Ludo are coming up. And now your parents. Everyone thinks we're getting married anyway, so staying would be the most natural thing in the world. I can protect you from the paparazzi."

Something clenched in my chest—not anger, not yet. It was the word *protect*. The way he said it so naturally, like it was obvious I needed protecting. Like it was his job. Like he knew best what was good for me. I knew that tone. I'd grown up with it. I pulled my hands back from his.

"I don't need your protection, William."

"But if I can shield you from the worst excesses of the press, why wouldn't you let me help?"

I stood, anger now rising.

"When the time is right for you to come riding in on your white horse to rescue me, my lord, you'll know about it. I don't need a hero."

William got to his feet, his face pleading.

"Petey, I'm sorry, I didn't mean—"

"I can look after myself. I've been doing it since I was a kid."

"I'm sorry, that's not what I meant. Come to bed. We can cuddle until you fall asleep."

I shook my head. "I've got to finish my pitch deck for Indira. She's expecting me to present to her in two days."

He grabbed hold of this like a life ring. "Great! Let me help you. Which idea are you going with? We can talk it through."

"No," I said, and it came out of my mouth more forcefully than I intended—but I was absolutely raging. "I need to do this by myself."

* * *

The next morning, despite having stayed up half the night, I still didn't have a big idea I loved enough to present to Indira. I had less than forty-eight hours to go. I walked into the Old Coach House to find her bouncing around like she was in an aerobics class, two lit cigarettes in her mouth and a spare tucked behind her ear. She was wearing the same trainers, black leggings, and oversized chunky knit jumper as yesterday. In her hand, she held a corrugated paper coffee cup. There were at least four empties on the desk. Even for her, she looked *really* unwell.

"Have you been to bed?" I asked.

Indira picked up the show's rule book and threw it at me. I caught it against my chest.

"We're fucked," she said, out of one side of her mouth.

"Why? What's happened?"

She pointed at the rule book I was busily trying to straighten out.

"That thing. Is. Fucked."

"OK," I said. I was carefully trying to assess the situation. If Indira had a problem, I needed to find a solution. "How can I help?"

"Read page forty-seven."

I turned the page and started to read it.

"Not out loud, for fuck's sake. What is this, a kindergarten?"

I slid into a chair in front of one of the computers, eyes not leaving the page. It was the section on deciding the winner. According to the rules, only a married couple could win the prize money—the point being that marriage was the definition of success in the Regency era. We couldn't have bachelors or spinsters walking away with the loot. In the event the show ended with more than one married couple, all the remaining cast would be invited to vote in a secret ballot. If no couple got more than fifty per cent of the vote in the first ballot, then the couple with the fewest votes would be eliminated until there was only one couple left.

"Do you see it?" Indira said, arms flailing, ash falling like the last days of Pompeii. "Of course you can fucking see it. You're a bright kid."

I wasn't sure I could see it. But Indira praising my abilities was like a shot of whatever they give horses to win races, direct into my arm— and I was determined to see it.

"It's a bit... dull," I said.

"Dull? It's apocalyptically anticlimactic. A secret fucking ballot? In Regency England?"

Phew, I'd landed on it.

"I presume we tart it up, though, right? Get Dorinda seriously glammed up. Give her a central role. Every cast member has to confess on camera how they're voting and why as they cast their ballot."

"*Boring*! I need visuals."

"Visuals. Right."

"Drama."

"Got it."

The cigarettes came out of Indira's mouth, clutched in her bird-like claws.

"I need tension. I need the audience at home so on the edge of their seats, so unable to tear themselves away, that bladders are exploding all over Britain. I need living rooms across the country showered in piss and blood. And as they're getting wheeled into an ambulance, I need them turning to their families shouting, *Fuck me, that was good television!* I cannot serve the people of Britain a secret... fucking... ballot."

The cigarettes were straight back in the mouth, glowing as brightly as the fire in the belly of Mount Etna.

"So, we're looking for—"

Indira huffed smoke out of her lungs. "A different way to end the series. Yes."

I could work with this. This was what I was here to do, after all. I might not have landed on a big idea for my own show yet, but I could at least prove my problem-solving talents with this one.

"So we're looking for something era appropriate, with great visuals, and with solid tension."

"Piss and blood, Petey Boy. Piss and blood."

Indira really did not look or sound well.

"Why don't you go have a lie-down, and I'll come back with some options this afternoon?"

"Sleep is for pussies. I want options now."

I sat back in my chair, trying to think of Regency-appropriate competitions—my fingers fidgeting with a biro.

"Something with horses?" I suggested. "A race?"

Indira shook her head. "Insurance."

"A card game of some sort?" I tapped the pen against the desk.

"Too many rules to explain. It loses the audience."

"Card cutting, then? Highest card wins."

"How can we build tension with that?"

I leapt out of my seat. "A billiards match!"

Indira was silent for a moment.

"Great atmospherics," she said. She seemed to be warming to the idea. "Plenty of rising tension. Wait, is billiards the one with all the red balls?"

"No, that's snooker. Billiards has three balls."

"OK, boring," Indira declared.

I slumped back down into my chair, picking at the plug in the end of the biro until it popped out.

Indira stubbed out her cigarettes. "Visually, you want to see shot after shot of balls being sunk, until there's one left and everything hangs on what happens next. The audience should be able to understand what's happening intuitively."

I put the nib between my teeth and plucked it free, leaving me with a long hollow tube. I spat the nib onto the desk and remembered a story William had told me.

"Of course, real 'era appropriate' would be a duel." I laughed.

Indira's eyes expanded like they were going supernova. "Could we?"

"Oh God, Indira. No!"

She was pacing around the Old Coach House. "What about paintball guns?"

Before I could reply, she was screaming into her walkie-talkie. "I need the props department, now! And get me the phone number for an armourer."

Chapter 28
William

I'd rather made a hash of things. It was the last day of filming for *The Love Manor*, and Petey had barely said two words to me since our silly little argument. He'd been coming in late, leaving early, and spending the precious hours in between downstairs, bashing away at his laptop. Which made today jolly uncomfortable because Indira had invited me, Mum, and Bramley to watch the filming of the big climax. We were sitting on the Great Lawn in front of the monitors, alongside Indira. Petey was marching back and forth in his trademark boiler suit, headset on, clipboard in hand, having what looked like a very serious conversation with Jonty and Armando.

"When do you think I should give them the acorns?" Mum asked.

"Who?"

"Jonty and Armando."

I looked around. Indira was distracted by her walkie-talkie. On the Great Lawn, Jonty and Armando were rehearsing. They were standing twenty paces apart, pointing pistols at each other, while Petey barked instructions.

"I should go now, I think."

"Right you are, darling." She slipped out of her seat and started heading towards them.

"Be sure to stand in between them," I called after her. "Ideally, you want to get caught in the crossfire!"

"Champagne, my lord," Bramley said, presenting a bottle of Tesco's Finest Prosecco.

"Not yet, Bramley. Let's save that for precisely the right moment."

"Who wants an acorn!" I heard my mother cry—immediately before two loud cracks of gunfire and a scream.

"*Now*, I think, Bramley."

All three of us got a dressing-down from "the armourer," who looked and sounded like a character from a Guy Ritchie film. For someone whose entire job is firing munitions with pinpoint accuracy, he wore Coke-bottle glasses and had a surprising number of missing fingers. Which was perhaps why both Jonty and Armando had missed my mother? In any case, we were confined to quarters for the rest of filming. Indira had to be talked out of duct-taping us into our chairs.

"She could do with a few days at your Aunty Karma's retreat," Mother whispered into my ear. "A good aura cleanse and kidney detox would do her the world of good."

I have to say, I was inclined to agree. Something about Indira smoking three cigarettes at once suggested not all was OK.

Finally, the moment had arrived. Dusk was, for the show's purposes, pretending to be dawn. Jonty and Armando were dressed in knee-high boots, black breeches, white shirtsleeves, waistcoats, and era-inappropriate safety goggles. They were standing back to back on the Great Lawn, paintball guns (which the show's art department had tinkered with to look like pistols) held upright in front of their noses. Standing between them, and well back, was Queen Dorinda Carter—in a gold-embroidered dress of purple silk, her hair braided and piled up on her head in a spectacular African beehive. Behind her sat the entire cast of *The Love Manor*.

Petey appeared at Indira's side and muttered something I couldn't hear. I glanced at him hopefully. His eyes briefly caught mine, but he looked away.

"And action!" Indira called.

Dorinda was imperious. "Gentlemen, you are here to settle a matter of honour. Are you prepared to proceed? Or will either party offer satisfaction?"

I leant over to Indira and whispered, "They can yield?"

"Petey Boy's idea," she murmured. "If they both yield, they split the winnings evenly. If they don't, the duel is on. Fucking brilliant TV."

"How do you know they won't simply split the winnings?"

"Because I've read their psychological profiles."

Dorinda reached a hand up in the air. "If you are prepared to offer satisfaction, turn around when I drop my handkerchief. If not, then remain as you are—but understand the consequences of your actions."

"Close-ups on Lola and Ridhi," Indira whispered into her headset.

Dorinda dropped her handkerchief.

Neither man turned.

"Let there be blood," Indira murmured. I can't be sure, but I thought I heard Petey say "Piss and blood." The two of them bumped fists.

"Gentlemen, take your positions."

Jonty and Armando each took a stride forward, then another, until they were twenty paces apart. A sharp growl came from beside me. Indira was crouching, hands on her knees, eyes forward and squinting, face almost as purple as Dorinda's dress. She was bouncing on her heels and breathing heavily, like you see women on the TV doing in prenatal classes.

"I don't think she's OK, you know," Mum said. "Do you think—"

"Gentlemen, cock your pistols," Dorinda began. I couldn't have been more on the edge of my seat if the hem had been sewn into my arsehole. "Rules are, first blood wins. If you both draw blood, we go again. You will fire on the count of three."

Indira let out a squeak that started audibly enough but quickly escalated into "dogs only" territory.

"One."

I glanced across at Petey, who was staring fixedly at the action playing out on the lawn.

"Two."

I looked across at Indira, who thumped her chest with her fist, her face purpled and constipated.

"Three."

Bang! Jonty and Armando fired their shots. Figuratively, everyone let the smoke clear. The armourer assessed both men, then delivered the results to Dorinda.

"Gentlemen, neither of you have been hit."

"Fuck *yes*," Indira said beside me. She had a fist to her mouth. She was bouncing up and down on the spot. Petey was looking at me, but when my eyes caught his, he looked away.

"You will fire on the count of three," Dorinda said. "One. Two. Three."

Bang! Bang!

Silence.

The armourer did his thing and reported to Dorinda.

"Gentlemen, neither of you have been hit. This is your third and final shot."

Indira was bouncing up and down on the spot like this was a Zumba class, her face so purple now it was almost black.

"Is she still breathing?" Mum muttered in my ear. "I'm worried about her."

"If one of you draws blood, you will win the full prize pool of one hundred and twenty-three thousand pounds," Dorinda said. "If neither of you draws blood, then you both go home empty-handed. If you both draw blood, then you split the prize pool. Are we understood."

Both men nodded.

"Gentlemen, cock your pistols. One. Two. Three."

BANG!

The whole scene seemed to happen in slow motion. Red paint burst across Armando's waistcoat, sending his shoulder back and knocking him to the ground. In the same instant, Ridhi was on her feet, running towards him. Jonty was checking himself over, hands patting down every part, looking for any signs of paint. A second later, Lola was throwing her legs around him and he was swinging her around on the lawn. Beside me, Indira's hand was clutching her chest, and she was crumpling to the ground.

"Medic!" I heard Petey shout. "Medic!"

Chapter 29
Petey

The rest of the night was a blur. The show's medics had been performing CPR and given Indira a couple of shocks with the defibrillator, but she was unconscious when the ambulance arrived. It did not look good. I'm not a doctor, I'm a TV producer, so I did the one thing I was qualified to do—I stepped up and took charge. I'd have been terrified, but there wasn't time to think. I was running on adrenaline all night. Though there were dark clouds over the production and no one really felt like celebrating, we filmed the Farewell Ball as planned. One last flash of colourful silk gowns and spectacular waistcoats—under disco lights in Buckford's Great Hall. An eight-piece string orchestra backed Dorinda as she sang Beyoncé's "Love on Top"—a track she'd also recorded in the studio so we could play it seamlessly over the closing images. Those images were a sequence Indira called "Carriages at Midnight." Cast members would walk down the front steps of the house to Buckford Hall's carriage court one last time. They would bow and curtsey to Jonty and Lola, then climb into the waiting carriages, and we'd film them waving goodbye as they disappeared up the drive. The final shot would be Lola and Jonty walking back into Buckford Hall, arm in arm, as if it were their home.

At the end of the drive, the cast found an ugly white marquee, where they could get changed back into their twenty-first-century clothes, then pile into a fleet of black Range Rovers to be taken to the Travelodge in Leicester, where they'd spend tomorrow with the aftercare team. But first, in the function room in the Travelodge, the party would continue—this time for the crew as well as the cast.

It was late when I was finally ready to leave Buckford Hall. I showered to wash away a truly awful day and gathered up my things from the folly. William was nowhere to be seen. I assumed he'd gone to the party in town. I checked the belvedere for any stray belongings and found myself burying my face in William's sheets, desperate for the smell of him. I'd been so angry with him that I'd made my last few days here a misery. But seeing Indira face mortality like that... I'd started to think about what was important. I went downstairs and sat at William's desk one last time and scribbled him a farewell note.

* * *

The party was in full swing by the time I checked into the Travelodge. There was two grand behind the bar, and everyone had clearly decided not to let it go to waste. It was getting rowdy. I didn't much feel like being there, but I had to show my face. The crew was all there. Bunny Winters was dancing with Hassan. Bramley was taking part in a limbo competition. William was nowhere to be seen.

"Petey Boy!" Jonty's unmistakable voice cut through the hubbub. "Looking for someone?"

"Nope."

He looked like he didn't believe me. "Any news on Indira?"

I shook my head. "She's in surgery now. Her sister's coming up from London. I don't expect to hear anything until tomorrow."

There was a terrible screeching sound, like someone was trying to tie two foxes into a knot.

"What is that... noise?"

"It's Lola!" Jonty said, face beaming. "Turns out she's *obsessed* with karaoke. Isn't she marvellous?"

"That's certainly one word for it."

Love was not only blind but clinically deaf, apparently. As I was about to stand upright to give my back a rest—the curse of tall people everywhere—Jonty looped an arm around my neck and pulled me down to eye level.

"I'm going to marry her, Petey Boy. For real this time. She's everything. I mean, have you seen those *ears*? She's the piece of me that's always been missing. I can't thank you enough for bringing us together."

I was thrilled for him, obviously, but very nervous for society as a whole.

"I hope you'll be very happy together," I said. "I'm sure you'll have a very happy, very... loud... life together."

"And I plan to fill her with a lot of very loud children."

"What a vivid way to say that, Jonty. Thank you for that image."

He laughed like a donkey being fed into a meat grinder, and I got a very good look at a couple of fillings.

"And what about you?"

"What about me?"

"Are you going to marry that prime aristocratic beef you're definitely not searching the crowd for right now?"

I frowned at him.

"You know the engagement was fake."

"I know," he said, pulling me closer still. "The engagement was fake, but the feelings aren't. I've seen the way you look at each other."

A screech pierced through the speakers, followed by a wail of feedback.

"Are you seriously going to tell me you're not going to give it a shot with old Dub-Dub?"

I shrugged. I wanted this conversation to be over—and not only because Jonty's breath smelt like a rubbish bin at a dog park on a hot summer's afternoon.

"We're not even talking to each other at the moment. I just want to go back to London, hug my gran, and see the boys. I don't know what impression you've got or why it's any of your business, Jonty, but their ain't anything going on between me and Lord Buckford."

"I think you're wrong."

"Pardon."

"I think you're scared."

"I grew up in the East End. Nothing scares me, bruv."

"This scares you, *bruv*."

"Are you mocking me?"

"Not at all. It's been a while since I've heard you speak like that. That's all."

"What are you saying?"

Jonty's mouth was back at my ear. "Listen, I know you. I've been on plenty of nights out with you and Ludo and the boys. You're the leader. The organiser. The group's fixer. Never an outward sign of weakness. But you don't feel in control of your feelings for Dub-Dub, and it scares you."

"Oh, piss off, Jonty." I jerked myself free of him.

"OK. But I'll say this—"

"You've said enough." I was ready to break the world record for throwing a posh twat across a bar.

"He deserves a shot." Jonty squared up, his eyes intense. "I've known Dub-Dub since we were thirteen. We've been through some shit together, man and boy, but one thing's always been true. If he loves you—whether you're a friend, family, a horse—he gives you his all. I think you need someone like that."

Jonty mussed his hands through my hair.

"And you deserve someone like that." He disappeared across the dance floor towards the stage, and I watched as Lola jumped down into his arms. They spun around, their faces in raptures, like they were the only two people in the venue. That was about all I could handle. I went up to my room to pass out until morning.

Chapter 30
William

I headed up to the belvedere hoping to find Petey. I'd gone to the after-party in town with Mum and Bramley, expecting to see him, hoping to put things right. But he didn't show, and after a couple of hours, I gave up. He wasn't here, either, though. His stuff was gone. A wet towel in the bathroom was the only sign he'd ever been here. I'd have sucked his DNA clean out of it if I thought I'd feel closer to him, if I thought it'd fill the hollow in my stomach. It had been such a stupid little fight. I'd been clumsy in the way I asked him to stay, but I still hoped he'd *want* to stay. I didn't understand why he'd flipped out.

The next morning, I stared at the calendar. I had a hundred and fifty-three days to save the estate, but I was wallowing in bed. Eventually, Bramley appeared—like a judgemental Victorian ghost.

"My lord, I thought you might wish to be informed the production company removal vans are here, and they're decanting all their props and will soon begin returning all the household chattels. I'm told the cameras and computer equipment will be uninstalled and collected by a team of specialists next week."

"Yes, of course." Aunty Karma's voice echoed through my head. "Just make sure they turn all the cameras off, will you?"

"Of course."

"You didn't happen to bring breakfast up with you, did you?"

"I'm afraid not, my lord. I wasn't aware wallowing was especially hungry work."

We were interrupted by the loud, violent whacking of metal on wood and the whinnying of horses.

"Achilles!" I said, leaping up from the bed and racing downstairs. In the stable yard, Hank—the show's horse handler—was struggling to load his Cleveland Bay mares into the horse float for their trip home.

"I don't think he wants us to go," Hank said, the words like a lance through my chest. I ran towards my faithful stallion.

In the stables, I found Achilles braying and striking the cobbles and his stall walls with his hooves. It took a full ten minutes after Hank's horse float had disappeared up the drive for Achilles to calm down. I was checking him over for injuries when Mother's voice echoed through the stables.

"William!"

I stuck my head up to see what she wanted.

"Darling, I'm taking the car into town."

"That seems a bit irresponsible, as you don't have a licence," I said.

"I know, that's why I'm taking Bramley."

"You can't take Bramley. Who's going to make sure all our shit is put back in the right place?"

"Well, it's your house, darling. You're the baron." Mum turned to walk away, muslin scarf flapping in the breeze behind her.

"Where are you going?"

She didn't answer.

It was several hours later when I finally made it back up to the folly, smelly, dirty, and still in my boxer shorts. I slumped into my father's armchair in the study—and noticed the drawer of the desk had been left open. There was a note inside.

Thank you for everything. It's going to be a hit. I'll see you in a year. Petey Boy x.

Below that was a PS.

Tackle the hard stuff. I believe in you.

Well, now I was even more confused. What did this mean? Was this an apology? A promise? I didn't know. All I knew was, it gave me hope. Now I had to make sure there was still a Buckford Hall for him to come back to, and not a tacky hotel.

Chapter 31
Petey

It was time to return to London, but there was one thing I had to do first. The taxi pulled up to Glenfield Hospital, where Indira was being treated at the cardiac unit.

"Anywhere here's fine, thanks, bruv."

As I paid, I looked out the window and saw Bunny Winters striding out of the hospital's main entrance to a car where Bramley was waiting with the door open. By the time I grabbed my receipt, they were gone. I had to drag my whole suitcase through the hospital. At first, I didn't think the nurse on the ward desk was going to let me in.

"She's had a heart attack and triple bypass surgery," he said. "She's very weak and shouldn't really be having visitors yet."

"I'm pretty certain she's already had a visitor," I said. "I've just seen the Dowager Baroness Buckford leaving the hospital."

The nurse leant across the desk, tapping a pen against his cheek to draw attention to his dimples. "Her ladyship is head of the board of trustees. Bunny can do whatever she likes. No one says no to her." Then he looked me up and down like I was a steak. "I bet no one ever says no to you, either, do they? Big tall lad like you."

I wasn't in the mood for flirting, but I was desperate to see Indira, so I batted my eyelashes and begged.

"It's room six, sweetheart. Down the corridor and on the left." He winked.

Indira looked terrible. She was surrounded by machines and screens. There were tubes everywhere. Her face was bloated, with dark rings under her eyes.

"Petey Boy," she said, her voice soft and croaky. "Exactly the man I need."

"That's a popular opinion right now."

"Huh?"

"Horny nurse on reception."

Indira smiled, weakly. "Did you come to pitch your show idea?"

"No! God no! That can wait until you're all better, obviously."

"You brought it with you, though."

I tapped my laptop bag. "A good producer is always prepared."

"I was dead on the lawn at one point yesterday," she said, struggling to speak. "I've had six hours of surgery. You thought I might want to hear your pitch?"

"I'm sorry." What had I been thinking? I felt awful for even mentioning it.

"Don't be. That's exactly the kind of bloodlessness that means you'll go far in this business."

I laughed.

"Listen, I want you to do something for me."

"Anything. Name it."

Indira waggled a hand, clearly struggling to find the strength to move it. I leant in, resting my hand on hers, being careful to avoid the catheters.

"Turn off the machine. I can't go on."

"What!" I pulled my hand back, horrified. "You're joking?"

"Of course I'm fucking joking. I wanted to see what your limit was."

If Indira was joking, she was going to be all right. I breathed a huge sigh of relief and flopped down into the visitor's chair.

"Hey, Petey Boy," she said.

"Yeah."

"Fuck me, that was great television."

I laughed, and she laughed, and she formed a fist with her hand and I gently bumped it.

"I need you to take charge of the edit."

"What?"

"I'm going to be in here for a week. Then, fucking get this, old mad tits Lady Buckford is treating me to a two-week retreat at a place about half an hour up the road."

"Sounds like a trap."

"No, it's really famous. Robbie Johnswagger and Cole Kennedy went there and both came out completely changed men." Indira had worked with both troubled rockstars on *Make Me a Pop Star*—Cole as a contestant and Robbie as a judge. "Hey, get this. The retreat is run by a couple of those fox hunt saboteurs."

"Are you sure you want to put your life in their hands?"

Indira smiled. "You know what the first thing I saw when I woke up after surgery was? My sister and my nephew, both in tears. Suraj possibly because he'd shoved quite a large Lego quite a long way up his nostril. A nurse had to fish it out. It was a whole thing. But they were scared, Petey Boy. That killed me. So I'm accepting this offer as the blessing that it is. Because... I'm fucking scared too."

I said I understood but reminded her I wasn't an editor. Indira said she had editors, she needed someone she trusted to oversee the edit. It was a huge responsibility—I wasn't sure I was ready. But Indira's voice was getting softer, weaker, harder to hear. I had exhausted her. There was no time to argue, I had to step up.

"OK," I said. "When I get back to London, I'll go into the Monkey Ginger offices—"

"No. Everything you need is in the Old Coach House at Buckford. I want you to work from there."

It was like a bullet. It hit fast and hard and then the shock reverberated through my body. Work from Buckford?

"But all the equipment is being collected next week."

She glared at me like I was dense. "So cancel the collection."

The door to the room swung open, and an officious-looking matron-type woman walked in. "All right, visit time is over, I'm afraid. Ms Murray needs to rest."

I walked up the corridor, processing everything that had happened. As I threw my suitcase into the boot of the taxi, my heart was fluttering with excitement. I slid into the back seat, trepidation washing through me. Suddenly, I had to face some things I thought I'd kicked into the long grass.

"Where to, mate?" the driver asked.

I took a deep breath. "Buckford Hall, please, driver."

Chapter 32
William

I was in the East Drawing Room, in my riding gear, standing at the window looking out across Home Field. I was trying to figure out where I could find about £300,000 to start the riding school, when I needed every penny to pay off the estate's tax debt. Petey's note was disintegrating in my pocket as I pawed it. There was a familiar clearing of a familiar throat. I turned to see Bramley, back in his rightful place, haunting a doorway and looking disappointed in the state of my personal appearance.

"Mr Topham is here, my lord."

My heart burst out of my chest and punched Bramley in the face.

"Well, show him in, man!"

"He's waiting in the drawing room, my lord."

"But I'm *in* the drawing room, man."

"Mr Topham is in the *West* Drawing Room, my lord. This appears to be the East Drawing Room."

"Bramley, you blind me with science. If you'd brought him to the East Drawing Room, it seems we could have saved ourselves a great deal of trouble."

"Apologies, my lord. Given recent... sensitivities... and given the fact Mr Topham has arrived with his travelling cases, I thought perhaps—"

"Cases?"

I bolted out of the room and through the Great Hall, skating across the chequerboard tiles and bursting through the doors into the West Drawing Room, startling my quarry. Petey stood upright, staring at me, face like a kid caught with his mitts in the biscuit tin. He was as beautiful and as tall and as bleached blond as ever. Suddenly, I was frozen to the spot. Petey was six feet away, but I couldn't move my legs.

"Hi," I said.

"Hi."

"Well, that year absolutely flew by." My hand was still in my pocket, fingers strangling whatever was left of Petey's note.

He winced, face sheepish. "Bit awkward, to be honest."

"Not at all. I'm thrilled to see you."

"Thrilled?" Petey said. "I thought you'd be mad at me."

I shook my head, perhaps a little too fiercely, given the room started to spin.

"Surprised, yes. Delighted, of course. But mad? Absolutely not. I don't think I could ever be mad with you."

Petey laughed. "Give it time. You'll get there. I promise."

I pointed to his bags.

"Are... you staying?" The hope must have been written across my face.

"That's the awkward part."

I grimaced. "Tea. Would tea help?"

Petey nodded, and I hollered for Bramley.

"No, don't bother Bramley."

"But I've already called him."

"I'm happy with the gas ring up in the folly," he said. "Actually, I'd prefer it. If that's OK with you?"

I smiled. Bramley would be shuffling towards us at pace on his two-hundred-year-old hips. I could hear the squeak getting closer by the second.

"Of course," I said. "I can't wait to see Bramley's face when you tell him you prefer my tea to his."

* * *

In the folly, I sent Petey Boy straight upstairs to the study while I boiled the kettle and made the tea. It meant I had a good ten minutes to gather my thoughts. It also meant Petey had time to do what I knew he would do, and snoop. After five minutes, I heard the unmistakable thwunk of my father's secret drawer being opened. My heart was thumping like a jackrabbit having a wank. I knew Petey would be reading a note that said: *If you're reading this, then you came back. Welcome home. I'm so glad you're here. x.* It was on Buckford letterhead and dated with today's date.

The cuckoo clock announced four o'clock as I climbed the stairs with the tea. Petey was sitting in his usual armchair with my note open in his hands.

"I might not have found this for a whole year," he said as I put his tea down in front of him.

"I know."

"But you knew you'd be happy to see me?"

"Yes."

His face had crumpled like a tissue, but he was refusing to cry. I didn't like seeing him so distressed. I reached across and grabbed his hand.

"Why do you have so much faith in me?"

I fished Petey's note out of my pocket. It was battered and looking worse for wear, but I carefully unfolded it and put it on the coffee table between us.

"You said you'd be back. You gave me your word."

"I'm sorry," he said, his hand reaching across to grab mine. "I'm sorry for the silent treatment. I'm sorry for making our last days together an absolute misery."

"It's OK. You're here now."

Petey seemed to cringe.

"I'm sorry too," I said. "I meant to invite you to stay because I wasn't ready for you to leave. I should have said that. I should have said I wanted to spend more time with you rather than trying to strong-arm you with stupid warnings about paparazzi. That was clumsy. Disrespectful."

Petey frowned and took a deep breath.

"When you grow up with really controlling parents, you either accept it and go with it, like my brother and sister did, or you rebel and become hyper-independent. So, yeah, you saying you wanted to protect me was kind of triggering."

"I'm sorry."

Petey shook his head. "It's not your fault. I think I was also a little scared, if I'm honest. I don't normally let people get close to me. I have friends, obviously, and my gran. But, William, I've never had a boyfriend. I've never *wanted* a boyfriend. I've let you get closer than anyone else. You're gorgeous and hilarious, and you're literally the first man who ever wanted to spend time with me for my mind and my personality, not just my body."

"To be clear, I am also very taken with your body."

"Noted. Thank you. The point is, when you suggested I stay, I think it freaked me out. So I started treating you like shit to make myself feel like I was still me. The old me, the me who doesn't get attached. Even when I was being a prick, I think I knew it was wrong, but I couldn't stop myself. I'm so sorry."

I leant closer to him. "But you came back."

Petey looked down at the note on the table. "I wrote that so you'd know I *wanted* to come back, if the show came back. It was pretty cowardly, really."

I brushed it away. "It gave me so much hope. What made you come back now?"

Petey got to his feet and started pacing.

"Well, this is the awkward bit."

"Is this where you tell me you've only popped back because you forgot your butt plug?"

"Oh shit, yes. I should probably grab that. I lent it to Bramley."

I laughed. My God, it felt good to laugh. It felt good to be making jokes with Petey again. So it rather worried me when his face turned serious. That's when he told me Indira was going to be recuperating for a couple of weeks at Aunty Karma's retreat, and she'd insisted he oversee the edit of *The Love Manor* from Buckford Hall.

"But that's wonderful news! She clearly trusts you."

"Yes, but don't you see, *that's* the reason I'm here."

Ah. Yes, I did see.

"But I want you to know, I really, really did want to come back here," he said. "I guess I needed fate to give me a little nudge. The courage. The excuse, maybe."

"Fate?" I said. "Why would it make sense for you to edit the show from here?"

My mind was in full Sherlock Holmes mode now—which must have been pretty impressive stuff for Petey to witness.

"The retreat is only thirty minutes up the road. So I guess it's not far for me to pop up there? But the equipment is still here, so…"

The old noodle was really whirring now, putting two and two together. "Seems a bit of a coincidence Indira's going to Aunty Karma's retreat, doesn't it?"

Petey frowned. "Well, no. Buckford is paying for it. I assumed it was your idea."

"My idea? I know nothing about it."

"But I saw your mother leaving the hospital."

I should have detected my mother's hand from the start. "We've been played," I said.

"We have?"

"Still, mustn't be upset. Mum comes from a very long line of meddling mamas. We didn't really stand a chance."

Realisation dawned across Petey's face. I nodded. He smiled.

"You're not angry with me, then?" he asked. I reached out and grabbed his hands. Part of me wondered if he would have come back without my mother's scheming, and whether I really would have had to wait a year to see him again. But he was standing here in front of me, and that counted for something.

"You're here. That's all I wanted."

"You don't mind if I stay?"

"Mind? I'd be delighted." I pulled him towards me and wrapped my arms around him, his eyes meeting mine. "I do have a favour to ask, though."

"Anything."

"If you're going to be sticking around for another few weeks, would you mind if we kept up the fake-engagement act a little longer? Only it's the Newton Bardon village fair next weekend, and I have to go. I can't bear the thought of everyone treating me like I've been jilted at the altar. I'd rather not spend the whole day being pulled aside for deep and meaningfuls and pretending to be heartbroken. Would you come along and play at being Lady Buckford for me?"

Petey smiled. "Of course! Do I get to judge jams or something?"

"There will be no shortage of things for you to judge. You're going to shake a lot of hands, and you're going to hand out a lot of little trophies."

Petey laughed, and his eyes sparkled. "I can't wait."

The thought of presenting ourselves to the entire Buckford community as a real, unified duo made my heart leap. I wove a hand up into Petey's hair and pulled him down to me until my lips were on his and the heat of his mouth was in mine.

Chapter 33
Petey

The next morning, after a long phone call with my gran, I sat at the large oak table in Buckford Hall's kitchen, having breakfast with William. It was blissful—the smell of toast, the steaming coffee pot, the sound of Bramley fighting with the orange juicer. William was naked, obviously, except for his red satin boxer shorts. As he ferried a toast soldier from his egg to his mouth, a large droplet of golden yolk dripped onto his chest and began making its way down his cleavage, narrowly missing the ring on the chain around his neck. I watched as he wiped it up with his finger, then popped his finger in his mouth.

Bramley put a jug of fresh orange juice on the table. William was sucking on his neck chain—I guessed in search of stray yolk. Bramley stared at him in thinly disguised disappointment. William noticed.

"Is there something the matter, Bramley?"

"No, my lord. I was merely going to ask whether you planned to move back into your usual bedchambers today? I prepared the room for you yesterday, but I note this morning your bed is unmolested."

It wasn't the only thing unmolested. Although we'd slept in each other's arms, the night was as chaste as every other night had been.

"Sorry, old thing," William said. "I think we might stick it out in the folly a bit longer. It's rather good fun, camping up in the belvedere."

Bramley shook his head in obvious disapproval.

William turned to me. "If that's all right? Unless you want to—"

"No, the folly is lovely. It feels like home. It *is* Buckford to me."

William winked and champed down on some yolky toast.

"Bramley, that reminds me. Chap's coming to install Wi-Fi in the folly on Friday. Can I leave you to look after him? I've got the art dealer from Wetherby's Auction House coming to value the paintings."

"Of course, my lord."

I leant over to William. "I thought the folly was screen-free?"

"Only because there was no Wi-Fi," he said. "But the study has to become a real working office. We've got a hundred and fifty-two days to save the estate. I need to start running things like a proper, modern business."

A wave of pride flushed through me, and I reached under the table and squeezed William's leg. He leant forward, lips puckered for a kiss.

I pointed to the corner of his mouth. "You have a bit of yolk."

"Oh!" His tongue darted into the corner to dig it out and, satisfied, the puckered lips were back. I laughed. "Absolutely not."

The telephone on the wall by the refrigerator rang. I'd never heard it do that before. Bramley answered the call. At that moment, Bunny drifted in, greying hair piled on top of her head, muslin scarf trailing behind her—smiling broadly. Her hands plunged straight into William's hair.

"Morning, darling." She massaged his head.

"Morning, Mother," William said, tilting his head back and puckering his lips again.

Bunny winced. "Absolutely not." I laughed. She kissed him on top of the head and said good morning to me. "Ooh, coffee." She rested a hand warmly on my shoulder as she drifted past to pour herself a mug.

"My lord." Bramley had the phone receiver buried in his apron. "It's a gentleman from the *Bulletin* newspaper."

"NO!" William, Bunny, and I all sang like a chorus.

Bramley put the receiver to his ear to deliver the bad news.

"We only plugged the bloody thing back in this morning," William said. "I'm regretting it already."

Bunny sat down and cut into a grapefruit.

"Not that it's not lovely to see you, Mum, but what are you doing here?"

"I thought, seeing as Petey's clearly staying—"

"And how might you know about that?" William said.

"The great goddess works in mysterious ways," she said. "I thought we should talk about who's doing what at the village fair. It'd be nice to split the workload three ways this year."

After breakfast I went across to the Old Coach House, where all the production equipment was still set up. All the fixed cameras were still in place in the house too.

In the Old Coach House, I found my fellow producers, Thandiwe and Haruto, freshly arrived from the Travelodge and already beavering away at their computers, sorting the footage we'd collected. We would spend the day working out narratives and sequences. Once we had those, we would send the instructions to our team of editors, who were working remotely from their living rooms, basements, crack dens, and so on.

At the end of the day, I returned to the folly to find William sitting at his desk in a white business shirt, sleeves rolled up to his elbows, face lit by the screen of a laptop. I almost did a double take.

"Is that new?"

This whole vision was new. Who was this guy?

"I've been making some investments," he said. "I had a meeting with the new accountant today. And the old one. Seemed only right to sack him face to face. But the new one, well, she hit me with some real talk. So it's down to business, I'm afraid."

That made me smile. I walked around the desk and sat on the edge of it, winding my arm around William's head and bringing my lips to his. His body felt so good against mine. I wanted him to pull me down onto the desk and swing his leg up over me, to feel the weight of him pressing down into my body. He looked so sexy in shirtsleeves. The cut was struggling to contain his chest. I ran a hand down the fabric and circled his nipple playfully.

"And how was your day?" he asked.

"I've had enough of looking at a screen for one day."

"Me too." William closed his laptop and stood. "Are you hungry?"

I was, but not for food.

I put on a shirt, at William's insistence, and we ate dinner in the dining room, at Bramley's insistence. There were candles and three courses and Bramley had lit a fire in the fireplace. I realised the pair of them were putting on a show to impress me. I was being wooed. My God, I felt special.

Over dinner, William told me what his new accountant had to say. It was really none of my business, but I enjoyed that he trusted me enough to tell me. I held his hand across the corner of the table. William didn't just need to find £4.3 million, he needed to find at least £12 million—and the target kept growing. The debt was accruing daily interest. He still had to pay tax on any money he raised, still had to fund the estate's ongoing operating costs, had to find capital to pay for any investments and improvements that would help ensure the estate was profitable long into the future, and had to find enough to cover the insurance costs of his new revenue streams. The mountain he had to climb had almost tripled in height, yet William seemed determined to reach the summit. He seemed upbeat, ready to meet the challenge. That made me feel incredibly proud of him, and I told him so.

"Former British Prime Minister Margaret Thatcher and a tarte au citron," William said, as we dug into Bramley's delicious dessert with our spoons.

"Sorry?"

"What's the link?"

"Oh!" I shovelled more dessert into my mouth to give myself thinking time.

"William Winters reporting there, on the proposed new statue to the late Prime Minister Margaret Thatcher. And from a tart who left a deeply bitter aftertaste to one that's so good you'll want to stick your nob in it. Bramley's in the kitchen next, with his lemon tart recipe."

William guffawed, nearly choking on his pie. "That is such a talent. I don't think I've ever met anyone as clever as you."

He may as well have called me a good boy and scratched my belly. I don't think I'd realised I had a praise kink until that moment, but there it was. I couldn't get enough. As I sat there, tummy way too full, staring at the thin white cotton shirt struggling to contain William's body, I wanted to climb him like a mountain lion.

Back at the folly, I was so horny I was scratching at my skin. When I came in from the bathroom in my briefs, William was still in his shirt and chinos, lying back on what was notionally my bed, propped up on his hands. His shirt was stretched so tight over his chest, at any second the thread holding the buttons was going to lose its battle and they were going to fire across the room like bullets. I was probably going to lose an eye. The cut of his new beige chinos made his package look huge, like it was the centre of the room, like everything else had been designed around it, like it was a sodding chandelier. We were waiting for the kettle to boil on the gas ring, but I didn't want tea. I wanted William.

I took a chance. He'd been wooing me all night, right? The lights were green this time, I was sure of it. I slid onto the bed, one knee either side of his thighs, feeling the heat of him between my legs. I crept up the bed towards him, my eyes never leaving his. I put my hand on his chest and pushed him down onto the bed. He did not resist. I leant over him; I kissed him. My hand found his buttons, and I undid his shirt.

"You look so sexy in this," I said.

"Golly."

I kissed his neck, his jaw, his collarbone. "Who knew dressed could be even sexier than undressed?"

"If that's true," he said, arching his back as I pulled his shirt tails free of his chinos, "why are you undressing me?"

"Because I want to feel close to you." I kissed my way down his chest, my mouth teasing one nipple, then the other.

"I want to feel close to you too," he said.

I let my crotch press into his, feeling his hardness against me. He wanted me. His body wanted me. He was aching for me as much as I was aching for him. I sat up, pressing my gusset into his cock, and undid my shirt and threw it across the room. William's hands caressed my chest. His fingers worked their way down my body. His hands, his big, powerful hands, held my waist.

"It's so tiny," he said, marvelling as he pressed my hips down onto him.

I slid a hand inside my trousers and grabbed myself, undoing the button with my other hand. "Do you want to see the rest?" He'd seen it all before, but never like this. Never with this heat burning between us. Never when I was offering myself to him like this.

"Petey, I..."

"It's OK."

But his face had changed, and I felt the moment slip away. I pulled my hand out of my pants and held his hips like he was holding mine.

"Petey, you remember when you said you'd never had a boyfriend?"

Where was this going?

"Well, I've never had a boyfriend either."

It took a full four seconds to register what he meant.

"You're... a virgin?"

William nodded, sheepishly, like a nervous boy.

"But... you're the Bisexual Baron Buckford?"

He shrugged. "Don't believe everything you read in the papers."

"You told me—"

"I told you I got caught with a couple on a bench in Berkeley Square. I didn't tell you what happened next."

"What happened?"

"She vomited on the Tube at South Kensington, and I rather went off the idea."

"Yeah, that'll do it." I slapped my hand to my forehead. "I can't believe you look like this and you're a virgin. Are you even bisexual?"

"I don't know, I've never met anyone I wanted to have sex with before."

I was speechless.

"Are you mad?" William said. He looked terrified. "You seem mad."

Oh God, he was being vulnerable with me, and I was failing. He didn't deserve that.

"No, absolutely not," I said, trying to wipe from my face whatever William had seen in it.

He propped himself back up on his hands, bringing his face closer to mine, his grey eyes pleading for understanding.

"But you mind. It bothers you."

"No. Surprises me, yes. But bothers me, no."

I tried to think what I would want William to say if the situations were reversed. My mind was racing. What did this mean? Was he asexual? Demisexual? Was he simply shy about sex?

"Do you *want* to have sex some day?" I said.

"Oh yes," he said, smiling, chest heaving. That was a good start.

"Would you like to have sex with *me* some day?"

William nodded, enthusiastically. "If you wouldn't mind. I mean, if it's not too much trouble."

I had ached to feel that close to William. I still ached for it. But breaking in a virgin? It wasn't something that had ever been on my to-do list. I always preferred my men incredibly experienced. This was

William, though. A beautiful gentle giant of a man. A huge-hearted, genuine, deep-feeling man. He'd as good as told me he'd been saving himself for the right person. He'd just told me that person was me.

"I would be honoured," I said, leaning in to kiss him.

He kissed me, hungrily, gratefully. "Thank you," he said.

Behind us, the kettle began to whistle.

"Is it OK if it's not tonight?"

I nodded. "Of course. You let me know when you're ready."

"Thank you. I'm... really full of lemon tart."

The rest of the week went in much the same pattern. Breakfast together, a day spent working on our various projects, dinner prepared by Bramley in the dining room, and then an evening alone together in the folly. It was the closest thing I'd experienced to domesticity in my whole life. The only thorn was the constant telephone calls from a very persistent journalist from *The Bulletin*, but we left Bramley to deal with those.

Chapter 34
William

It was Friday morning, the day before the village fair and a hundred and forty-eight days before Halloween. I was in the kitchen, raiding the pantry for ginger nut biscuits, when Buckford Hall's doorbell rang. I looked at my watch. The fellow from Wetherby's Auction House had arrived very early.

"*Bramley!*" I hollered, before remembering my faithful chief operating officer was busy with the team from the internet company, getting Buckford Hall fully Wi-Fi'ed. I was going to have to pull on my big boy pants and answer my own door. Still, we all had to make sacrifices if we were going to save the estate. I dashed through the house to the front door—stopping to check my hair in the mirror and brush a few biscuit crumbs off my crisp white shirt. Thanks to Bramley, who was thrilled with my new-found sartorial professionalism, my shirt and my tan chinos were freshly pressed, my Chelsea boots were nicely polished, and the simple rust-brown tie that was trying to throttle me to death was tied in a perfect double Windsor. I had drawn the line at the tweed blazer Bramley had suggested. The tie was enough. I smiled at my reflection, sucked the biscuit out of my teeth, and opened the front door.

"Lord Buckford?" an amiable but scruffy chap standing at the top of my stairs said.

"'Tis I," I said, and I have no idea why. I'd never answered my own door before. "You must be the fellow from Wetherby's. Call me William."

"Wetherby's?"

"The auction house?"

I extended my hand, and he shook it.

"Yes, of course. Call me Gary," he said, and he hooked a thumb over his shoulder to where his colleague was snapping photos of the house. "This is Astrid. She's here to do the photographs."

"For the catalogue? Come in, come in. Shall we start in the West Drawing Room?"

"We'll start wherever you like, William," Gary said, pulling a notepad from his satchel. "You're in charge. I'll make a few notes as we go."

I marched them into the middle of the drawing room and pointed at the paintings on the wall.

"I thought the Stubbs, the two Reynolds could go."

"The Stubbs *and* the two Reynolds, you say?"

"Yes, I thought that should raise a bit."

Gary spun around to face me, his expression suggesting I was mad.

"I know, it's a shame to get rid of the Stubbs. She's a beautiful buckskin mare." I pointed to the picture by the door we'd come through. "But we've still got the John Boultbee over there. He was local, so it would be more of a shame to part with that one."

"How much are you hoping to raise?" Gary asked.

I shrugged. "Hopefully, somewhere north of twelve million. Every time I talk to the accountant, the number goes up. I'll take your advice on what's possible."

Gary's eyes bulged like he'd hit the jackpot. Well they might. Wetherby's was earning ten per cent on anything we sold. I was going to have to sell extra paintings to pay the commission on the other paintings.

"Let me show you the Long Gallery. That's really the motherlode."

As we climbed the stairs, Gary explained buyers wanted to know the story behind a work.

"A good story can really sell for a premium," he said.

"We have files and files of provenance in the library. Receipts, the lot."

"Forgive me, William," Gary said. "We need to create a bit of a buzz! Something to cause a stir. In the market."

"Well, all the portraits of creepy children are dead relatives. They weren't dead at the time, you understand, even though some of them look it. They're very much dead now, I assure you. Half of them are in the family mausoleum, if anyone wants to check for... bone structure... or something?"

We summited the stairs, and I pushed open the doors to the Long Gallery.

Gary shook his head. "What I mean to say is, why are you selling these cherished pieces of your family history?"

"Oh, I see!" I pointed to the terrifying Holbein of Queen Elizabeth I. "Well, she's not *my* family history at all. She's only a distant cousin. The three Holbeins and a lot of other old tat were bought by the ninth baron in the Victorian era. He'd massively extended the house and needed some artwork to really achieve the gothic horror aesthetic he was apparently going for."

"I'm sorry, William, you misunderstand me," Gary said. "Why are you selling them?"

I pointed to a portrait of a buxom and bewigged relative by Joshua Reynolds.

"Well, I haven't been comfortable with *that* painting ever since my mother told me she walked in on my grandfather masturbating to it."

Gary's eyes lit up. "I like the sound of that story. Tell me that one."

"There's not much more to it. He was off his rocker by then."

Gary's pencil was scribbling away madly.

"Is this the sort of thing you want?" I asked.

"It's wonderful colour. But tell me, William, why do you need to raise twelve million?"

That gave me pause. I tried to wave his enquiry away. "It's the usual story. You know how it is."

"Gambling debts?" he said with a slow, knowing nod.

"Well, no."

"A dissolute lifestyle, then?"

"No. Not that either."

"Are you being bled dry by mistresses?"

Why did an auctioneer need to know this? I shook my head.

"Blackmail?"

"What kinds of stories are you reading, man? It's to pay a bloody tax bill."

"Ah." Gary smiled sympathetically. "Now that *is* a common story. How much did HMRC get you for, out of interest?"

"Four point three," I said.

Gary whistled.

"No kidding."

Over the next hour, I pointed at paintings, Gary took notes, and Astrid took photographs.

"You need to create a buzz," Gary kept saying. His enthusiasm was infectious, and by the time we were done, I'd quite warmed to the scruffy little man—and we'd identified nineteen paintings to sell.

"Something's just occurred to me," Gary said, palm of his hand smacking against his forehead. We were standing in the Great Hall in front of the big Gainsborough—a painting I'd refused to sell. "Did I read in the newspapers that you recently got engaged?"

Oh, good lord. What choice did I have but to admit it?

"Many congratulations!" Gary beamed, his hand shooting out to shake mine. "Where is the lucky fellow. Is he here?"

I nodded. "He's working."

Gary's hand smacked his forehead again. "You know how we could *really* make a buzz for your auction? If you want to make a premium."

"I want to make a premium, Gary," I said. "Tell me."

"All this publicity you've had around getting engaged, well, we could leverage it in our marketing." He called Astrid over. "What do you think, Astrid? Could you take a photo of the baron and his fiancé that really sells precisely what a once in a lifetime opportunity this auction will be?"

"Course." Astrid nodded. She pointed to the fireplace. "I'd set yous up over 'ere. Looking all in love."

This was getting out of hand. Petey and I weren't engaged. Now we were going to pose for a publicity photo suggesting we were very much in love and getting married, all to flog a few paintings?

"I don't think—"

"Art collectors from all over the world will hear about this auction. It really is genius."

"Genius," Astrid added.

I shook my head. "No, I'm sorry. I can't ask Petey to—"

"Oh, William," Gary said. "He does *know* about this little financial strife you're in, doesn't he? You're not hiding it from him?"

"Of course not. He knows all about it. He's very supportive!"

I was starting to go off the man again. Gary held his hands up in surrender.

"Forgive my impertinence, William. I thought it would be a terrible way to start married life, with a great big lie. But if Petey's supportive, then, no harm in asking him if he'll join us for a photo now, is there? Think of the buzz!"

As I stood there, I *did* think of the buzz. I didn't like it.

"No," I said. "I'm afraid not."

Gary looked genuinely disappointed. I was starting to want the man out of my house.

"Let's at least get a photo of you before we go," Astrid said.

"For the catalogue," Gary added.

I let them take their photograph, then escorted them back to the front door. As I waved goodbye to them from the steps in the carriage court, I felt this enormous sense of relief for a job well done. It was only a few minutes later, when the doorbell summoned me back to those same stone steps, that my heart started to sink. A man in a sharp blue suit handed me his card, doffed his trilby hat, and introduced himself.

"George Wetherby, my lord. Wetherby's Auction House," he said. "Sorry I'm a few minutes late."

Chapter 35
Petey

The Saturday morning of the village fair, I woke early to my phone beeping with messages. I was so unused to having Wi-Fi in the folly that it was completely disorienting. When I opened my eyes to find William gone—rather than wrapped around me, as I'd expected—it felt worryingly like the start of a zombie film. He'd been weird all day yesterday. He'd said he was stressed about the village fair, so I'd let it rest. But now he'd left without saying goodbye? I reached for my phone to see a string of messages from Sunny.

Sunny: *Holy shit, I'm so sorry.*

The next message was the cover of the morning's *Bulletin*, with the headline "BISEXUAL BARON BROKE."

Sunny: *There are FOUR pages inside. Hang on.*

The snapshots of the newspaper kept coming, filling up my screen. I scrolled through, unable to focus on more than scattered words: "Bisexual baron finds love, but could lose home," "five centuries of history go under the hammer," "fiancé a pillar of strength," "father and brother killed in a light plane crash," "grandfather a renowned local pervert," "the trash TV twink is the son of Sir Edward Topham, KC."

How? How had this happened? After everything William had told me about his experiences with the press, I couldn't believe he'd given an interview to *The Bulletin*. But there he was, staring back at me, in a photograph taken in the East Drawing Room, wearing the clothes he was wearing yesterday. He was quoted throughout the story.

Sunny: *I used to work with Gary Ashworth. He's old skool tabloid. How'd he blag his way in?*

Sunny: *Let me know if there's anything I can do xx*

* * *

I found William in the stable yard, washing Achilles. He was wearing rugby shorts and steel-capped boots and nothing else. Both man and horse were wet and sudsy. William saw me approaching but couldn't bring himself to make eye contact.

"Morning," I called out.

William shuffled around behind his horse. "Good morning."

"Is it?"

I stood before Achilles, rubbing the beautiful animal's nose, wondering if he knew his owner was an idiot.

"Is there anything you maybe forgot to tell me about yesterday, William?"

There was a long pause.

"Ah," he said.

"Ah," I replied.

William's head appeared beside me, face sheepish, hands wringing the water out of a cloth.

"Is it *bad*?"

"Bad?" I said—only containing my outrage so as not to spook Achilles. "Are you fucking insane? What were you thinking?"

William's chest heaved like he was swallowing a hiccup. Then he did it again. He was choking down tears. My anger dissolved.

"Hey, hey, hey." I put my arms around him, and he nestled into my shoulder. "Tell me what happened."

"You're going to think I'm such an idiot," he said.

We sat side by side on a hay bale as William filled me in on the previous morning.

"Why didn't you tell me?"

"If I tell you that, you're going to think I'm even more stupid than you already do."

"I seriously doubt that," I said. We both frowned. "I didn't mean that the way it sounded, I promise."

"This past week, you've seemed so... *proud*... of everything I've been doing. The way I've got all professionalised and got stuck in and got—"

"Dressed."

"Exactly. The fact you seemed impressed made me feel good. It was a confidence boost. I wanted to do well for you. At dinner each night, I couldn't wait to update you on what I'd achieved."

It was incredibly sweet. I wove my fingers through William's and brought his hand to my lips to kiss it. His cheeks were wet.

"And then I go and do something stupid and prove I'm a himbo on horseback after all."

"You're not a himbo," I said. "I never thought that. I'm sorry I said it. But if you are, you're *my* himbo. I am proud of you for what you're achieving."

William shook his head. "It's humiliating. I'm a dumb rugby jock who's unfit to be the lord of Buckford Hall, and thanks to that newspaper article, now everyone knows it. And today, I have to spend the whole day with my community, knowing they'll all be thinking *Well, he's clearly useless, we're better off without him anyway*."

"They won't," I said.

"They will."

"No, they'll be thinking the new Lady Buckford looks fantastic in that vintage Westwood coat."

"You aren't?"

"I bloody well am. I've got prizes to hand out. Jumaane couriered it up from London especially."

William laughed. "I love it. I know you'll look beautiful."

"And I'll be right there beside you, whenever you need me. We're a team, remember?"

William rested his head against mine. "Thank you."

"I *am* proud of you, William." I wiped his wet cheeks with the cuff of my sleeve and kissed him. "And I'm going to be so proud to be seen on your arm today, in the village, in front of everyone, in defiance of the crap that's been printed. The Buckfords are a united team."

I kissed him gently on the lips. Then swung a leg around and straddled him, kissing him more deeply—his hands gripping my waist and pulling me down onto him.

"So tiny," he said. He nodded towards Achilles. "I do have to finish this, though. You're not the only one who needs to look their best today."

"Achilles is coming to the fair?"

"Coming? He's the star! Which reminds me. Did you happen to see if Bramley has finished polishing my suit of armour?"

"Pardon?"

Chapter 36
William

The sun was shining, children were running around squealing with delight, and the sweet smell of sugar filled the air. Newton Bardon Common was alive. Large marquees were buzzing with deliveries of things in want of judging—cakes, jams, flowers, poultry, handicrafts, and rudely shaped vegetables. The great and the good of the village were throwing balls at coconuts, dipping hands into the tombola, and shooting corks from wonky rifles to win highly flammable prizes. I was peering out at it all like a coward from the safety of the jauntily medieval red-and-blue-striped tent that was my base camp for the annual re-enactment of the Battle of Buckford Field. I stood at the tent flap, worrying it with my fingers.

Petey rested his chin on my shoulder. "I'm meant to be judging jam in forty-five minutes. Shall we go show our faces to your people?"

"Please don't call them my people."

"Well, aren't they? You literally own the village."

"I don't own the people, though."

A fellow in a Yorkist uniform walked past the tent and doffed his helmet in acknowledgement. "Morning, my lord."

"Morning, Andy. I hear young Matthew is joining us for the first time this year."

"That he is."

"Well, he'll make an adorable addition to the battlefield. Tell him if he can fight his way to me, I'll kill him myself."

"Thank you, my lord. That'll make his day."

As Andy left, Petey ran a hand up into my hair playfully. "Not your people, hey?"

I kissed him on the forehead. "Charles the First probably thought they were *his* people, and look what they did to him."

Petey laughed. "Wasn't he a first-rate arsehole, though? Are you expecting to be beheaded?"

"No, much like the jam, I'm expecting to be judged. I'm afraid they'll think I've come up short."

"Well, if they behead you, you probably will."

I groaned. Petey smiled and kissed me on the nose. But the truth was, I really was worried. That article would have confirmed what everyone must already have been thinking: William Winters was a dumb jock who'd be the last of the Buckford Winterses.

Petey's hand slid into mine.

"You're going to be absolutely fine," he said. "You look bloody gorgeous. The women will all be swooning after you, the men will all be questioning their sexuality, and I expect even a few of the chickens will be having unnatural thoughts while you judge them."

I was wearing my new uniform—teamed, this time, with an air force blue blazer Bramley insisted I wear. Petey, meanwhile, was wearing an asymmetrical red tartan coat that fit like a glove, over what I can only describe as Mickey Mouse trousers.

"Besides, it's me who should be nervous," Petey said. "This is my chance to make a good first impression. I don't want to blow it."

"You recall this is a *fake* engagement, right?"

"That's hardly the point."

I squeezed his hand. "You look gorgeous. They're going to love you."

Petey kissed me, then stepped out into the daylight, dragging me along behind him. We walked up to Birdie Craddoch, a tweedy woman from my grandfather's generation, at the tombola. I introduced her to Petey, and she curtsied.

"No, please don't do that," he said—getting the hang of the Buckford way of handling formality. I handed Mrs Craddoch my two-pound coin to exchange for a ticket. She refused to take it.

"I insist."

Mrs Craddoch leant into me, her hand folded around mine, and whispered in my ear.

"Your money's no good here, my lord."

She winked, slid a yellow ticket into my palm, and turned to speak to the next person in line.

"That was weird," I said to Petey as we walked away.

"What was?"

But before I could answer, he was dashing over to the shooting gallery. When he reached it, he turned back to face me, splaying himself playfully across the counter of pop guns, eyes full of mischief.

"Can you shoot?" he said. "I know your family don't do guns and violence."

"Can *you* shoot?" I said as I reached him. "No, don't tell me. Had your first shoot-out with the cops in an East End alleyway at five years old, brought down your first policeman single-handed at ten. The gang calls you Dead Eye Pete."

The shooting gallery was being run by Noah, the village electrician, who made a couple of uncomplimentary comments about the state of my wiring. Nevertheless, I dug around in my pocket, fished out a couple of two-pound coins, and handed them over. We took our shots. The rifles were so wonky my first cork nearly took off my ear. Petey didn't fare much better, although his last shot did skim the edge of the baked bean tin and made it wobble. Noah walked over to it and gave it a bit of a nudge, and the tin fell.

"Congratulations, sir!" he called out, loud enough for the whole village to hear. "We have a winner!"

"No, we don't," I said as Petey took receipt of an enormous stuffed yellow duck, smile beaming across his face. "This is fraud."

"Everyone wins a prize," Noah said loudly. Then he leant over to me and grabbed my hand as if he was going to shake it, and I felt my coins tumble back into my palm. "My wife and I wish you all the very best for your impending nuptials, my lord. We hope you'll be very happy together."

I tried to hand him back the money, but he wouldn't take it.

"I'll come around next week and do a free survey on your wiring. A little wedding gift from the missus and me."

I was so gobsmacked I could barely speak, but Petey thanked him profusely and pecked him on the cheek. Noah blushed like a spanked buttock. Petey drifted off towards a stall selling cotton candy and doughnuts. I waved at Gurpreet, the village chemist, who was manning the machine. His wife, Harpreet, was on the till. They were both filled with congratulations on our impending wedding.

"What would you like?"

Petey got a stick of candyfloss and I got a box of six doughnuts, but when it came time for reckoning, Harpreet's hands went up.

"Absolutely not, William. Your money is no good here."

"But—"

"I will not hear of it. Please."

The same thing happened at the coffee hut, the coconut shy, and the hook-a-duck. By the time we had got around all the stalls, Petey was high on sugar and I almost had more money in my pocket than when I started.

"They're meant to be raising funds for good causes," I said.

"Clearly they think you're a good cause!"

But I struggled to see how denying the local nursery or the village school two pounds benefited anybody. I'd have rather they had it than the taxman.

Judging duty started at eleven. We bumped into Mum by the floral marquee. She was on flower-and-suggestive-vegetable duty this year. Petey had bagsied the jams and preserves.

"I'm jealous," I told him as I deposited him at the right marquee. "Mrs Craddoch does an incredible red onion chutney. She wins every year. Can't get the recipe out of her."

"I'll keep a taste bud out for it." Petey pecked me on the cheek. "Where are you off to now?"

"Poultry shed." I pointed over my shoulder. "Somewhere in there is the best cock in the village, and it's my job to find it."

From the chickens, ducks, and pigeons it was on to the cakes, scones, and biscuits—which had to do double duty as lunch because by one o'clock, I was back at my medieval tent, being trussed into my suit of armour by the ever-faithful Bramley. I'd been shoehorned into sabaton, greave, cuisse and tasset, fauld, plackart, breastplate, and pauldron. I only had my gauntlets and helm to slide on when the bloated crimson face of Horatio Blunt appeared through the tent flaps.

"You absolute prick," he said.

"Lovely to see you, too, Horatio."

"This isn't going to work, you know?"

I had no idea what he was talking about and said so. Horatio produced a copy of *The Bulletin*, held it aloft, and slammed it into his open hand.

"Bramley, dear fellow, could you give us a moment? Perhaps go check Achilles hasn't wheedled his way out of his barding again."

He gave me a weary glance, passing me my sword on his way out the door. He'd never been subtle, Bramley.

"What isn't going to work?" I enquired.

"Don't be coy, William, it doesn't suit you."

"But does this suit suit me? That's the only question of importance today," I said, pointing at my armour and hoping to drive him insane.

"I know what you're doing." Horatio was sneering, spittle flecking my previously spotless armour. I hadn't seen a face that red since, well, since Indira's heart burst all over the Great Lawn. "You've planted this little story in the paper in order to flush out other potential buyers. You're trying to inflate the price. But I will not have it, William. I *will not*!"

He hit me on my right pauldron with his rolled-up newspaper.

"You realise this was made to withstand the blunt force of metal?"

"My clients have offered you a fair price, Dub-Dub. A very fair price indeed."

"Oh, we're back to Dub-Dub now. Over our little fit of pique, are we?"

I was, very deliberately, riling him up.

"And as a gesture of my client's enduring goodwill, they have this morning increased their offer by a further five million pounds, on the condition you withdraw the house from the market today."

I shook my head. "Alas, I can't do that, Horatio."

The head was rattling now, great chunks of spittle flying everywhere, face completely blue like that kid in *Willy Wonka*.

"Why not?" he raged.

"Because—and this does seem to be a point you've failed to understand at every juncture, dear chap, which really is an appalling oversight for someone in your line of business—it's not bloody well on the market. It's never been on the market. It's not going to be on the market. My family home will never be a hotel!"

That's when the name-calling started.

"You are a joke, William. You're humiliating yourself. You're not a quarter of the man your brother was. Or your father."

Fury welled inside me. Back at Petersham College, Horatio had led the gang of bullies who haunted my every waking move—and many of my nightmares. He and his little friends had been responsible for me seeking refuge in the school library and then, when I saw how he never picked on the beefy lads on the rugby team, for taking up rugger. He still knew how to press my buttons, and he was bashing at them with his fist now.

"It won't work, Horatio," I growled. "Now piss off back to Daddy and tell him you've failed. Yet again."

That got him.

"You've always been an idiot, William, but at least now everyone can see how stupid you really are. I could have saved you from all this. I *tried* to save you from all this. If you'd sold the estate when I first came to you, I could have spared you all this embarrassment."

My parents taught me never to choose violence, but in that moment, the only thing stopping me bashing Horatio over the head with the hilt of my sword was the vision of Petey appearing behind him through the tent flaps. Apparently, no one had ever taught Petey not to choose violence because he calmly tapped Horatio on the shoulder and, when he turned around, planted his fist into the odious man's eye socket.

Horatio fell to the floor, clutching his hands to his face and threatening to sue. Petey picked the newspaper off the ground and stood over Horatio like an East End heavy in a gangster film.

"You know who I am," he said with menace. He pointed to the newspaper article. "You know who my people are. You come for me, mate, and we're coming for you. And we'll do you slowly, fingernail by fingernail, until you wish you'd never been born. Now I reckon, prima facie, William's already got a dozen cases against you, civil and criminal. Enough to tie you up in court for years. I don't even have to break your legs. What will my old man find once he starts grubbing about in your private affairs? You better hope you're squeaky clean, bruv. Or you might be spending a lot of time as a guest of His Majesty. Now, I don't know your people, but I reckon they'd probably consider you a bit of a failure when they visit you in Wormwood Scrubs. So why don't you stop cowering on the ground, stop making threats you're never going to follow through on, and fuck right off, you pathetic little pisswank."

Horatio jumped to his feet and scuttled out across the common.

I stared at Petey in awe.

"What have I witnessed?"

Petey calmly unhooked the tent flap, shutting out the outside world, so the two of us were alone.

"Are you OK?" he said, grabbing my hand, his voice back to normal.

"Holy shit, that was hot. I mean, I would never condone violence. I'm certainly glad you didn't have access to my sword. But *wow!* You beat up my school bully."

My erection was bashing against the inside of my armour like a battering ram. Petey wove his hands behind my neck and pulled me towards him, his eyes blazing with intensity.

"I want you to listen to me, William. You are *not* a failure. You're magnificent. The people here love you and respect you and want you to succeed. So do I. I am *so* proud to be your fake fiancé."

I let my sword clatter to the ground, clasped my hands around Petey's jaw, and dragged him into a deep, passionate kiss. As we pulled apart, Petey started jumping up and down, hands flapping, face contorted in disgust.

"Ew, ew, ew! I just invoked my parents. I've literally never done that in my entire life. I feel so *diiiiiiiirty*."

I didn't feel dirty. I felt incredibly turned on. A switch had been flicked inside my brain.

Chapter 37
Petey

The brassy crackle of a medieval fanfare pierced the air, nearly making me jump out of my skin. I was sitting on a hay bale overlooking a huge expanse of common that had been roped off for the re-enactment. Around me, hundreds of locals chattered and squealed with excitement.

"There you are, Petey darling."

It was Bunny Winters, pushing her way through the crowds with coffee. She plonked herself down beside me and handed me a cardboard cup that was as hot as the centre of the sun. As my fingerprints melted off my hand, I thanked her. The trumpets burst into life again. This time I could see them. There were three buglers, dressed like medieval heralds, marching towards us. Behind them, drummers, beating out their warmongering tune.

"Golly, it's exciting, isn't it?" Bunny said.

"I don't really understand what's going on," I confessed.

Bunny looked shocked. "The Battle of Buckford Field changed the course of our nation's history. You've heard of the Wars of the Roses, at least?"

I nodded. "The wars between the house of York and the house of Lancaster for the English throne."

Bunny seemed pleased.

"Richard the Third was killed up the road at the Battle of Bosworth Field in 1485. The Battle of Buckford Field took place the day before. The Lancastrians were encamped in the ancient oak wood, which was no doubt slightly less ancient back then, when they saw the Yorkists crossing the ford on the River Buck. Where the Long Water is now."

"Got it." I made the mistake of sipping my coffee, scalding my mouth.

"The Lancastrians—lead by Richard de Valois—attacked. They waited until the last man was across and they were boxed in between the hill and the river, and barrelled across Home Field on their horses and slaughtered them. It significantly weakened the Yorkist forces. Anyway, every year since at least the ninth baron's time, they've re-enacted the battle on the day of the village fair. William is playing Richard de Valois, obviously."

"I see," I said, my tongue gingerly exploring the roof of my mouth to see what was left of it.

On the field, the soldiers were taking their places. The sun was glinting off suits of armour, poleaxes, and swords. Not everyone was in full armour. Some were in maille (you don't call it chain mail, I discovered, if you want to stay in William's good books), most wore livery coats (don't call them tabards, for the same reason). All wore helmets—I thought that probably had more to do with modern health and safety than historical accuracy.

"For clarity, so I don't make a massive faux pas and find myself beheaded, which side are we on?"

"Catherine de Valois was queen consort to Henry the Fifth. We're Lancastrians. The ones on the right."

I recognised the name de Valois. It was the bit of William's surname he never used.

"Holy shit, is William descended from Henry the Fifth?"

"Oh goodness no. Nothing like that. There's no English royal blood in William's veins. Sorry to disappoint you."

I shrugged.

"Just the French royal blood," Bunny said, leaving me astonished. But before I could ask more, the trumpets were blowing again and the men were on the move, the clink-clank of metal echoing across the field. It was already awesome before William came riding in on Achilles, both in full battle gear, with his sword aloft, rousing his men to charge. The enormous white stallion was thundering across the field, the gold fleur-de-lis embroidered on the red and blue of the cloth that draped his flanks fluttering in the wind. Behind him, a rank of archers loosed their rubber-headed arrows, and the whole crowd counted down from five to one together—obviously a much-loved tradition—until a swathe of Yorkist men clutched their chests or arms or heads and fell to the ground, or bravely struggled on. Soon the village common was alive with the sounds of battle. Of men roaring in courage and wailing in pain, of swords clashing and horses whinnying. I sat there, unable to take my eyes off the spectacle. All the TV producer in my brain could think was, this would make great television. I put my coffee down, took out my phone, and started recording.

"I'm going to get a different angle," I told Bunny, and crept along the rope separating us from the action until I found a good vantage point, away from the crowd, where I could film without disturbing anyone.

A few minutes later the field was littered with dead Yorkists. I watched as a small boy in black-and-white livery, ten if he was a day, limped bravely towards William. He was dragging one leg, his left arm held against his chest as if it were broken. His sword was held out in his right hand. I was willing to bet that boy's name was Matthew and his father's name was Andy. William circled Achilles around him, then dismounted some twenty feet away and marched across the battlefield towards him with his sword at the ready.

"He's very impressive, isn't he?" A man's voice. Not one I recognised. I glanced across. He was suited but scruffy.

"The little boy?" I said. "He's brilliant." And he was. He and William were circling each other, swords extended, waiting to see who would strike the first blow. William was twice his height and six times his weight.

"Not him," the man said. "Your fella."

"Sorry, have we met?"

The man shook his head. "I don't think so. I've done a bit of business with William in the past, though."

On the field, Matthew struck the first blow, the clank of metal on metal slicing the air. William batted it away, and Matthew went again. William pretended to be knocked back on his heels, and the little boy drove home his advantage, pressing forward. Then William lurched towards him, roaring like a lion as he swung the sword down—only for Matthew to dodge out of his way.

"Have you set a date for the wedding yet?" the man said.

"Sorry?"

"It's the talk of the village. I was wondering if you'd chosen a date."

"Not yet," I said, annoyed but not wanting to be rude.

On the field, young Matthew struck a blow against William's leg, and His Lordship was stumbling around like a pro wrestler, milking the moment for all it was worth. The crowd was on their feet, jumping up and down, cheering.

The man stepped closer. I took a step away. "I only ask because there was no engagement announcement in *The Times*, and I noticed you haven't applied for a marriage licence yet."

"Pardon?"

I properly stopped to look at him then. His face was familiar. Where had I seen it?

On the field, Matthew was stumbling around as if exhausted. He fell to one knee, then both knees. William, also feigning exhaustion, put a hand under his helmet and ripped it from his head, tossing it aside. The crowd roared. William was rounding on his prey. A woman shouted, "Get up, Matthew! Run him through!" The boy crept forward, head hanging, sword on the ground, as if accepting his fate. William played the crowd, raising a gauntleted hand to his ear, as if he couldn't hear them, or as if he wanted to know if they were ready for the terminal act. The crowd bayed for blood. But then—as William was about to strike—Matthew thrust his sword up, up, up. It glanced off William's armour, and he made out he had been pierced in the flank. The crowd whooped and hollered and stamped their feet.

"What I can't work out," the man said as William raised his sword, "is how long you two have actually known each other."

William plunged his sword into Matthew's belly, and the boy fell. All around us the crowd cheered. The trumpets started playing. All I could do was stare at the man who had the audacity to ask these kinds of questions. I stopped filming, put my phone in my pocket. I was about to ask him who the bloody hell he thought he was when I realised I already knew.

"You're Gary Ashworth." I'd seen his photo byline in *The Bulletin*. The man smiled. It was slimy and insincere. "I think you've had quite enough out of William and me for one day, mate."

"I have a few questions, though, Peter. Because there's a few things don't quite add up."

"Our private life is none of your business."

I glanced at the field, where William had young Matthew on his shoulder, surrounded by dozens of cheering re-enactors. All over the common, ovaries were exploding.

"I understand," Gary said. "But when's the first time you ever came to Buckford Hall?"

"Again, that's not your business."

"Oh, but it literally is. My business is the truth, Peter, and you ain't telling these people the truth. Are you now?"

I swallowed, my Adam's apple slowly descending below my collar before reappearing holding a flashing neon sign that said *guilty*.

"No announcement. No marriage licence. No evidence you'd even heard of Buckford Hall before you started filming *The Love Manor*. Not to mention a string of gentlemen in London with some very interesting stories to tell about the man who has supposedly won Lord Buckford's heart."

"You absolute snake." My fists clenched. Was I about to punch my second person for the day? In front of the whole village? In Vivienne Westwood?

"What do you want, Mr Ashworth?" I sneered.

"I want a story for tomorrow's newspaper. I don't mind which story it is. I want a nice big Sunday read. An exclusive. I *could* write the inside story of the Bisexual Baron Buckford's soon-to-be-wedded bliss. Assuming this engagement is real, of course. Or I could always write up the surprising stories I've been told about what you get up to on your Friday nights in Vauxhall."

My blood was thumping so loudly through my temples, I didn't hear the thunder of hooves until Achilles was almost on me. Gary Ashworth's body flew across the grass like a skittle. William reached a hand down to me. I grabbed it and he swung me up into the saddle behind him. His hair was windswept, his breathing heavy. I wrapped my arms around his armoured waist. His sword was pointed squarely at the reporter on the ground.

"Did he threaten you?" William asked me.

"Yes." And then I whispered, "He knows. He wants a story or he's going to print it— and worse."

It was only then I looked around. The whole village was staring, slack-jawed and gobsmacked. Gary Ashworth was on the ground, his hand up to his face. William circled Achilles around, sheathed his sword, and addressed the whole village.

"Let it be known that I, William Stanley Leaf Richard George Winters-de Valois-Winters, the seventeenth Baron Buckford, *love* this man. I will *marry* this man. I intend to spend my *life* with this man. Make no mistake, if any man tries to come between us or threatens the incredible happiness ahead of us, I will hunt them to the ends of the earth and I will exact a terrible price from them." William pointed a gauntleted finger in the direction of Gary Ashworth. "And that includes members of the press."

I was flagstaff rigid. Achilles turned on a tight rein.

"How was that?" William whispered over his shoulder.

"Sexy as hell. That French royal blood really tells."

"Mother's been telling tales, I see."

"Let's get out of here," I muttered.

"What?"

"Carry me off into the sunset, for crying out loud."

"Right you are!"

As we galloped across the common, I leant into William's ear. "Did you mean it?"

"What's that?"

"That you love me. Did you mean it?"

"Of course I did. I think you know that."

As Achilles's hooves trod the road back to Buckford Hall, every cell in my body was bursting with a sensation I'd never experienced before. I couldn't name it, but it felt the way I imagined the earth must feel in spring, when it explodes with new life. Overwhelmed, I cried.

Chapter 38
William

I was in the bathroom at Buckford Hall, freshly showered, wearing my red satin boxers, giving myself a pep talk in the mirror. I'd declared my love in front of the whole village, my mother, and that bloody reporter from *The Bulletin*. It was a whole, complete, indisputable fact. I loved Petey. Over these weeks together in the folly, living like an old married couple in private and pretending to be engaged in public, I'd come to know him intimately. His kiss. The way his body felt against mine at night. The smell of his clothes after a day of work, his hair after he'd washed it, his body in the funk of the bed in the morning. It all drove me wild. He'd rewired bits of my brain. When I heard the folly door open each evening, my whole body responded. If I was a whippet, my tail would have been knocking books clean off the shelves. When Petey was going back to London, I'd been miserable. When fate intervened—with lashings of assistance from Bunny Winters—and bought us an extra few weeks, I felt incredible relief. Because it felt right for him to be here. Like he belonged here, with me. I had never given my body to anyone before, not because I was afraid or virtuous. I just hadn't met anyone I wanted to do that with before. I'd known, ever since Berkeley Square, that I couldn't fall into bed with someone I didn't love. And *this* was love. And it was time.

There was a knock at the door.

"I thought I gave you the night off, Bramley? You should be six pints in at the village pub by now and trying to charm that chutney recipe out of Birdie Craddoch."

"It's not Bramley."

My heart fluttered.

"Come in," I said, still bent over the sink, hands resting on the vanity.

The door opened, and Petey's eyes sized me up before landing on mine in the mirror.

"That really is the world's most magnificent arse," he said.

"Thank you."

He was freshly showered and had a towel slung low around those glorious hips. He held up his phone and waved it at me. "I thought you might want to know, we're going viral."

I let my head slump. "How bad is it?"

Petey rested an arm on my back, and I watched the footage of today's little scene play out on his phone.

"If we ignore the cynical alpha bros calling you a 'beta cuck'—"

"Yes, I think we can safely ignore those."

"Then based on the comments of the queers, the girlies, the fantasy nerds, and anyone who's ever read a Saddle Club book—in fact, everyone else except some bloke from the Richard the Third Society, who was a bit of a dick—general opinion seems to be we're the greatest love story the internet has seen in at least a couple of weeks."

I sighed, looking at myself in the mirror. My face was tired.

"I don't want to be famous, Petey. I never asked for this attention. I want a quiet, honest life with the man I love."

"This will blow over," he said. "All of it. We can face it tomorrow. Together. But tonight, I want you to hold me in your arms and tell me again and again that you love me. Can you do that?"

I grinned. "I would be honoured, my liege."

"Good." Petey slapped my arse. "I'm probably going to want to nibble on that. So you know."

Then he turned around, let his towel drop, and strode out into the corridor. I nearly slipped on the wet tiles rushing to watch his cute bubble butt bounce up the hall to the folly. But I didn't follow him. I spent a few more minutes at the mirror psyching myself up. I loved Petey, and I was going to show him exactly how much. I jumped up and down a few times and belted my chest with my fists, like I was preparing to run onto the rugby pitch. I shook my head, loosened my neck. Amped and ready for the big match, I ran up the corridor to the folly.

Chapter 39
Petey

I had found the folly's stash of candles and lit a dozen of them. William came bounding up the stairs to the belvedere like it was Christmas morning, to find me posed on the bed with the giant yellow stuffed duck I'd won at the village fair hiding my crotch. It stopped him dead in his tracks.

"That thing is definitely flammable," he said.

"Should I get rid of the candles or the duck?"

"The duck."

I threw it at him, and he tossed it down the stairs.

"I thought you were going to be naked under there," he said, disappointed.

"Isn't it better to have something to unwrap?"

William's hands rubbed my feet at the end of the bed. He bent down and kissed them, then kissed his way up my body.

"You're beautiful," he said, lingering over my belly.

"Well, you looked *very* sexy today." I ran my fingers into his hair, and William rubbed his face into my pants, breathing in deeply. "Where did you learn to wield a sword like that?"

"I play *Dungeons and Dragons*."

"Don't you use dice for that?"

"Sometimes."

I hooked my legs around him. "Being rescued by a literal knight in shining armour was, without a doubt, the hottest thing that has ever happened to me."

"I thought you didn't want me to protect you," he said, tongue circling my nipples.

I pawed at the muscles of his back. "I'll let you off this once. Don't do it again."

"I can't promise that," he said. "I protect the things I love with my body and my heart. So do you, as it turns out. I've been wanting to deck Horatio since I was thirteen."

I laughed, pulling him towards me. He kissed me, and I felt his hardness digging into my stomach for barely a moment before he leapt up.

"I need to pop downstairs and get something."

He reappeared a few seconds later with a tube of lube in one hand and some condoms in the other, proudly holding them up like he'd caught a couple of fish.

"I thought we might... um..."

I nodded. "If you're ready."

"I'm *very* ready."

We kissed for a while and took it slowly, exploring each other's bodies in the candlelight. Lips. Tongues. Fingers. When it got stuffy, William opened the windows, letting the cool breeze flow over us, tickling our skin and blowing out most of the candles. It was lightly raining, and the petrichor made it feel primal and sensual, like the Buckford earth itself was our bed.

When the moment came, William was kneeling over me, one hand buried in the pillow beside my head. His auburn hair was falling in front of his face, his neck chain was dangling above me, his eyes were locked onto mine. I felt him at my entrance and pulled my knees higher.

"Are you sure?" I asked.

"I've never been so sure about anything in my life."

Tenderly, he nestled his way into me. I wrapped my legs around his back and pulled him down onto me. His eyes were wide, full of wonder. Not greed. Not lust. Not the raw carnality I expected. But awe and reverence and love. His body pressed me into the mattress and I relaxed onto him, welcoming him home.

"You feel amazing," he said as he began to slowly rock against me. "This is amazing."

I wound my arms around his head, pulling his face to mine.

"It gets better," I said, tensing my diaphragm, ready to roll further onto him.

"How? How could this get better?"

"Push in deeper."

"I don't want to hurt you."

"You won't, I promise. Push deeper."

He did, and as I felt him nudge through my inner tightness, I gasped for air.

"Are you OK?"

"Never better. Don't stop. I never want you to stop."

My body had ached for William so long. I had craved him. But when I had imagined this moment, I had no idea I would feel this complete, this whole. It wasn't only that he was inside me, that we were finally physically as one, but he was overwhelming all my senses, like a drug I was powerless to resist. I yielded, completely. I loved him, and I wanted to ride this wave of ecstasy for as long as possible.

It was not to be.

"I'm sorry," William said, pulling his head back, eyes full of apology. "I'm sorry, I can't stop it."

I smiled. "It's fine, my sweet boy. Fill me up."

He shuddered into me, his face contorting in pleasure and joy. It was beautiful. As the pulsations ebbed away, he kissed me and collapsed onto me. I wove my fingers into his hair, content to feel the weight of him on top of me.

"Sorry that was a little... quick," he said.

I giggled. "We have plenty of time. We can go again in a minute."

"Oh, we absolutely will." William laughed. He pointed down to where our bodies were still joined. "Should I leave this thing plugged in to recharge, or...?"

I grinned. "Leave him where he is for now," I said, unable to bear the thought of not feeling him there. "We can rustle him up a new raincoat in a minute."

William smiled. I kissed his forehead. It was salty and damp with sweat.

"I love you," I said. I'd never said those words to anyone before.

His eyes searched mine. He leant on one elbow and traced his fingers along the side of my face. "Really?"

"Really."

He smiled—and I felt complete.

Chapter 40
William

Nothing could have wiped the smile from my face, but Bramley was trying. The coffee was practically strychnine, my dippy eggs were cooked right through, and every time I called his name, I was met with the sharp sound of air being sucked through teeth. If I were a betting man, I'd have said my humble retainer was hungover.

"Fun night in the village, Brammers?" I asked, feeling jovial despite the sub-par petit-déjeuner.

Bramley put the heel of his hand to his temple before responding. "Yes, my lord."

"Could I trouble you for a couple more eggs, dear fellow? Not that these aren't delicious, but I've got a bit of DIY to do later, and I thought I'd save them to bash in some nails."

"Of course, my lord."

Mum drifted in, resting her hands on my shoulders and kissing me on the head.

"Morning, darling!"

Cue the sound of teeth sucking.

"Your aura is different today. You seem *happy*."

She knew. Of course she did. How did she always know? She twisted around me to see my face, lifting my chin towards her.

"*Oh!*" she said. "Oh, William, I'm thrilled for you."

"Mum, please don't."

"I told you the great goddess was sending you a blessing. Was it passionate?"

"Please don't ask that."

She ran her fingers through my hair. "When your father and I used to make love—"

"Dear God, stop, you horrendous woman."

"Very well." Mum shrugged. "Ooh, coffee."

She sat down beside me and poured herself a cup. I considered warning her it was strong enough to give her generalised muscle spasms and respiratory failure, but Mother was an old hippie. There wasn't a naturally occurring drug her body hadn't metabolised in industrial quantities. She reached for a grapefruit.

"And where is your lover this morning, darling?"

In fact, I'd left Petey sleeping soundly while I went in search of sustenance. It turns out making love all night really burns up the calories. By seven o'clock I was so ravenous I considered boiling my own eggs, before coming to my senses and waking Bramley. I showered, got dressed, and left Petey a note in the secret drawer of my father's old desk: *I love you, I love you, I love you. I am yours, forever. WW. xxxxxxx.*

"If you mean me, I'm right here," Petey said, his voice coming from the doorway. His hand rested on my shoulder, sending electricity sparking through my body. He pecked my cheek. Well, I wasn't having that. My lips were on his in half a second—my hand in his hair, pulling his mouth down onto mine. It was only Mother wistfully sighing that reminded me to choose decorum. When I finally released his face, Petey didn't look as thrilled as I'd hoped.

"It looks like Gary Ashworth got his front page after all."

Dread washed through me, my mood crashing to earth. Petey held his phone, screen shining. Why couldn't the bloody papers leave me alone?

"What does it say?"

"They're very excited about having 'exclusive pictures of the social media sensation everyone is talking about.'"

"Exclusive pictures?"

"They must have had a photographer there yesterday too."

The telephone rang, and Bramley made the sucking sound again before answering it.

"If that's the press, tell them to sod off," I said.

Petey Boy dropped into a chair and rattled off a few key phrases from *The Bulletin*'s article: "KNIGHT AND GAY!" "SUITOR OF ARMOUR," "Bisexual Baron Buckford's romantic love declaration," "happy couple in battle to save historic family home."

Bramley cleared his throat, phone receiver buried in his apron. "It's Mr Armando Conti, my lord."

"Who?"

Petey frowned. "Last seen duelling Jonty on the Great Lawn."

"Ah."

Bramley continued: "He says he saw yesterday's article about the auction and would like to discuss a business proposal with you."

Petey and I exchanged brief glances. Curious, I took the call on the new phone line in the hallway. Armando said he'd been devastated to read of my financial straits and asked if I was looking for investors to help get things back on track. I was so touched, I could have cried. Then he dropped the number he was willing to invest, and I blubbed like it was the first day of boarding school.

"Actually, I do have a project you might be interested in," I said.

The doorbell rang, and I watched Bramley shuffle through, palms pressed to the side of his head. Before long he shuffled back with something in his arms.

Ten minutes later we were all in the kitchen again.

"It looks like the riding school is on," I said, to whoops of applause from Mum and Petey—and the sound of air being sucked through Bramley's teeth. "Assuming we can raise enough from the art sale to keep the place, that is. Who was at the front door, Bramley?"

"Mrs Howes, from the village, my lord. She delivered a casserole."

"A casserole?"

"It's a kind of stew, my lord."

"Yes, I know that. But why?"

"I think she thinks she's helping, my lord."

The phone and the doorbell rang constantly all morning. The phone with people offering promises of help, the door with people from Newton Bardon inexplicably bringing cakes, pies, lasagnas, and curries. The phone rang again as I was boiling the kettle for tea, but as I'd sent Bramley back to bed, I was forced to answer it myself.

"Buckford Hall!" I announced theatrically.

"Is that Lord Buckford?" a woman's voice asked.

"'Tis I!"

"I don't know if you remember me. I'm Zoë. From *The Love Manor*."

"Of course!" I said, but I didn't.

"I want in. I am in love with your brand, your message, and I want to collab."

Zoë was apparently a travel blogger, and she had more than two million followers on TikTok and Instagram. She wanted to film a tour of Buckford—and she wanted me and Petey in it.

"My followers love to explore new places. You'll have visitors from all over the world."

"The house isn't open to the public, I'm afraid."

There was a horrified silence on the end of the phone.

"Are you absolutely insane?"

"With these genes? Highly probable. The fifth baron was a noted lunatic—"

"You're sitting on a gold mine. People are gonna want to see where that swoony knight in shining armour declared his love in front of the whole world. Open those gates and start charging."

I liked the sound of that. Not least because she said I was swoony. I mean, *swoony*? Gosh! So I agreed to the "collab" and thanked her profusely. I was busily re-boiling the kettle and wondering whether the Old Gatekeeper's Cottage could be turned into a ticket booth when the kitchen doorbell rang. As I'd answered my own phone so masterfully, I felt emboldened to have a go at the door. It was Andy, from the village.

"You know you're welcome to use the front door?" I said. "It's got a lovely big knocker."

"Cheers, William. I prefer the tradesman's entrance."

"What's the matter? You don't like big knockers?"

Andy's belly laugh rattled the teacups.

"How's young Matthew this morning?"

"Won't shut up. You've created a monster."

"That's the spirit."

I offered Andy elevenses, and we sat at the kitchen table, tucking into the fine apple turnover Mrs Craddoch had delivered.

Andy scooped four heaped teaspoons of sugar into his tea.

"Half the village has been here this morning, offering their support," I said. "It's all very touching."

Andy cleared his throat. "I expect they're wanting to help. On account of the estate's money troubles. Actually, that's why I'm here."

"You haven't brought a casserole, have you? Only we're full to the gunwales."

"I wanted to speak to you about the estate's financial problems."

My chest tightened.

"We wondered if you were planning to sell the village?"

"Oh gosh, no. My family has always felt the village was rightfully part of Buckford. So if you're worried I'll sell it to the Blunts, I never would."

"Actually, William, we were hoping you would sell it to *us*."

"Oh."

"We know you need the capital, and to be honest, we'd like the security—the peace of mind—for ourselves, for our families. I'd like young Matthew to be able to inherit a house, like you inherited yours."

Not sure I'd wish that on the lad, I thought.

I swigged my tea as Andy made his case. He was here representing all eighty tenants. Most wanted the option to buy their cottage, though not all could afford it right away.

I looked into Andy's hopeful face. The people of Newton Bardon had been so loyal and so wonderful to our family over the years. They'd put up with Grandfather's proclivities and my father's eccentricities, and now they were enduring my incompetence. This community was their home as much as it was mine and my family's. But...

"Let me think about it," I said, a knot forming in my stomach. "I need to speak to my accountant."

"That's all we can ask, William. We know you'll always do the right thing by us."

No pressure. Andy downed his tea in one manly gulp and put his mug on the table, his face a beaming smile. I smiled back, but I'm afraid I had to force it.

Chapter 41
Petey

Later that afternoon, I took a break from editing and went looking for William. Eventually, I spotted him sitting on Lady Caroline's Bridge, staring back at the house like a brooding hero from an Emily Brontë fever dream. His face broke into a smile when he saw me walking around the Long Water.

"Been looking for you everywhere."

He pulled me onto his lap, the warmth of his body radiating into mine as he wrapped his arms around me. I brushed his hair from his face, and we kissed.

"You all right?" I asked when we came up for air.

"Big day, really."

"Mourning the loss of your innocence?"

He slapped my butt.

"That's one thing I'm definitely not mourning." His voice was soft. "It's around twenty weeks until Halloween. One hundred and forty-six days to pay the tax bill—or all this is gone. Oh, and the accountant called. We need to find another million."

"You'll pay it," I said firmly. "You're tackling the hard stuff. I'm proud of you. You're going to make it."

He sighed.

"The tenants have asked if they can buy their houses from the estate."

"Well, that's wonderful!"

He shook his head.

"The estate needs ongoing revenue. The rent accounts for forty per cent of my income. If I sell the cottages..."

You'd think his tenants had shot his dog and poisoned the well, the way he was carrying on.

"But it'd be a lot of money," I said, flipping the narrative for him. "You can invest it in other ways to make more."

"Maybe."

I eyeballed him.

"And it's the right thing to do. People should be able to own their own homes."

William rolled his eyes. "All right, steady on, Karl Marx. I know that."

"My grandparents bought their council flat through Right to Buy in the eighties. It was huge for them. Completely changed their lives."

William ran his hand through my hair. His face was still sad.

"You really miss your gran, don't you?"

"More than my mother misses the death penalty." Staying on at Buckford after filming meant I hadn't got home to see Gran. I'd spoken to her on the phone, but I missed her hugs. Suddenly, I felt overwhelmed by a need to see her. "I think I might go down for a few days. See her, see the boys."

William's face fell, and his shoulders slumped. I'd forgotten for a moment I was meant to be listening to his problems right now, not talking about mine.

"Hey, don't worry. We'll find a way to save the estate and help your tenants."

William brightened a little. "We?"

"Of course."

He broke into a wide grin. Like he'd found an extra toy in his Happy Meal and it had completed a treasured set. Suddenly, I was being scooped up and spun around and around, William's lips on mine. When he finally planted me on the ground, his hands gripped my waist.

"Actually, Zoë had a good suggestion." Apparently, William had spoken to half the cast of *The Love Manor* today, and Zoë had recommended opening the house to the public.

"It's a fabulous idea. You can probably get huge grants for doing it too."

William started pacing along the bridge, ideas tumbling out of him. "I do like the thought of breathing a bit of life into the old girl. This place is meant to be buzzing with people. When my parents had the place, this was a real party house."

I sat down on the stone bench, watching him pace. This was when William was most beautiful—when something sparked that enthusiasm in him.

"You need a marketing strategy to sell what makes Buckford unique," I said. An idea struck me. "What would be amazing is if we could bring the history of the place to life."

"You want to do a séance in the family mausoleum?"

I rolled my eyes. "Why don't we re-enact the Battle of Buckford Field again, but on the actual field where it originally happened? Think of the footage. It would make an awesome promo video to help get the punters in, and it'd be a spectacular way to sell the historical importance of the estate."

William stood upright. "Do you think it'd work?"

"I literally produce TV for a living. Believe me, it'll work."

"Then I'm in."

He hadn't hesitated for a second. All the air seemed to leave my chest. My eyes began to sting. I threw my body around his and kissed him like I'd never kissed anyone in my life.

"Golly," he said as my lips left his. "I'm dizzy. What was that for?"

"For believing in me."

William's eyes searched my face, and I knew he understood.

"Why don't we hold the re-enactment on the same day as your father's car club visit?" he said. "It'll look great on camera. I know it'll impress your parents."

"How?"

"Let Edward and Angelica see you doing what you do," he said, "because you are magnificent to watch when you're in the zone. It'll knock their socks off. I know it will."

My chest hollowed again. "You really think so?"

"I do."

I pulled him into another kiss—even more passionate than the last.

"Gosh, that was a real loin-stirrer. What was that one for?"

"For being you. For loving me."

I reached into my pocket and pulled out the message William had left me.

"You found my note?"

"I did."

"I hope I spelt all the kisses right."

The rain started to fall then—heavily, steadily. The house across the water disappeared behind a misty grey curtain.

"We're going to have to wait this out," he said, starting to unbutton my boiler suit.

My hand snaked down inside his waistband. "However will we fill the time, my lord?"

"I have one or two ideas."

* * *

We lay there in the afterglow, the rain still falling around us. Absently, I played with the ring on William's necklace.

"Why don't you wear this?"

William tensed. "Because it's not mine."

"Was it your dad's?"

He nodded. "And his father's before him. It's worn by the baron."

"Aren't you the baron?"

William stared up at the stone ceiling. "I don't feel entitled to wear it. I haven't earned it."

I pulled back to look at him properly. "I think you've fundamentally misunderstood how inherited privilege works in this country. Someone dies, you win the lottery. That's the whole point."

"Great men do great things," William said quietly. "Richard de Valois won battles. The ninth baron built this house. My father created the nature reserve. What have I done?"

"Inspired an entire village to make casseroles? Convinced half the cast of *The Love Manor* to donate their talents and invest their money?"

"That's not me," William said. "That's the house."

"Bollocks. Do you know how much I'd kill to have the people in my life believe in me the way everyone believes in you? You're probably more qualified to wear that ring than half the men who've ever worn it."

"Steady on, those are still my ancestors."

I reached for the clasp of his necklace. "Just put it on."

William's hands wrapped firmly around mine. "No. Not until I've earned it."

His eyes were steely, determined. There was a grit in him I hadn't seen before. I didn't agree with his logic, but I had to admire it. The stupid sexy stubborn himbo.

Chapter 42
William

It was a Friday afternoon and Petey and I were in the folly, waiting for Sunny and Ludo to arrive. Guests would be an essential distraction from shagging, which I had taken to with the zeal of a convert. We'd had so much sex since Saturday night, we'd had to drive into the village twice to buy bedroom supplies, and Petey had been unable to bend over with confidence since about Tuesday. I was hovering at the porthole window, waiting to see a taxi coming down the drive. Petey was busy at his laptop, working on new show ideas to pitch to Indira. What he didn't know was, I had a surprise for him—and keeping it had almost sent me stark raving bonkers. Not a little bit bonkers. I mean the-fifth-baron-plucking-his-own-fingernail-out-to-use-as-a-quill level of bonkers. There were more guests in that taxi than Petey was anticipating.

"What about a show based on making cosplay costumes?" he said, apparently struck by inspiration. "I've just watched a video of a guy who made a fully transformable *Transformers* outfit. It's incredible."

Inspiration struck me then too. "What would it take to get you to dress up in a slutty little vest and a pair of Daisy Dukes, like Megan Fox in that movie?"

Petey's eyes narrowed. "I feel like we've accidentally unlocked a core memory for teenage William there."

I let my eyebrows bounce. "I'm not hearing a no."

The taxi appeared on the horizon. I nearly burst out of my own skin.

"They're here!"

Petey dashed out to greet them so fast his shadow was still on the stairs while his body was bounding across the carriage court. I raced to catch up to him and was bolting out the front door when I heard Petey shouting, "Gran! Gran!"

His arms were wrapped so tight around the old girl's frail-looking frame, he might have snapped her.

"What are you doing here?"

Petey's gran, Peggy, clasped her hands to her grandson's face.

"Orright, my boy? Thought I'd better check in on you, didn't I? Make sure you're eating right. Maybe pocket a bit of posh silver to flog down the Portobello Road."

Petey laughed. I did, too—rather more nervously. But it brought untold joy to the old ticker to know how happy seeing his gran made Petey. I introduced myself to Sunny—who didn't even attempt to bow—and made myself useful by helping him get the cases out of the boot. Jonty's older brother, Ludo, paid the cabby, and we said our hellos and well-mets as the taxi drove off. Then the three of us turned as one to look at the family reunion still underway in the carriage court.

Petey had tears streaming down his cheeks.

"Bugger me," Sunny said. "That's one of the signs of the apocalypse, isn't it?"

"I can definitely hear frogs," Ludo added. "We could be in real trouble here."

I shook my head. "Where does he get this reputation from? He's been blubbing every five minutes since he got here."

Sunny and Ludo stared at me in apparent disbelief.

"Someone's finally cracked him," Sunny said.

"I doubt he's still under warranty," Ludo added.

Petey, realising he had an audience, finally released Peggy. Mentally, I was patting down all her bones, looking for fractures. At last, he introduced us. Peggy made to curtsy.

"No, don't do that," Petey and I said in unison. That made me grin.

Petey pointed to his gran's knitting bag, sitting on top of the cases.

"Are you... staying?" he asked.

I put my hand on Petey's shoulder. "Peggy has graciously agreed to be our guest for the next week. She's going back with your folks in the Jag next Sunday."

"You're kidding?"

"Surprise!"

"Oh, William!" He threw his arms and legs around me, kissing me. Now I was the one risking snapped bones.

"For a fake engagement, things seem to be going remarkably well," Ludo observed.

"Is he trying to suck out a filling?" Sunny added.

"Ain't it bloomin' marvellous?" Peggy said.

I liked her immediately.

* * *

Sunny and Ludo were here to check out the house, specifically the chapel, to see if it might work for their wedding. So, after cups of tea all around, I launched into the tour I'd been mentally rehearsing all morning. If this went well, it might herald Buckford's future as a wedding venue for hire. I was dressed in what Petey now called my uniform—a crisp white Oxford shirt, tan chinos, and the russet tie that I refused to get rid of, even though it bore heavy scars from two nights earlier, when Petey had tied me to a banister with it before whipping my nipples with a riding crop.

"This is the Great Hall," I announced, gesturing upward as we entered. "The chandeliers were originally designed for Napoleon's palace at Malmaison. Supposedly, he had them based on Josephine's breasts—which, I take it, must have been absolutely gigantic and reeked of tallow. They were electrified in my grandfather's day. The chandeliers, that is, not Josephine's breasts. Although with Grandad's reputation, that would have been advisable too."

I caught Petey trying not to laugh and felt my confidence grow.

"Is that a Gainsborough?" Ludo asked, pointing at the huge landscape above the fireplace.

I said it was, feeling rather pleased he'd noticed. I pointed to the lake. "It's a hay cart crossing the River Buck. A couple of years before Capability Brown diverted it to create the Long Water."

"Is it one of the works you're selling?" Ludo was studying it with real appreciation.

A lead weight formed in my gut. "No. Yes. No. Well, only if things get desperate. Most of the artwork is dreadful, but that one feels like it belongs with the house."

Petey's hand slid into mine. It was enough to steady me.

As we moved through to the West Drawing Room, Peggy's arm was hooked into Petey's, and the way he kept glancing down at her, checking she was all right, made me want to kiss him all over again.

"This is the perfect breakout area for your guests when they've had enough of dancing," I explained to Sunny and Ludo. "There's a door right out onto the sunken garden, which was originally designed for courting couples. Or if you really want to put your back into it and properly ruin somebody, it's only a short walk to the hedge maze."

"Very posh," Peggy said. "We used to make do with an alleyway round the back of the boozer if we wanted a tumble."

Everyone's jaw hit the floor—and Peggy screeched with laughter.

The chapel was where I truly hoped the house would sell herself. It was on the ground floor, tucked near the stables, and the light through the stained glass always made it feel somehow both ancient and alive. Generations of Buckfords had been married here, but never anyone from outside the family.

"The chapel can seat eighty guests comfortably," I said, walking Sunny and Ludo up to the business end while Peggy and Petey settled into a pew at the back. "The altar is fourteenth century—salvaged from a monastery after the dissolution. The stained glass is all original." I was pointing up to my ancestor, Richard de Valois, kneeling before the king—light shining gold through his crown—feeling like I was making excellent headway, when I felt something damp under my arm. I was sweating like a hog in December who'd realised his calendar was remarkably clear in January. I clamped my arms to my sides.

"It's gorgeous," Ludo said, pointing to the window.

Sunny was squinting. "Why's he giving the king a head job?"

Ludo whacked him.

"And the acoustics in here are incredible," I said. "When my sister got married here a few years ago, she had a string quartet. Couldn't have sounded more magnificent if your head was stuffed inside the cello."

Sunny looked around the chapel, taking it all in—the carved pews, the stone columns, the pools of candy-coloured light drenching the floor. Then he glanced at Ludo, and something passed between them. One of those couple moments where an entire conversation happens in a flash of eyes.

Sunny turned back to me. "We're sold."

My heart almost stopped. "Really?"

"Really." Sunny blushed, his face going almost as red as his hair. "Actually, we sort of assumed it would be perfect, and—"

Ludo chimed in. "We've already applied for the marriage licence, listing Buckford as the venue. All we needed was to confirm the date with your availability."

"When are you thinking?" I asked, nervously. "Not to put too fine a point on it, it has to be this side of Halloween."

"Six weeks from now," Ludo said.

Relief flooded through me.

"Will you have us?" Sunny asked.

"Of course!" I threw my arms out to pull them into a hug, got a whiff of my "eau de Dub-Dub," and clamped them back to my sides before I knocked anyone out. "We'd be honoured."

We shook hands on it. Petey jumped up from his pew and hugged me. Sunny and Ludo were wrapped in an embrace. Even Peggy was clapping and cheering. I hoped, desperately, these boys would be the first of many public weddings at Buckford. I'd been through the numbers with the estate's new accountant. With the venue hire, accommodation, and food packages we'd designed, the baseline profit after expenses and tax on each wedding would add £32,000 to the coffers. Ten or twelve of those a year would be a huge boost to the Buckford economy. If I got the chance. I had to save the estate first.

Chapter 43
Petey

Bramley had prepared a three-course meal and raided the cellar. He was in his element—suited up like a proper old-fashioned butler, with black coat-tails and white gloves, giving us the full silver service treatment.

Afterwards, we retired to the East Drawing Room for brandy or, in my case, a glass of sherry—as my tastes don't run to piss-coloured methylated spirits. Everyone was blotto, including Gran, who could really put it away. She and Bunny tucked themselves in a corner, bonding over Reggie and Ronnie Kray for some unknown reason—the pair of them were getting along like a forest fire. Sunny, Ludo, William, and I were sprawled across a couple of sofas. We had worked out Sunny and Ludo were old friends of William's godparents—they'd all worked together to uncover a corruption scandal at the heart of government a couple of years earlier. Apparently, Karma was a demon of the dark web. It's always the ones you least expect.

"So, how long until you have to pitch to Indira?" Sunny asked.

I grimaced. "Two weeks."

"You don't look keen. I thought this was your big dream?"

"It is. But I don't have an idea big enough yet."

"What's your best one, at the moment?" Ludo asked.

"A show called *The Great Real Estate Gamble*. Picture this. An apartment block. Six identical flats. Six couples. All competing to renovate their apartment as best they can on a tight budget. The catch? The renovation decisions they make are decided on the flip of a coin, or the roll of a dice. They're making big design decisions based on a constant game of chance. Which wallpaper? It's heads or tails. Do they get to buy the tiles they want? Only if they roll a six. The twist? If they win their game of chance, they can either buy the wallpaper or the tiles they want, or they can choose to sabotage their competitors instead. At the end, all the flats go on the market, and the one that gets the highest offer wins."

Ludo sucked air in through his teeth. Sunny was doing his best to smile supportively, but he seemed to have developed a tic in his right eye.

"It's terrible, isn't it?"

"Nooooo!" Ludo said, too quickly. "Jolly clever. I'd certainly never have thought of it. Would you, Sunny?"

Sunny glared at his fiancé. "I would watch *any* TV show you made, Petey Boy. I'm sure it'll be huge."

I knew it wasn't a strong concept. Not yet. But it could be. I needed time to work on it.

The conversation turned to Sunny's old employer, *The Bulletin*, and its obsession with the Bisexual Baron Buckford.

"It was bad enough when it was me," William said. "But when they went after Petey, too, I saw red. Thank God we managed to kill it off."

Sunny looked at me with concern, his journalist's instincts obviously kicking in. "What does he mean they went after you?"

I glanced over at Gran to make sure she wasn't listening. She was still deep in conversation with Bunny.

"Your old mate Gary Ashworth says he's got people on the record telling stories about me," I said, quietly. "Visiting Vauxhall."

Sunny's and Ludo's eyes went wide.

"He threatened to print it unless we gave him a better story," William added, his hand grasping mine. "Luckily, we did."

"Accidentally, mind you," I said.

Sunny's face was grim. "It might have killed it for now. But if Gary Ashworth has that story in his back pocket, he'll keep threatening to pull it out every time he wants something."

"That's blackmail!" William said.

"That's how it works," Sunny said. "Do you know he definitely has the story?"

I shook my head. "No idea. It could be a bluff."

"Seems like a weird thing for him to know," Ludo said.

"I agree," Sunny replied. "But either way, there's only one thing you can do. Get a superinjunction."

"Does that work?"

Sunny nodded. "I can't see why not. You would not believe the tales of affairs, children born on the wrong side of the bed, and eye-watering personal proclivities journalists know about but can't print. You'd be horrified by the names of the beloved national figures involved."

"Like who?" William said, leaning in for the gossip.

"I can't tell you."

"Why not?"

Sunny frowned. "Superinjunctions."

"Ah. Yes, I see your point."

Ludo cleared his throat. "If there's no public interest defence, you can jolly well suppress most things."

"You're not public figures," Sunny added. "So I imagine you might have grounds for an injunction for privacy reasons." He took a sip of his brandy and turned to look at me directly. "Know any good lawyers, Petey?"

I groaned. "How are we defining 'good'?"

I looked at William. It was there in his eyes—the question, the hope, the understanding. He knew how I felt about asking my family for anything. I couldn't call my father. I couldn't admit I needed his help. I couldn't face his disappointment, his disdain. I'd rather let Gary Ashworth print and be damned.

There was a loud clapping of hands, and everyone turned to look at Bunny Winters.

"Right, who's for Scrabble?"

* * *

Bramley drove Sunny and Ludo to Leicester, where they were staying with Sunny's mum, and I took Gran upstairs to the yellow bedroom. She looked frail, but she was up those stairs like a rat up a drainpipe. Couldn't wait to get into her nightie and roll around in that four-poster bed, complaining someone had put a pea under her mattress. I tucked her in and sat on the edge of the bed.

"I wish the girls from the market could see me now," she said. "Imagine the look on Dolly Nollis's face, seeing Margaret Topham lying here in fine sheets in a grand country house, like Lady Muck. That'd shut her up. The smug cow."

"Isn't she dead?"

"Not dead enough. I hope she's up there watching." Gran stuck a middle finger up at the ceiling. It was fun seeing her like this. She almost seemed youthful.

"What do Edward and Angelica think about... this whole situation?" I asked. "You being here. *Me* being here?"

"Petey Boy, your parents are the biggest snobs I've ever met. They think you're marrying a baron. They're delighted."

"But their names keep appearing in the papers alongside mine."

Gran laughed. "I think having an aristocrat for a future son-in-law makes up for it. Your father's walking around like he's being elevated to the House of Lords."

Of course my father was making this all about him.

"How do you think they'll take it when they find out it's not real?" I asked.

Gran was quiet for a moment, studying my face. Then she said, softly: "Isn't it real? It looks pretty real to me."

I opened my mouth to argue, then closed it. She was right. The engagement was fake, but the feelings were definitely real. What had started as a lie had, somewhere along the way, become the truest thing in my life.

"You done well, ain't you, Petey Boy?"

My chest burnt, a blush heating my face.

"He's amazing, isn't he?"

Gran laughed. "If they'd built them like that when I was young, my hips would have been completely shattered by the time I was your age."

"Gran!" Now my face was so red I must have looked like a lobster in the pot.

She slapped my hand. "Don't become a prude now, just because you landed a toff. You think I don't know what you used to get up to with boys in the bushes down in Weavers Fields, when you should have been upstairs doing your homework?"

I stared at her, horrified.

"Don't look so surprised, Petey Boy. I might be old now, but I was young in the swinging sixties."

I tried to shake off what she'd said. We sat in silence, as the horrors of my misspent teen years came flooding back.

"How's it gonna work, then, Petey Boy?"

It was the question I'd been avoiding. "I don't know, Gran."

"Has he got a place in London?"

I shook my head.

"I thought all the toffs had a big gaff in the West End. Like in *Upstairs, Downstairs*."

"William hasn't been to London for three years."

"Hasn't been to London? But it's the centre of the world."

I shrugged, not sure how to explain it. "He... seems to think it's cursed. Or he's cursed, perhaps."

Gran threw her head back in disbelief. "You'll have to fix that, Petey Boy. What kind of future can you have together if he's scared of your home town?"

The dull ache I'd been ignoring for weeks sharpened. Trust Gran to come right out with the practicalities.

"Oh dear, have I put my foot in it?"

I brought her hand to my mouth and kissed it. "No. You're right."

My whole life was in London. Gran, my career, my friends. I belonged in London, and William clearly belonged here. What was I meant to do? Give everything up and move to Buckford?

"You'll work it out," Gran said. "If you boys want to be together, you'll find a way. But I'll tell you this for free, Petey Boy. The way that lad looks at you, he's well and truly gone. I mean, he called your old man to get permission to bust me out of prison. He sent your mates to collect me, arranged the train ticket, and he's given me the nicest room in the house. It's bigger than the flat where I spent my whole married life. He's mad for you. What's more, you're mad for him. That's got to count for something."

"How'd you figure?"

"Because you're already speaking like a proper toff."

"Oh, piss off."

"You are!"

"You're drunk, Margaret." She was right, though. I'd found myself needing to speak like a London roadman less and less. I hadn't even noticed it at first, but the more comfortable I got at Buckford, the less natural it felt, and it had melted away. I leant down and kissed Gran on her forehead. "You get some sleep. I love you."

"I love you, too, Petey Boy."

I turned off the lamp and slipped out of the room.

Chapter 44
William

There were footsteps on the stairs, and Petey's face appeared. He was stunning. Freshly showered, hair still damp, in tiny black boxer briefs.

"Aw, those aren't Daisy Dukes."

"I'm not ruining my only pair of jeans so you can live out your teenage fantasy."

"It's a very *adult* fantasy."

"I bet. Sometimes I forget you're bisexual."

"Who said I'm bisexual?" We both knew the answer.

"Aren't you?"

I shook my head. "I'm Petey-sexual."

He smiled, and I held my arms out. He climbed onto the mattress and collapsed back into me. I wrapped him up in a hug, rolling onto him and smothering him—showering him in kisses. It was true. "Petey" was as much definition as my sexuality would ever need. I loved him so much my body ached. So the fact we only had another week or so left together before he would have to return to London had started haunting my thoughts like a spectre. I tried to shake it off, not wanting Petey to sense anything was wrong.

"Can I say," I said, "your gran is magnificent."

Petey smiled. "She's my favourite person in the whole world."

"I know. But, I mean, I've literally never known anyone to beat Mum at Scrabble, and your gran did it three times on the hoof. It was spectacular."

"Your mum took it well, I thought."

"There were twice as many tiles on the board as there should be by the end of that last game. How on earth did Peggy win?"

"Oh, she cheated."

"No way!"

"I gave Gran the heads-up, so she volunteered to score. She's a maths whizz. Kept adding percentages onto her score when your mum wasn't looking."

"She out-cheated Bunny Winters? Incredible." I kissed my way around Petey's neck. "I can see where you get your smarts from."

Petey smiled. It was beautiful. I smooched my way across his body. With everything going on, it had felt good to bask in the simple pleasure of family. But even better to be alone and basking in the pleasures of Petey.

"You did great today," Petey said. "I'm very proud of you."

Pride burst from my chest like that alien in, well, *Alien*.

"Thank you."

"I can't believe my gran is here," he said. "I don't know how to thank you."

"I do." For a split second, I toyed with asking him to ask his father about getting that superinjunction Sunny told us about. Then at least the press would be off our backs and I could breathe a little easier. But it would have meant a fight, and that would have ruined an amazing day. Instead, I slipped my hand under the pillow and pulled out the filthy note Petey had left in my father's desk drawer. "I thought we could start here."

Petey smiled, his fingers reaching up to curl around the piece of paper. "You want to *start* there? We're growing in confidence, aren't we?" His legs wound around my back, and I grabbed his waist, pulling him tight against me. "How about we build up to it," he said, his mouth hot against mine.

"Could do," I said, the fabric of my boxers sliding against his hardness. I wormed my hand inside the elastic of his briefs and tugged them down. "But a promise is a promise. We keep our word in this house."

Petey's laugh turned into a gasp as I kissed my way down his body—and then we didn't need any more words at all. But even as I wrapped myself around him, held him, filled him, loved him, the spectre was there.

Chapter 45
Petey

A drone shot of Jonty and Lola kissing on the steps of Buckford Hall slowly pulled back to reveal the house in all its twinkling nighttime glory. Music swirled around our winners, then the screen cut to black and the credits rolled. Haruto and Thandiwe erupted into whoops of applause.

"That's it, we're done," Thandiwe cheered, dragging me out of my chair so we could dance in the middle of the Old Coach House. I spun her around under my arm. She was really going for it. I couldn't keep up. She frowned.

"I thought you were gay, why you dancing so white?"

"I'm sorry, I'm tall. I dance like a giraffe on ice."

A champagne cork popped. Haruto had found a bottle in the fridge.

"Since when did we have champagne?"

He bounced his shoulders. "It had a note on it from your boyfriend."

I dashed over, plucked the envelope from the tangle of wire and foil, and ripped it open.

Congratulations on the last day of your edit! That overpowering smell is impending BAFTA glory! (Actually, it's probably horse shit. But underneath that, I definitely detect strong undertones of BAFTA.) So proud of you. WW xxxxxxx.

God, he was so thoughtful. My lip quivered. Haruto shoved a glass of bubbles into my hand, and Thandiwe switched to a party playlist. The landline rang. Haruto answered it. I couldn't believe we had finished. In a week, Indira would watch our edit. Looking at what we had created, I knew we had a hit on our hands. She was going to love it. At least I hoped so—because I was now officially unemployed.

"Derek wants his duck back," Haruto said, rousing me from my thoughts. "Asked to come up tomorrow. I said that was fine."

I looked at him.

"Tomorrow?"

"Is that OK?"

Tomorrow was the summer solstice. The stone circle would be mobbed with revellers, the drive would be full of my father's Jaguar car club, and two hundred battle re-enactors would be pretending to belt the shit out of one another on Home Field. The estate couldn't be busier if we turned it into an IKEA and offered free pony rides to the kids in the crèche.

"Sure," I said. What was one more person to add to the chaos?

William marched past the window without stopping to wave or touch me up. Something had to be wrong. I stuck my head out the door and caught him just before he disappeared into the stables.

"You OK?"

He turned to look at me. "I need to get out of the house. I'm going for a ride." His voice was tight, and it worried me.

"Has something happened?" I walked towards him. "Has Gran said something, because she can be a bit of a menace—"

"Your gran's fine. Last I saw her she was playing Hungry Hungry Hippos at the Dower House with Mum."

I reached for his hand. "Then what's up? You're scaring me."

"Wetherby's Auction House has set the date for the art sale. It's going to be held here, in the Great Hall, on the twenty-first of September."

My shoulders relaxed.

"But that's great news." And it was. *The Love Manor* would already be going to air by then, which was excellent publicity, and it gave the cheques time to clear before Halloween, when William had to pay HMRC.

"They want me to do some press for the release of the catalogue."

"OK." That seemed logical. I waited for the great revelation that explained William's mouth looking like someone had pissed in it.

"I'm not doing it."

"William—"

"I don't know anything about the art. What am I supposed to say?"

"You say whatever you need to say to generate interest in the auction. Tell your story—"

"Everyone's already heard my story," William snapped.

I stepped back. *This* wasn't the William I was used to. "If you want to save Buckford, you have to tackle the hard stuff."

His arms flew wide, his face red. "What do you think I've been doing day in and day out?"

I tried to hug him, but he pulled away.

"I want a quiet life," he said.

"You can have one. Once we get through the auction."

"Don't you remember what Sunny said? If we go seeking media attention, we give them carte blanche to invade our lives forever."

"That's not exactly what he said—"

"I can't risk it."

"It's a few interviews about some paintings. You don't have to talk about us, your family, or—"

"It won't be enough. They'll want more. I'll end up piling on more lies to cover the ridiculous lie we're already caught in. I'm trying to protect us before things get worse. One of us has to."

The words landed like a slap. My kindness evaporated.

"I don't need you to protect me."

"You do, Petey." He was agitated, arms flailing. "Have you got the injunction Sunny mentioned? Have you called your father?"

My jaw clenched. I hadn't. He knew that. We hadn't spoken about it, but he knew it.

"How dare you?" If I could have picked him up and flung him into his dung cart, I would have.

"I'm not judging you for it," he said, hands pumping invisible brakes.

"You just did. What do you know about it? What do you know about any of it?"

"I know that you can't ask for his help." William's stormy eyes softened. "And I don't blame you for that. I don't question it. But if that door is closed to us, then the only door open to us is privacy. So no, I don't want to do any interviews."

My God. This arsehole. Even when he was being a total dick, he was trying to be honourable. He'd white-knighted me into a corner right as I was dialling up my fire-breathing-dragon setting to "toasty."

"William, I'm sorry, I wasn't—"

But he was already shaking his head, already backing toward the stables.

"I need to clear my head. I'm going for a ride."

I watched him disappear through the barn-style doors, fisting my hands in my pockets to stop them trembling. I didn't chase him. I turned on my heels and went back into the Old Coach House.

"Is everything all right?" Thandiwe asked.

Haruto handed me my glass of champagne. "You look like you could use this."

I downed it in one. "Have we got anything stronger?"

Haruto refilled my glass. Thandiwe turned down the music. This should have been my moment of triumph, but instead, I felt like I'd dropped something precious and watched it smash on the floor.

Chapter 46
William

I rode Achilles hard across Home Field and through the ancient oak woodland to Buckford Hill—the place I always found it easiest to breathe. But when I got there, I found three old women dressed in rags, standing in the stone circle. As a fantasy reader, it rang alarm bells. I dismounted, letting Achilles roam, and nodded at each of them in turn.

"Peggy. Aunty Karma. Mother."

Mum rushed over to me, raking her hands through my hair. "William, my poor baby, have you been crying?"

"Certainly not, you batty old crone." I pulled myself free of her, hoping to restore a little dignity. "You're perfectly aware it's high pollen season. It's hay fever. What are you all doing up here, anyway? You appear to have forgotten your cauldron."

"Preparing for the solstice," Mother said.

Aunty Karma grabbed my jaw and peered into my eyes like she was inspecting my soul.

"We are at the summer's peak, William. Before the turn to darkness. Everything must change."

I squinted. "Is that Byron? I was never very good with the Romantic poets."

"There's a lot weighing on your spirit, William," Aunty Karma said. "You should come along tonight. Let the night air cleanse you before the dawn that must come."

I wasn't in the mood for this batshittery. I was in the mood for wallowing in self-pity. But Karma was right, there was a lot weighing me down. A fresh wave of tears spilt hot down my cheeks.

"What is it, darling?" Mum said.

I clenched my jaw to stop my lip trembling—and it all tumbled out. Everything I was worried about. The estate, the tax bill, the auction, the bloody press, the fact we'd lied to everyone about our engagement.

"Is that everything?" Karma asked.

Mum shook her head. "Come on, spit it out."

"He's finished his big edit," I said, finally. "He's going to film the promo for Buckford tomorrow and work on it next week, but then his reason for being here is gone. This time next week, he'll be on his way to London, and I don't want to lose him. But I want him to achieve his dreams. He's so determined about his pitch for Indira that I can't see a way for us to build a life together—not when I so clearly need to be here. I love him. And I can't have it all."

"Have you asked Petey Boy what *he* wants?" Peggy said.

"Pardon?"

"Not being funny, but have you two actually discussed what you want? Or have you been so busy playing hide the sausage you forgot to ask?"

I sniffled, then wiped my nose on my sleeve, giving myself time to process this extraordinary statement.

"I know what he wants," I said. "He spends all his free time coming up with TV show ideas that'll take him back to London."

"So he told you he wants to go back to London?"

I nodded. "As good as."

Mother was shaking her head. "Oh, William. I raised you to be smarter than that. The trouble with you, darling, is you think love means shielding people from hurt—like that knight in your books." Her voice softened. "But you couldn't shield your father or your brother. You can't shield Petey either. You have to trust him to make the right choice for himself. That's love."

The words landed like a punch to the gut. I looked away, blinking the tears from my eyes.

"But what if he makes the wrong choice?" I was acutely aware of how small and pathetic I sounded.

"Which choice is the wrong one?" Peggy asked.

"If he chooses—" But I didn't have the answer, and that was the problem. What was right for me wasn't right for him.

Aunty Karma squeezed my forearm. "The strength of any marriage—"

"We're not married," I muttered. "We're not even engaged."

She waved it away. "The strength of any marriage of souls is in the togetherness. Taking on everything *together*. As a partnership."

"That's it," Mum said. "You need to work together, otherwise you're not really partners, you're two people circulating in each other's orbit."

"So, you think I should..." I let the sentence trail off, inviting one of these witches to deliver their words of wisdom with a little more clarity.

"Talk to him, you bloody idiot," Aunty Karma said.

"Ask him what he wants," Mum said.

"You might be surprised," Peggy added.

Imagine the power these women could summon if they'd brought their bloody cauldron.

* * *

The stable yard was quiet when I returned. The Old Coach House was empty; everyone had gone. The champagne bottle sat abandoned on the desk. Petey wasn't in the folly either. Eventually, I found him in the East Drawing Room, curled up on the sofa with his laptop. He looked up when I entered, his eyebrows raised almost in a dare. The guilt made my chest ache.

"Hi," I said, somewhat gingerly.

"Hi."

I crossed the room and sat beside him on the sofa, resting a hand on his socked foot.

"I'm sorry," I said. "For how I spoke to you. For trying to make decisions for you. For bringing up your father. All of it. I was freaking out. I'm sorry."

Petey's eyes softened. He closed his laptop and put it on the coffee table. "You pulled away from me. You've never done that before. You scared me, William."

"I know. I'm sorry." I reached for his hand. "I was scared too."

"About the interviews?"

"No. I mean, yes. But not really." I took a deep breath. "I'm scared you're leaving, and I don't know how to ask you to stay. I love you, Petey. I want a future with you. I want you here, at Buckford, with me. Not because I need to protect you and I can do that here, but because I can't imagine my life without you in it."

Petey's thumb rubbed the back of my hand.

"I've been so happy here with you. It's been magical. All of it."

Hope flared in my chest—but then Petey wouldn't meet my eyes.

"But I can't stay. My whole career is in London. I've worked so hard for it. I can't give it up. What if we don't work out? Could you imagine? Then I'd have lost *everything*. My parents already think I'm a disaster."

Sod his bloody parents. I wanted to tear strips off them for what they'd done to this beautiful man and his sense of himself and his place in the world.

"I've never wanted a future with anyone before," he said. "Well, except for Timothée Chalamet, but that was a phase and a very confusing time."

I nodded. "That movie has a lot to answer for."

"No kidding. The point is, I never even let myself imagine a future with anyone until I met you. Now all I want is a future with you. But I can't see how it works, how we can both be happy. We might have to do the long-distance thing for a while. See how it goes." The thought of it killed me—but at least it wasn't the end. He wasn't giving up on us. That gave me hope. He must have seen the strain on my face. "Tackle the hard stuff, remember?"

"We'll find a way," I said, sliding down onto the rug and onto one knee. "I give you my word, my liege."

Petey smiled. It was small and sad—then cheeky. "I can't even tell you how cringey that is. Every single time. Shivers."

"I know. But it's a whole thing now. I can't stop it."

Petey pulled me into a kiss that tasted like relief and melancholy.

"But I am going to have to go back to London next week," he said. "I have to start looking for work. But I… don't know when I'll be back after that."

My heart clenched. "I know."

Petey tucked a stray lock of hair behind my ear. "I'm not going to disappear on you, you know?" he said.

"Again, you mean?"

"Ouch." He held out his little finger. "When it's time to go, I swear, we'll talk about it. Properly. Together."

"Together," I echoed, hooking my finger into his.

I crawled back up onto the sofa and slid in behind Petey, wrapping my arms around him, feeling him sink back into me—like we could stop time if we held each other tight enough.

Outside, preparations for the solstice were underway. Tomorrow, the estate would be full of people, full of noise, full of celebration. But for now, it was the two of us, and the heart-rending knowledge that sometimes love can't solve everything—but it's enough to keep you trying.

Chapter 47
Petey

I woke to an empty bed and a madhouse. The kitchen had been turned into a makeshift cafeteria for the solstice revellers, most of whom were still encamped on the Great Lawn. Bunny was ladling out soup into cups for grateful pagans. Spotting me, she waved me over.

"Peter, darling, would you like vegetable broth or miso?" she said as Karma shoved a recyclable heat-proof cup into one of my hands and a bread roll into the other. "They're exactly the same, but with the miso you've got a one-in-fifty chance of scoring a tiny piece of tofu."

I wasn't awake enough for this. I opted for the miso. Mine was tofu-free. No favouritism here. Then I spied my gran making tea. She was in her eighties, had been up since before dawn, had climbed a hill to watch the sun rise, and now she was doling out cups of tea and chattering away to the punters like she'd spent her life running a greasy spoon. Where did she find the energy? I kissed her on the cheek, and she introduced me to a couple of pagans.

"This is my grandson. He's going to be a duchess."

The women giggled, and I rolled my eyes. "Don't mind her. She's off her meds."

"You cheeky bugger!"

I had to get on. It was going to be a big day—and the filming wasn't the only reason. William was going to meet my parents. Dread dragged through my guts like an anchor.

"Careful you don't wear yourself out, Gran. You're not as young as you used to be."

"Don't you worry about me. I'd much rather be doing this than rotting in front of a telly in prison." The other women's eyeballs boggled. "Besides, Bunny says she knows the perfect way for us all to unwind once we're done."

Why did that make me nervous?

I headed for the Old Coach House, where Haruto and Thandiwe were waiting for me. I'd asked them to stay an extra day to help me on this shoot. I was paying them cash in hand. They were both heading back to London and unemployment until their next gig came up, so they'd jumped at it. I was very grateful. The carriage court was filled with Range Rovers, trucks, and horse floats. In the stable yard, dozens of people were grooming horses, preparing them for the day's big re-enactment. Some of the people were already wearing their Tudor-style liveries. I searched for William but couldn't find him.

"If you're looking for your fella," a stranger called out, "he's setting up tents in the field."

I waved a bread roll at him in thanks and dashed back to the Old Coach House as quickly as I could without spilling my soup. As I marched through the door, two faces turned to look at me. Haruto and Thandiwe already had their cameras in hand, going through their checks.

"We need to start filming, guys," I said. "It's bonkers out there."

"I know," Thandiwe said. "Have you seen the Great Lawn?"

I hadn't.

Haruto was shaking his head. "They're literally dancing around maypoles."

I felt a buzz of electricity in my gut. My producer's instinct was telling me we had something very special on our hands.

"Film it," I said. "Film it all. Whatever happens today, I want *everything* on tape. We need to be everywhere."

* * *

A couple of hours later, I had cleared the last of the horse floats out of the carriage court to make way for the arrival of my parents and the North London Jaguar Car Club. I had also set up my camera on a tripod, framing the shot to capture the convoy's arrival. I pressed the button on my headset.

"Haruto, is the drone up?"

"Affirmative."

A glint of something sparkled on the horizon, catching my eye. I looked up to see the first of the Jags coming down the drive. My father's Jag. My stomach was churning like my nerves were holding a rave. I thought I might barf. I hit record right as someone slapped my arse.

"You're so sexy in that headset."

I turned to see William. He winked. He was wearing a green tweed suit, hair neatly combed down into place under a matching flat cap, looking every bit the lord of the manor. I'd never seen him look so... aristocratic. I laughed. He frowned.

"Why are you dressed like that?"

"We're putting on a show, aren't we?"

"You're going to be in a suit of armour later. How many ridiculous outfits have you got planned for this video?"

"I meant a show for your parents. This is what they're expecting, isn't it?"

I looked at him. "Oh my God, you're nervous."

"Of course I'm nervous, they're your parents." At least we were in this together.

"So, you've dressed up like Toad of Toad Hall to impress them? What's next? Are you planning to lend my father your best driving goggles? Have you hired a Labrador for the occasion?"

Bramley emerged from the house dressed in full Buckford livery, carrying a tray of sherry glasses to offer around.

I couldn't contain my laughter.

"Stop it," William said. "I'm trying to make a good impression, all right?"

"You look like a walking advertisement for the Tory party." I kissed him on the cheek. The convoy was nearly at the carriage court, and I could hear the drone buzzing overhead. My hands were shaking now. I really hoped Haruto and Thandiwe were getting all this. "You better take your place, my lord. You *don't* need to impress them, you numpty. They were already fawning over you before they met you. I'm the one who's meant to be impressing them today, remember?"

There was a cackle of laughter from high above the carriage court, and I looked up to see Gran and Bunny leaning out a second-storey gabled window, still dressed like aged nymphs, waving down at us. William waved back.

"You say that," he said out of the side of his mouth. "But at some point, quite soon, your parents are going to realise my mother and my godmother have got your grandmother royally stoned."

"What?"

"And it might take all the tweedy respectability we can muster to get ourselves out of that one."

William took his place on Buckford Hall's steps and—head reeling, at a loss what else to do—I turned my camera around to capture him waving and smiling as the cars parked up.

My parents climbed out of my father's 1967 Series 1 E-Type roadster. They, too, were in tweed. "Oh, for Christ's sake," I muttered. My father took off his leather driving gloves and strode over to meet William. Mother came around the car and joined him. They bowed and curtsied.

"No, please, don't do that," I heard William say. "We don't stand on ceremony here."

I couldn't see their faces, but I could imagine my parents' horror. Ceremony was what they were all about. "You're practically family," William added—and my parents' backs straightened. Well played, my lord. My parents hadn't even spotted me. My whole body was tingling with nerves. I shoved my hands in my pockets to still them, but they were shaking so bad I looked like I was having a wank, so I removed them again.

"How was the drive up, Sir Edward?"

"Good clear run. Noticed the handbrake's a bit dicky again when we stopped at the Northampton services, but nothing material."

"Yoooooohooooooo, Edwaaaaard!"

Everyone looked up to see Gran hanging out the window. My father waved up to her uncomfortably.

"I hope my mother hasn't been too much trouble," I heard him say.

"Not at all! We've loved having her here. Peggy fits right in. She and my mother are thick as thieves."

Were my parents going to spot me at *any* point? Were they going to look for me? Clearly not. William waved me over, and I sidled up beside him.

"Here he is, the man of the moment—my hero," William said. He put an arm round me and kissed my cheek.

"Hello, Mother. Father." I tried, but I couldn't put any warmth into it.

"Oh, Peter, why are you dressed in those tatty old overalls? Couldn't you have made an effort? You knew we were coming."

William squeezed me tighter. "Doesn't he look fabulous in his uniform. You know whenever Petey is boiler-suited up like Churchill, he means business." William leant in conspiratorially to my father. "I'll show you the Churchill Bedroom later. And, Sir Edward, remind me to show you the stack of empties the great man left behind. The fourteenth baron was so astonished he kept them all, stacked up in the cellar like a shrine. It's not on the usual tour." My father was preening now. "I hear you like a nice Bordeaux. We can grab a 1995 Château Margaux while we're down there." William was playing my father like a fiddle. He squeezed my shoulder again. "Petey Boy's on the clock today, aren't you, baby? You know, of course, that he's making a video to promote the house on social media and something called the internet."

"Thank you for signing the release forms," I said. My mother's nose curled. It had definitely been my father's ego that signed the form. I bet they had a blazing row about it.

"Buckford's opening to the public!" William continued. "Petey's an actual genius with this sort of thing. I'd never have thought of a promo video myself. The sheer depth of talent—I don't know what I'd do without him. You must be very proud of him."

My parents looked at each other meaningfully. My heart stopped.

"Of course," my father said.

"Terribly," my mother added.

The lying bastards.

The other Jags had emptied now, and a queue had formed to meet my fake fiancé. A group of at least twenty women in barely there muslin dresses appeared and started dancing in witchy free form through the crowd and the cars, to satisfyingly astonished faces. I tried not to giggle, and I could feel William doing the same.

"I should get back to it," I said. "I'm not meant to be *in* the footage."

"All right, babe," William said. He'd never called me babe. Literally everyone was acting right now. He leant into my ear and squeezed my butt. "Isn't this fun? Gah! I love you, *so much*." And then he kissed me—passionately—in front of my parents, and the North London Jaguar Car Club, and the pagans, and my film crew, and Bramley. A wolf whistle cracked the air from above. I was so embarrassed my knees almost gave way. As I slunk away, I heard Bramley offer my parents "a restorative sherry" and point them towards the sunken garden, where sandwiches and light refreshments had been laid on especially.

"The Dowager Mrs Topham will be down to join you momentarily," Bramley said.

Not if I could help it.

The plan for the next couple of hours was for the car club to split into two groups. One lot would have individual photos taken with their cars out the front of Buckford Hall, while William took the other lot on a private guided tour of the house. Then they would swap around. At the end, all the classic cars would be parked on the Great Lawn, sparkling in the sunshine, lined up on the slopes either side of the Long Water. It would make for a magnificent shot back up the lake towards the house. Then everyone would gather at the edge of Home Field to watch the re-enactment. All fine in theory, but at some point my parents were going to find Gran stoned out of her nut—and who knew what the resulting explosion of outrage would level in its wake.

I walked into the house to find bedlam. The kitchen was filled with chattering women from the village, all of whom had volunteered to make sandwiches to feed the five thousand. There was a Blitz-like spirit, if you didn't count the pagan drifting between them, smoke wafting from burning sage held high above her head. No one seemed to be paying her the least bit of attention. The women turned to see me and bowed their heads.

"No, please don't do that."

I grabbed three bottles of water, then I headed upstairs to the servants' quarters, where I found Gran, Bunny, and Karma sitting on a rug on the floor, in a gale of laughter.

"What's so funny?" I asked, putting the water down on a table.

"Men," Karma said, wiping her eyes.

I looked at the ashtray between them. There were at least three roaches in there.

"My God, how much have you had to smoke?"

"It's all right, Petey darling. It's natural."

"It's illegal," I said.

Three faces stopped and turned to face me.

"When did you get so stuffy?" Gran said.

I eyeballed her. "Mother and Father are here."

"We saw."

"They can't see you like this. I need you to stay up here until you've sobered up a bit." I pointed at Bunny and Karma. "And you two help her out, please. Give her water. Help her walk it off or something."

Karma was squinting at me through the smoke rising from the joint between her fingers.

"You seem very tense, Petey," she said. "Your whole energy has changed."

"Funny that."

"So serious," Bunny said. "Come and have a little toke, darling."

I marched over, whipped the joint out of Karma's hand, stubbed it out in the ashtray, and eyeballed the lot of them.

"Stay here and sober up, for Christ's sake," I said.

A mocking, sing-song "ooooo-ooooooooooo" filled the room.

"This is a really important day for William. And for me. We need everyone to be on their game. We need your support."

Bunny swallowed, her face turned serious. "Yes, darling. You're quite right."

"Thank you."

"The re-enactment is at one o'clock. I'll see you all then—and not a minute before. Sober. Are we clear?"

Three serious faces nodded. As I marched out into the hall, I heard them burst into laughter again.

"Men!"

"He's going to make a brilliant duchess."

I hadn't even got to the bottom of the stairs when the three of them bounded past me, muslin trailing behind them.

"What did I just tell you?"

"Sorry, darling," Bunny replied, "we've got the munchies."

Derek appeared from a doorway holding up a piece of paper with a photograph on it.

"I don't suppose you ladies have seen my duck anywhere, have you?"

The sound of clanking metal filled the corridor.

"Make way for the King's Guard!" a man shouted. I turned to see a line of soldiers marching towards me. I stepped aside to let them pass, and the leader lifted his helmet. It was Andy from the village.

"Don't suppose you could point us to the loos, could you?"

As I watched a trail of Tudor soldiers march up the stairs towards the servants' quarters like something out of *Bedknobs and Broomsticks*, and looked back to see three stoned pagan witches trying to console a distraught man in search of his duck, and as I heard the bawdy revelry coming from the kitchen, inspiration struck. Here it was, the idea I'd been looking for all this time. It was fully formed, and it was brilliant.

Chapter 48
William

From the field of dead Yorkists, a hero stumbled towards me, his sword aloft. I squinted through my helmet, trying to get a clear view. I didn't recognise the man. Who had they selected to do battle with de Valois?

"Hello, Dub-Dub," the soldier said, ripping off his helmet.

"You have got to be kidding," I said, removing mine too. "Horatio, what are you doing here?"

All the fun of the moment had instantly evaporated, replaced by the stink of mutual contempt. We circled each other, our swords raised.

"It was the only way I could get to speak with you." He lifted his sword and drove it down towards me. I deflected it easily.

"And now I get to kill you. Did you think this through, Horatio?" I swung around, giving him the full weight of my sword against his— and his clattered to the ground. "Fighting Richard de Valois is meant to be an honour. How did you convince everyone to let you do it?"

"It turns out they all wanted to see me murdered as enthusiastically as you do," he said, hand scrabbling for his hilt. "Bit crushing for the old ego, to be honest."

"What do you want?" I drove my sword into the ground between his legs, inches from his cock. The crowd roared. He looked up at me, astonished.

"You know what I want."

"I'm not selling the estate." I pulled my sword free and walked away, giving him time to get to his feet. "Not to become a hotel, and especially not if it means you get your hands on the village."

"My buyers have put their offer up again. You could walk away with at least fifty million in your pocket after you've paid all your father's debts."

"I'm not selling."

"Don't be stupid, Dub-Dub."

I turned and ran towards him, sword aloft, and brought it down right above his head. Horatio barely had time to block it before I split his skull in two.

"Are you sure?" He twisted away from me.

"I'm sure." We circled each other, swords at the ready.

"I had a reporter from *The Bulletin* come to speak to me the other day. He was asking some very interesting questions about you and Peter. What would all these people think if they found out you'd been lying to them?"

I swallowed—then gritted my teeth and adjusted my grip on my sword.

"You don't get to threaten me, Horatio."

He scowled and hunched his shoulders. "Not enough to convince you? Then what if I tell them all about Peter's whoring instead."

Rage erupted out of me like lava. I swung at Horatio's feet, and he stumbled back onto the dirt. The crowd cheered.

"If you sell now, they never need to know. You can leave with your head still held relatively high." He dug his heels into the ground and slid backwards across the grass like a crab.

"I will never sell."

He tried to get to his feet, but I knocked him back on his arse with my foot. He hadn't expected physical contact, and anger flared in his eyes.

"You *will* sell the estate, Dub-Dub. Buckford Hall is going to become a hotel. It's what my father wants—and my father always gets what he wants in the end. You just have to decide how much humiliation you can withstand until he does."

I swung my sword around, preparing to strike, but stopped as realisation dawned. I looked into my old school bully's eyes, his face contorted with fury.

"How much humiliation have you had to withstand at the hands of your father, Horatio?" I asked.

A flash of recognition. For a second, the mask dropped. I'd seen him and he knew it. I thought I'd broken him. But his eyes narrowed, his teeth gritted, and he kicked his legs wildly, trying to knock me off my feet.

"At least my father's alive!"

That was it. I'd had enough. I lifted my sword high above my head and brought it down heavily, sinking the blade into the space between Horatio's torso and his arm. Our battle had reached its climax, and the crowd roared their delight. I put my foot against Horatio's chest, extracted my sword, and pushed him back onto the dirt. I stood over him, my shadow eclipsing his face.

"The greatest gift my father ever gave me was the knowledge he loved me unconditionally," I said. "I hope you get to experience what that's like some day. Before it's too late."

Then, to rapturous applause, I mounted Achilles and galloped across the field to where the audience had been watching. Petey was standing to the side, his camera on its tripod, trained on me. I beckoned him forward, certain in what I needed to do.

"People of Newton Bardon," I said. "Friends." I dismounted, and Petey stepped towards me. I put my arm around him. "I have something I need to say to you all." The crowd hushed, and I swallowed down my jitters. "Petey and I aren't actually engaged. We never have been."

There was stony silence. I couldn't read what it meant, but it scared me. So I explained about *The Love Manor*, the reasons for our deceit, and how the story had accidentally spread out into the real world.

"I never meant to lie to you all," I said. "It was something that got out of control."

"So you're not getting married?" Mrs Craddoch called out across the crowd.

I shook my head. "No, I'm sorry. We're not."

"Shame on you!" she shouted, and guilt pierced my heart, sharp as an assassin's stiletto. I was never getting that red onion chutney recipe now. "I've already made my dress," she said—and several people laughed.

"I've let you all believe a lie, and I'm sorry," I said. "I haven't lived up to the high standards I expect of myself, or that you should demand from me."

"But you love him, right?" Gurpreet, the village chemist, called out.

"I do. Very much. That wasn't a lie."

"Then not to put too fine a point on it, William. Who gives a shit?"

Now *everybody* laughed.

Petey and I looked at each other. I was *so* confused.

"So you don't mind?" I asked the crowd. A chorus of "no" came back.

I felt a heavy hand on my shoulder. It was Andy. I spun around to find all the re-enactment crew standing behind me. Andy removed his helmet.

"Two weeks ago, William, you killed my ten-year-old son, Matthew, on the village green. It was the happiest day of his life and one of the proudest moments of mine. How many men can say that? All these people here, we know who you are. Inside." He tapped his finger against his armoured chest. "And we all rate you, mate. You might have a fancy title and a big house, and eye-watering debt, and thighs my missus won't shut up about, but you're one of us. Which is why we all gave that arsehole from the newspaper absolutely nothing when he came around last week and told us all you weren't really engaged."

"You're kidding? I've been sweating bullets about this for weeks."

Andy shook his head. All the men and women in livery and armour behind him were doing the same. I looked around to see the entire crowd apparently in agreement.

"But I lied. Aren't there any consequences?"

Andy crossed his arms. "Well, you know what we want. Sell us our homes and we'll say no more about it. Deal?"

I glanced over my shoulder to where Horatio was sat slumped in Home Field, looking broken, defeated. Then I looked at all the faces staring back at me—people who'd lived in these cottages for generations, who'd protected me from the press, who'd embraced Petey without question or hesitation, and who'd turned out for a mad weekend of chaos merely because I'd asked. People who deserved to own their own homes.

"Deal," I said, and stuck out my hand.

Andy shook it, his gauntleted grip firm, and the crowd erupted into applause.

I had no idea how I was going to replace the long-term income the estate would lose by agreeing to a fire sale of the cottages. But if I didn't manage to save the estate in the next hundred and thirty-three days, it wouldn't matter—because I wouldn't be in a position to live up to the promise I'd made.

"Well, that was easy." Petey's breath was warm against my ear. "Two problems crossed off the to-do list in one go." He pointed a finger across the field to where his father was pushing his way through the crowds towards us with a face like thunder. "That one might be a bit harder."

Great, yet another reason to feel terrible. Today was meant to be all about making Petey's parents see how brilliant he was. What were they going to make of this ridiculous display?

"You go," I said. "If you can find my mother, send her this way." I sensed her witchy charms could be indispensable. She was always so good at wrangling men of a certain age.

"She's out searching for Derek's duck."

"Christ. How stoned is she?"

"Lord Buckford, I'd like a word," Sir Edward Topham called across the crowd.

"Go," I said, pecking Petey on the cheek. He didn't need to be asked twice. I raised a hand, acknowledging Sir Edward's claim on my time.

"That's it, Peter," Sir Edward bellowed. "Run away from your responsibilities, like you always do."

A moment later, red-faced and puffing with exertion, he stood in front of me.

"My lord."

"Sir Edward."

"On behalf of the whole family, please accept my sincere apologies for my son's behaviour," he said.

"Pardon?" He was lucky I'd left my sword on Home Field.

"What did he do to make you call it off?"

A general silence descended upon the immediate area. I suggested we walk towards the water's edge, where we wouldn't be overheard.

"I didn't call it off, we were never engaged."

"Yes, I heard you. Clearly a cock and bull story for the villagers. You don't expect me to believe that, do you? I know my son, and I know he'll have done something to screw this up. He always does."

Wow. "Nothing could be further from the truth, I assure you." My sword hand was itching.

Something over my shoulder caught Edward's eye. "No, get away from there, you little oik!" he bellowed. I swung around to see young Matthew, a few metres away, hand poised over the shiny navy blue paintwork of Sir Edward's precious roadster. "It's not for touching with greasy little hands. Show some respect."

Matthew looked like he was about to cry.

"Excellent slaughtering today, young Matthew," I called out to him. "You did your family proud."

The boy smiled. "Fanks, William!"

"Go find Bramley and tell him I said to crack out the good chocolate. If he doesn't believe you, the password is *gusset*."

"Fanks, William!"

Matthew gave me a toothless grin and two big thumbs up. I turned back to Sir Edward.

"Greasy fingerprints polish out," I said. He didn't appear to hear me.

"Listen, we can settle this between us—like gentlemen. What will it cost for you to reconsider? Name your price."

"Are you trying to bribe me into marrying your son?"

Edward's eyes bulged. "That's an ugly word. Think of it as a wedding present."

"Jesus Christ, it's a dowry. You're offering me a dowry to take Petey off your hands."

"I wouldn't put it like that. I know you need the money—"

"I'm not interested in your money." The words came out harder than I intended, but I'd been richly insulted. "And I don't need a financial incentive to be with Petey."

"You said you care for him—"

"Care for him?" I was outraged now. "I love him. I am madly, completely, utterly in love with him. Do you have any idea who your son is? He's the most spectacularly talented, creative, funny, smart, and beautiful man I have ever clapped my eyes on. I wake up every day astounded someone so objectively and demonstrably brilliant could fall in love with someone like me."

"Don't be ridiculous, you're a baron!"

I stood there, flabbergasted. It took me a moment to speak.

"Is that who I am?"

"Of course it is." Edward waved a hand in the air, apparently indicating the house, the estate.

I shook my head.

"Sir Edward, I'm a twenty-five-year-old former fly half for a semi-professional Welsh rugby team you've definitely never heard of. That was my career before all this. Did you know? I'm also a fantasy-reading geek who can empty a pub with his opinions on the works of D. R. R. Fanshaw. And don't even get me started on Brandon Osmond's *A Kingdom of Vipers and Valour* series because you'll regret that you did. I'm also a level six human paladin with an oath of devotion. These are my passions, by the way. Oh, and let's not forget, I'm a common or garden-variety himbo on horseback. I'm a son and a brother, an uncle and a godson, and I'm a lover. To your son, as it happens. I am all of these things *before* I am a baron. Petey understands that. He sees me, not a title—which is how we prefer things around here."

I paused to give that time to sink in, but Sir Edward appeared unmoved—which was annoying because I thought I'd been jolly eloquent. So I put the metaphorical gloves back on and delivered the blow I knew would land.

"The fact you think a title matters more than the soul of a person, the fact you think it would take a financial incentive to make your son worth loving, Sir Edward, says more about you than it does about him."

Sir Edward's face went as red as a shiny new cricket ball. "How dare you—"

I held up a hand. "I'm not telling you how to be a father. That's between the two of you. But I won't stand here and let you talk about

Petey like he's a burden, or a problem to be solved, or something you need to pay someone to take off your hands. He deserves better than that."

Peggy stepped out from behind Sir Edward's back. I hadn't seen her approach, had no idea how long she'd been listening.

"It's true, Teddy," she said. "You're my son and I love you, but you're an arsehole to that boy."

The heat was now visibly rising from beneath Sir Edward's collar. His blood was bubbling away like raspberry jam on a stovetop.

"As if I would take parenting advice from you, Mother," he sneered. Then he stopped, and squinted at her. "Dear God, are you high?"

This was not a conversation I needed to be a part of. I turned to make my exit, only to be greeted by a wall of feathers and flapping wings. Derek's duck was scrambling across the lawn, flying over Jaguars—with my mother, still dressed like a geriatric nymph, in hot pursuit.

"Someone help me grab this duck," she wailed—and a horde of men in Tudor battledress rallied to the cause, descending on Gerald and the water's edge. One man in the burgundy-and-blue livery of the Duke of Gloucester made a leap for him, but the duck flapped high into the air and landed on the other side of a car. There were three roadsters with their roofs down in a row, and the duck scrambled through the first, my mother leaping over the door and across the seats trying to nab the bird. Gerald flapped his wings and flew over to the next Jaguar, and my mother—with an esprit that defied her years and how stoned she was—followed along doggedly, arms outstretched. Men were falling all over themselves to keep up and to catch the duck, which leapt into the belly of the next car.

"Not on my leather seats!" Sir Edward cried. At which point my mother looked up, got her leg caught in her muslin dress, stumbled, pitched forward into Sir Edward's Jag, and struggled to pick herself up. She stood and fell, and stood, and tumbled out of the car onto the lawn, and stood again.

"I'm all right!" she said—as Gerald finally managed to take flight and make his bid for freedom. "I'm all right!"

And everyone watched in disbelief as, behind her, Sir Edward's beloved 1967 Series 1 E-Type Jaguar roadster rolled silently into the Long Water.

Chapter 49
Petey

The following Tuesday afternoon, I was in the Old Coach House editing footage of two hundred men in Tudor battledress dragging a classic Jag out of a lake like they'd challenged it to a tug of war. Haruto had captured the whole disaster on the drone—Bunny scrambling through the cars after the duck, the stumble that must have knocked the handbrake loose, and the slow inevitable roll of the car into the water. Thandiwe had caught the close-up of my father's face as the only thing in this world he truly loved entered the water and sank like a stone. I had watched it at least four hundred times. My parents had taken the train home with Gran, who was still high and singing "Octopus's Garden" on a loop, I think to torture my father. The Jag had gone back on a tow truck.

William, dressed in his riding gear, popped his head around the door. I quickly turned my screen off and pulled my headphones down.

"Not suspicious at all," he said, stepping into the room. He was filthy and sweaty.

"I don't want you to see it until it's finished."

William stood behind me, hands on my shoulders, kissing my neck.

"You absolutely reek," I said.

"Of horse and leather and manliness?" He slid a hand down to my crotch and gripped it like he was testing an avocado for ripeness.

"Of horse shit," I protested. "Come on, off you go. I have work to do." I shrugged myself free.

"You don't even know what I want yet."

"I have a fair idea, and you're not getting it until you've showered."

William shook his head. "Aunty Karma called. Derek has checked into the retreat for a few weeks."

I turned. "Like, willingly? Or did she abduct him?"

William laughed. "It's all above board. He's in good hands. Plus, she's doing it for free."

"How does she make any money?" I asked. "Indira spent two weeks there for free."

"Believe me, she's doing fine. She's helped enough big-name celebrities to fill Wembley Stadium. Those who can afford to pay, pay."

William perched himself on my desk, his leg brushing mine. "Speaking of Indira, I have bad news."

I did not like the sound of this. She was meant to be coming to Buckford in the morning to hear my pitch.

"Is she still unwell?"

"She's fine, but she's heading straight back to London to be with her sister and nephew. She says if you want to pitch, you'll have to go to her office on Friday."

William and I exchanged glances. He hooked a finger through mine. We had a deadline now. It was time for me to go home. But it was OK—because I had a plan. If I could pull it off, we could be together at Buckford for at least part of the year, for who knows how long before we needed to worry about it again.

"I need to get back to work," I said, squeezing his hand.

Chapter 50
William

P etey came bounding into the folly and up the stairs, face as bright and flushed as a freshly smacked arse.

"Check your email," he said.

I was sitting at my laptop at Father's desk, trying not to scream at a note from my accountant about urgent renovation costs that had upped the amount we needed to raise from the art auction to £13.9 million—so I was glad of the distraction. That it involved Petey looking pleased as punch was a delectable bonus.

"Is it finished?" I asked.

Petey nodded. Well, I didn't need to be told twice. I stood decisively, yanked the cable out, snapped the laptop shut.

"I think this deserves a bigger screen, don't you?" I said, tucking the computer under my arm.

I grabbed Petey's hand, and we dashed barefoot through the house to the East Drawing Room, where after five minutes faffing about with cables, I was finally able to share my screen on the big TV. Then we sank into the sofa, bodies tight together, holding each other's hands, arseholes clenched in vivid anticipation, and pressed play on the promo video. As a drone shot coming down the drive towards the house filled the screen, I was fizzing with so much excitement I farted. Two minutes later, I was so completely convinced Buckford was the ideal place for a fun family day out, I wished I had a family I could take along to see it myself.

"Well, what do you think?"

"It's fabulous. Beyond fabulous. You can barely tell the house is a rapidly deteriorating death trap."

"Good, because I have another surprise for you."

"What is it?"

"You'll see. Give me a sec."

Petey disappeared into his phone, then told me to check my email again.

"A *second* video?" I said. "You really are value for money. You've just earned yourself an excellent Google review."

I pressed play. Buckford appeared on the screen again—this time a drone shot along the Long Water. Rousing string music filled the room, followed by a voice-over extolling the house's five-hundred-year history, its royal visitors and Capability Brown landscape.

"That voice-over artist sounds sexy as hell."

"It's me."

"Oh, I thought it was Attenborough."

Petey punched me playfully in the arm.

The voice-over continued: "But Buckford Hall carries a secret."

I looked at Petey, a tad confused. "What is this?"

"You'll see."

The screen filled with various broken and battered bits of the house—leaky taps, buckets catching drips, caution tape on the cellar door.

"Who put that there?"

"It's for effect."

"It's a Halloween decoration."

"Listen."

The voice-over lowered in pitch. "After centuries as a great glory of England, Buckford Hall has run out of money. It's up to one man to save it."

It was like a boot to the solar plexus.

I appeared on screen in full armour, doing battle with Horatio Blunt.

"William Winters is the seventeenth Baron Buckford," the voice-over said. "And he'll do anything to save his family's home. Literally anything. No matter how outrageous."

What followed was a montage of the events of the weekend, with cameos from my mother, Aunty Karma, Bramley, and even Sir Edward. There was footage of Peggy dancing on the kitchen table, leading volunteers in a chorus of "Knees Up Mother Brown."

I frowned at the angle and realised the footage had been taken from one of the fixed cameras in the ceiling.

"Are they still on?"

Petey looked sheepish. "I turned them back on. Only for the weekend. The footage was too incredible to lose."

The air in the room turned cold.

"So, they didn't know they were on camera?"

"Everyone signed a release form—"

"For the promotional video. Not for whatever this is."

The video cut to Aunty Karma on the staircase with her arm around Derek, who was bawling his eyes out into her shoulder. I whacked the space bar on my computer so hard the video not only stopped, it cowered in the corner.

"That's a private conversation," I said. "A counselling session with an unwell man." Petey's eyes flicked away, unable to meet mine. "What have you done?"

He retreated to the end of the couch.

"What else is in this video?"

"Nothing! I'm sorry."

But I could tell from his eyes he was lying. I restarted the video. The footage cut to me fighting with Petey's father.

"Really? You put that in there?"

"William, I'm sorry." His eyes were wet. "I know it was private, but... no one has ever stood up for me like that. You look amazing. Like a real hero."

I crossed the room, steadying myself on the mantel.

"I was trying to make your father understand who you are. And you not only recorded it, you edited it into, into—oh my God, this is your pitch, isn't it?"

On screen, the video was building to a crescendo. Me slaughtering Horatio Blunt, Edward's Jag sinking into the lake, Peggy accepting rousing applause from the kitchen volunteers.

The voice-over continued: "Join the dashing Lord Buckford, and a cast of colourful characters, as he channels the fighting spirit of his ancestors to save his family home—penny by penny, brick by brick, battle by battle."

The words *Saving the Love Manor* flashed up on the screen over footage of me in my armour, the wind lightly tickling my hair.

The screen went black.

I couldn't speak.

It was easier to breathe at the bottom of a ruck than it was right now.

"Well, what do you think?" Petey asked, his voice small.

I turned to look at him.

"What do I think?" The words cracked. "You secretly filmed me. My family. Your family. The entire community. Everyone I care about. You recorded private conversations." I pointed at the blank screen of the TV. "This is exactly what *The Bulletin* does. Violates privacy for entertainment."

Petey's face went white.

"That's not... I'm not..."

"How is it any different?"

"Because I love you!" Petey was on his feet, his voice breaking. "I was trying to find a way for us to be together. This is it. If Indira goes for this, I can be here during filming. We can be together. This is me fighting for us, William."

"If this is you fighting for us, what does you fighting against us look like? Volunteering the house as a nuclear testing sight? Ripping my heart out to make a casserole?"

"William—"

"You've violated everyone's trust."

"It's *just* a pitch. None of this goes on TV. But I can take anything you want out of this edit. Anything anyone's uncomfortable with. I'll destroy the footage. I promise. No one will ever see it."

It wasn't enough.

"You can't pitch this show. *I* can't do this show."

Petey's face crumpled. "You can't be serious."

"I don't want to live my life on camera. I don't want to live in public."

"But we'd have control. Don't you see? We'd control the narrative. We'd have a PR team."

"Why didn't you ask me before you did all this?"

"I wanted to surprise you."

"By making a major decision about my life without asking me?" Tears were streaming down Petey's face.

"Please, don't be angry."

"I'm not angry. I'm just... really disappointed."

The words hung in the air. Petey's face changed. His eyes shuttered. He dashed out of the room. I started to give chase, then stopped. He needed space. We both did. I stood there, feeling completely empty. My hands were shaking. I meant everything I'd said. But I still loved him.

I needed to clear my head. I needed Achilles.

* * *

Two hours later, my stallion was exhausted and I had calmed down. Petey had made a mess of things, but at least he was trying—and he was trying *for us*. I could see why he might think the show was a good idea. It was a very Petey solution. I just wished he'd spoken to me about it first. I felt terrible about where we'd left things. It was time to have a proper conversation. I bounded up to the folly, but Petey wasn't there. I tried his bathroom, the East Drawing Room, the kitchen. Nothing.

"Can I help you, my lord," Bramley asked, one hand up the arse of a dead pheasant.

"Have you seen Petey anywhere?"

"Mr Topham has returned to London, my lord."

My stomach hollowed. "What?"

"He said he left you a note."

I bolted upstairs to Father's desk and bashed away at it, trying to get the mechanism to work.

"Bastard thing!" I shoved it but it wouldn't open, so I kicked the desk—then fell to the floor, gripping my foot in agony. My father's voice drifted through my head: The drawer required gentle coaxing, you had to caress it. I took three long breaths and tried again. The drawer popped open. My hand shook as I extracted the note:

William,

You were right. I should have asked you before making you the centre of my pitch. I should have asked before turning on the cameras. I violated your trust. I am no better than the Bulletin. I am sorry.

I know I promised I wouldn't disappear again but I can't stay at Buckford knowing you're disappointed in me. I've spent my whole life hearing that word from my parents. Hearing it from you was more than I could bear.

I've gone back to London. I don't know what the future holds for us, William. But I know I love you. I'm sorry I let you down.

PB. xxx

A tear fell onto the paper, and the ink began to smear.

How could I have been so stupid? Petey had spent his whole life hearing *I'm disappointed* from his parents, and I'd said exactly the same thing. Now he was gone. I'd let him slip through my fingers.

Chapter 51
Petey

Ten minutes into my pitch, Indira hadn't lit a single cigarette. "...then, when the couples think they understand the rules, we pull the rug out from under them completely with something I like to call 'The One-Armed Budget.' Instead of the ten grand they think they're getting to renovate their bathrooms, we pull out a slot machine. They pull the lever, whatever it lands on, that's how much they're working with."

Indira sat opposite me in the Monkey Ginger offices, leaning across her desk, face resting on one hand. She looked bored. It was terrifying.

"So, let me get this right," Indira said. "At the end of this, we're left trying to flog six really ugly, poorly renovated flats?" Put like that, it didn't sound great. "With the country in a housing crisis?"

Indira's face scrunched. This was a bad sign.

"Wait, it gets better. So, the couples can all sabotage each other—"

"Listen, Petey Boy." She closed my laptop and slid it across her desk towards me. "I don't want to make programmes like this anymore."

"Huh?"

"I want to make programmes that do less *harm*. Narrowboat holidays with ageing national treasures, that kind of thing. Film the *Women's Institute Cookbook* being cooked by women from the Women's Institute. You know what I mean?"

I didn't. She'd lost the plot.

"Gentle television," she said. "This type of show—shows that exploit people or pit them against one another—it isn't for me anymore. It's not the kind of energy I want to put out into the world."

What the hell had Karma done to her at that retreat? I sat upright. This was potentially a massive problem.

"Wait, what about *The Love Manor*?" I said, terrified of the answer.

"I won't be pitching a second season to Channel Three."

"But... what about William? He's relying on that show for the income, for the estate."

"Look, I'm sorry for your boyfriend. If Channel Three is willing to cough up two hundred grand for the format, they can have it. But I won't be making it. I'm sorry, Petey."

The room seemed to tilt. *The Love Manor* was my only logical route back to William. What now?

"You need to tell him," I said.

"William? Yes, of course. I'm sorry, Petey. I know none of this is what you wanted to hear."

I walked out of Indira's offices into a rainy summer's day in London's Soho. I felt empty. As I drifted along a wet Brewer Street without an umbrella, past the boutiques and red telephone boxes, reality hit me like a flood. I'd violated William's trust for a pitch I couldn't use, I'd run away to sell an idea Indira didn't want, and now the one show that could have taken me home to Buckford was cancelled. I'd lost everything. William hadn't called. Maybe he was relieved I'd gone? I'd spent the past few days replaying the fight—the look on his face when he'd said he was disappointed. Still, it had been gutless to run away. Now I had no William, no prospects, no opportunities, and nothing on the horizon except lunch with my parents on Sunday. The answer, clearly, was drink. At least I was in London. I pulled out my phone and messaged the Brent Boys group chat.

Petey Boy: *Heading to Miss Timmy's for cocktails and a fat slice of occasion cake. Get. Your. Arses. There.*

Jumaane: *Will be with you in ten. xxx*

Sunny: *Will be shitfaced with you in twenty. xx*

Nick: *Drinking while gay? I'm in. xx*

Chapter 52
William

I was miserable. It was Friday night, and I was bunkered down in the Dower House. Mother and I had eaten an unholy amount of chocolate, and I was lying on her couch in my boxers, my head in her lap, surrounded by discarded Lindt ball wrappers, while she gently stroked my hair. That great goddess of hers was suspiciously quiet, precisely when I could have used an insight or two. That Petey had left without saying goodbye had hurt, but at least we'd had the promise of him returning in a year for the next season of *The Love Manor*. Then a call from Indira, and even that small hope vanished. I couldn't have been more gutted if I'd had my brains dashed out against a rock and been filleted by a fastidious angler. I'd read Petey's note a thousand times. He must have pitched his idea by now. That was meant to be today. I'd thought I might hear from him, but I hadn't. I'd picked up the phone to call him a dozen times, but I couldn't imagine how to get the words right. We had too much to say.

"You know, you could always sell the place, darling," Mum said.

I was so shocked I put my chocolate back in its wrapper and placed it on the coffee table. "You can't be serious."

"Of course I'm serious. You can take the money, buy a lovely flat in London, and be young, with your lover. Build a life together."

"But... Buckford is our family history. Our legacy."

"It's the past, darling," she said, still stroking my hair. "The past is gone. It's not coming back. The world has moved on from this place and what it represents. It's just stuff. It doesn't matter."

Was she short-circuiting or something? Did she need switching off and on again? My father and brother were interred in the mausoleum. I'd grown up here. She'd raised her family here.

"But it's our home."

"It's been a wonderful home. A fabulous adventure. But if it's over, we'll survive. We don't need it."

I sat up and looked at her in astonishment.

"I have a duty to preserve it."

"Do you?"

"What about Callum?" My nephew would expect to inherit.

"Life offers no guarantees. Callum is part of a future that hasn't happened yet," Mum said, plucking my chocolate from its wrapper. "You don't know what he'll want. He might want it less than you do. Lord knows your father never wanted it. How long does this go on for? How many generations must carry this burden?"

Mum popped the chocolate in her mouth, her eyebrows raised in expectation of an answer. I didn't have one. I lay back down on her lap, and her hands returned to combing through my hair. Silence fell between us, interrupted only by the gentle clatter of a Scrabble tile coming loose from its hiding place under the dining table.

"I can't be apart from him," I said, after a few minutes. "This is killing me."

"Then go get him."

Mum made it sound so *simple*. Sell Buckford and move to London? Build a life there together? Could I really do it? And could I really be the one to end five hundred years of history?

I sat up. "I need to think."

"And shower, darling. Before you do anything. Please shower."

Chapter 53
Petey

By midnight, Miss Timmy's was absolutely heaving. From the stage, Sandy Crotch, the venue's resident drag queen, was delighting the crowd of drunken homosexuals with a medley of Judy Garland and Liza Minnelli tunes. Ludo had bolted for the edge of the stage the second Sandy started belting out Judy's "Get Happy," and the rest of us were working our way through our seventh bottle of champagne.

"To be clear, because I'm well confused," Jumaane said, "have you actually broken up with Baron Fuckboy?"

I shook my head. Then nodded. Then shook my head again.

"That's really cleared that up."

"I didn't mean to," I said. "But... maybe? We fought—"

"And then instead of staying to talk it through like an adult, you did a runner?"

When he said it like that, I felt like an idiot. "Yeah, but... you should have seen his face. He really *hated* me."

Stav swirled his red wine around in his glass.

"But what did he actually say to you?"

"He said he was disappointed in me."

"On account of you violating the privacy of several hundred people by secretly filming them?"

"Well, don't say it like that."

"Like what?" Stav sipped his wine.

"Like a lawyer."

"I am a lawyer."

"Yes, but it's not like I really did anything wrong."

"Unless you count Article Eight of the Human Rights Act 1998," Stav said. "And the multiple potential GDPR violations, the possible defamation suits and intellectual property issues, and if you wanked to any of the footage, the voyeurism charges under the Sexual Offences Act 2003."

I looked at him, appalled. "I'm *so* glad you're here."

Sandy's medley switched to Liza Minnelli's "Losing My Mind."

"Well, what did he say when you spoke to him afterwards?" Sunny asked.

I slumped back against the banquette, my head lolling from side to side.

"You have spoken to him, right?"

I couldn't make eye contact with him.

The boys all groaned.

"I love you, mate," Jumaane said, "but you're a bloody bellend."

Dav topped up my champagne. "Is there a *reason* you haven't called?"

"He doesn't have a mobile phone."

The boys groaned again.

"But he does *have* a phone," Sunny said. "And an email. And probably a pigeon loft. I mean, it seems like the kind of gaff that has one."

"Oh, sod off," I said, draining my glass.

I went to top it up, but Dav plucked the bottle from my hand.

"Do you want to fix things with him?"

"Of course I do," I said quietly. "But it's such a mess. I've fucked everything up."

"You can't avoid him forever," Nick said. "Sunny and Ludo are literally getting married at your boyfriend's house in a few weeks' time."

My stomach hollowed. I'd forgotten about the wedding.

"Plus," Jumaane said, "Stav has already planned a full year's worth of country house weekend getaways."

Stav nodded. "Done the menus, selected the wines, bought the tweed."

"They won't be anywhere near as fun without you," Jumaane said.

"But to be clear," Sunny added, "we *will* still go without you."

I looked around the table at my friends, a lump in my throat. "You'd really come and visit?"

Jumaane rolled his eyes. "You can't get rid of us by moving to a party house in the sticks."

"That's the opposite of how you get rid of us," Sunny said.

"Although it is how you get rid of me," Nick added. "Unless this five-hundred-year-old house has a lift?"

On the stage, Sandy Crotch switched to Judy Garland's "The Man That Got Away." This medley was starting to feel personal. I had to get out of here. I needed to stop talking about William, thinking about him. He hadn't called. He was clearly still furious with me. I'd ruined everything.

"I want to go dancing," I announced to the table.

Stav shook his head. "I don't think they'll let you into Hades in the state you're in."

Was he an idiot? "Why would we go to that crèche? We'll go to Vauxhall, like we always do."

Sunny frowned. "You want to go to a sex club?"

"The sex isn't compulsory, Sunshine," I said. "You can go there to dance, you know."

Stav knocked back his red wine. "I'm no Sigmund Freud, but that seems like super self-destructive behaviour."

We bickered about where to go next until Sandy reached the *Cabaret* part of her medley. She was singing "Maybe This Time" when Sunny asked for the bill. By the time we dragged Ludo away from the stage, she was closing with "Cabaret" itself, and the gays were screaming their approval.

"Where are we headed?" Ludo asked as we stepped out into the fresh air of Old Compton Street.

"Vauxhall," I replied. "And I don't want to leave until Sunday."

Chapter 54
William

The bluebells had long since died off. I walked up to the stone circle to look out over the estate. My naked feet were claggy with mud. I'd wanted to feel close to the earth, but in reality, it meant playing hopscotch around the shit Achilles had festooned along the bridle trail. The day was overcast, and the breeze was cool against the bare skin of my chest and legs. My face was damp from tears that hadn't stopped in days. The estate always looked so beautiful from here: the Long Water reflecting the sky, the house nestled between the two hills like a shiny new coin between a pair of glorious buttocks. I turned my back on all of it and looked east to the family mausoleum. I closed my eyes, sucking the fresh air deep into my lungs, and—when I had summoned the courage—scrambled down the rocks and through the forest.

I sat there for ages, on the floor, in the mortuary chapel above the crypt, letting the weight of my ancestors' judgement press me into the stone. I needed to confess to the dead that I was contemplating the unthinkable.

"I know you'll think I've failed," I said, as if they could hear me.

"But Mum is right. Living is for the living. Why am I living for the dead?"

Mum had been here, too, it seemed. There was a glass jar filled with foxgloves and ox-eye daisies. My fingers traced the names of my father and my brother, carved by the stonemason into the memorial plaque so recently it looked as if it had been finished yesterday. Their deaths felt as fresh as yesterday yet somehow also a lifetime ago.

"You would have been so much better at this than me," I told my brother.

"And you"—I tapped my father's name with my finger—"you have a lot to answer for. It's as if you'd never heard of a savings account. Or tax. Or living within one's means. But I'm proud to be your son. I love you, Dad. I miss you every day. And if, *if,* I sell the estate, I know you would understand. Because I'd be doing it for love."

Petey's face flashed through my mind. His laugh. His cheeky grin. The way his hip bones were sharp enough to slice through the elastic of his briefs and how right they felt in my hands whenever I pulled him towards me. The look on his face when I'd told him I was disappointed. That note: *I don't know what the future holds for us, William. But I know I love you.* I had to try, surely? Even if it all came to nothing or he didn't want me anymore, I had to try.

When I emerged, it was starting to drizzle and I was beginning to regret my lack of clothing. There was no buzzer in the mausoleum to summon help (probably because it would have scared the shit out of the staff if it ever rung—and believe me, as someone who was once a teenage boy, my brother and I would have been ringing it all the time) so I had to make the best of it. I trekked along the river path until I reached the Long Water. As the heavens opened up, I took shelter in Lady Caroline's Bridge and pressed the button to summon Bramley. As I sat there, looking back at the house, waiting for my trusty chief operating officer to appear, my eye was caught by a movement on the water. It was Derek's duck. He was followed by a mallard and a dozen ducklings. My heart filled with joy, and tears sprang from my eyes again. No wonder he didn't want to get caught. He had too many reasons to stay.

"Good for you, mate," I said. "You're an ecological disaster, but good for you."

A few minutes later, Bramley arrived with a towel, an umbrella, and a hip flask.

"Thank you, Brammers," I said, wrapping myself in the towel.

"A pleasure, my lord." I took a swig of the brandy and felt liquid fire all the way down to my gut. Derek's duck was standing by the water's edge, supervising his babies scrambling up the bank—as if he was counting each precious soul to safety.

Love. It was a future worth fighting for. And realising that, logically everything else fell into place. I had clarity. But I was also terrified.

"How would you feel about moving to London, Bramley?"

The old man smiled. "Sounds like an adventure, my lord."

I blinked, astonished. "You wouldn't mind?"

"I adore London, my lord. Great things always happen in London."

No, they didn't. I snatched the flask and sniffed it. "How much of this have you had? That city is cursed, man."

Bramley's eyebrows went up. "If I might speak plainly, my lord?"

I nodded, urging him to explain himself.

"You're the fourth baron I've had the privilege to serve—"

"If you're going to compare me to my forefathers, I'm not sure I can bear to hear it."

"The first was your great-grandfather, who went to London a freshly minted lord and rose to hold two of the great offices of state. A confidant of Churchill, he was a towering statesman who brought much credit and lustre to this house. The second was your grandfather, who came back from London with investments that saw this house safely through a period when many great houses were sold off.

The third was your father, who came back from London with your mother—who is the best thing that has happened to this estate all my fifty years here. Oh yes, very good things happen to this family when the baron goes to London, my lord."

"Golly." That was quite the speech. I took a swig of the brandy. Then another. And one more for luck. "So you don't think the place is cursed?"

"No, my lord."

Holy shit, I was going to do this, wasn't I?

"And you'd come with me, wouldn't you, if I moved to London."

The man bowed slightly, smiling broadly. "Of course, my lord."

I hit the bottle one last time and sucked in a deep breath.

Tackle the hard stuff.

I straightened. "Bramley, I need you to pack me a bag."

"Very good, my lord. Shall I let Mr Topham know our intended time of arrival?"

"Yes. *No!* Let's surprise him." And as I looked at the wise old bird, an idea struck. "And get the horse trailer ready, will you?"

A few minutes later, in the kitchen of the house my family had called home for more than five hundred years, I picked up the phone and dialled a number I had never dreamt I'd call.

"Horatio? It's William."

* * *

Later that evening, I was standing in Jonty's back garden in suburban North London, while Bramley made himself at home in the Boche family kitchen with Lola, and Achilles nibbled on Jonty's mother's marigolds.

"And the reason you brought the horse?" he said, holding a bottle of champagne and two glasses, with a concerned look on his face.

"He's part of my big romantic gesture—my plan to win Petey back."

"Horse crucial to the whole show, is it?"

"It's romantic."

"It's ruining the lawn."

"Sorry, old chum. But, you see, the day Petey and I properly got together, it was after I'd swooped in on Achilles, in my suit of armour, to rescue him from the gutter press." I remembered too late that Jonty's family owned a newspaper empire. "Sorry."

"Don't mention it."

"Then I was in all my armour the day I slew the dragon that is Petey's father. Thought I cut rather a dashing figure. So thought it'd be romantic, you know, to do it again."

Jonty looked stunned.

"Don't you think three times is a bit much? Why not do something else. For a bit of variety. You know, tone it down a bit."

If Jonty, of all people, is telling you to tone something down, then you jolly well know it needs toning down.

"You think I should forget the armour?"

Jonty nodded. "It's a start."

We sat on the patio of Jonty's summer house—his little bachelor pad in the rear of his parents' garden—knocking back the champagne. It was one of those orange-red dusks, and the first few stars were peeking through the polluted London sky. I shuddered, unable to quite shuck the belief I was tempting fate by being here.

"Well, not that it's not wonderful to see you, Dub-Dub, and in the capital, no less. But not to put too fine a point on it, why are you here? And *why* do you need to make a big romantic gesture?"

I spilt all. I told Jonty about the promo video, about *Saving the Love Manor*, about the secret filming, about telling Petey I was disappointed in him, about him leaving without saying goodbye.

"You said you were disappointed in him?"

"I know."

"You've met his parents?"

"I know."

"No wonder you got the old smoke bomb exit. Golly. You've heard nothing since?"

I shook my head. Jonty clucked and tut-tutted.

"Well, of course, you know what I'm thinking now?"

Honestly, how could anyone ever guess what Jonty was thinking?

"Show me the bloody video, man."

I pulled out my new mobile phone. Jonty nearly dropped his champagne. "What. The. Actual—"

"I know, got it this afternoon," I said. "I'm making a few changes."

I pulled up the email with the video and played it, Jonty's eyes widening with every new frame. When it was finished, he stood up, face astonished.

"Dub-Dub, this is bloody fantastic. This is a sure-fire hit. The public will lap it up. You said no to this?"

"He violated everyone's privacy."

"We can work around that. It's only a pitch." Jonty cupped a hand to his mouth. "Lolz, baby. I need you. Come quickly."

Lola slid open the kitchen window. "I need you, too, baby!"

"Come quickly, baby. Bring your laptop. Dub-Dub needs you to edit something."

"Give me a minute, baby." She slid the window shut. The pair of them were ridiculous.

"What are you up to?"

"Saving your arse. Seriously, Dub-Dub, are you as batty as your grandfather? This is your chance to save the estate, earn pots of money, and become a household name into the bargain."

"I don't want to become a household name. Besides, I'm selling the estate."

Jonty *actually* dropped his champagne glass.

"Why?"

"To be with Petey. Here. In London."

Jonty was wide-eyed in horror, arms outstretched. "You're out of your sodding tree. Sell the estate? To move to London? You hate London. I had to check the calendar to make sure it wasn't April Fool's Day when you rang the old Boche family doorbell."

"I can come to terms with London if it means Petey and I can be together."

Jonty yanked my phone out of my hand and bashed a finger into the screen. "No, *this* is how you can be together. You can have everything you want. Petey. Buckford. A jolly good dose of shagger's knob that'll last the rest of your life. All you have to do is say yes."

"What about the press intrusion—"

"I *am* the press! We can help you with the press. It is an eminently solvable problem. Everyone from Beyoncé to Emma Thompson to that Jonas Brother with the weird teeth deals with the media. I'm an online influencer. This is what I do. Plus, Lola is a genius. Who do you think came up with our strategy for winning *The Love Manor*? Why didn't you ask for help?"

I opened my mouth. Closed it. I had no answer. It had never occurred to me.

Achilles took a shit on the lawn.

"Sorry," I said. "I'll clear that up in the morning."

"It's OK, my parents are in Cannes."

Lola appeared on the patio with her laptop. "What's up, baby?"

Three bottles of champagne later, the video had been reedited to remove the offending material and the two of them had knuckled out a media strategy. They had a new plan. But it meant being very brave indeed. And though I'd been brave enough to risk London, I wasn't sure I was courageous enough for what Jonty and Lola had cooked up.

Chapter 55
Petey

T*he Bulletin* had photographed me going into Crucifix on Friday night, and by Sunday it was all over the gossip pages. The mood at my parent's house was funereal. Or would have been, if funerals involved my father shouting. The whole Topham clan was sitting around the living room—my awful parents, my odious brother, his odious wife, my all-right-on-her-day sister, her even-more-odious husband, and my gran. I was still so hungover, every time my tongue moved in my mouth it was like a cactus being dragged across another cactus. I wished for death to take me, if only for the peace and quiet.

"What were you thinking, Peter, visiting a place like that?" my father bellowed. "You're marrying a member of the aristocracy."

Everyone else had their faces buried in their phones, reading about my disgrace. Everyone except Gran, whose hand was on my knee.

"We're *not* engaged. We were never engaged. How many times?"

My parents were struggling to process that fact.

"A minor detail. It's obvious you care for each other. So why would you visit this... this... house of ill repute? What do you think Buckford is going to say when he sees this report?"

It was a good question. I had no idea, and it was churning my guts up. Yet I only had myself to blame. If I'd listened to Sunny's advice, if I'd got an injunction as insurance against *The Bulletin*'s threats, I wouldn't be in this situation. Frustrated with myself and my pride, I did what any sensible son would do and took my impotent rage out on my father.

"For a lawyer you're very quick to convict," I said, looking up at him. "Nothing happened. I went to a club and I danced with my friends. End of."

"It's a sex club!"

"It's a *night*club."

"Where people have sex!" my mother wailed. "Animals. Disgusting."

Now was not the time to admit I had usually been one of those animals and I had loved every disgusting minute of it.

"Nothing happened!" I shouted. The sound of it reverberated around my head like it was bouncing around a canyon, and I thought I would throw up. "Nothing was ever going to happen. All I did was dance with my friends."

My father was stabbing a finger into his phone. "The paper says otherwise."

"The paper is lying."

"Then we sue for defamation, Pete," my sister Kathy said.

"Yes," Mother said, eyes brightening. "Let's take them to the cleaners."

I shook my head. "And make myself an even bigger target? No, thank you."

My father had one arm resting authoritatively on the mantelpiece. "Peter, wrapping them up in years of expensive legal disputes is precisely how we make them go away."

"I don't want your help." The words came out in a sneer, accurately capturing my contempt.

"You have to fight them, Peter," Mother said. "Show some mettle. Or you're going to lose your fiancé."

"For fuck's sake, he's not my fiancé. He never was."

"But he's good for you," she said.

"He's put a stop to you talking like a barrow boy," my father chimed in. "And he clearly cares for you—"

"He's not going to want to marry you now, anyway," my brother said. "You've been ruined."

Rage was bubbling up inside me. I couldn't take it anymore. "Can any of you hear yourselves? You're a bunch of judgemental pricks. Why do I have to fit into this tiny heteronormative box? Why aren't I good enough for you as I am?"

They might have always been outwardly OK with me being gay, but it felt like they were demanding I be a certain kind of gay.

My mother threw her hands up. "Look where your lifestyle has got you, Peter."

Father shook his head. "And now you need our help getting yourself out of the mess you've got yourself in."

"I don't want your help."

"You need it!"

"It's a bit bloody late to get a superinjunction now, anyway," I railed. "I'm all over the paper already."

"Superinjunction?" my brother scoffed. "Was that your plan? Pathetic."

I turned to face him, my anger white hot. "And maybe if my family didn't always treat me like this, I could have come to one of you and asked for help."

"It wouldn't have worked," my sister Kathy said, matter-of-factly. "You'd need to show not only a major breach of privacy but an immediate risk of harm—"

"And what is this but a major breach of privacy?"

My brother laughed, loud and mocking. "That ship sailed the second your boyfriend made his little public declaration."

"Sunny said—"

My brother's laugh split the air again. "Maybe you shouldn't take legal advice from a journalist?"

I slumped into the sofa, utterly defeated. It was pointless, hopeless. Gran squeezed my knee. If I looked at her, I'd cry.

"Let me help," Kathy said, sitting forward on the sofa.

"It's too late to do anything anyway, apparently," I huffed.

She shook her head. "We can still tie them up in litigation. If you won't accept Dad's help, let me handle the legal side. Please, Pete."

Her eyes were pleading. She seemed to actually care about me, and not the family name or the idea of being related to a baron or making sure I live by the rules.

Gran tapped my leg. Finally, I looked at her—and her eyes were filled with the supportive, loving, steely determination I had relied on my whole life.

"Let your sister help," she said. "As old Reggie Kray used to say, 'save yourself a headache tomorrow and shoot the fucker in the head today.'"

I laughed despite myself.

My sister-in-law looked up from her phone. "Can anyone hear a horse?"

Everyone's heads tilted towards the window. Sure enough, I could hear the click-clack of horseshoes on bitumen in the distance.

"Funeral?" Kathy suggested.

"They're too early, I'm still alive," Gran said.

"It's only one horse," my brother said. "Not a full hearse."

I ran to the front door in time to see Achilles rounding the corner into my parent's driveway. William was astride, high in the saddle, bare-chested, wearing nothing but his red satin boxer shorts.

Behind me, my mother gasped. "Good God."

"What are you doing here?" I said, heart thudding in my chest. My family piled out onto the porch.

"I called Horatio Blunt," he said. "I agreed to sell everything. Well, not the village. The tenants still get the village."

There was a collective sharp intake of breath behind me.

"You did what?"

William hopped down. His feet were bare. He held the reins out, and Kathy stepped forward to take them. William cupped my arms, his eyes burning with a passionate intensity.

"All that matters is you," he said. He was shaking. "I want to be with *you*."

"But Buckford means everything to you."

"No, *you* mean everything to me."

My knees buckled. Only William's grip held me up. He was willing to give up everything for me?

My mother muttered something.

"He obviously hasn't seen it yet," my father replied under his breath.

Oh God. They were right. He can't have heard.

"William, *The Bulletin*. They're saying I... listen, it's not true, you have to believe me—"

William pulled me into him, cradling me. "I don't care what the papers say. I know you. I know your heart. I know the papers. I know who I believe. I will *always* believe you."

Relief washed through me. I nuzzled into William's neck. William pulled me tight against his bare chest. I could feel his heart hammering.

"You'd really give it all up, for me?"

"Every square inch. I'm moving to London to be with you. If you'll have me?"

I pulled away so I could see his eyes. He meant what he said, but I could see the grief, the sacrifice. He could never be happy in London. Buckford would always be calling to him, to the iron in his blood, and it would be too late.

"I... don't want you to sell," I said. The words slipped out so quickly I hadn't thought about them, but I meant them with my whole heart. "Not for me. Do it for you, if you want to. But I can't... I couldn't... please don't put that on my shoulders."

William frowned. He studied me for a moment, as if he was considering something. "Jonty said you'd say that."

"You've seen Jonty?"

"Stayed with him last night."

William was still frowning. "He and Lola did suggest a plan B."

"A plan for what?" I wasn't sure I trusted any plan devised by Jonty. Although Lola was a smart cookie.

"You'll see." William's hand dived into Achilles's saddlebag, and he pulled out a mobile phone.

"When did you get that?"

"Yesterday," he said, painstakingly tapping out a message. "Thought I might need it in London. Not that the reception is any better here than at Buckford."

The wait was killing me. "What's plan B?"

"Be patient. You'll see." He slipped the phone back into the bag.

"Is there a reason you brought Achilles?"

William's head bobbed around. "It seemed romantic."

I pointed at his boxer shorts. "And these?"

He shrugged. "My suit of armour is back at Jonty's place."

I laughed. "Of course. You didn't think maybe your riding gear, or a shirt and chinos—"

Gran cackled. "Your dangly bits fell out when you jumped off your horse."

William grimaced. "So sorry, Peggy."

"Don't be, son. Very nice it was too."

We ignored my mother's sharp intake of air and my father's sigh of frustration.

Gran turned to my sister. "More meat than a butcher's window." Then she turned back to my parents. "Are we having lunch or what?"

***

A couple of hours later, after the most awkward meal of my life, a black Range Rover pulled up in the road outside the house. William peeked through the net curtains, then raced to the front door. Having refused my mother's offer of a robe, he was still in his boxers. It had kept everyone uncomfortable the entire meal, and I loved him for that. I followed him outside. When the car door opened, Indira Murray stepped out. What the hell was she doing here? Indira was wearing yoga pants and trainers and shifted her sunglasses on top of her head to better eyeball William in his boxer shorts. As she walked up the drive, she circled a finger at Achilles, who had destroyed my parents' front garden.

"This is so over the top, William. We'll make a TV producer out of you yet."

I couldn't quite believe my eyes. "Why are you here?"

"*Saving the Love Manor*," she said. "It's brilliant, Petey. I want to make it."

I looked at William. I was shocked and confused.

"So, second confession for the day," he said. "I *may* have sent Indira your pitch for *Saving the Love Manor*. When I sent that message earlier. That's our plan B. I'm sorry, perhaps I should have asked. You're not angry, are you?"

Should I be angry? Words didn't come. My body was numb.

"But what about the privacy issues?"

"Lola reedited it," William said. "It's fine now. And it's absolutely amazing, Petey."

The rest of the household had now followed us outside and were standing on the porch.

"I came straight here so I could tell you to your face," Indira said. "I want you to executive produce it. As we agreed. If you still want to?"

I spluttered. "Yes. Yes, of course I still want to. But I thought you didn't want to make this type of TV anymore?"

"Petey Boy, there's enough compelling drama going on at that house without needing to exploit anybody for entertainment. This is exactly the kind of TV show I want to be making. I do have one condition, though."

My heart stopped.

She turned to look at my gran. "Peggy. I want you in the show. You're television gold. We'd need you at Buckford during filming."

My parents gasped. There was muttering behind me.

William looked at me, then at Gran. "In that case, Peggy, would you like to come live at Buckford full-time? The place doesn't feel right without you."

"You're busting me out of prison?" Gran clapped her hands together in prayer. "If Petey Boy's going, I'm going too! You know, my husband always said I had the legs of a film star."

"You cannot be seriously considering this?" my father moaned.

"You watch me, Teddy."

My mother inhaled sharply. "What will people say?"

"There's something else," Indira said. "*The Love Manor*. I'm willing to sell you two the format rights. If you want to make it?"

The clattering sound of my jaw hitting the pavement could be heard several streets away.

"Really?"

"Of course."

"But..." I looked at William. "We can't afford that, can we?"

William seemed thoughtful. "Would making two shows from Buckford be enough to keep you in Leicestershire full-time?"

With my gran there too? Sure, I'd miss London and I'd miss my friends, but they would visit. This was a chance to make my career, to really be someone in television. It was a chance to be with William. I nodded. It was more than enough. It was everything.

William smiled. "Then I'm sure we can sell another painting."

"Wait," I said, looking back at Indira. "If I make *The Love Manor*, doesn't that still put the wrong kind of energy out into the world?"

She shrugged. "Two hundred grand is two hundred grand. I have a nephew who needs a lot of care."

I turned back to William. He rolled his bottom lip through his teeth. "So, which future shall we take? Are you coming up to Buckford or am I coming down to London? It's your choice."

I had thought everything I wanted in the world was in London, but the future I really wanted was now waiting for me at Buckford Hall. I shook my head in disbelief. "What do you think?"

I kissed him then. Thoroughly, deeply, passionately. I kissed him like it was the first kiss of the rest of our lives. I kissed him in love and gratitude and awe. I kissed him like my whole family weren't watching.

"Well, this is uncomfortable," my brother said.

"Anyone for a cup of tea?" my mother asked.

William and I pulled apart.

"Can't stay, I'm afraid," William said. "I need to telephone Horatio Blunt and tell him it's all off."

I laughed. "I want to be there when you make that call."

"Then I have to see a bloke about a horse. A dozen of them, actually. I'm buying the Cleveland Bay mares. For the riding school."

Achilles whinnied in what I swear was delight. William untied the white stallion from the rowan tree in my parents' front yard and mounted him.

"Sorry about the garden," he said, wincing as he took in the damage.

Then he reached down, giving me his hand and one stirrup, and swung me up into the saddle behind him.

"But we can have tea next time," William said. "At our place."

At. Our. Place.

I wrapped my arms around his waist, leaning my cheek against the bare skin of his shoulder, and breathed him in.

"You could always come up in the Jag," William added. Then he pulled on Achilles's reins, and we turned towards home.

Chapter 56
William

The morning sun streamed in through the folly windows, warming my face. I blinked into the light, and my heart skipped to see the gentle sweeping curve of Petey's bare back and the round of his buttocks in the bed beside me. I folded an arm over and pulled him towards me. He woke and stretched, rolling over to face me, kicking a leg across my thigh to pull himself closer. Slowly, his eyes opened.

"Good morning, beautiful," I said.

He smiled. "Am I still dreaming? I can't believe I'm here."

The stench hit me like a lorry. I tried not to breathe it in. Petey noticed.

"Morning breath?"

I grimaced apologetically.

"Hang on, I have a trick to fix that."

Petey rolled on top of me. He began kissing my nipples, then slowly worked his way down my body until suddenly the warmth of his mouth was around me.

"I'm beginning to suspect this isn't a medically approved treatment for morning breath," I said.

Petey looked up at me, his blue eyes glittering with mischief. "Nine out of ten doctors recommend it."

"How does it cure it?"

"It doesn't. It means my breath is several feet away from your face."

I laughed and reached down to pull him back up towards me. "I don't care. Come here."

Then I kissed him properly and rolled myself on top of him, pinning him down. Petey wrapped his legs around my back and playfully wiggled his hips.

"You really are a stink pig!"

Petey waggled his eyebrows seductively, looping his arms around my neck.

"I don't know about that," I said, trying not to breathe in—and I scooped him up. Petey squealed with delight, his naked body hugging mine like a baby koala. I shuffled along the mattress on my knees, then stood at the end of the bed and carried him down the stairs.

"Holy shit, that's hot," Petey said.

"You know what's *really* hot? Toothpaste."

I carried him into the bathroom. Once minty fresh, we stepped into the shower together. The hot water beat against my back. I pressed Petey against the tiles and kissed him until we were both breathless. When we finally emerged—the hot water tank completely drained—we towelled each other dry.

"We didn't really get a chance to speak yesterday," Petey said, rubbing the water out of his hair.

It was true. Between getting Achilles back in the horse trailer, grabbing some things from Petey's flat, and buying my obsessively horny stallion twelve new girlfriends, it had been a long and busy day—and all of it chaperoned by a very smug Bramley. When we'd finally got home, we'd let our bodies do the talking.

I put my foot up on the ledge of the bath to dry between my toes. "You want to know why I agreed to plan B?"

"Well, yes." Petey perched his bare bum against the vanity. "You were adamant you didn't want to be on TV."

"Jonty and Lola convinced me the media is manageable. They talked me through how they use them. You were right, we'd have a whole PR team to act as go-betweens. The estate is private property, so we can control access. Don't get me wrong, I'm absolutely terrified. Haven't pooped in forty-eight hours."

Petey laughed. I looked up at him until our eyes met.

"I thought I'd lost you, Petey, and it was the worst feeling in the world. I knew I would do whatever it took to be with you again." I stood up and dropped the towel, closing the gap between us. "I hope you can see that."

Petey smiled. "I can. I'm incredibly grateful."

I pulled him into a hug.

"You don't need to be grateful for anything," I said. "We're a team. Your dreams are my dreams."

"Same." Petey's fingers fiddled with the ring on the chain around my neck. He was building up to something.

"What is it?"

"I've been thinking. If you can compromise, so can I. We should get Kathy to help us with the legal stuff. Defamation suits, at least. Whatever it takes."

I couldn't control my smile.

"What?" Petey said. "What's so funny?"

"Nothing's funny. I'm proud of you."

"For mooching free legal representation off my sister?"

I kissed him. It was a stealth attack. Took him completely by surprise. The British Army would do well to study it.

"Asking your family for help is *big*."

"They're still horrible people."

"Agreed. That lunch was the longest two hours of my life."

"The point is," Petey said, "I would do anything for you too."

"I know."

I looked into Petey's eyes.

"I love you," I said. "And I will be your liege man of life and limb, and I promise to serve you faithfully, with worldly honour."

Petey's grin lit up his whole face.

"I love you, too, my lord," he said, pecking me on the lips. "So we're clear, that is still incredibly cringey."

I tapped him on the butt. "Come on, get dressed, get your camera. We've got a hundred and twenty-four days to save the estate."

Chapter 57
Petey

Bang! The Wetherby's auctioneer bought his gavel down on the sale of another piece of Buckford's horrendous art collection.

"Sold to the lady in the pink hat for eight hundred and fifty thousand pounds."

The Great Hall was full to bursting with collectors, media, and the *Saving the Love Manor* film crew. There was real excitement about the auction—and not only in the room. Thanks to a little marketing push from Jonty, Zoë, Ellie, Armando, and the other *Love Manor* influencers, the Buckford art auction had captured global attention. A bank of phones had been installed along one wall to accommodate overseas bidders. The auction was going to be the final episode of season one of *Saving the Love Manor*—and it was the biggest episode we'd recorded since the one featuring Sunny and Ludo's wedding several weeks earlier (and, thanks to Sunny's mum, that one had BAFTA written all over it). I'd been running around barking directions at my team through my headset but circled back to where William was sitting with his mum, his Aunty Karma, and Gran. They were all wearing hats decorated in acorns. For luck, apparently.

It was good TV—if Indira could convince one of the channels to buy it.

"How are we going?" I asked.

"Not good," William said, eyes full of concern. I reached for his hand, and he grabbed mine, putting it to his mouth and kissing it.

Gran looked up from her notepad, where she was keeping tally of the numbers.

"We've raised eight point five million quid so far," she said. "Which is a lot of carrots, to be fair."

She was right. It was wild to be throwing around these kinds of numbers so casually, let alone to be worried they weren't nearly enough. The house was a money pit, with a long list of essential repairs. The target we needed to raise had been shifting northwards constantly, with the accountant revealing (on camera, obviously) the final amount we needed to gross was £14.6 million. Ten per cent of anything raised today went to Wetherby's Auction House, and twenty per cent would go in capital gains tax. We needed £4.3 million to cover the original tax bill, £130,000 to cover the interest, and the rest to fund repairs and William's plans for the estate, including buying the rights to *The Love Manor*. But the trouble with selling the art was, much like selling the village, we could only do it once. This auction was our first and last hope. Everything depended on it.

"Next, a beautiful buckskin mare by George Stubbs," the auctioneer announced. "Where shall we start the bidding? Do I have any takers at three hundred thousand?"

"How many pictures left?" I asked

Bunny leant over to whisper in my ear. "The Stubbs, the two Reynoldses, and the Holbein," she said.

"What will be will be," Karma said. Which wasn't exactly encouraging.

I squatted down beside William. He turned to look at me. "Whatever happens, we will make this work," I said. "You and me. Together."

William nodded. "We're a team." He squeezed my hand.

"I need to get back to it," I said—conscious a camera was trained on William and our family to capture their every reaction. I slipped back into the shadows, like a good producer, to watch from a bank of monitors.

The Stubbs went for £720,000.

The first Reynolds went for £610,000. The second for £820,000.

On the monitor, I could see William looking agitated as the bidding began on the final painting— the creepy Holbein of Queen Elizabeth the Undead. He was biting his thumbnail, his hands shaking, his knees bouncing. Bunny put her arm around his shoulder. I wanted to be there beside him, but I had a job to do. Everything rested on this painting. When the gavel fell, it had sold for £2.2 million. The air left my lungs. That only took us to £12.85 million—almost £2 million short of our goal. My eyes were glued to William on the monitor. He looked devastated. I knew how he felt.

The Wetherby's auctioneer told everyone the sale had concluded. The room filled with the sounds of chairs scraping on floorboards and people murmuring. This was it. We'd done well, but we'd come up short. We could pay the tax bill, but the future of Buckford Hall was far from secure if we couldn't fund the projects that would bring in long-term income. I watched my beautiful man on the monitor, my heart breaking for him. Suddenly, he sat upright, shoulders back. He turned to face the camera, his eyes boring directly into mine through the lens with an intensity that must have come direct from the French kings. He gave an almost imperceptible nod, then stood.

"Just a moment!" he called out to the room. My heart was thumping.

I hit the button on my headset. "Thandiwe, stay on William. Haruto, get crowd reactions."

The room hushed.

"I have a late addition to the catalogue." William pointed to the painting on the wall high above the auctioneer's head. "What will you give me for Thomas Gainsborough's 'Crossing the Buck'?"

The auctioneer's face split into a beaming smile. The room broke into a hubbub of frenetic activity. Camera flashes went off everywhere. At the bank of phones, attendants were scrambling to call back their international bidders. Amid all this chaos, William calmly sat back down in his chair, looked straight down the lens of the camera at me again—and winked.

The painting had been behind the auctioneer all morning—everyone had had hours to admire it. The bidding was fierce. I listened intently as the numbers climbed. One million. Two million. My body was so awash with adrenaline I couldn't feel my teeth. Three million. Four. Five. Six. I watched William's face on the monitor, eyes wet but steely with determination. He was selling this painting for *us*. Not only to save the estate but so we could build a future together here, so we could both follow our dreams and march through the world side by side, hand in hand. I was already crying when the hammer finally fell. The big Gainsborough had sold for £8.6 million.

William roared like he'd won a rugby final, fists punching the air. I thought for a second he was going to rip the shirt clean off his chest—which would have been great TV. Instead, he picked Bunny up and swung her around in circles. He kissed Karma on both cheeks and gently kissed my gran on the back of the hand, like a proper gentleman. Then... then he came running towards me—and I threw off my headset and leapt into his arms.

"You did it," I said, hot tears burning my cheeks. "You saved the estate."

"*We* saved the estate," he said. "We did it together."

My heart burst with love and pride and joy. I held William's jaw in my hands, already wet from his tears, and I kissed him.

Chapter 58
William

That evening, we took our celebrations to the top of Buckford Hill and lit a bonfire to mark Mabon, the autumn equinox.

"Please, Mother, will you put some clothes on?" I cried from my perch—sitting with my back against one of the standing stones, snuggled up with Petey. Mum, Karma, and Peggy were dancing around drunkenly in various states of undress.

"Another cider, my lord?" Bramley asked. He'd sloughed off his jacket and was in his shirtsleeves. I very nearly lectured him about standards, but everyone deserves a night off.

"No, thank you, Brammers."

"It wasn't a question, my lord." He thrust the bottle into my hand and joined the women in the dancing.

I turned to Petey Boy. "Are you sure you want to join this madhouse?"

He smiled. "I've never been so sure of anything in my life."

Petey took the cider from my hand and took a swig. The bonfire flickered, making his face glow orange and gold. He was so incredibly beautiful.

"What's the equinox all about, anyway?" he asked.

"Well, it's when the night and the day are the same length."

"I know that. But what are we celebrating?"

"Apart from a successful auction? Saving the estate? Your gran moving in with us? *The Love Manor* being a box office smash hit for Channel Three, a second season almost in the bag—"

Petey's grin widened. It couldn't have been cheekier if it was buried in my backside. "Actually, I've got some news on that front."

I raised an inquisitive eyebrow.

"Indira called. Channel Three are picking up *Saving the Love Manor*." I leapt up, heart filled with joy. "They saw the rushes from the auction today and offered for it on the spot. She's inking the deal now."

"We should tell everyone!"

"No," Petey said, reaching out an arm and pulling me back down to him. "Not yet. We'll tell them tomorrow. Once the deal is done."

I resumed my perch beside him, putting an arm around his shoulder and kissing his cheek. "I'm prou—"

Petey cut me off. "I know." He kissed me softly, sweetly, on the lips. "It means the world to me."

I booped him on his adorable little nose and took a swig of the cider.

"You never answered my question. What are we celebrating? What is Mabon all about?"

"Ah, well." I was nuzzled beneath his jaw. "It's the time of year when we show gratitude for the harvest and all its abundance. It's a time to honour the ancestors. And to let go of things that no longer serve us."

"Like the trees letting go of the leaves?" Petey asked.

"Exactly." I sat upright. "Or horrendous paintings."

"We do have a *lot* of very empty walls now."

"I have no regrets."

Petey turned my face to meet his. He leant in and I thought he was going to kiss me, but instead, he pulled my necklace out from inside my shirt and over my head.

"Speaking of honouring the ancestors," he said, undoing the clasp on the chain, letting my ring go free. "I think it's time you wore this."

Before I could protest, he grabbed my hand and slid the ring onto my pinkie finger.

"You've earned it."

I looked down at the circle of onyx in the band of gold. My father's ring. My grandfather's ring. His father's ring. Generations of Barons Buckford. Now it was mine. Not because I'd inherited, but because I had earned it.

"I'm proud of you too," Petey said.

A tear rolled down my cheek. I cupped my hands around Petey's jaw and pulled his face towards mine, gently kissing his lips—then kissing him more passionately.

"I love you," I said. "*So* much."

Petey's eyes sparkled. "I love you too."

Three grown witches made noises like mocking schoolchildren.

"Shall we get out of here?" Petey asked.

I nodded. "Let's go down into the ancient oak woodland and fuck like wildlings," I said. "I know just the place."

THE END.

Also in the series

The Paper Boys
The Silly Season (free novella)
Going Solo
Something Borrowed (to be released in 2027)

Subscribe to my newsletter.
https://www.dpclarence.com/newsletter/

Acknowledgments

I was reading a lot of P. G. Wodehouse when I started writing this book, and I think it shows. So thank you to that great master for the timeless lessons in writing comedy.

A lot of people helped make this book infinitely better. First among them, as always, is my old school chum Beejay Silcox—to whom this book is dedicated. I write books for a living. Beejay critiques books for a living. I am immensely proud of her achievements and honoured to call her my friend. We often wish we could go back in time together to our old high school and tell those awkward, nerdy misfits that things would turn out not just OK, but great. And I love that for those kids. (Also, that era was peak Spice Girls, and who wouldn't want to revisit that?)

Thank you to my incredible beta reader team, including Jen and Alex (who tried valiantly to help with the demisexual representation in particular), Derek (the KC, who helped me with the legalities of super-injunctions—I hope he forgives me for fudging the law for the sake of good storytelling), Yvette Davies (whose page-turning thriller *The Twin Sister* is a brilliant read, and I encourage you to buy it immediately), and the wonderful Rose and Andrea (both tireless champions of my books and treasured Insta-friends).

Special thanks to Stuart, who provided excellent insights into the world of medieval re-enactment. Rest assured that where I got something wrong, it was all my fault, not Stuart's. (For example, having written it, I could not deprive young Matthew of his valiant death in one-on-one combat with William simply because, in the real world, no insurer would let a ten-year-old anywhere near a re-enactment battlefield.)

As always, big, big thanks to my dedicated band of professionals: my development editor, Natasha Bell, who waded through my draft manuscript with a newborn on her hip because she is a legend; my cover designer, Bailey McGinn, who has the patience of that patient thing people are always saying is patient; Valerie Gomez, for once again creating the beautiful chapter images; my copy editor, proofreader, and all-round beaut sort, Elyse Lyon; and my dear friend and proofreader-for-life, Wendy Wood.

Special thanks, as ever, to the Nashers writing group for their unfailing support and friendship, including Ann, Lou, and Nia.

Thank you to my husband, Luke, for letting me write all weekend when we could be spending time together. To my dog, Pablo, for refusing to let me write when we could be spending time together. And to my incredible nibling, Hail, whose light brings so much joy to my life. One day this empire will be all yours. Let's hope I live long enough for it to actually make money.

Finally, to you: thank you for reading *Much Obliged*. Please rate and review this book on whatever platforms you prefer. And if you really, really loved it, let me know. I'd love to hear from you. I'm at **dan@dpclarence.com**.

Be queer and mighty, always.

D. P. Clarence
14 February 2026

About the Author

D. P. Clarence (Dan to his friends—including you, dear reader) was a journalist for a long, long time before finally deciding to bite the bullet and do the thing he'd always wanted to do—write books about boys kissing other boys.

His debut novel was *The Paper Boys*, the first book in the Brent Boys series, starring Sunny and Ludo. The free novella, *The Silly Season*, follows what happens to Sunny and Ludo next. *Much Obliged* is the third full novel in the series.

Dan is an avid reader of everything from rom-coms to literary fiction—but he especially loves LGBTQ+ fiction and historical romance. You can see what he's been reading lately on Instagram and Goodreads.

Originally from Australia, he lives in London with his husband and their very smiley corgi.

www.ingramcontent.com/pod-product-compliance
Lightning Source LLC
LaVergne TN
LVHW041618060526
838200LV00040B/1336